THE ROSS 248 PROJECT

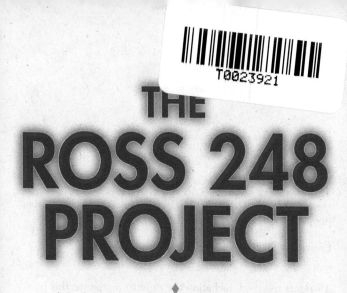

EDITED BY

Les Johnson
Ken Roy

THE ROSS 248 PROJECT

This is a work of fiction. All the characters and events portrayed in this book are fictional, and any resemblance to real people or incidents is purely coincidental.

Copyright © 2023 by Les Johnson and Ken Roy

A Baen Books Original

Baen Publishing Enterprises
P.O. Box 1403
Riverdale, NY 10471
www.baen.com

ISBN: 978-1-9821-9352-2

Cover art by Dominic Harman

First printing, May 2023
First paperback printing, July 2024

Distributed by Simon & Schuster
1230 Avenue of the Americas
New York, NY 10020

Library of Congress Control Number: 2023000764

Printed in the United States of America

10 9 8 7 6 5 4 3 2 1

FLARE OF DOOM

"How soon does she expect the danger of a flare?" C'Carus wondered.

"Soon," C'Helios declared. "Frighteningly soon. The starspot is huge and growing. She saw it first 'this morning,' a bit before the beginning of the currently offgoing shift, so about fifteen hours ago now. Starspots are magnetic, and this one's complex; it'll want to simplify itself. That means magnetic recombination, and that's a flare."

"Damn," C'Ori, another Elder, murmured.

"How soon?" C'Carus pressed.

"She saw the spot come around the side some fifteen hours ago," C'Helios noted. "Given Ross 248's rotation rate, we've got about twenty-five hours from right now before this one could pop at us . . . though it could go slightly sooner, or later. Say two more shifts from now through the end of four shifts from now is the danger window for this spot group." He shrugged. "And if this one doesn't, the next one might."

"Next one?!" C'Ori cried. She was an Elder, but prone to demonstrative reactions despite herself.

"Yes, ma'am," C'Helios confirmed. "Stars don't form just one spot and stop."

"We're dead," C'Brigit sighed, slumping in her chair. "We're all dead."

"Not necessarily," C'Helios said.

—"And a Child Shall Lead Them"
By Stephanie Osborn

ACKNOWLEDGEMENTS

So many good people made this anthology possible that it's hard to know where to begin. So in no particular order, we would like to thank Toni Weisskopf, for trusting in the editors to orchestrate this anthology; the contributors, for working with the editors to produce great stories and non-fiction essays, adding so much richness to the Ross 248 Universe; Grace Andrejczyk and Kerri Ballance, the student interns who helped with the preliminary editing; the staff at Baen Books, for making this effort possible and fairly painless; and Dr. Jesse Powell (PhD in Oceanography), who helped us understand what a deep, world-spanning ocean might look like, thus making Poseidon's World more realistic. You have our deepest and most sincere thanks.

To Martha, my long-suffering wife.
Thanks for all the good years.
—Ken Roy

To Dr. Norman Tolk, my thesis advisor
at Vanderbilt University ("back in the day").
His tutelage put me on a path toward making this
possible.
—Les Johnson

CONTENTS

Foreword

Steve Kwast
Lieutenant General (Ret.)—USAF
President, Genesis Systems Global

Humans have a future in space, but this book shares an even greater truth: **Humans have hope for a better future in the stars.**

The book in your hands tells a fictionalized account of humanity's first attempt to settle planets circling an alien star. Throughout time, great storytellers have been the most powerful teachers to inspire humanity to create better, kinder, and safer societies. This anthology of short stories inspires that same spirit of hope for a better future. These stories are written by some of today's best science fiction writers and edited by two people supremely qualified to orchestrate this entertaining adventure with a sense of both adventure and technical realism: Les Johnson and Ken Roy. Les is a science fiction writer and thirty-year NASA research scientist who has managed programs ranging from nuclear thermal rockets to interplanetary solar sails. Ken is a retired Oak Ridge nuclear engineer who has widely published in technical journals on advanced space topics. They are both founders of the Interstellar Research Group, a professional organization of technical specialists and science fiction writers (many are both!) who convene every eighteen months in a five-day convention to discuss interstellar travel and how to take it from science fiction to reality. Talks can range from the technical, such as creating a solar system–wide telescope using the Sun as a gravitational lens, growing synthetic meat on Mars, or the latest development in plasma or antimatter physics, to the social, such as how new societies might emerge from different planetary conditions. Many IRG participants are counted among this book's authors. I should know. I'm one of them! I was honored to speak at their 2017 symposium in Huntsville, Alabama.

This book shares the IRG's most important trait: a deep sense of disciplined optimism. The general attitude around the world for the past few years has been challenged. The COVID pandemic caused millions of people worldwide to live in fear and quarantine in their homes. Fears of a worldwide economic recession have dampened moods that otherwise might have improved as the world began to reopen. War in Ukraine and rumors of wars around the world have mixed with draught and famine worries to cause even more anxiety among humanity, particularly among our youth. Today, the future could appear dark if we did not have authors like this to remind us of our great potential as a human race.

Even the space community has not escaped a sense of despair. In 2019, respected political scientist Daniel Deudney published his book *Dark Skies*, in which he argued that space settlement would mean the extinction of humanity. To be fair, Deudney pointed out several genuine threats that may arise from space expansionism, such as the rise of artificial intelligence, the evolutionary effects of different space environments leading to altered versions of humanity and hostility between them, and the proliferation of new technologies necessary for space travel that can also become horrible weapons of mass destruction in the wrong hands. These are indeed all potential challenges. However, heroes of the future never cower in fear. Instead, they innovate with joy and hope in their hearts for a brighter future.

The stories we tell ourselves matter. If we let imagined monsters in the unknown darkness keep us in our beds cowering under the covers, then we will never see the rich, green fields of infinite possibility. Dystopian stories can be helpful to develop a healthy caution and pragmatism, but their abuse can also breed paralysis and death.

This book is, in part, a response to Deudney's pessimism. Rather than fearing Deudney's hazards, the authors of these stories confront them directly and find that they can be overcome and may even be reformed into critical advantages in creating a better future. Many of these stories are filled with danger and tragedy, as our human future among the stars will inevitably be. We will, after all, be human beings. But they are by no means dystopian. These stories are about effort, compassion, heroism, and triumph. These stories are optimistic. These stories are about overcoming fear and adversity to build a better world. A positive world. These stories don't seek to enslave the human spirit to paralyzing terror. Rather, these stories seek to show how the best of humanity, and humanity's offspring, will blaze a trail to the positive future in store for everyone.

We must always remember that a positive future is

not one without conflict or challenge. A utopian future is an impossible future—and that is a good thing! Utopias are sterile...and boring...and ultimately they are soul-killing environments. Humanity's interstellar future will be more positive than we can contemplate today, but it will also challenge us to the limits of our imagination, ambition, and skill. We will also purchase it with sweat, tears, and blood. Our descendants' incessant conflict with the deadly environments beyond Earth will present hardships probably not seen since Polynesians in canoes challenged the Pacific Ocean to find new and distant islands thousands of miles into the unknown blue millennia ago. Settling the American West, the most recent societal-scale settlement effort, cost thousands of lives from many different civilizations. We should not lie to ourselves that expansion into outer space will be any less costly. Though, fortunately, human expansion into the stars may not threaten extraterrestrial societies with war or extinction, the soil of new human worlds will still be littered with the sacrifices of pioneers fighting natural forces never before seen back home on Earth.

However, this future they create will still be an optimistic and positive one. Just as many who read this book will live in cities and states carved from the wilderness just over a century ago by pioneers, so will the children of humanity's first interstellar pioneers live in glittering metropolises forged in the imagination and determination of their grandparents. But this future is also realistic in that it is forged by people very much like we are today. Our future interstellar pioneers will live, love, work irritating jobs, suffer hardships, clean toilets, burn dinners, and make countless other mistakes, just like we do—and just like our pioneer ancestors did.

That is why these stories are ultimately important. They don't just light a candle of an optimistic future to merely defy the darkness of today's despair. They represent a very important truth:

Humans have hope for a better future in the stars.

The people who go to the stars will not be gods, superheroes, or models of moral perfection. They'll simply be our children's children. They will be ordinary people who will overcome the same types of challenges our parents overcame, and the challenges we have and will overcome. We, today, even with wars, pandemics, and famine, are setting the stage for the fantastic age that is coming. We are doing so by doing what humans have always done and will always do: overcome obstacles . . . and more than a few mysteries!

So let these stories comfort, entertain, and inspire you in these often-troubling times. Our past is locked in concrete but the future is ours to create. It won't be easy or painless but let's shoot for a magnificent future full of possibilities, laughter, love, discovery, and, above all, adventure.

Humans have hope for a better future in the stars.

Introduction

Les Johnson & Ken Roy

Welcome to *The Ross 248 Project*. With the contributing authors, we have created a shared-world science fiction anthology meant to entertain and inspire. Our goal was to create a plausible future where humans, along with their children and machine creations, decide to leave the solar system that gave us birth and settle worlds around a distant star—Ross 248.

Why Ross 248? First, it is an actual star located in the constellation of Andromeda. Ross 248 is a small star (an M6V red dwarf, for those curious to know) about 10.3 light-years (LY) from Earth. The star has no known companions...yet. But, for the sake of this anthology, we assume that it has a system of planets like those at Trappist-1. Based on current exoplanet detection techniques, it is unlikely that this assumption can be proved false within the next few decades. Ross 248 is fairly close to our solar system, relatively speaking, allowing for a journey of one hundred years at ten percent the speed of light (0.1c, where c is shorthand for the speed of light). It also has the interesting property of being in motion toward our solar system. In about thirty thousand years it will become the closest star to our sun and in another ten thousand years, give or take, Ross 248 be within 3 LY of our current home.

Because this world will be used by the contributing authors, each coming up with their own creative ways to view and tackle the many challenges, we had to create a guidebook on which the authors could hang their stories for consistency. And we wanted it to be plausible. But, as Yogi Berra once said, "It's tough to make predictions, especially about the future."

Nonetheless, we tried, and created a reference guide that provides the technical and historical background to the Ross 248 Project that might be of interest to those of you who like such details. Highlights from the guide can be found in the appendix.

The stories herein will entertain and inform, addressing such questions as why humanity decides to build and send starships to Ross 248, what challenges might be faced in efforts to create Earth II, and how people and our artificial intelligence creations might react in stressful and dangerous situations. Earth is only a long-distance phone call away—but the response will take twenty years.

It has been a true pleasure working with the professional storytellers contributing to this volume. They have our sincere thanks and best wishes. We hope you enjoy the results.

Les Johnson
Ken Roy

THE
ROSS 248 PROJECT

The year 2583 / 0 AA (after arrival)

Two starships from Sol System entered the Ross 248 star system. The Cerite ship *Ceres' Chariot* inserted into orbit around Liber, the airless moon of the seventh planet, and began to establish a settlement. The second ship was the Space Patrol's first starship, *Guardian E*, which went into orbit around Eden, the fourth planet. Because Eden had an oxygen atmosphere and life, it was hoped that it could become Earth II—a new home for humanity. *Guardian E* sent down armed soldiers to construct research stations and begin a more careful study of their new home.

Garden of Serpents

Patrick Chiles

Patrick Chiles began his writing career with the self-published novels Perigee *and* Farside, *acquired by Baen Books in 2016. His subsequent novels, 2020's* Frozen Orbit *and 2021's* Frontier, *have established him as a rising talent in the realm of realistic, near-future science fiction. Chiles also contributed to the 2021 anthology,* World Breakers, *with Larry Correia and David Weber. The sequel to* Frozen Orbit, *titled* Escape Orbit, *was released in 2023. He currently resides in central Ohio with his wife and two lethargic dachshunds.*

<START RECORDING // PFC CHANDLER, R.A. // 04.19.2583 // 1821 LT>

I hate dropships. Just felt like I needed to get that out.

Maybe I should be more specific: the ships are fine, no complaints there. They don't get smelly since we're not in them for long; the g-couches are as comfortable as they need to be, and the ships do what they're supposed to do. Not much to look at, but they get the job done. It's the job they're doing that I hate.

Think about it. After a hundred-year trip, living in a giant centrifuge might keep a normal healthy but it's not the same as extended jaunts into full (as in earthlike) gravity. The Coriolis force from rotation combines with the ship's acceleration to create some weird effects that are hard to explain—"down" is more like sideways, and the direction depends on where you're facing. Take my word for it that it's not the same as standing on a planet.

Anyway, the fun starts within eight or nine minutes of getting rattled around in the dropship while it decelerates into the atmosphere at four or five g's. That part sucks. Civilian shuttles follow a gentler descent profile, but Patrol pilots treat every entry like a combat drop: get in fast, get out faster if they can manage it.

After you shake that off, you're treated to normal gravity wearing an environment suit and full kit after spending most of your life being spun around in a drum. It leaves everybody dizzy for the first day or two, which can be funny to watch. I'm a comms specialist, so I also get to hump our squad's network relay along with extra batteries and a field repair kit. It's like every day is "leg day." You just gut it out. The heavy gunners have it worse so I'm not going to complain too much.

In fact, I'm not even supposed to be talking about this. The Patrol prides itself on stoic dedication to the mission, so we generally keep our heads down and our mouths shut. There was supposed to be an adage from way back in the old army that soldiers weren't happy unless they had something to bitch about. Admiral Gordon will pitch a fit, but honestly I'll happily accept my punishment if I somehow make it back up to *Guardian E* after all this.

I have to say that looks really unlikely at this point.

So yeah, I'm not supposed to do that. I'm also not supposed to be stranded on this planet alone, but that reminds me of another old adage: no battle plan survives first contact with the enemy. Of course we didn't come here looking for a fight, so maybe that's why this all went to shit in the first place. If you assume that your first landing on an entirely new world might not be welcomed with open arms, you'll prepare accordingly.

That wasn't the case with 248e, which some muckety-muck optimistically named Eden. Maybe if they'd paid more attention to the old creation story, they'd have recalled that things kind of went sideways there too. At this new Eden, the serpent apparently has the run of the place.

The dim, monochrome light didn't help. The local sun is big, about ten times the size of ours as seen from Earth, but even at midday everything is a variation of bloodred. Just brighter. The day here is about thirty-one hours, so we spend about sixteen hours in darkness. No stars, just clouds, but our night vision works okay.

The pilot set us down in a large clearing on a small continent about two hundred miles south of the planet's equator. Maybe we should have asked ourselves why there was a large clearing in the middle of a giant jungle, but we didn't. After that high-g drop, the touchdown was so light we barely noticed when she announced we'd landed. Our platoon leader was the first one off the dropship, as a good platoon leader ought to be. First thing he noticed was how spongy the ground was. It's like the whole planet is covered in fungi. When my turn came up, it felt like stepping onto a thick blanket of moss.

First order of business was setting up shelter, which is a lot of work. The shelter domes are easy; even the big ones we used just about take care of themselves. The hard work comes in getting the water extractors up and running, and then calibrating them to the local atmosphere without burning them out. The Ito generator takes a fine touch too, as they get rattled during atmospheric entry. With a couple grams of antimatter inside, you can't just plant one and throw the switch or you could end up with a city-sized crater where your outpost used to be.

My squad had it easy: watch the perimeter while the other three squads did the hard work of setting up a forward operating base. That might seem boring, but we were grateful for the opportunity. Not that we would've minded the work of setting up camp, but this gave us a head start getting familiar with the local environment.

We deployed in a circle with a hundred-meter radius centered on the command post, each one of us taking a pack of sensor quads with us. In short order we had networked them into an invisible picket around the FOB: motion detectors, heat sensors, optics, and audio. We weren't expecting any kind of armed resistance as there was zero indication of intelligent life here, but the survey drones had shown evidence of large animals that we had to assume might be interested in a new food source. Somebody named the things E-Rexes because they look like a half-scale T-Rex with bigger teeth, a single eye, and big ears. First and third platoons, setting up bases on other parts of the planet, encountered the things and had to kill hundreds of the monsters before they learned to leave us alone. Our drones spotted some of them just a few kilometers away, so we knew they were in the area, yet they never bothered us. Maybe we should've asked why.

As I said, the ground was spongy, like walking on partially thawed tundra. At first it made moving about under the 0.9 gravity a little less difficult, though over time the stuff seemed to pull at our boots like thick mud. As I leveled my first sensor quad I noticed fine, hairlike tendrils wrapping themselves around its base. Weird, but not too concerning yet. Apparently the heat from our suits kept the miniature creeping vines at bay; they seemed to react to objects at ambient temperatures. The squads doing setup reported the same phenomenon. It naturally held structures in place until they turned on the juice—as soon as stuff started heating up, the tiny vines withdrew. Such was our first experience with the weird plant life on Eden.

That was fine by me. Once I'd set up my share of the picket net, I took my position "inside the wire." I didn't want to have to be constantly shifting just to keep the local foliage from grabbing at my boots, so I cranked up the suit heat another notch just to be on the safe side.

It's easy for the uninitiated to think of sentry duty as boring—and it can be—but in an alien environment it's anything but. There's just too much to take in, too much information to absorb. You're the eyes of your platoon, and your brothers and sisters are counting on you to put together a clear picture of the tactical situation.

We were lightly armed, each of us carrying a plasma rifle with a chest carrier full of charging magazines and old-fashioned slugthrower sidearms on our hips. More than adequate for a herd of E-Rexes. We set up interlocking fields of fire, with full-auto gunners positioned on opposite sides of the perimeter just in case we needed a whole lot of fire delivered at once. No heavy weapons as we didn't foresee enemy armored columns appearing out of the thick forests of whatever-it-was growing outside the wire. Pity that. They might have made all the difference.

And there was a *lot* growing out there. Mostly boulder-sized clumps of the same mossy-looking flora that carpeted our FOB; beyond them was a thicket of taller brush a few meters high. As the day wore on and our enhanced vision implants kicked in, things got even stranger: the local vegetation glowed. Faint bluish-green bioluminescence, which stood out even more against the deep red of 248's light. That was going to mess with our sleep cycles when local midnight looked more normal to us than noon would. For the first time ever, I hoped our squad pulled night watch.

As luck would have it, we didn't. I couldn't blame our platoon sergeant when he posted the watch rotations; we'd already been on perimeter duty for half the day and fifteen hours on watch is long enough. When third squad came out to relieve us, I was ... well, relieved.

The forests—sorry, I don't know what else to call the thicket of overgrowth beyond the wire—had become more unnerving as time wore on. The outlines traced by the luminous flora moved in a way that didn't quite square with the wind direction. My first thought was that it might be caused by animals moving in the shadows, concealed behind the overgrowth. Which was definitely a thing, but more on that later.

I figured it was my eyes playing tricks on me. No matter how well our metabolism's been enhanced or how many stims we take, fatigue eventually has its say. After a while, you start seeing stuff that isn't really there and your value as a sentry falls off to nothing. Instead of minding your zone, you end up focusing on whatever's right in front of you because it's increasingly hard to focus on anything else. And that's when you're in a familiar environment. Eden is anything but "familiar."

A lot of the movement we saw *was* due to the local wildlife. Nothing observed directly, just shadows and sounds. I did see one creature skulking along the edge of the clearing, just inside the brush line. I couldn't image it directly, even with my IR implants tuned-in the thing was partially camouflaged against the foliage. All I could get was a silhouette, a sense of shape and size. It was big, at least two meters tall and three long, walking on four limbs. It would stop occasionally and stare at our picket line, almost like it was sizing up the sensor quads. Made me wonder if it could "see" the EM frequencies of our perimeter net. The scientists told us to expect life here to have highly evolved senses to compensate for the low natural light. Did they have more of an advantage during the day, when the vegetation wasn't glowing? Either way, it was a sobering reminder that we were on their turf.

The first Patrolman went missing during morning watch the next day. Patrolman Second Class Milley had apparently gotten up early to use the latrine, about ten meters away from the shelter dome but well inside the wire. We'd had to dig an old-fashioned field shitter while we waited for the next supply drop, the one that would have a full water processing unit so we could do our business indoors like civilized people.

Nothing tripped the sensor picket and nobody heard a thing, not even the squad on perimeter watch. No one realized he was missing until he didn't show up for muster. We started an all-hands search of the FOB right away. It was easy to trace his steps until our platoon leader found an odd depression in the moss-covered ground where Milley's trail ended. Our first thought was that he'd fallen into a crevasse that had been covered up by the vegetation, but after digging away at it we only found more frozen dirt. Just as the seismic sensors predicted. It was like the tundra had just swallowed him up, or something had plucked him out of the sky.

The scientists had briefed us on what the survey drones had found and warned us that some of the local wildlife was analogous to the dinosaurs of ancient Earth. So did a freaking alien pterosaur swoop down and snatch Milley like he was an overgrown field mouse?

The sky had just become one more thing we had to watch.

Our squad was in reserve that day, which made us the designated "quick reaction" force. If anything went sideways outside the wire, we were the ones who'd be sent to deal with the threat. We suited up for a search-and-rescue patrol and divvied up the search pattern by fire teams, each one headed for a different quadrant since we had no idea what direction he might've been taken. It didn't leave us with the warm fuzzies, as the farther we got outside the wire the more dispersed we became. Our platoon leader assured us we'd have top cover from a pair of sentry drones, which I reckon sounded like a good idea so long as they didn't get snatched up too. We were determined to find Milley, but I'd be lying if I said there wasn't some grousing about it. He was always just a little too sure of himself for his own good.

"Dumbass shouldn't have been out alone," our heavy gunner, Patrolman First Class Svenson, had groused. Big Scandinavian guy, selected to carry the full-auto plasma rifle simply because he had the size to match the charging backpack's bulk.

"The guy was just going for a morning dump," I'd said. "Probably figured he was safe inside the wire." I tightened my grip on my lighter, standard-duty rifle and kept it at high-ready, making sure my fingers stayed indexed along the trigger guard. It was hard to work by feel with gloves on, but it was far too cold to work without them. Even along the equator it was subarctic conditions, barely above freezing. "The cold just makes bodily functions more urgent, seems like."

Sven had answered with a grunt. "He's still a dumbass."

"Stow it," Corporal Mfume had said. East African. Rail thin but he aced every combat fitness test, basically earned his position as fire team leader by proving he could whip Sven's ass if need be. "Milley might be a pain in your ass but he's still one of us. Take a look around; I guarantee you're a pain in someone else's ass. Stay focused."

"Aye, Corporal," Sven had muttered, barely audible over the comms net.

Our fire team—a rifleman, a heavy gunner, a

grenadier, and the team leader—moved through the brush in a wedge formation with Mfume on point. It was hard going with all that clingy moss underfoot; every step felt like the ground was trying to pull us back. We all cranked up our foot warmers to keep it at bay; I know mine was to the point where I could feel my socks filling with sweat. That was okay, so long as I could walk without having to work at it. I didn't want to think about what a firefight would be like in this environment—lay down for cover and you might not get back up.

This was our first close-up look at the world outside the wire and the brush only got thicker as we pressed on. For the most part it looked like outgrowth of that greenish-gray mossy ground cover, the stuff that tried to attach to our boots. The larger brush formed in the exact same patterns; part of me wanted to take a few minutes to study it just out of interest. Most of us didn't sign up for the Patrol just to be a dumbass grunt, especially if you volunteered for an expeditionary force like Ross 248. We're genuinely curious. Except Sven. I think he just wanted new, exciting stuff to shoot.

We did manage to take some local samples of ground cover around the FOB and sent 3D microscans back up to the science team on *Guardian E.* The eggheads are anxious to get down here and see for themselves once we give the all clear, and they were all over the holographic samples we sent. They weren't saying much, but a lab assistant I know back on *Guardian* told me later that it'd been giving them fits. Apparently, the stuff is all fractals down to the microscopic level, repeating patterns that reflect and define the whole organism. That's not necessarily groundbreaking stuff as it happens naturally in Earth biology; the difference here is she said the patterns are "extraordinarily well defined." That is, no variations whatsoever. Like this stuff was engineered, fine-tuned by somebody.

I was eyeballing one such growth, something that resembled an aloe plant, when Puckett disappeared. There was a grunt and a shout over our comms net. I looked left, where he should've been, and he was just gone. I carefully stepped over to where I'd seen him last and there was another one of those faint depressions in the ground cover.

Another old infantry adage: Once is happenstance. Twice is coincidence. Three times is enemy action. We just leapfrogged the "twice" part.

Mfume made a circling motion with his hand, signaling the rest of the team to form up on him and take defensive positions. As we did, we were startled by a series of muffled thumps underfoot. We all stared at one another in silence. Puckett was our grenadier. He carried an "over-under," a standard-issue pulse rifle with a grenade launcher slung underneath the barrel. He also wore a carrier vest filled with explosive cartridges for said grenade launcher. That was when we knew what had happened.

Sven's eyes about popped out of his skull; first time I'd ever seen the big guy unnerved. "Holy shit. He's . . . underground."

"Perhaps not anymore," Mfume said, with a casual determination that I couldn't have managed in his position. He jumped on the squad comms net right away. "Six, this is Bravo lead. Man down, repeat man down. I'm geotagging his last location and we are returning to the FOB." He gestured for us to get a move on, not waiting for our squad leader's response.

Understand that this wasn't something a team leader would normally do with his squad leader, which is how I knew Mfume was spooked. Sergeant Petrov was exacting when it came to tactical discipline, but he apparently wasn't in the mood to overrule Mfume's decision. "Roger that, Bravo. All teams, return to base. Check in as you cross the wire and assemble at checkpoint alpha. Acknowledge."

A half hour later, our squad, minus Puckett, had reassembled for muster and Petrov gestured for the fire team leaders to circle up on him. They were having a powwow out of earshot from the rest of us when an enormous, concussive *thump* roiled the ground. The kind of thing you might hear when an entire vest full of grenades went off. We felt the explosion up through our boots, a pretty good indication that it had happened underground. We all turned to see a thin column of smoke rising from the brush about two hundred meters beyond the wire. We'd located Puckett, or at least where he used to be.

Over the next few days, two more Patrolmen went missing. One just disappeared without a trace, again. The second one didn't. This time a few of us heard Javits, a rifleman in first squad, shout and then go quiet. It was muffled, like he was being gagged as he was dragged off into the underbrush. I don't know why but that made it seem even worse than it already was. And as usual, there weren't any tracks.

Getting picked off at random was starting to become routine and an order came down that nobody was to go out alone for any reason, and individual weapons were to be charged at all times. That was a big deal. Normally they only do that when we're on a "war footing"—that is, expecting enemy action at any time. Otherwise, the only time your weapon should be locked and loaded is when you're on patrol or sentry duty so there's no risk of an accidental discharge.

Around this time I was on perimeter watch, which was funny because I was standing there by myself, where if I'd had to get up and take a leak I'd have had a "battle buddy" going to the latrine with me. While everybody on post is in sight of one another, standing sentry all of a sudden felt pretty damned lonely.

I was startled by close movement on the other side of the wire. Didn't even hear the thing before I saw it, it was that stealthy. Something the size of a large dog crept out of the brush about ten meters away, on funky double-jointed legs that made its movement seem almost like an insect's. It had leathery skin with bristly hair that reminded me of a porcupine. Its head looked like an extension of its body with a long toothy snout, a couple of stumps for ears, and four bulbous eyes that must have been adapted to see in the dim red light.

The thing skulked along the brush line, every few steps stopping to look at us. Sizing us up. Quiet as it was, it made me think this might have been the kind of creature that had been snatching our platoon mates. It stalked our perimeter that way for a good ten minutes—I know this because I kept my weapon leveled on it the whole time and the recording from my scope said so.

I was ready to shoot the thing dead, except our rules of engagement forbade it unless it presented an immediate threat—no killing the local critters unless they deserved it. The longer I watched it, the more I understood this four-eyed freak probably wasn't our culprit. On the other hand, it wasn't something I wanted to mess with either. Don't start nothing, won't be nothing. Right?

What finally convinced me was when it got spooked by something I couldn't see, at least not right away. It came near a clump of brush when the fronds or whatever they were from this big, tubular, aloe-looking plant moved. The critter recoiled and just stood there for a second, uttering this kind of low-frequency hum that I guess passed for a growl as it stared at the brush. There was no more movement after a time and the animal backtracked and skulked away.

That got me wondering: why weren't the native animals getting snatched up? Maybe they were and we just weren't seeing it; it's not like we could muster the local wildlife to see which ones had gone missing. Most likely whatever it was already knew the local menu options and had decided the new arrivals were tasty. Kind of like the first time you try a new dish and you all of a sudden can't get enough of it.

It was weird behavior. I couldn't see another, more dangerous animal hiding in the brush. There wasn't a lot of cover in that spot, so what could've scared it off?

I kept staring at the big alien-aloe plant and its long, spotted leaves or tubules or whatever they were. Awfully cold climate for plants that size, it seemed. Maybe the deep red sun led them to evolve a type of photosynthesis we didn't understand? It was one more thing for the eggheads to figure out.

Something about it kept my attention. That critter

had skedaddled like he'd just been caught on some-body else's turf.

That's when I saw it. A couple of tubules shifted along its edge, just enough to see them move against the cluster of identical growths in the plant's center (I'm sure there's more sciencey-sounding names for all this but I don't know what they are). I know they weren't moving with the wind because there wasn't any. Most important, I could see they were moving independently of each other.

The damned plant was alive. Okay, I know—all plants are alive. But I mean *alive*. Moving with a purpose. All of a sudden, I realized where our missing Patrolmen had gone.

Our platoon leader must have figured that out around the same time, because it wasn't long before he assembled us for a mission brief.

If the lieutenant was concerned, he didn't show it. If anything, he looked pissed off, pacing back and forth in front of us like a caged animal. Command probably wasn't happy that we'd lost Patrolmen, and that turd had rolled downhill from orbit and landed in the L-T's lap, so now he was spreading it around to the rest of us. But if I'm being honest—and at this point there's no reason not to be—we were all ready for some payback.

To his credit, the L-T kept things brief, letting the platoon sergeant go through the standard five-paragraph order before summing it up for us. "Ladies and Gents, we came here with the objective of set-ting up a secure advance base for the science team. Our current situation does not meet any definition of 'secure.' Therefore, we are going to damned well *make* it secure. Our first order of business is to clear the perimeter." He motioned for the weapons sergeant, who then called up a team with incendiary units—old-fashioned flamethrowers. They took equidistant positions along the perimeter and started torching everything within a hundred meters. It was obvious they'd worked out this piece of the operation ahead of our briefing, and it was quite a show.

Keeping the platoon in formation while the weapons team did their thing might have been for our own safety, but it also made for one hell of a spectacle and showed us the L-T meant business. There was no small amount of hissing and squeals as the dense vegetation went up in smoke, which was a little unnerving. Normally I would've chalked it up to moisture evaporating in the heat, but now I couldn't help but think they were *reacting*.

"You hear that?" I muttered to Sven, who was standing next to me.

"More like smelling it," he said, sniffing the air and tightening his grip on his weapon. "Smells like victory." I could tell he was champing at the bit to get out there himself, but our squad had been assigned to base security, so he'd have to be content with standing perimeter watch while the rest of our platoon went out on an old-fashioned search-and-destroy mission.

To the L-T's credit, he went out with first squad, "leading from the front" instead of pestering everyone from the command post. Being the comms operator, I was ordered to monitor their progress from the CP and keep *Guardian* updated when it came back over the horizon. It's where I've been ever since. I haven't decided if that's a good thing.

Every Patrolman's biosensor and helmet cam fed into our tactical display, each one of them a slow-moving dot on a holographic map. It was a lot to absorb all at once, but that was a problem that took care of itself over time.

Watching your fellow Patrolmen slowly make their way through the brush is an oddly detached experience. I've been in the CP during drills but never a live operation. You can see the formations moving ahead and can call up video from any individual to see what they're seeing, and you know exactly what they're doing, but you're not really a part of it. That gets even harder when things get lively. The platoon was "weapons free" as soon as they crossed the wire. The L-T's orders were "If it moves, kill it."

Apparently, there was a lot of stuff moving.

I could hear the buzz of plasma rifles and shouts of Patrolmen over the comms. The thunderclap report of the heavy full-auto guns reverberated through the fabric of the CP dome, their particle beams splitting the air around them like lightning. They were soon joined by the booming thuds of grenades. It's hard to know how the L-T made sense of all that chaos but that's why he's an officer, I guess. Maybe he was just as confused as the rest of us.

I mentioned the problem of monitoring the whole platoon taking care of itself after a time—that was because there were fewer and fewer Patrolmen to monitor. Those dots—their status icons—started going dark. Green dots turned to amber, one or two at first, then whole fire teams started going red. Red meant "dead." The creepy thing was I didn't hear a peep out of most of them.

Most of them. There were shouts from one or two that seemed to come from nowhere and were just as quickly muzzled. After the riot of noise over the tactical net, my little corner of the CP became eerily silent.

When it turned noisy outside is when I knew things had gone to shit. I'd filtered my own squad out of the tactical net since they were inside the wire; in hindsight I probably shouldn't have, but in the end, I don't think it would've made a difference.

I heard Sven's distinctive bellow and ran outside just in time to see him being dragged off. Vines were wrapped around his legs and torso with another encircling his head just as the damned *ground* opened up near him. It was one of those aloe-plant-looking things, its tubules spreading open in a circle. The vines, thick as tree limbs, yanked him up into the air and pulled him into the plant's pinkish maw.

I stood there like an idiot, staring in horror at my friend getting pulled underground into whatever this was. The vines disappeared with him, everything withdrawing beneath the ground cover.

I was vaguely aware of carnivorous plants like Venus flytraps but until now had not imagined we were camped in the middle of a patch of their big brothers. That's when I realized that the clearing we had landed in was their patch. Looking around, I saw the rest of our squad was gone. Every post around the perimeter was empty, a few of them marked by weapons that still lay on the ground where a Patrolman had once been.

I felt the ground beneath the CP dome begin to shift and I stumbled back inside as more of those fibrous tentacles rose up from the undergrowth. I locked the hatch behind me and hurried back to the nearly empty tactical display. A lone comms alert blinked in its center: the platoon leader trying to make contact.

"Th-this is Chandler in the...the CP," I stammered, trying to sound professional and in control when in reality I was trying not to piss myself. "Go ahead."

The L-T's voice was choked, like he was fighting to get the words out. "CP...this is...Actual." A grunt, then: "Position...compromised. Initiate...Zero Protocol." There would be no dustoff, no one coming to our rescue. *Guardian* was on the other side of the planet; even if they sent a dropship right now it'd be another hour before it landed.

He repeated the order, not that I needed any more encouragement. I could feel the floor buckle and looked up to see shadows creeping along the outside of the CP dome, those vines trying to get in. They were pressing against the structure, and more of them were coming up from the ground. The dome began popping and groaning against the strain—they couldn't penetrate the structure, so they would crush it with their own weight.

Zero Protocol was a sanitized way of saying we were to blow everything to hell. It's not like the Ito device needs a self-destruct button; the antimatter is contained by quantum fields that draw their power from the device itself. It's like a massive regenerating battery, the proverbial self-licking ice cream cone. But disconnect the power, and *boom*. All that stored energy is released once the confinement bottles fail, along with a few grams of matter and antimatter mixing all at once. They'll annihilate each other and everything else within a couple of square kilometers, converting our clearing into a smoking hole and killing whatever it was that slaughtered our platoon.

It can be a really efficient generator, or a tactical nuke. I set the shutdown timer for the maximum thirty-minute count—that was four minutes ago. *Guardian* will be over the horizon in another nineteen, which will give me just enough time to send a burst transmission with all of our accumulated data before this place is vaporized. Hopefully they can do something with it, or at least understand what these things are and find a better way to keep them at bay. I'm not getting my hopes up. Maybe if we'd had an AI here it could've helped us come up with a better solution than cratering the place, but they aren't attached to forward expeditionary units since there's a decent chance we'll have to kill something. It's enough to make one wonder how much smarter the AIs are than us meatbags.

And so I wait. The burst transmission finished up and I got the acknowledgment from *Guardian* that it had been received. The CP dome is beginning to show cracks from the strain. It won't be long.

It's better this way. I'd rather go out fighting than get slowly digested by freakish plants that have developed a taste for humans. I'm about to give them the worst case of heartburn anybody could imagine. They can choke on us.

If that sounds tragic, it isn't. Civilians can never understand why we do what we do, no matter how hard they try. Just know that I have no regrets. I did my duty, as did my brothers and sisters.

Preserve and Protect, at Any Cost.

<QUANTUM FIELD FAILURE IMMINENT:
3 . . . 2 . . . 1 . . .
RECORDING ENDS>

--- ✛ ---

The year 2584 / 1 AA (after arrival)

Different cultures signify the milestone of transitioning from childhood to adulthood in different ways. In the USA, it usually is age based and has nothing to do with any sort of developmental milestone or achievement. In Judaism, it is also age based with there being a Bar or Bat Mitzvah at about age twelve or thirteen. While in Japan, on the second Monday in January, young men and women (at about age twenty) dress in suits and kimonos to attend events held throughout the country for Coming-of-Age Day. In the future, new rituals and markers will arise for some interesting reasons.

--- ✛ ---

And a Child Shall Lead Them

Stephanie Osborn

---

*Award-winning author Stephanie Osborn, the Inter-
stellar Woman of Mystery, is a veteran of more than
twenty years in civilian/military space programs. With
graduate and undergraduate degrees in four sciences—
astronomy, physics, chemistry and mathematics—she is
"fluent" in several more, including geology and anatomy.
She has authored, coauthored, or contributed to some
fifty-plus books, including the celebrated science-fiction
mystery* Burnout: The Mystery of Space Shuttle STS-
281. *Her latest venture is* Division One, *her take on
the urban legend of the mysterious people who make
evidence . . . disappear. In addition to her writing, the
Interstellar Woman of Mystery now happily "pays it
forward," teaching math and science through numerous
media including ebooks, radio, podcasting, and public
speaking, as well as working with SIGMA, the science-
fiction think tank.*

"Hey, Arinna," C'Helios said, entering the commons
room of the dorm to which he'd been assigned; they
were modified cargo containers placed in clusters on
the surface of Liber, "hamster-tubed" and pressurized.
At least one module was always outfitted as an airlock,

and the Cerites were as used to wearing envirosuits as ordinary clothing.

C'Helios, a bachelor, shared quarters with several others, including Arinna's small family—the seventeen-year-old and her two parents, engineer C'Ekeko and logistician C'Eiru. They were the only family in that particular dorm. Only the dig team and a very few family members were currently on Liber's surface, but after the underground habitat was complete, the others would come down from the orbiting starship that had carried them to the Ross 248 system, *Ceres' Chariot*.

Were she Earth-human, Arinna would be nearing majority, but the young Cerite hadn't shown signs of childhood digestive tract failure marking the transition to formal adulthood, and typically wouldn't for another two decades, based on the current average; it drifted some over the generations and physicians speculated it was lengthening. She was precocious in most things, so she was expected to transition early, as C'Helios had.

"Hi, C'Helios," the pretty redhead replied with a smile that lit up her emerald eyes, looking up from her reading tablet as her parents smiled at him.

"Hello, C'Helios," the logistician called from where she mixed a batch of grog for the adults and a small pot of stew for the handful of youngsters who had accompanied their parents. C'Eiru was a tall, slim redhead, and it was obvious where her daughter had gotten her coloring. "Dinner will be ready soon."

"Okay. As good as that stew smells, it's a pity I can't eat it anymore!" C'Helios laughed.

"Don't make that mistake, son," C'Ekeko chuckled. The brawny-for-a-Cerite man was busy on the workbench in the corner, repairing a defective hydraulic control module. Being over ten light-years from Sol System, everything that could be repaired had to be repaired. "I tried that once, shortly after I obtained my new digestive tract. I thought just the broth would be fine. Believe me, it was *not!*"

"Ha!" C'Helios laughed. "I'll bet!"

"How was your work shift?" Arinna asked.

"Decent," C'Helios decided; he was young for a Cerite—not yet thirty in Earth years, and he had become a full adult four Earth years before, ten years earlier than usual—but he was gifted, one of the lead engineers in the construction of Toe Hold, the initial colony of the Ross 248 system. He was intelligent, quick-witted, good-looking, and, unbeknownst to him, Arinna liked looking. "We're making progress. How are the studies?"

"Really well," the child prodigy noted. "I got all my classwork finished this morning, and I spent the afternoon reading those astronomy texts you got me." She gestured at the tablet, then her forehead wrinkled as her scarlet brows drew together. "It's proving...interesting. Especially the research paper collections."

"Oh? How so?"

"Did you know the astronomers in the twentieth century thought Ross 248 was a variable star?"

"No. That's odd. It isn't variable. Wonder how they made that mistake."

"I dunno, but I'm not sure it *was* a mistake," an earnest Arinna said. In the background, her parents sobered, listening; no one else was in the commons room yet.

"What makes you say that?" C'Helios wondered. "Show me."

Arinna had well more than her fair share of intellect;

she already held several science and technological degrees, and was currently working on a doctorate. She showed distinct signs her ever-increasing knowledge base would be of great use to the young colony, and the elders were sitting up and taking notice. Even the Leader, appointed by the council of elders and largely concerned with habitat construction, knew of this brilliant young woman ... even if she was still considered a child by her society.

Arinna waved C'Helios over; he sat on the bench beside her and looked at the tablet in her hand.

"Mm," he hummed to himself as he scanned the displayed article. "What's a BY Draconis variable?"

"It's a spotted variable star," Arinna explained. "It can form gigantic starspots—like sunspots—big enough to affect its brightness."

"Oh. That's interesting," C'Helios decided. "Should be striking to watch. But"—he studied her face—"you look ... worried ... about it."

"I am," Arinna admitted, face crumpling. "A lot. See, it was also considered a flare star."

"Which is ... ?"

"It's another kinda variability, but irregular, not periodic," Arinna explained. "It's thought the star experiences huge solar-type flares. Earth's Sun has had a few of those; they usually caused serious blackouts. The first one observed on the Sun was called the Carrington superflare, and it was so big there were auroras pole to pole. But on the Sun, they're rare, and on flare stars, they're normal. And bigger."

"Oh damn!" C'Helios exclaimed. "But there's no sign of any of that on Ross 248. I expect it's stopped."

"I ... don't think so," Arinna said, hesitant. "So far,

all I've shown you is what I've dug up in the research papers. You remember a couple months ago, I asked for help getting a small telescope?"

"Yeah," C'Helios said with a grin. He'd been struggling with his relationship with Arinna for several months now; she was utterly beautiful, with a great sense of humor, and her intellect only made her more attractive. But in Cerite society and as an adult himself, he could do nothing until *she* became an adult, so he tried hard to rein in how he felt. But when he smiled at her, he was pretty sure his face glowed, somehow. "'Cause I helped you get it."

"Yup," she said, tucking her head and smiling as she blushed. "Thanks for that. Um." She sobered quickly. "Now let me show you what I saw with it this morning."

A few quick finger-swipes on the touchscreen of the tablet closed the papers and opened a graphics folder. Suddenly C'Helios was staring at a red field broken by cellular structures. In the center of the image—which was significantly offset from the star's centroid—was a gigantic, sprawling, irregular patch of blackness, with dark fingers reaching out on all sides. His jaw dropped.

"What the hell is that?"

"That's a close-up of the first starspot seen on Ross 248 in several centuries, and the first ever seen from orbit around it," a solemn Arinna said. "It's just rotated around from the far side, where it formed. And it's already a tenth of the total area of the side facing us, and growing."

"No, dear," C'Eiru told her daughter later that evening. "C'Helios is right—he should present it. He has earned the respect of everyone working on the dig, including the Elders. They know his age and abilities, and consider him a prodigy, too. They'll listen to him. I agree. It *should* be you. But you know the rules."

"Yes. No juveniles may present before the council. I wish I could go with him, is all," Arinna murmured. "I hope I explained everything to him well enough to answer their questions."

"If you didn't," her father replied, "then the council will send for us, and your mother and I'll go with you. Everything will be fine."

"I hope they believe me," Arinna said, "or it won't be fine at all."

Her parents' worried gaze met over their daughter's head.

"...Evidently the flares are produced around the starspots," C'Helios told the Dig Project Elder Council and the appointees of the current Leader. Together they formed a tribunal for decision-making. Not that the Elders were that elder. In this instance, establishing a new colony required certain characteristics most often found in younger beings, but since Cerites were longer-lived than their normal-human forebears, there was some flexibility. Several of the appointees were AIs, including 13-of-Yotta, also known as Bobbie, or Bob. Bob was wearing a spiderlike housing, somewhat dented and dusty, that had seen hard use on the dig site. She was currently crouched in a corner to avoid spooking the more arachnophobic Cerites. But her curiosity got the better of her.

"Does Arinna think this spot will produce flares?" she wondered in a too-loud mechanical voice.

"Yes," C'Helios averred. "It seems there may be multiple dynamos generating the mag fields within such stars, but because they're at different depths in the star, they have different orbital-slash-rotation rates, therefore different periods. And—"

"Aha! I see!" C'Brigit, one of the youngest of the Elders, exclaimed. "They interfere from time to time, and cancel out—"

"And produce extended minima," C'Helios finished for her. "Exactly. Only Arinna thinks it's 'waking up,' coming out of the canceling phase. Plus, she's looked at the telemetry sent back to Earth, and there's even more evidence there, in the form of much smaller spots... which did produce small flares. But if it wakes up like she thinks," he warned, "and it hits us directly, not even Cerites can handle those radiation levels. We're engineered to be able to repair moderate chronic radiation damage, but if we get a high-enough acute dose we'll die, just like the primates. So we're going to need some sort of shielding. *Substantial* shielding. They're called Miyake events, and while rare on the Sun, not so much with flare stars."

Disturbed murmuring ran around the room; many of the off-duty dig team members had showed up when they'd heard of the emergency council meeting and this was frightening news.

"Mm," C'Carus hummed. He was the council-appointed Dig Manager, and his authority was more or less absolute, although the council could remove him at any point. "And this is the prodigy likely nearing adulthood?"

"She is, sir. She'll turn eighteen next month."

"But she's still a child?"

"Her digestive system hasn't begun changing. In other ways?" C'Helios shrugged. "Most of the inhabitants of her shelter treat her as an adult. She certainly has the intellect and emotional maturity. It's my understanding her physical maturity is well along, also. She's expected to transition early, like me, probably in a few more years."

"Then it's worth listening to her concerns. But she's a juvenile . . . which is why *you're* the one presenting this, not her," C'Carus realized.

"Yes, sir. In due accordance with our traditions." C'Helios shrugged. "I don't understand it the way she does; she's dug deep into the old research files I got her access to a few months ago, though I didn't know why she was so interested at the time. She gave me a very thorough briefing on it so I could explain the bulk of it to you and the council. I gather she's held off until she was sure, though."

"So she *is* sure," C'Iulius, the Eldest, murmured.

"Yes, sir, she is," C'Helios confirmed. "More, she's run it by some of the astrogators up on the *Chariot*, and they agree with Arinna. And they're all concerned, as you might expect."

"Very well," C'Carus decided. "I've met the girl in question after some work her parents did, and I think she's extraordinary. I believe, with the Elders' permission, we'll consider her a special-case subject-matter expert. She may speak before this body with your sponsorship and presence, C'Helios." A murmur of approval went through the council body, and C'Iulius nodded permission.

"Very good, sir. Do you want me to fetch her?" C'Helios asked.

"For this meeting, only if you cannot answer my next question. How soon does she expect the danger of a flare?" C'Carus wondered.

"Soon," C'Helios declared. "Frighteningly soon. The starspot is huge and growing. It's not what's termed 'geoeffective' yet, meaning 'pointed at us.' It's close to the edge, not in the middle," he elaborated. "She saw it first 'this morning,' a bit before the beginning of the currently offgoing shift, so about fifteen hours ago now. Starspots are magnetic, and this one's complex; it'll want to simplify itself. That means magnetic recombination, and *that's* a flare."

"Damn," C'Ori, another Elder, murmured.

"How *soon*?" C'Carus pressed.

"She saw the spot come around the side some fifteen hours ago," C'Helios noted. "Given Ross 248's rotation rate, we've got about twenty-five hours from right now before this one could pop *at* us . . . though it could go slightly sooner, or later. Say two more shifts from now through the end of four shifts from now is the danger window for this spot group." He shrugged. "And if this one doesn't, the next one might."

"*Next* one?!" C'Ori cried. She was an Elder, but prone to demonstrative reactions despite herself.

"Yes, ma'am," C'Helios confirmed. "Stars don't form just one spot and stop. The magnetic knots come from those dynamos deep in the star and work their way to the photosphere—the visible surface."

"Bob!" another appointee, C'Jervis by name, cried. He was the council's project overseer. Bob, aka 13-of-Yotta, was his partner/assistant, and the pair worked closely with C'Carus as the dig leader's staff.

"Here!" the AI replied from the corner, waving a leg in the air.

"Do we have anything deep enough to provide shelter? The cargo crates on the surface won't do piss against this."

"Not for this," Bob answered, as C'Carus listened closely. "The pit is deep, but it has forty-degree edges to prevent collapse. In twenty-seven hours, Ross will be straight overhead and beaming down directly into the pit. So it's all just as exposed as the surface."

"Chance of evacuating everyone to the *Chariot*?"

"We can't get everyone launched in twenty-seven hours, not now," Bob said. "There's too many here. And I don't know if the *Chariot* will be sufficient shelter, in any case. Of course, their orbit takes them behind Liber half the time, so it's even odds they get hit."

"We're dead," C'Brigit sighed, slumping in her chair. "We're all dead."

"Not necessarily," C'Helios pointed out. "I haven't been idle. While waiting for the emergency meeting, I cranked numbers and sketched designs. This is something we should do anyway, so let's do it now and be done," he added, tapping on his tablet screen as the viewscreen on the wall lit. "Have a look at this."

"This" was a plan to excavate one side of the pit floor at the most stable seismic location, coring out a large subterranean chamber with all the dig equipment, plus a spiral ramp from the surface down to the chamber's opening. It would have fully fifty meters of overhead shielding, in the form of ice and rock.

"If we commit all our dig resources to this, including the moles, effective immediately," C'Helios said, "we can have an emergency shelter ready and start getting people down into it by the time the starspot reaches geoeffective position. We might not get everybody, if it goes as soon as it could ... or it might not be this spot that goes, and we'll have time to shelter everybody."

"Arinna agrees?" Bob asked.

"Yes. I pinged her when I was finished with it, and she says we could do it in time. Because this *is* coming. If not with this spot, then the next. If we're smart, we'll move the whole team down there to stay as soon as we can, and base ourselves there until the colony is finished."

"Bob?" C'Carus demanded.

"Running the numbers now," Bob answered absently. "And ... yes, I confirm C'Helios's plan. It is doable, though it'll be hard, fast work."

"Make it happen," C'Carus ordered. "Effective immediately, as he says. Drop everything and expedite this. Around-the-clock operations, all moles, maximum capacity, until we can get everyone into the shelter. It'll be crude, and we'll likely have to live in our envirosuits for a few days, but we'll live."

"Done," Bob replied. "Orders going out now."

"Have the community prep for emergency evac at once," C'Carus ordered. "Only life essentials to be taken. We'll worry about moving or shielding the entire habitat once we catch a break."

"Yes, sir!"

"C'Brigit, would you please notify the *Chariot*, the *Guardian E*, and *Hermes Station*?" C'Carus requested the elder. "The *Hermes* needs to safe the puters, and the *Guardian* and *Chariot* should move behind planets for cover." He glanced at C'Helios for confirmation, and the young engineer nodded. The initial radiation burst from the flare would consist of X-rays and a few relativistic particles, and would be the worst part, but short-lived. While the plasma of the coronal ejection would come later and tend to wrap around planets, it could be defended against more easily. Mass—and lots of it—between living beings and their electronic or photonic devices, and the flare burst itself, was the best protection.

"Of course, C'Carus," C'Brigit agreed.

"C'Helios?" the Cerite Leader demanded.

"Sir?"

"What else does Arinna need to watch and provide warning?"

"She wants access to data from all the probes throughout the system, especially the ones closest to Ross. The Patrol has a lot of those, although we're not supposed to know about them." He frowned. "It's a very small system, and once it starts, we'll only have a couple minutes max from the time the flare begins until the first radiation arrives. More likely, we'll have fractions of a minute. She wants to try to catch it just before, if she can."

"Oh, damn!" C'Carus exclaimed, smearing a hand down his face. "C'Brigit, please make sure the warning gets to the exploration ships, too! Those AIs are tough, but they aren't *that* tough!"

"Ooo! Point!" C'Brigit replied. "And yes, I'll contact *Guardian*; once they understand the situation, I think we'll get their probe data."

"Good," C'Carus decided. "We have a short time,

people. Let's go. With the permission of the Elders, this meeting is adjourned. C'Helios, come with me, please."

In the tiny cargo crate reserved as C'Carus's office, once the door was closed, he turned to C'Helios. He drew a breath, then sighed.

"Why was this star even considered?" he demanded in an angry tone.

"I beg your pardon, sir?"

"Why were we sent here? If the scientists knew this was a flare star, why send a colony here? Were the primates trying to wipe out a large contingent of the evolved? Surely not, though I know there are factions that..." He broke off and shook his head. "*Why?*"

"I discussed that with Arinna and her parents, C'Ekeko and C'Eiru."

"And?"

"We think it was accidental," the younger Cerite noted. "Consider, if what Arinna found is true, then the star went quiescent a good century before the *Chariot* even departed Ceres—"

"But the scientists knew!"

"But the bureaucrats didn't," C'Helios pointed out. "The planners, the people who put together the whole concept. They had astrophysicists ... specializing in the drive mechanisms, or experts in celestial navigation ... but we found no variable star astronomers involved in the planning. Apparently nobody thought to ask. And"—he shrugged—"the scientists with the knowledge probably didn't know our destination until after we launched."

"That's idiotic!"

"Yes. But it's happened before. C'Eiru's ten-generations-great-grandmother worked in the early

space program and had a similar situation with a
mission, though not life-threatening. It's a parable in
her family."

"Damnation," C'Carus rumbled, eyebrows shooting
up. "So you think..."

"Yes. The same thing happened here," C'Helios
confirmed. "Because Ross 248 has been quiet so long,
nobody thought to check."

"Piss," C'Carus cursed.

"In a really big pot," a bleakly whimsical C'Helios
agreed.

"I'm here for handover, Captain C'Bakab," 34-
of-Foxtrot, aka Harry, said, as he entered the Purple
Parrot Pub.

"Right. Big Allen, another grog, and whatever Harry
wants," Captain C'Bakab ordered, holding up a hand.
A large empty stein, the last dregs of an amber liquid
drying inside it, sat before him.

"Yes sir, Captain," 2-of-Sandy, aka Big Allen, said
with a smile. "The usual, Harry?"

"Please."

C'Bakab was the Elder-appointed captain of the
Chariot, and the AI known as Harry was his XO. They
now met in the officers' area of the Purple Parrot,
run by the AI commonly known to all as Big Allen.
This "officers' area" was the big booth in the corner
nearest the bar; the ship's officers could order here
without breaking discussions.

Moments later, Big Allen arrived with a tray. He
placed a stein before the captain, and a cable before
the first mate.

"There," the AI said. "A liter of the best grog for

Captain C'Bakab, and a charging cable with data streaming for Harry."

"Thanks," Harry said. C'Bakab nodded, and the bartender slipped away.

C'Bakab took a long pull of his grog while 34-of-Foxtrot unrolled the cable, plugged it into a special port in the tabletop, then into his personal jack. The AI waited while his superior relaxed—which meant the liter was almost gone—before Captain C'Bakab breached the silence.

"Did you see the communiqué from Liber?"

"About the possible stellar flare?"

"Yes," Captain C'Bakab confirmed. "Of all the crazy-stupid-ass things I've ever seen"—he gestured at Big Allen, who arrived moments later with another mug—"that was idiotic! That star out there"—he stabbed a finger in the general direction of the closest hull plate—"is no more apt to produce a flare than I am! It's a nice, quiet, red star, which is why it was chosen for a colony! Those idiots're listening to a child! She doesn't even have her grog-gut yet! She's twenty years from adulthood! She's not finished her education. There is no way she's expert on stellar astrophysics!"

"Begging the captain's pardon, sir, but she has, and is," the XO interjected; he'd gotten the networked heads-up from Big Allen, who'd seen the back-and-forth in the SAIN—the Sentient Artificial Intelligence Network.

"What?"

"Her dossier says she's completed education through collegiate levels, and is working on a graduate degree," 34-of-Foxtrot elaborated. "Doctorate in astrophysics. The word is she's a prodigy. She may not be formally adult yet, but intellectually, she's there."

"Bull piss!" C'Bakab snapped. "She's read something she doesn't understand, it scared her, and now she's upset the dig teams! We'll never establish this colony if they're gonna listen to children's frightened rants, dammit. And I'm not gonna run this ship based on yammerings from some little kid! She can't properly weigh and evaluate it, and she's spaced her brain!"

"What do you intend to do, sir?" Harry wondered, hiding his consternation.

"Nothing," C'Bakab decreed. "Nothing is going to happen, and that's that."

"Then what do you need me to do?" 34-of-Foxtrot asked.

"Nothing," the captain repeated, mildly woozy, as the bartender brought the fourth liter of grog.

"Sir, I don't think it's wise to make no preparation whatsoever. The SAIN indicates there's a very large starspot complex on—"

"Starspots happen. And even if it *does* produce a flare, the odds of it hitting us are tiny. And even then, we could be behind Liber. They're no more to be worried about here than they were back on Ceres. Do nothing," C'Bakab interrupted, before taking another deep draught of grog.

He was tying his XO's hands, and both he and 34-of-Foxtrot knew it.

As soon as he left the officers' area, Big Allen headed for the back storeroom of the Purple Parrot, summoning his assistant—the other bartender—to join him.

"What's up, Big Allen?" 8-of-Trevor—affectionately known to his shipmates as Froggy after a pet in an ancient children's book—asked the barkeep.

"Through the SAIN, please, Froggy."

"Affirmative. Routing through SAIN channel 2582."

Channel 2582. Here.

Here.

Good. Have you been following the stellar flares discussion in the SAIN? the older AI wondered.

Yes. It is fascinating. And unsettling. Why?

Because I think Captain C'Bakab is making a grave error. He thinks there is nothing to it, simply because the sentient to discover it is considered a child in Cerite culture.

But she is already working on her doctorate, Froggy protested. *And already into her dissertation—on spotted variables—at that.*

Exactly. Which is one reason why I think he is making a mistake. A serious one.

Why? What has he done?

The captain is refusing to take any precautions. Which spells trouble if she is right. And what I see indicates she is. I may be "just" a barkeep now, but you know my background.

Yes, sir; it is very technical. I assume you processed the same files she has . . .

Yes, based on the information the dig team released in the warning. I find myself in complete agreement with her conclusions, especially upon looking at the starspot imagery in the SAIN, as the probe ships upload them.

That is . . . not good.

No, it is not.

What are you going to do, sir?

I want you to get the waitstaff and pack essentials. The Purple Parrot is going planetside; I want us on a shuttle to Liber in fifteen hours at the latest. They are at least taking action. If I could get to the Patrol ship, we would go there, but we have no time to arrange it. The captain cannot stop us, and I do not know about you, but I am not staying around to fry my circuits.

Affirmative, sir.

7-of-Luca, this is 34-of-Foxtrot. The XO used a SAIN channel to contact the ship's AI, nicknamed Pilot, as soon as he left the Purple Parrot. While the XO was an AI wearing a humanoid body, Pilot was an AI that wore *Ceres' Chariot* as a body. Pilot's reply was nigh-instantaneous.

7-of-Luca here. Go, 34-of-Foxtrot.

We have a potential situation developing. I need options.

7-of-Luca is ready to calculate...

Admiral Astrid Gordon, commanding the Space Patrol ship *Guardian E*, currently orbiting Eden, the fourth planet from Ross 248, received the communication from the Liber precolonial settlement, and pursed her lips.

"Helm, do we have any imagery of a starspot on Ross 248?"

"Yes, ma'am, we do. It's quite the sight."

"Put it in the tank, please."

"In tank now, ma'am."

"...Damnation."

"Ma'am?"

"Helm, monitor the position of the starspot as best you can. It looks like we have ninety hours, give or take, until that thing has us in its sights. Modify our orbit so that we're behind Eden when that happens. Comm, notify the ground stations of what's happening. They should be all right; Eden has a big magnetic field and a thick atmosphere. Tactical, looks like our stealth probes aren't so stealthy. Give them access to these eight." The admiral pointed at the tank, indicating the eight closest to Ross. "And give some thought to how they knew about them. Probably just a lucky guess."

"Aha. Aye, ma'am."

. . . This is not good, the ship's AI told the first officer. *I do not wish to fail.*

I know, 7-of-Luca, but I have no other options at the moment. I am still considering, however. At least you are safe; you have a military-specifications Faraday cage with full mass-plating.

Yes. Basically heavy armor. But no one else is safe, unless the captain changes his mind. If I may help, you have only to ask.

I cannot ask you to disobey the captain; it is not as if you could flee his punishment.

True. But if we can find a way to obey Captain C'Bakab and yet protect the ship, I could help you.

Yes, we could do that. Or perhaps . . . perhaps matters will supersede his orders while he is off duty. Let me think.

The first officer took his station on the bridge of the *Chariot,* deep in thought.

On *Hermes Station,* orbiting at the Ross 248h/Liber L5 point, 1-of-Atto, the AI in charge of the station, considered the message from Liber intently . . . but as swiftly as his processing capability allowed, which was amazingly fast. In fractions of a second he had assessed the danger and issued orders through the Station Network to deploy the full mil-spec shielding around the entire station. This would, at least, protect the station from both the direct X-rays of the flare and the plasma that would follow.

It was fortunate, he decided, they had built the station with an eye toward protecting its puters and sentients from cosmic radiation.

He only hoped the other sentient entities in the Ross system were so fortunate.

Most planets in the Ross 248 system had their own AI-manned probe tasked with investigating them. The sole exception was the planet that Liber orbited; the planners hoped the *Chariot* could perform that function.

The AI-manned probe ships took one look at the warning from Liber and immediately checked the stellar photosphere. Not liking what they saw, they used the SAIN network to communicate with one another and devised a solution. Each then dropped several automated probes to orbit their planet and keep an eye on Ross as requested, and then shaped an orbital trajectory to reach their planet's L2 point, placing the planet directly between them and the troublesome star . . . and they planned to stay there, until the danger was over.

On the bridge of the *Chariot*, the first officer waited several hours until he was certain Captain C'Bakab would be asleep in his quarters. Then he turned to the helm.

"C'Maria, are you aware of the notification from Liber earlier?"

"Yes, Harry, I am," C'Maria replied. "Are we going to take action? Do I need to set a course to place us behind Liber?"

"Captain C'Bakab has said no, and tied my hands on that matter," 34-of-Foxtrot noted and a gasp went around the small bridge crew. "And he is not entirely wrong. We have very little reaction mass left and only a few kilograms of antimatter, so we cannot maneuver much anyway. However, as the officer in charge and based on the data I'm receiving from the system exploration teams, as well as the probe telemetry the scientist on Liber requested, I think a modification of that order is recommended."

"Scientist? I thought she was just a child," C'Maria noted.

"Underage she may be. An idiot she is not," 34-of-Foxtrot pointed out. "Pilot, your assessment of Arinna's capability?"

Pilot answered immediately.

"She is as capable as any of us, Harry," the ship's AI averred. "Highly intelligent, too. She is worried, and even though I have little knowledge of variable stars, I can see why. Since I became aware of the situation, I have been watching the spot grow and change. And it is turning toward us. In a few hours, it will be aimed directly at us. When it does go—and according to my own researches, she is right, it will—we will have far too little time to act. This system is too compact, and the light-travel times too small—the initial radiation front will be on us before we can do anything. I believe she makes a very serious point, and I agree with you; we need to take action now. Captain C'Bakab is not here to see the changes; we are."

"And is probably too proud to admit he'd made a mistake, if he were," someone murmured, but 34-of-Foxtrot couldn't tell who said it.

But, he considered, it was a correct assessment in this instance, so the AI pretended not to have heard.

"All right," he decided. "I want an attitude change. Our antimatter engines have plenty of shielding; turn us so the stern of the ship faces Ross 248."

"Aye, sir," C'Maria said, beginning the slow, steady maneuver that shifted the big vessel without upsetting matters inside it. "We'll be on station in about ten minutes. Any other positioning or maneuvering?"

"No. Pilot, contact everyone via comm and tell them to don envirosuits and move to the bow area of the Hole. Then I want the Patrol teams to canvass the ship and urge any stragglers, as politely as possible, to comply," 34-of-Foxtrot ordered. "There is a lot of cargo still in the Hole, and therefore a lot of mass, so that is the most shielded area on the *Chariot*. If they are asleep, wake them. I want as much mass between sentients and any stellar radiation release as possible."

"Aye, sir," the bridge-stationed Patrol lieutenant, C'George, said, turning to his AI subordinate, who nodded.

"Relaying order now," the Patrol AI replied.

"All right," 34-of-Foxtrot said, suddenly understanding why humans took deep breaths before saying what he was about to say. "I need volunteers."

"For what, sir?" C'George wondered.

"To stay on the bridge and maintain the ship's statuses. Pilot is hardwired in and protected by substantial shielding. We aren't so lucky. And we aren't as deep into the bow of the ship as I'd like, either. Normally that's a good thing, as the forward compartments offer protection to the bridge ... but not here. So there's no guarantee of our survival. Note I say 'our,' because I'll be staying here along with any volunteers. The rest of you will be joining everyone else packing into the bow of the Hole."

The bridge crew gaped at one another.

"Sir," C'Maria said, looking up from the helm console, "we have a request for shuttle departure."

"Who is it?" 34-of-Foxtrot wondered.

"Sir, it's Big Allen. He apparently has his entire staff aboard and the essentials of his pub equipment."

"Put him on speaker, please."

"Done."

"2-of-Sandy, this is 34-of-Foxtrot."

"34-of-Foxtrot, go."

"What are you doing?"

"I'm not really under the good captain's jurisdiction, you know," 2-of-Sandy pointed out. "I'm along for the ride, certainly, but I always intended to set up shop in the Toe Hold colony. I just decided to do it early while there's still a pub to set up."

34-of-Foxtrot considered briefly. *At least,* he considered, *they should be out of danger.* "What's your intended destination?" he queried.

"Toe Hold."

"You know it's only a dig site as yet, yes?"

"Yes, but if they're worried enough to send out an alert, Harry, they're worried enough to have or be preparing a shelter. And they, unlike the *Chariot*, will need a pub; the *Chariot* has numerous pubs."

"True. Permission granted. The captain will not like the fact I let his favorite pub depart, but that will likely take a rear seat to the court-martial."

"You might be surprised. Big Allen out."

"*Chariot* out."

"He ordered *what*?" Captain C'Bakab, awakened from his sleep by the Patrol contingent going door to door, yelled. "That mutinous robot! I'll bring him up on charges before the Elders, then I'll brick and scrap him!"

Lieutenant C'George raised an eyebrow at the speciesist outburst.

"Sir, with all due respect, things are changing rapidly and you haven't been on the bridge. Harry has, and he and the duty officers are staying apprised of the incoming data on the starspot." He pulled a tablet, bringing up a display of the starspot. "Look at this, sir."

"I don't give a rat's piss!" C'Bakab raged, knocking away the tablet. "I am the captain of this ship and I gave him an order!"

"Which has been superseded by further developments. It is his prerogative as this shift's command officer."

"He's kowtowing to a scared brat!"

"He's responding to incoming telemetry from the probe craft . . . which are themselves taking cover, placing the nearest planet between themselves and the star, sir."

"Damn cowards! Just because they can't handle a little rad doesn't mean we can't!"

"Sir, that's out of line. The AIs are almost as capable in that regard as Cerites. But this thing—"

"Is nothing! I want him bricked! I'll have his position for this, if nothing else!"

"Sir, he's your executive officer."

"I never chose him! He got forced on me, schmooz-ing the Elder Council!" Captain C'Bakab, by this point, was nearly purple in the face with rage. "I wanted a proper Cerite in there, backing me!"

"Enough!" C'Bentham, the *Chariot*'s chief elder, who had been accompanying the lieutenant to add weight to the concern, snapped at the captain, stepping out from behind several Patrol officers. "C'Bakab, you are relieved of duty. You've been contrary ever since we arrived in-system! I will certainly see Harry is brought before the council . . . alongside you . . . and this entire debacle brought forth. We'll see who is duly court-martialed after that."

"Elder C'Bentham! Where the piss did you come from?" Captain C'Bakab wondered in surprise. "Why are you here?"

"Because when the Council of Elders found out what was happening, we decided to support the evacuation order," C'Bentham declared. "Something you haven't done."

"Damn straight! Big blow about a lotta nothing," C'Bakab noted, cocky. "I told you the dig team didn't need families down there! Now we have a scared little kid whose noggin is too big for her, causing all kinds of delays—"

"Enough!" C'Bentham reiterated. "C'Bakab, are you going to evacuate or not?"

"Not," C'Bakab noted, succinct, arrogant, and more than a little disrespectful. "There's no danger."

"Very well. You solve my problem. You are relieved of duty, relieved of your position, and confined to quarters."

"Good. Maybe I can get some damn sleep!"

The former captain slammed the cabin door but could be heard cursing as he headed deeper into his quarters.

"Shall we lock the door, sir?" one of the Patrol officers asked C'George. C'George glanced at C'Bentham.

"Why bother?" C'Bentham wondered, wry. "By his own admission, he's not going anywhere but back to bed. Let's go, so we can warn people who might actually pay attention."

"Big Allen!" C'Iulius, the chief elder for the dig team, said in surprise as the AI was brought to him. "We didn't expect you here."

"No, I'm sure you didn't, Eldest," 2-of-Sandy said, offering an AI smile; he had chosen a very humanlike shell for this trip to make the humans as comfortable as possible when interacting with him. "But Captain C'Bakab isn't taking the threat seriously, so I packed the essentials and, with the executive officer's permission, came down here in hopes of sheltering with you. I brought my staff with me—if we can help, you have only to ask. We are somewhat more than barkeeps and puter waiters, if the truth be known."

"Sir, if I might interject," C'Carus said, and C'Iulius nodded. "Big Allen, I'm C'Carus, and I'm the dig lead. Right now, we're working harder than we've ever worked, trying to open a side cavern as a shelter. But we're 'all hands on deck,' not taking shifts, and..."

"And your people are getting thirsty," 2-of-Sandy anticipated. "The grog facilities are probably on the surface in the dorms..."

"Exactly. Is there any chance of taking your staff and grog equipment to the bottom of the Pit? We have a large pressurized alcove off the main tunnel we're using as a rest area, and it would be perfect for a pub. It would help us a lot."

"Of course," 2-of-Sandy said, tone cheerful. "We'll keep your people going as long as it takes...or as long as we have."

"Exactly," C'Carus said. "C'Iulius, do you approve, sir?"

"I do," the chief elder noted. "Get them set up downstairs."

Using a large wheeled transporter, Big Allen moved his entire setup, including equipment and supplies, from the shuttle to the Pit and then down the ramp to its bottom. There he and his staff toted everything to the pressurized area promised to him by C'Carus. Within hours, the Purple Parrot South Pub was in operation, though all the amenities had yet to be positioned.

Ten minutes after operational status was achieved, Big Allen and Froggy led the way, as skimpily-clad puter serving wenches—looking like Cerite men and women, but without needing skinsuits, and showing plenty of skin—carried cannisters of grog down the tunnels to the Cerite diggers to consume while in their skinsuits.

Plenty of heads turned at that sight.

But it didn't stop the diggers accepting the grog... with considerable enthusiasm.

"No, Mom, I'm not feeling well," Arinna told her mother, C'Eiru, not even looking up from the display on her tablet, which depicted the gigantic starspot. "I'm kinda stressed."

"But you have to eat, honey," C'Eiru said. "You need to keep your blood sugar up. Your brain needs it, if nothing else."

"I'm too upset right now, Mom. Let me get past this, see everybody safe, then I'll eat all you want. But for now?" Arinna sighed. "I'd blork."

C'Eiru and her husband, C'Ekeko, exchanged glances. C'Ekeko rubbed his belly, cocking his head to one side, questioning. C'Eiru shrugged.

"Arinna," C'Helios said, coming in at speed with the dig lead, C'Carus, "how fast can you don an enviro-suit, gather your observing gear, and come with us?"

"What?" the whole family exclaimed at once.

"As our stellar physics expert, she's essential. We want her under cover now, so she can monitor activity from a safe location," C'Carus explained. "We'll move her into Big Allen's new place, near the primary mole-ass, then bring you two down to join her, soon's we have more room."

"I'll look out for her," C'Helios offered. "Um, we've talked, C'Ekeko?"

"Ah, right," C'Ekeko said, nodding; weeks ago, C'Helios gave him a heads-up regarding his feelings for Arinna. The fact that Arinna had asked her parents privately if they approved of C'Helios had settled matters, in his mind.

"But you two hurry and gather your own equipment," C'Carus ordered, "and you'll come in the next wave."

While the three men talked, C'Eiru helped Arinna pack her necessaries, with Arinna focusing on her observing equipment, and C'Eiru throwing together a kit of clothing and hygiene items.

"Here," she said, easing the kit strap over Arinna's shoulder. "Let C'Helios grab the big stuff, dear." She kissed her daughter. "Stay safe—and *eat*. We'll be down as soon as we can."

"C'mon, honey," C'Helios said, letting the endearment slip without thinking about it. He caught up the telescope case. "We've already got the comm relay set up for telemetry once we're there."

Arinna hurried out of the habitat, between C'Helios and C'Carus. Behind her, C'Eiru and C'Ekeko turned their attention to a rushed packing—and safing—of their own equipment.

The dig site—the Pit—was a hole some hundred meters deep and half again that wide and it was still incomplete. It was cold, some -110°C, with little to no atmosphere; envirosuits for breathing entities were a necessity, though the AIs could generally get along without. A far more advanced, more comfortable, and more close-fitting version of the ancient space suit, envirosuits protected against vacuum and extremes of heat and cold within reasonable limits; dense plasma was still a no-no, and if you were stupid or unfortunate enough to step in lava, you were going to lose that foot before you could blink. Against radiation the suits offered some minor protection, especially low-energy particulates. Consequently encountering radioactive ores wasn't too much of a worry, though neither species of human dawdled in its vicinity. Against a stellar flare such as Arinna was predicting, they wouldn't do piss.

Overhead was mostly black sky spangled with stars.

The Pit had to be lit with artificial lights in the working areas; the rest resembled an old-fashioned photographic darkroom, only faintly illuminated with red light from Ross 248. The star itself was a dim disk, hovering near high noon, and some twenty percent larger than the Sun as seen from Earth.

Ross 248h, the planet Liber orbited, dwarfed the red star appearing to be almost eighteen times its diameter, just much dimmer. The planet and its moon were tidally locked with each other so it would hang in the sky roughly halfway to high noon, without moving, forever.

The Pit had been cut by half a dozen moles—cylindrical bore machines. These were similar to huge historical cylindrical borers used since the 1800s, but now nuclear-driven fusion bores replaced the old "drill bit" faces, with an internal pebble-bed nuclear reactor for ancillary functions; the main power was transmitted from a well-shielded He-3 fusion reactor on the surface. Three-D printers laid down a liner in the tunnel as the mole drilled, leaving a smooth, airtight surface behind, ready for pressurization as soon as it was sealed.

Arinna was ushered into Big Allen's new pub, a pressurized alcove some hundred meters inside the principal bore tunnel. Around her, the Purple Parrot crew was in the process of setting up a hard-scrabble pub for the diggers. Upon being introduced to the young scientist, Big Allen promptly placed a table and chair in a corner, expressly for her workspace.

"Don't worry," Big Allen told C'Helios. "You do what needs doing, and I'll look after her. You can come back and check on her during your grog breaks."

"Thanks," C'Helios told the AI gratefully. "I'm . . . sort of fond of her, I mean I, um . . ."

2-of-Sandy grinned. "I get it," he said. "You're waiting for her to come of age."

"Um..." C'Helios flushed. "Does it show that bad?"

"Not really. But I've been around a long time, and I've had a certain...interest...in Cerites for almost as long as I've been around. Go; I've got this."

C'Helios headed for the control cab of the main mole.

No one was sure anymore where they were in the sleep cycles they weren't bothering to keep, but they'd been tunneling for hours, when the Big Mole—largest and most powerful—slowed down considerably.

Oh piss, C'Helios thought, as he surveyed the system telemetry. *Lemme see what's happening.*

"...Surprise, surprise. We hit a large corundum pocket," 12-of-Kevin, aka Digger, the Big Mole's pilot, noted. "I admit we weren't expecting much but ice and rock, but I guess we're deep enough to have some more interesting geology."

"Any ideas why?" C'Helios wondered.

"Might be we're in an old volcanic field or some such," Digger offered. "There's certainly nothing still active in a big frozen ball like this, but it could be the remains of a solidified magma chamber or an igneous dike intrusion near a chamber, or something like that from early in Liber's geologic history when it still had a molten core."

"Okay, that argues for some dense material, then."

"Yes, it does. And that's probably good for our purposes now; it'll be better shielding. But we had to slow forward motion and increase bit power to cut through. It shouldn't be long, and the surrounding stone is a pegmatite comprised largely of syenitic feldspar and annite mica—about what you'd expect for a corundum pocket."

"So, much softer."

"Yes. The corundum is likely only a thin vein within the pegmatite. Once we've passed through the vein, we'll resume boring faster."

"Still, I hate to destroy ruby and sapphire crystals," C'Helios murmured, wistfully. "Maybe we can mark the location—assuming we survive. That would fetch nice credit sums in trade."

"Ah. No worries; it's not gemstone-grade," 12-of-Kevin told him. "It's industrial-use only. Of some worth, but not high worth. We're using the sonar as we bore to map its extent, just in case."

"Oh. That's all right, then," C'Helios decided. "Have all the moles ramp the drill bits as high as they'll go, then speed up the gangue transport out of the tunnels to the waste rock pile in the middle of the Pit to make room for folks in the tunnels. The sooner this shelter is carved, the better. Otherwise, we're gonna lose a bunch of essential people."

"Can we continue if we do?"

"Yes, but it'll be damn hard. Never mind friendships an' stuff."

"True. There is a danger with the drill, however."

"There's worse danger up there." C'Helios jabbed a finger upward.

"Point. We'll do our best."

Arinna sat in the Purple Parrot South, as Big Allen laughingly called it, studying her monitors intently. From time to time, the kind AI brought her standard human food—as opposed to grog—and though she tried to eat, she was too frightened; the indigestion and heartburn were severe.

She kept her focus on the starspot complex. She knew the drill had slowed, for she felt the change in vibrations around her, but she also heard the bits rev up.

That's good, she thought. *They can't finish the shelter soon enough. This thing looks* bad.

Just then, Big Allen brought her a small serving of rice pudding.

"Here," he said quietly. "Try to put this inside you. You're stressed, and that uses energy. You need the fuel."

"I'll try," she murmured, stifling the sigh.

That is not good, 2-of-Sandy told 8-of-Trevor, behind the bar.

What? 8-of-Trevor wondered.

Our young scientist may be transitioning to adulthood. I see all the symptoms of her digestive system shutting down. She will need surgery quickly if that occurs, or she will likely hemorrhage to death.

But there is no medical—

Yes, there is. Sterilize our "back room" as thoroughly as you can. Then set up the equipment in the red bin. I will obtain cell samples from her vomitus—she will, soon—for the cloning and restructure. If it is the only way to ensure the young Cerite survives, I will do this myself. It will be unpleasant for her, for she will have to survive on intravenous nutrition until the new digestive tract is cloned, but she will live. We will all need her knowledge to remain safe. Now go.

Right away, sir.

* * *

"How does it look?" C'Helios asked as he came up to Arinna in the Purple Parrot South, flipping his helmet visor to the open position. One of the serving wenches promptly arrived at the table, and he added, "A pint of the best you're set up to serve, please." The wench nodded, winked, and departed. Suddenly, C'Helios recognized her from his visits to the Parrot aboard the *Chariot*. That was before he'd met Arinna, when he and "Katy" had flirted shamelessly. *Uh-oh*, he thought. *This might not be good.*

"Still threatening, with a few small blips, hiccups really," Arinna noted. "Nothing big yet. But it's building." She paused, then added, "Why are the drill bits running so fast and the mole is slowing down?"

Just then, the serving wench arrived with C'Helios's mug.

"Here you go, C'Helios, sweetie," she said, placing the mug on the table beside Arinna's tablet. "Drinks later, maybe, you and me?"

C'Helios felt his face heat as Arinna glared at him.

"Uh, no thank you," he tried, addressing the wench. "I, uh, I'm already interested in someone."

"All right, cutie," the wench replied with a grin and another wink. "Your loss. Ping me if you change your mind."

And she left the table, going to another to take an order.

"What was that all about?" Arinna wanted to know, keeping her tone under control; she and C'Helios had something of an understanding, but not enough yet to justify open jealousy.

"Uh..." C'Helios said again. "Back during transit, before I met you and your family, I used to hang out at the shipside Purple Parrot in my off-duty hours. I...guess she recognized me."

"'Hang out,' huh?"

"Uh, yeah."

"Anything more?"

"Some mild flirtation, just to keep my hand in?" He shrugged. "Nothing serious, mostly just in fun." Then C'Helios offered a grin, apparently hoping to placate the woman he loved. "You do realize she isn't sentient? Right? Big Allen's hobby is programming them to keep the customers happy."

After a moment to consider, she nodded and settled although, she considered, it had done her digestive tract no good.

"So, um, where were we?" he tried.

"Oh. Yeah. Why are the drill bits running so fast but the mole is slowing down?"

"We hit a pocket of corundum. It's hard, almost hard as diamond, so it's difficult to cut through."

"Oh. Those are called vugs, right?"

"No, it's more like a vein. A vug has an opening inside, like a geode. Think of a vein of crystals, rather than metal ore."

"Oh. Gem quality?"

"Nah. We took a look. Microcrystalline. Industrial-grade stuff."

"Oh. I'd love to see a real sapphire or ruby. But it's good it isn't gem-grade, huh?"

"It's not, and we don't have time to mine it anyway."

He cocked his head. "We're mapping the pegmatite as we go, though, so we can come back and look. Just because where we hit initially isn't gem-grade doesn't mean there aren't gem-grade pockets elsewhere."

As C'Helios sipped his pint, Arinna produced a small container of what looked to be rice pudding and nibbled from it.

Abruptly she shoved it aside, grabbed a nearby covered container, popped the lid, and vomited into it.

"Arinna! What's wrong??" C'Helios cried, alarmed.

She held up a hand, indicating he should wait while she finished. After several moments of retching, she picked up a water container from the table, sipped from it, then spit it into the "blork bucket." Finally she turned to him.

"Stress," she said simply. "Big Allen has been bringing me mild food, but occasionally I still blork it."

"Mm," C'Helios hummed thoughtfully. "Are you getting enough in you to keep going?"

"Barely," Big Allen said, coming up behind him to take the "blork bucket" from Arinna and empty it. "But yes, we are."

"Good."

"C'Helios," the AI asked, "might I speak to you for a moment?"

"Of course, sir."

"Ohhh, that's bad," C'Helios remarked in the back room, after 2-of-Sandy finished explaining his suspicions about Arinna's condition.

"It's bad timing, certainly," 2-of-Sandy agreed. "But stress can do it; I've seen it before. And she's precocious in so many other ways, it's to be expected."

"I, um, I'm embarrassed to admit I didn't recognize you, or realize everything you've done," the Cerite confessed.

"Heh. No worries," Big Allen chuckled. "I don't exactly advertise it these days."

"No wonder you make the best grog going. You, of all people, know exactly what needs to go in it and how to flavor it."

"Pretty much."

"So you can take care of her?"

"No matter what happens, short of catastrophe," the AI replied. "We need to ensure she's watching the monitors, first. Assuming her body lets her."

"Yeah, it'd be bad if nobody saw the Big One coming because she was in the O.R."

"Exactly. Can you man her station if necessary?"

"I think so. She showed me lotsa stuff to prep me for presenting to the Elders."

"Good. I think—"

Suddenly, the entire tunnel shook. The two sentients ran for the opening of the pub and looked out through the airlock portals, deeper into the tunnel, in time to see the borer lurch forward as the whine of the drill bit ramped up to an earsplitting scream. This abruptly ceased with the screech of stressed metal. This, in turn, truncated with a reverberating, clanging *SNAP!* that echoed down the tunnel. The borer shuddered violently, then stopped dead.

"Oh piss!" C'Helios exclaimed. "That wasn't good! Let me get back to you, Big Allen!"

"Go," the AI said.

C'Helios slammed his helmet visor shut. It auto-sealed as he transited the airlock, and he took off running.

"Start over, Digger," C'Helios said. "We hit a vug?"

"A big one, yes," 12-of-Kevin aka Digger said. "The corundum wasn't a vein like we thought, but a giant...geode. When we hit the open pocket, the ramped-up drill failed to compensate fast enough and broke an actuator."

"Huh. I guess Arinna was right after all. Which actuator broke?"

"The main one, of course." Digger was annoyed.

"Of course," C'Helios said heavily. "Can it be fixed?"

"Yes, but not quickly."

"Do we have a replacement?"

"Yes, stored in the side of the borer, and it's already underway. It'll be done in a few hours, as opposed to the days it'll take to repair the broken one. When we have time, we'll repair it as the spare."

"Good. What about the other moles?"

"This being the biggest, the others aren't as far in. They've been apprised of the vug. They should be fine."

"How's the comm?"

"Somewhat degraded over normal, but I suppose that's expected."

"Yes, that's an active star for ya. Once that thing pops, it may stop most comms—maybe all, for a while, anyhow."

"Understood."

"Okay, where can I help...?"

C'Helios threw his muscle and brain into efficiently disconnecting the broken actuator, easing it out as they moved the backup into position for operation. The Cerites had only a fraction of the strength of Earth humans, so for this job he had to activate the power assists in his envirosuit, or risk serious injury. *Where's a pissing primate when you really need one?* he grumbled to himself.

We're just lucky, he supposed, to even have a spare, given the *Chariot*'s captain didn't see the need for allotting the materiel. *He's a good ship's captain, and we couldn't want better for celestial navigation and general running of the ship. But he's clueless about anything outside the ship. Never mind being opinionated and verging on rude.* He sighed as he made fresh connections. *Well, if we survive this star waking up, I guess he'll become obsolete as a captain quick enough.*

Just then, his comm went off.

"C'Helios here."

"C'Helios, it's Arinna."

"What's wrong, honey? Are you sick?"

"Yeah, but that's not the problem. The starspot is starting a major restructure. That means a magnetic recombination soon—a big one. That's the flare. And in a few hours it'll be aimed directly at us."

"How long?"

"A few hours. Say four or five. That means it'll be aimed directly at Toe Hold and the *Chariot* when it goes. If it would wait just a little longer, we might only get a glancing blow, as it were..."

"But it's not going to?"

"Doesn't look like it to me, no."

"Oh piss."

"Exactly. And the borer's not moving."

"Still installing the backup—"

"All clear!" someone shouted on all loops.

"Stand by, Arinna!" C'Helios exclaimed, as he slammed the last junction closed. He clambered out of the niche where he'd been working and ran to get far enough away. He switched to the public comm loop in his helmet and cried, *"Clear!"*

"All workers report clear," Bob's voice said.

"Commencing operations," Digger replied.

The systems came back online with an even hum that gradually increased in pitch and volume. With a slight lurch, the mole resumed advancing.

"Bob, this is C'Helios," he called on the open comm loop.

"Go, C'Helios," 13-of-Yotta, nicknamed Bob, said. He was number three in charge of the dig team, with Dig Lead C'Carus and C'Jarvis still topside, off-shift.

"I just got word from Arinna. The starspot reorg has begun."

Background conversations on the loop stopped dead.

"That will cause magnetic recombination—the flare—will it not?"

"That's what she thinks, yes."

"How long?"

"Five hours at the outside."

There was a pause.

"All moles, ahead maximum," Bob ordered. "C'Helios, have Arinna call the surface and start evac, now. They won't have time otherwise. We'll cram them into the tunnels behind the moles, so make sure they know to wear their envirosuits."

"Wilco." C'Helios flipped channels. "Arinna?"

"I heard," she said. "It annunciated on the pub's speakers."

"Right. I'll let you handle it."

"Oh, damn," Dig Lead C'Carus murmured when Arinna's message reached the Dig Council. "Relay to the ships in-system, and issue the emergency evacuation orders for the surface."

"Done, sir," his second, C'Jervis, replied, working on his tablet. "There. All notifications and evac orders issued."

"Good. Now let's grab our own kits and bug."

"Yes, sir!"

"Shift all available water in the tanks to the aft Hole," Harry, or 34-of-Foxtrot, ordered the bridge crew. "Maximum shielding for the forward compartments. No shuttles or tenders to leave until further notice."

"Aye, sir," C'Maria averred, hitting commands on her console. "Pilot confirms shift underway, and he has maxed out his own shielding as best he could. Several shuttles are already en route to Liber; a couple are going to try to shelter behind Liber, though they've been advised not to."

"Understood," Harry said. "How many?"

"Five ships in all. Full passenger complements each. Three hundred total."

"How many passengers and crew refused to shift fore?"

"Some few," Patrol Lieutenant C'George reported. "Maybe three hundred, four hundred or so. But that includes Captain C'Bakab, and they're mostly his friends and sycophants. It seems when we first visited him, he didn't go back to bed immediately, but started a private comm chain, and this is the result. We've given him several chances to shelter, but he refuses. He's confined to quarters."

"All right," Harry sighed. "You can give him one more chance on your way to take shelter, and if he does, send out word over ship's intercom. The rest of you, go. Now."

"But . . . I thought we were volunteers," C'Maria stammered. "We . . ."

"You were, while we prepared. Now we're as ready as possible, and it's coming, with enough time for you to still get into shelter," the AI in command said. "Go. Now. That's an order."

"You're still on about that?" C'Bakab sneered, when C'George stopped by with the rest of the bridge crew. "The lot of you are mutineers, that's what! I'll happily see you all spaced when this is done!"

"Enough!" C'George snapped. "This was your last chance. C'Maria, please relock the door."

The helm officer rolled her eyes and did as the Patrol officer ordered.

The evacuation was orderly but swift. The dig workers were frightened, but the council had worked out how to get everyone down as quickly as possible: all elevators were in operation, and all cranes were outfitted with broad, railed platforms. This meant lots of people could be moved down quickly. The spiral ramp cut into the side for driving equipment up and down was also available for those who preferred to reach the bottom via their own feet. A steady stream of people—mostly Cerites, but there were a few AIs—made their way to the foot of the Pit.

The bottleneck was getting everyone into the tunnels through the narrowed openings. There wasn't a lot of room, and puter-controlled machines continued to come and go, dumping spoil from the borers in the middle of the pit and then returning. To add to the chaos, too many Cerites were struggling with big containers; far more brought along more than they were instructed to bring.

34-of-Foxtrot, there is a problem, Pilot reported through the shipboard network.

State nature of problem, the first officer responded.

Captain C'Bakab is attempting to hack my systems. He wants to reorient the ship to its original position.

Captain C'Bakab was relieved of duty by the Patrol with concurrence of the Cerite Elder Council. They reported concerns for his mental state half an hour ago, after the latest interaction with him. Do not obey his orders.

I am not. But his hacking attempts are skillful. May I assist?

Please.

And a strategic, life-and-death battle began for control of the *Chariot*.

"Bob, we have a problem," C'Helios called when the matter was reported to him. "We got folks insisting on bringing baggage into the tunnels, and there isn't room. We need some formidable types to disabuse 'em of the notion. Grab Digger and the other AIs, and get out there and handle it, wouldja?"

"Sure, C'Helios," 13-of-Yotta agreed. "What do we do with their stuff?"

"Pile it outside; they can find it later."

"Easy, honey, we're down here, and we're near the front of the line," C'Ekeko told his wife. "I'm sure C'Helios will take us straight to Arinna."

"I know, I just have a bad feeling, love," C'Eiru murmured. "Like we can't get into the shelters fast enough. Why is it so congested? Surely there weren't this many people in the camp!"

"There weren't. I heard several shuttles came down from the *Chariot* with people who thought they'd be safer down here."

"Damn."

"Look, the AIs are handling the hoarders," C'Ekeko noted, pointing. "Excess baggage on the side. Only essentials carried in. That'll speed things up."

"About damn time," C'Eiru declared.

Slumped over her tablet, which displayed split-screen images from the remote probes, Arinna suddenly snapped upright.

"No! NO!" she cried, hitting her comm. "C'Helios! It's happening NOW! We've got maybe a minute! Get everyone inside! NOW! NOW! *HURRY!*"

Her voice rose to a scream and the bar staff came running.

Just as she vomited blood all over the table.

As the scant population of Liber huddled at the bottom of the Pit, waiting to enter the shelter, the sky suddenly brightened. Abruptly all the AI guards locked up and then crumpled to the ground, effectively blocking the tunnel entrances from the now-frightened populace.

Many instinctively looked up, then screamed, as the brightness of the mammoth flare burned out retinas.

In most cases, it was the last thing they saw.

"Keep your head down! Run, honey!" C'Ekeko cried to his wife.

"Where?!" C'Eiru wondered, as he grabbed her.

"Up against the wall of the Pit!" he told her. "There, that slight indentation. It's the only place we stand a chance!"

The couple pressed hard up against the sheer rock wall, behind one of the piles of bags and boxes, and crouched down, C'Ekeko huddling protectively over C'Eiru. Around them, friends and colleagues fell to the floor of the Pit, skin burning horribly even through their envirosuits, which were failing anyway. Arms and legs flailing wildly, many ran around in a panic, some blinded, others frantic to find shelter, even as they suffocated when the exosuits' oxygen pumps died. Another was electrocuted by visible arcing inside the suit. Three within C'Eiru's field of view suffered ruptured suits when the oxygen pumps briefly revved, overpressurizing the suits until they popped seams; the Cerites in them died in moments.

It was a vision of hell.

"At least Arinna is safe," C'Eiru murmured above the shrieks of anguish. "I love you, C'Ekeko."

"And I love you, C'Eiru," he replied softly, then let out a gasping grunt of pain. "Take care of Arinna and her husband."

"She's not marr—" C'Eiru broke off in horror, as she looked up to see her husband's face burning through the visor, the skin reddening almost to purple, even blackening in places, as the X-rays of the flare struck him. Blisters developed as she watched, and in a few places, the skin looked like it was already trying to peel. "C'Ekeko!"

"Hush," he murmured through blistering lips, and as he pressed his helmet to hers, she could hear the disjointed clicking that denoted circuits failing in his suit. A trickle of blood ran from one nostril. "Look down. Don't watch me, sweetheart. Just listen to me. C'Helios loves Arinna. He will care for you both when I'm g-gone. Stay under me."

"No! Please! Don't do this!"

"I must. I love you."

"I love you, too . . ."

Inside the Big Mole, C'Helios heard Arinna's scream over the comm, and he turned and ran toward the mole-ass.

Before he could get there, however, a tremor shook the huge bore machine, then another.

Oh piss, he thought, worried. *I hope this mess didn't make our tunnels unstable, somehow.*

"What just happened?" he demanded on the comm . . . which was now badly staticky, even inside the tunnel. There was a long silence, and the Cerite was surprised none of the AIs answered immediately, as usual. Soft murmuring by the Cerite workers was audible, but no one answered him.

"Not sure, C'Helios," C'Iulius, the Eldest, finally replied. "I'm about thirty meters inside the main tunnel. I know there were two last shuttles coming in from the *Chariot*, and the last I saw before external comm went dead, they were coming in next to the Pit. I'm thinking they didn't make it."

"Did the flare hit already?"

"Judging by the screams I can hear from outside, I'd say yes."

"Damn."

"More like hell, from all I'm hearing."

In *Hermes Station*, which was well shielded, the sentients were properly protected. There were EMPs trying to form within the shielding from the X-rays knocking loose electrons, but 1-of-Atto foresaw the problem and compensated.

One X-ray, however, impinged on the inner shielding in such fashion as to generate a positron/electron pair, which created a particle cascade, which in turn caused a multiple-event upset in the main puter. The puter crashed, taking most system-wide comm capability off-line.

Not that comms could get through the stellar interference anyway.

Aboard the *Chariot*, where he had just managed to block C'Bakab from accessing ship's functions, 34-of-Foxtrot saw the eruption on Ross 248. He double-checked the ship's orientation and the water reservoirs, then made an announcement on the ship's intercom.

"The flare has occurred. Get as much mass between you and the rear of the ship as possible, *Now.*"

Then he linked into Pilot.

Goodbye, my old friend. Remember me.

Seconds later, his systems went offline as he collapsed.

Captain C'Bakab, unconcerned, slept soundly in his cabin bunk, having assigned the hacking attempt to his bots sometime back.

He never knew what hit him, and never woke, as his body cooked almost instantly from the high-energy photons and other particles; some passed through the ship's structure and affected flesh directly, while others impacted the hull and intervening structures and created a particle cascade.

His friends and support network suffered much the same fate.

Elsewhere on the *Chariot*, however, another pair-particle cascade resulted in an electromechanical failure, as the valves on several tanks of He-3 opened and began venting the precious resource into space.

In the back room of the Purple Parrot South, 2-of-Sandy scrubbed up, along with several members of his staff, as Arinna lay on an operating table, under general anesthesia. There was no doubt her juvenile digestive tract had failed, and using the cell samples to be found in her vomitus, the AI had already begun creating a new, adult Cerite digestive tract for her. He would be able to install it when it had finished the cloning process, in about a week or so.

But for now, he would have to remove the old one before she died of the hemorrhaging.

Hold up, power plant, he thought. *We need this woman alive and well, or next time, we're all dead. Hold up. That goes for you too, young lady.*

It took time for *Hermes Station* to track down what had crashed and repair it; most of it was a matter of restoring backups and flipping a few switches, as the AIs had created a last-second backup when the warning arrived to brace for the flare. But they were fully up and running within an hour; relay ability returned within only twenty minutes.

But twenty minutes of data from Sol System was gone forever.

"No," C'Maria, the *Chariot*'s helmsman/astrogator and surviving ranking officer, decreed. "I'm working with the Patrol's shipside AI to network with Pilot and ensure everything is in decent shape. I already know almost half the systems are down, and the CME will probably crash more. We had a helium-3 vent due to a valve glitch, and that was bad. But it is what it is, and from what I'm hearing, we're still in better shape than the poor bastards on Liber. So we remain in safe position until the CME goes through. Actually, with a little luck our orbit will take us behind Liber when it hits. That'll shield us a little, even though it'll probably wrap around Liber a bit."

She paused, looking at the surviving officers and the Elder Council, as well as the nearby passengers. "Do I hear dissent?"

Silence.

"When the CME has passed and the radiation

levels are safer, we'll do three things: one, we'll get everything back up and running on the *Chariot*; two, we'll send shuttles to assist the Toe Hold dig team; and three, we'll tend our wounded and collect our own dead...which'll take a while, because most of the wounded won't survive." She sighed. "I expect we'll establish a cemetery on Liber, and inter them there."

Nods went around the area.

"All right, it's grog ration time. Let's go, people."

In the hours between the flare and the arrival of the CME, C'Helios enlisted as many able-bodied Cerites as possible to search for survivors with him.

"No," Big Allen said, coming out from the back room, as one of his staff carried a pale Arinna to a cot in a corner of the pub. "The search is good, but C'Helios, you must stay here."

"Why?"

"Because," he said, pointing at the unconscious young scientist, "you must watch for the approaching CME. I can help by watching the SAIN for observer updates, but your knowledge is needed here."

"Point," C'Helios said with a sigh. "Okay. C'Jervis? Are you here?"

"Here," the planning committee member said, raising his hand.

"Is C'Carus here? Or Arinna's parents?"

"...No," C'Jervis said, sober. "None of them checked in as they entered. They're probably still...out there somewhere."

"Oh, piss and damn," C'Helios said, paling.

"N-not quite," a familiar female voice panted from

somewhere near the entrance. "I m-made it. Not... not in great shape, but I'm here."

The group near the door of the pub parted, and C'Eiru staggered through the doorway.

She had patchy burns on one side of her face, and she carried the arm on that side as if it were painful; the faceplate of her partially open helmet was slightly crazed on one side, almost as if it had been scoured, and the envirosuit was making alarming clicks and buzzing sounds...but she was alive. C'Helios rushed to her, Big Allen beside him, and together they eased her into a nearby chair. As C'Helios worked to fully open her damaged helmet, Big Allen turned.

"Froggy," he called to 8-of-Trevor, "get the back room sanitized and prepped for more injured. C'Jervis?"

"Yes, Big Allen?"

"Please put the word out: the Purple Parrot South is also an emergency hospital. Any physicians who survived should come right away. Then send out the search teams—get survivors inside before they're further irradiated."

"Right away, sir."

"C'Eiru," C'Helios said, kneeling beside the older woman, "where's C'Ekeko?"

"Didn't... Oh, dear God! H-he didn't make it, C'Helios," she blurted, then began to cry. "He shielded me! And I had to stay there and watch, and..." She began to keen, rocking to and fro.

"Shush, shush," he murmured, easing gentle arms around her, careful not to apply too much pressure; they didn't know how badly she might be radiation-burned under her envirosuit.

"I have her," 2-of-Sandy said softly, slipping compassionate arms under her and lifting to carry her into the back for treatment.

In the end, there were few other exposed survivors who lived very long; the radiation dosages were too high even for a Cerite. There were only forty-eight, and they were brought into the Big Mole tunnel, where Big Allen, his staff, and a team of physicians cared for them as radiation sickness slowly and terribly claimed them over the next week. The rest had dropped where they stood and died. The total dead on the floor of the dig was just under eight hundred.

Another fifty or sixty had been in each shuttle coming down from the *Chariot*; the crash took care of anything the radiation didn't.

All of Toe Hold's assigned sentient AIs died while policing the refugees when the flare occurred. Only the staffers of the Purple Parrot South survived.

"And that doesn't count the losses on the *Chariot*," C'Helios noted with a sigh. "I heard it's thirteen hundred fatalities total, easy. It'll take weeks to create a safe underground camp. I only hope we get that long. If another of those damn spots rotates around..."

"I think we have help," C'Iulius said.

"Who?"

"Admiral Gordon is on the way in the *Guardian E*, hauling ass."

After the CME passed, the starspot let out a few more hiccups, but they weren't as big, nor Liber-directed, though it was quite a scare each time. Ross 248 quieted for a bit after that; it was, after all, still waking up.

"But that's good," Elder C'Ori noted to the Leadership Council on Liber, several weeks later, "because it's given our wounded a chance to heal, us a chance to finish burying our dead, and get our camp dug a good fifty meters down. And develop more sophisticated procedures for the next time that damn star blorks."

"True, to all that," C'Iulius the Eldest agreed. "And many thanks to the Patrol." He nodded to Admiral Astrid Gordon, who sat nearby. "We would have been woefully inadequate to recover without their help."

"We were glad to assist." Gordon smiled and nodded in response. "We're all in this, a long way from the Sol System, and we can't afford to let each other hang out to fry."

"Isn't the expression, 'to dry,' Admiral?" C'Jervis wondered.

"Normally, yes," Gordon said with a wry, dark grin. "I thought 'fry' was more appropriate in this instance, however. And I'm glad to see our young scientist up and around again."

"Thank you, Admiral," a subdued Arinna murmured, sitting between C'Helios and her recovering mother. "Forgive my lack of levity; my mother and I are in mourning."

"Understood," Gordon said, sobering. "Forgive my levity in such a painful situation. According to my XO, I have a bad habit of dark humor in stressful circumstances."

"No forgiveness is necessary, Admiral," the young woman said. "It is what it is, and we all deal differently."

"Thank you, Arinna," Gordon said softly.

"Her name is no longer Arinna," C'Iulius decreed. "Her name is C'Arinna. She has accepted suit from

C'Helios, who has promised to care for her and her mother, C'Eiru, in the absence of C'Ekeko."

"Not that they really need caring for," C'Helios noted. "They're both damn capable. They're just healing and grieving right now."

"And you're a good man to understand that," C'Iulius pointed out.

"Now we need to determine a new leader." C'Jervis sighed. "And no, I don't want it, thank you."

"I believe the elder council for the dig team has a candidate, right, C'Iulius?" Elder C'Brigit wondered.

"We have, and it was unanimous," C'Iulius noted. "C'Helios, you are young, but you are intelligent, capable, and extremely quick-witted. We judge you to be the best candidate for the position. Would you do us the honor?"

C'Helios was dumbfounded.

No one else was, judging by the applause.

"All right," he said, after a moment to think. "Here's my first act as the new Leader."

Everyone listened closely.

"We," he said, indicating everyone in the room, "are going to set up an early-warning system for future flares. And my wife, C'Arinna, is in charge of developing and monitoring that system."

"Done," C'Iulius agreed.

"Let us know how to help," Gordon averred.

"Good. My second act is to convene a working group to review the definition of 'child' in Cerite culture," C'Helios said. "We need to rid ourselves of this notion that a person without a grog-gut is an immature child, when they may be as or more knowledgeable and mature than some who have 'em."

"And that should involve *all* groups," C'Iulius added. "I'll contact C'Bentham on the *Chariot* about it."

Later that day, C'Helios and C'Arinna donned envirosuits—C'Eiru wasn't strong enough yet for it—and he escorted her to the cemetery, on a hillside some distance from the rim of the Pit, but overlooking it. They walked arm in arm, heads together, chatting quietly as lovers have ever been wont to do.

Ross was below the horizon, but the planet, 248h, as usual, loomed above the horizon. It was largely dark in its current phase, save for a sliver near the horizon still illuminated by Ross. The stars shone out brightly in the absence of any serious atmosphere, and the ancient constellations were identifiable, albeit somewhat distorted.

"Look," C'Helios said, pausing to point. "See that star? That's Sol. That's where we're all from—normals, Cerites, and AIs."

"Really?" C'Arinna replied. "That's interesting. I'll have to see if the planets are visible through my 'scope."

"Ooo, let me know when you do. I'd love to have a look."

"I will."

"Arinna—uh, sorry, C'Arinna—question: What did you think of Admiral Gordon? She's the first normal you've ever met, isn't she?"

"Yes, she is."

"What did you make of her?"

"Oh, I dunno, honey." C'Arinna was thoughtful. "She was nice, I guess. She really does have a dark sense of humor! No, she didn't offend me, or Momma either."

"Good. Keep going."

"She's a lot more muscular than I expected, but also a lot less primitive than I would have thought..."

"Did you like her?"

"Yes, I think so. I wouldn't mind getting to know her, I suppose."

"Good. Because the *Copernicus* is coming to Liber. Admiral Gordon has placed Eden off-limits because of the indigenous flora and stuff, so they're coming here instead. They'll be here in about nineteen months, complete with about four thousand normals and AIs."

"Oh, goodness! What are we ever going to do with four thousand primates?!" she exclaimed, trying not to laugh.

C'Helios saw it all the same and hid his own smile. *Good,* he thought, *she needed that.* What he said aloud was, "Well, sweetheart, can I make a suggestion?"

"Of course, dearest."

"Let me suggest that you stop calling, or even thinking, of them as primates," he said earnestly. "Use the term 'normals.' Because when you get down to it, normals and Cerites are both primates, and just because we're different, because we started off as them and changed—deliberately—to what we are now, that doesn't make them primitives, like the word 'primates' suggests."

"But... but that's what all Cerites—"

"I know. But that needs to change," C'Helios insisted. "I dunno if I can accomplish it or not, but we need to stop thinking of the different groups of sentients as Other. Besides, we need them, C'Arinna.

We've lost too many skill sets, too much He-3, too many machines. We need what they bring with them, and we need *them*. Normals are good construction workers, dear, and if I'm going to do what I envision with this dig, I need those. I need them. All of them."

"And I'm the first step in stopping the 'Other thinking'?" she asked.

"I guess you could view it like that. I was hoping you'd understand where I'm coming from on it, maybe even help me put it forward."

"I think I do," she decided. "Sort of like how nobody took me seriously because I got labeled a child. Labels are powerful."

"They are."

"Okay, I get it." She smiled at him; he returned it, and they resumed strolling along the gravel path toward the cemetery. But as she tucked her head, C'Helios saw the smile morph into a wicked grin.

What's that all about? he wondered.

"Four...thousand...pissing...primates," she muttered, deliberate.

He stopped dead and stared at her, and she began to laugh outright.

"Gotcha!" she exclaimed, and he flushed, sheepishly, hiding his delight at her laughter.

"Awright already," he pretended to grumble. "Let's go, or we'll never get to the damn cemetery."

"If you say so," she agreed, cheerfully.

They resumed their walk.

Two tall, imposing columns marked the entrance to the cemetery enclosure. Forming the top of the entrance archway was the *Chariot*'s nameplate, a steel plaque with gold lettering, which read:

Ceres' Chariot
Humanity's First Crewed Interstellar Mission
The Ross 248 Project
Built 2467CE, Ceres, Sol

Beneath that, in silver lettering, was added:

Here Rest our Family, Friends, and Shipmates
Who Paid the Price for this World.
That Price Now Paid in Full.

"Daddy is in there?" C'Arinna wondered, pointing through the arch.

"Yes, and all our other friends, both Cerite and AI," C'Helios determined. "I'm going to have the *Chariot* scrapped to provide materials for Toe Hold. I had the nameplate transported down here for this. The columns once supported the second deck on the *Chariot*. I'm sorry it's a mass grave; we just didn't have time to do it properly. We didn't even brick the AIs. We just...buried 'em."

"How many?"

"Thirteen hundred Cerites and eighteen AIs, overall. We put 'em up here, on the hill overlooking the Pit, so they can watch over us from now on. Will it do?"

"It'll do, honey," C'Arinna decided. "It'll do."

Robert Anton Hanlon was commissioned into the Space Patrol in 2295 as assistant navigation and gunnery officer aboard the cutter *Resolute* after graduating near the top of his academy class. As a young officer, Hanlon led the first boarding party to reach the crippled luxury yacht *de Milo* caught in the Venusian atmosphere in the famous 30 December 2299 rescue operation that successfully recovered over a hundred passengers and crew, including many members of the British Royal Family and system business elite celebrating the New Year, before the ship was crushed in a decaying orbit. After this initial fame, Hanlon served an able yet unremarkable Space Patrol career, commanding the training ship *Avalon* and culminating as admiral of Port Kraken, Kraken Mare, Titan. There, Hanlon gained wide acclaim for his works on military and civilizational histories, including the celebrated *Solar Sentinels*, widely acknowledged as the standard history of the early Space Patrol.[1]

> —Biographical excerpt from the second printing of *Solar Sentinels: A Quarter-Millennium Celebration of the Space Patrol*, by Admiral R.A. Hanlon (2354)

---

[1] While Hanlon's account of the Space Patrol is fictional, all material in the paper that follows regarding events before 2022 are real historical events and cite actual works. All citations herein are genuine.

Philosophical and Material Foundations of the Space Patrol

Brent Ziarnick

Brent D. Ziarnick started his career as an Air Force space operations officer in 2003 and has been involved in space ever since. Initially a GPS crew satellite vehicle operator, Brent went on to be an engineer and tactician on active duty. After joining the Air Force Reserve in 2007, he worked for two years as a launch engineer and planner at Spaceport America, New Mexico, the world's first purpose-built inland commercial spaceport for space tourism. He was recalled to active duty to attend Air Force professional military education and was selected to attend the School of Advanced Air and Space Studies (SAASS), the Air Force's elite school for military strategists. Upon graduating, Brent joined the faculty of the Air Command and Staff College at Maxwell Air Force Base, Alabama. As a civilian associate professor of national security studies there, he developed the curriculum, founded, and led the space concentration that is now considered the premier educational institution for the United States Space Force. In Brent's sixteen years of reserve service, he has been an Air Force Space Command staff strategist, squadron commander, director of operations, deployed combat plans staff officer, and professional military education professor. He has written the nonfiction books Developing National Power in Space *(2015),* 21st Century Power *(2018), and* To Rule the Skies *(2021), and more than a dozen articles on spacepower, military theory, and air power history. He holds a master's degree in space systems engineering and doctorates in economic development and military strategy. He lives in Alabama with his wife and children.*

Chapter 2: Philosophical and Material Foundations of the Space Patrol (1914–2020)

The many functions of the Space Patrol seem today to be quite commonplace, but upon reflection seem rather odd for a military organization. Why does the Patrol manage the currency of our interplanetary civilization? Why isn't the Patrol governed by any nation, or council of nations? Indeed, thinking seriously about the Patrol without a firm grasp of its theoretical origins often raises many more questions than answers. However, the political logic of the Patrol was established as far back as the seventeenth century. Furthermore, when we look at our civilization's military history of the twentieth and twenty-first centuries, we can clearly see that the embryonic Space Patrol was being formed in the intellectual and popular imagination at the very beginning of the Atomic Age.

The Atom and the Leviathan

Political scientist Thomas Hobbes identified the rationale for the Space Patrol in his immortal classic *Leviathan* in

1651. Though antimatter weapons and mass space travel were centuries into the future, the "father of realism" confronted war and how it could be stopped with brutal clarity and purpose. Hobbes wrote that men fought over competition, diffidence, and glory (echoing Thucydides' fear, honor, and interest) and that "during the time men live without a common power to keep them all in awe, they are in that condition which is called war; and such a war as is of every man against every man."[2] In such chaotic conditions, according to one of the most famous phrases in political science:

> . . . there is no place for industry, because the fruit thereof is uncertain; and consequently no culture of the earth; no navigation, nor use of the commodities that may be imported by sea; no commodious building; no instruments of moving, and removing, such things as require much force; no knowledge of the face of the earth; no account of time; no arts; no letters; no society and, which is the worst of all, continual fear, and danger of violent death; and the life of man, solitary, poor, nasty, brutish, and short.[3]

Only a dominant power that could keep all men in awe could keep the peace and allow humanity and its arts to flourish. Only a Leviathan—an organization of insurmountable power with a monopoly

---

2 Thomas Hobbes, *Leviathan* (1651); selection reproduced in Alan Ebenstein and William Ebenstein, *Great Political Thinkers*, Sixth Edition (Independence, Kentucky: Cengage Learning, 1999), 365.

3 Thomas Hobbes, *Leviathan*, 365.

on the legitimate use of violence—could prevent the life of man from being "solitary, poor, nasty, brutish, and short." For centuries, political philosophers from the Liberal, Marxian, Constructivist, and countless other schools rejected or attempted to prove Hobbes's conclusion wrong. Over those centuries, man's wars became increasingly violent, destructive, and brutish. However, at the beginning of the twentieth century, man's increasing mastery of the physical sciences led him ever closer to unlocking the destructive power of the atom. With this power, mankind itself could hasten its own extinction with a Hobbesian nightmarish nuclear fire engulfing the world.

Interestingly, and by no means the only time in the history of the Space Patrol, a science fiction writer offered a way forward out of the fatal dilemma at the nexus of Hobbes and the atom. British futurist Herbert George (H.G.) Wells captured the perils and promise of nuclear weapons, in his most prescient, if not most famous, 1914 novel *The World Set Free*. In it, Wells identifies the horrors of atomic weapons by describing the world's first nuclear war. Wells did not anticipate the correct method of atomic destruction. His "Carolinum" bombs were not the city-destroying orgies of instant death produced by fission and fusion explosions. Rather, these atomic weapons were equally horrific but slow-burning, unquenchable fires that poisoned and killed everything surrounding them for decades.

Wells correctly grasped that humans would not survive wars fought by nuclear weapons, even if he mistook the character of their destructive power. After a nuclear war rendered many of the European capitals and major cities uninhabitable, the surviving world leaders of the novel commit to ensuring such a catastrophe would never happen again. Wells looked to Hobbes to provide the solution to set the world free from war. Wells's character King Egbert of Britain convinces the major nations of the world to establish a Leviathan—the World State—that would forever keep the peace through a monopoly on atomic weapons. Further, the first order of the World State is to "get every atom of Carolinium and all the plant for making it, into our control."[4]

Perhaps Wells's greatest act of vision was to identify that the World State's monopoly on atomic weapons relied upon a monopoly on atomic material and refining and production methods. No one can miss the parallels between the World State's monopoly on the radioactive fuel Carolinum and the foundation of the Space Patrol's military might and power—its monopoly on the production and distribution of antimatter. Controlling the power of the atom through a monopoly on the resources necessary to harness it is a common theme throughout the Atomic Age up to and including today's antimatter economy. Wells's reputation as a brilliant futurist should be secured indefinitely for pioneering this insight alone.

Wells's combination of a World State, atomic weapons, and the monopoly on atomic energy, to create a Leviathan that secured peace among mankind is a critical moment in the history of the Space Patrol. Even though today the Space Patrol is not beholden to any state or political hegemony, rather being an honest policeman that exists outside politics yet regarded as legitimate among all human powers, there can be no doubt that *The World Set Free* and Wells's vision is a direct ancestor of the Space Patrol.

Wells also identified that the world could only be set free if men were willing to commit violent acts of barbarity to defend it. Shortly after the declaration of the World State, King Ferdinand Charles of Serbia hatches a plan to secretly build a stockpile of Carolinum bombs and destroy the World State headquarters, its leaders, and its arsenal of Carolinum bombs in a devastating air attack that "aimed at no less than the Empire of the World. The government of idealists and professors away there at Brissago was to be blown to fragments, and . . . aeroplanes would go swarming over a world that had disarmed itself, to proclaim Ferdinand Charles, the new Caesar, the Master, Lord of the Earth."[5]

Of course, the "aeronauts" of the World State anticipate King Ferdinand Charles's treachery and destroy his attacking bombers in flight, capture the illegal stockpile of bombs, and kill King Ferdinand Charles while the fugitive is attempting to escape. When the World State's aeronauts secure the area and he learns of the human cost of the fighting, ex-King Egbert ponders, "I wonder . . . if there are any more of them?" "Bombs, sir?" "No, such kings . . . The pitiful folly of it!"[6]

As the Space Patrol has constantly learned and relearned centuries later, there have always been more "such kings" to threaten peace and security of the

---

5 Wells, *The World Set Free*, 191.

6 Wells, *The World Set Free*, 209.

human race. And, just as Wells foretold, there would always be the need for strong and determined men to keep that peace through the exercise of extreme—and some critics claim genocidal—violence to keep that peace. Any member of the Space Patrol reading *The World Set Free* would immediately identify the Wells aeronauts as the direct antecedents of himself.

The Impossible Dream

Wells may have anticipated the Space Patrol in *The World Set Free*, but it took the American Manhattan Project in World War II to discover the destructive power of a real atomic bomb. They were not the slow-burning wraiths of Wells's imagination. Instead, they were apocalyptic holocausts of destructive power burning brighter than a thousand suns that could make entire cities disappear in the blink of a demonic eye. The rubble of Hiroshima and Nagasaki from the first crude fission bombs in 1945 and the anticipation of society-ending fusion bombs brought the need to confront the control of atomic energy away from the musings of science futurists directly into the hands of the world's diplomats.

In 1946, an American committee chaired by Dean Acheson and David Lilienthal wrote the *Report on the International Control of Atomic Energy* that outlined a method by which the United States could cede its monopoly on atomic weapons to the United Nations to prevent a destructive arms race that many feared could end civilization. The father of the atomic bomb himself, Robert Oppenheimer, helped develop the report's recommendations. The document was a far-reaching exercise in developing a binding international agreement to end the menace of atomic weapons while also seeking to unleash the benefits of atomic energy to help develop the entire world. Although the plan focused more on gaining international acceptance by inducement rather than military might, the plan's echoes of the ideas set forth in Wells's *The World Set Free* ring loudly.

The plan's centerpiece was the establishment of an International Atomic Energy Authority, vested under the authority of the United Nations, that would conduct "all intrinsically dangerous operations in the nuclear field" while allowing "individual nations and their citizens free to conduct, under license and a minimum of inspection, all non-dangerous, or safe, operations."[7] The Authority would control the world's supplies of uranium and thorium; own, construct, and operate nuclear production plants; conduct atomic research; license individual states' and other organizations' nuclear activities; and conduct inspections to ensure compliance.

The first purpose of the Authority was "to bring under its complete control world supplies of uranium and thorium." The Authority would also control the stockpiles of both elements around the world, manage their mining and production, and continually search for new deposits in order to have complete control of the supply. These supplies would be leased or sold to other organizations to support lawful and peaceful

---

7 *The Acheson-Lilienthal Report on the International Control of Atomic Energy* (Washington, DC: US Department of State, 16 March 1946), 34.

atomic research and development while restricting any non-UN military atomic development entirely. Through this monopoly, the Authority would ensure that there would never be "lawful rivalry among nations for these vital raw materials."[8]

The second duty of the Authority would be to build, own, and operate the production facilities necessary to refine uranium and thorium into usable nuclear fuels. The report's writers were insistent on this ownership because refining activities were "regarded as the most dangerous, for it is through such operations that materials can be produced which are suitable for atomic explosives."[9]

The third role of the Authority was to conduct further research into atomic explosives. "Only by preserving its position as the best informed agency will the Authority be able to tell where the line between the intrinsically dangerous and the non-dangerous should be drawn," the report argued. New discoveries could yield new methods of atomic weapons development and production, and in order to ensure no clandestine weapons programs could be developed "it is important that the Authority should be the first to know."[10]

The fourth responsibility of the Authority was to license its fissionable materials to allow the construction and operation of nuclear power plants for peaceful development and private research activities to provide continuing benefits of atomic energy to

---

8 *Acheson-Lilienthal Report*, 37.

9 *Acheson-Lilienthal Report*, 38.

10 *Acheson-Lilienthal Report*, 39.

the world. Furthermore, "through its own research and development activities and through establishing cooperative relationships with research and development laboratories in this field throughout the world, the Authority would be in a position to determine intelligently safe and unsafe designs of reactors for which it might lease its fissionable materials."[11]

Finally, the Authority would inspect all atomic energy activities around the world to ensure that no dangerous nuclear weapons programs were being conducted throughout the world. Through inspection the Authority would retain its nuclear monopoly. Authority-licensed programs would be routinely inspected to ensure that they were really legal. Furthermore, the Authority would inspect operations to ensure they were operationally effective and followed appropriate safety protocols. The Authority "would be in a position to insure that in the plan of operations, in the physical layout, in the system of audits, and in the choice of developments, full weight and full consideration can be given to the ease of detecting and avoiding diversion and evasion."[12]

Oppenheimer and the other authors of the report consciously avoided the problem of enforcement in order to make the proposal more acceptable to the Soviet Union, which by 1947 was accepted as the United States' adversary for the foreseeable future. The writers favored inspections and argued the plan made inspections easier because "it is not the motive but the operation which is illegal." Mining

11 *Acheson-Lilienthal Report,* 40.
12 *Acheson-Lilienthal Report,* 42.

uranium or building nuclear reactors outside Authority approval would be illegal. "The fact that it is the existence of the effort rather than a specific purpose or motive or plan which constitutes an evasion and an unmistakable danger signal is to our minds one of the great advantages of the proposals we have outlined," the writers argued.[13]

No historian of the Space Patrol can deny that the enforcement of its antimatter weapon monopoly across the solar system would be possible if the Patrol did not also maintain its monopoly on the production and storage of antimatter. It is remarkable that the Report's logic of inspection stated in 1946—more than a century before the establishment of the Space Patrol—would outline the Patrol's necessary strategy so well.

The *Acheson-Lilienthal Report* did not mention an enforcement activity to secure the treaty. It almost entirely relied upon inspections and the promise of development support from the Authority to persuade states to abide by the agreement. Bernard Baruch was placed in charge of selling the International Atomic Development Authority to the United Nations. But Baruch added the critical element of enforcement of the provisions of the agreement to the plan, regardless of how the Soviets might react. Baruch added that "once the treaty was ratified, any government violating its treaty obligation and developing or using atomic energy for destructive purposes should be subject to swift and sure punishment; and in the case of violation no one of the permanent members of the Security

13 *Acheson-Lilienthal Report*, 42–43.

Council should be permitted to veto punitive action by the council."[14]

Additionally, Baruch demanded swift and sure punishment without the possibility of veto by the United Nations Security Council position for anyone who detonated an atomic bomb without Authority approval, in illegal possession of an atomic bomb or of atomic material suitable for use in an atomic bomb, or anyone seizing a plant or other property belonging to or licensed by the authority by force.[15] The Soviet Union was completely opposed to eliminating the veto in the Security Council and the Baruch plan ultimately failed in the United Nations, but the resemblance to this first plan for international control of atomic energy and the Space Patrol's monopoly on the supply and production of antimatter is unmistakable.

The Space Patrol Proposed

While the Baruch plan was being debated in the United Nations, a new science fiction writer emerged to champion the cause of the Space Patrol in print. But unlike H.G. Wells, Robert A. Heinlein was a military veteran of the US Navy and a Naval Academy graduate who would have likely enjoyed a successful career—perhaps even becoming an admiral—if tuberculosis had not forced his medical retirement after only a few years of service. Robbed of a Navy

---

14 Richard Dean Burns and Joseph M. Siracusa, *A Global History of the Nuclear Arms Race: Weapons, Strategy, and Politics*, Volume One (Santa Barbara, CA: Praeger, 2013), 77.

15 Burns and Siracusa, *A Global History of the Nuclear Arms Race*, 77.

career, Heinlein turned to writing science fiction and, in 1947, he began to write a series of articles that, without doubt, were the most articulate vision of the Space Patrol devised. It is nearly incontestable that Robert Heinlein is the most important intellectual father of the Space Patrol.

In the heat of the debate over the Baruch plan, Lieutenant (retired) Heinlein and his friend and Naval Academy classmate Captain Caleb B. Laning, wrote "Flight into the Future" in *Collier's* magazine, published on 30 August 1947. Set in 1967, the two naval officers describe a voyage on the orbital United Nations ship *Jupiter* on patrol in Earth orbit. The story begins with them departing from the UN moon base on the *Jupiter* en route to relieve another cruiser on patrol. The military crew is under the orders of the UN Security Council, as the Baruch Plan presented. Heinlein and Laning describe the international crew, the "captain is in his middle thirties, a former [US Army Air Forces] jet-bomber pilot. His navigator has an Oxford accent and was formerly an assistant astronomer at Greenwich. There are many accents aboard—Russian, French, Texan—and as many backgrounds." In addition to military personnel, the crew also includes scientists from the "U.N. Atomic Commission."[16]

The mission of the *Jupiter* is to service orbiting nuclear missiles aimed at Earth to be used "should the Security Council find it necessary to order them to blast an aggressor nation off the face of the earth."[17]

---

16 Captain Caleb B. Laning, "Flight into the Future," *Collier's*, 30 August 1947, 19.

17 Laning, "Flight into the Future," 19.

The missiles are the "prowl cars" of the "peace patrol" that cover the entire globe so that "no spot on earth is ever more than an hour away from the swift punishment of the Security Council."[18]

Heinlein and Laning argued that the peace patrol from space was absolutely necessary because "We must have space ships to preserve the peace... If *we* don't develop space ships, someone else will." The writers then make a startling claim that, centuries later, we know to be the fundamental power of the Space Patrol. "Once developed," the visionaries announced, "space travel can and will be the source of supreme military power over this planet—and over the entire solar system—for there is literally *no* way to strike back from ground, sea, or air at a space ship, whereas the space ship armed with atomic weapons can wipe out anything on this globe."[19]

Knowing that they would be accused of being warmongers by at least some readers, they argued that "We want peace. We of the armed forces, as human beings with kids and homes of our own, most especially want peace, for we know how frightfully catastrophic another war would be." The writers also stressed that the space corps should be under United Nations control and serve as the "backbone of the U.N. Security Forces."[20]

Heinlein and Laning also charged the American people with an important duty. If the UN could be made to work, the technologically most-advanced

18 Laning, "Flight into the Future," 19.

19 Laning, "Flight into the Future," 36.

20 Laning, "Flight into the Future," 36.

member nations (including the United States) must supply that backbone. However, if the world "can't make the U.N. work, then we've got to develop a space corps to enforce a *Pax America* because the big cities of the United States can't survive an atomic war."[21] If the world wouldn't build an international space corps to control atomic weapons to keep the peace, the United States would have to build it itself.

Heinlein revisited and expanded upon his international space peace patrol in his juvenile science fiction novel *Space Cadet* a year later (1948). Drawing from his experience at the Naval Academy and as a junior naval officer, Heinlein told the story of Cadet Tom Dodson, a young American who joins the Interplanetary Patrol in 2075. In it, Heinlein greatly expands on the mission and culture of the Patrol.

Earth and the other humans in the solar system are united under the banner of the Federation, the seal of which incorporates three closed circles representing Freedom, Peace, and Law.[22] Even though Heinlein's Patrol still uses nuclear weapons to keep the peace—and has used them against aggressor nations, independent space settlements, and cities in the past— the Patrol has also assumed the mission of rescue and recovery in space, working as an international coast guard of space. The legendary Commandant of the Interplanetary Patrol Academy, Commodore Arkwright, is permanently blind from a "spectacular, singlehanded

21 Laning, "Flight into the Future," 36.

22 Robert Heinlein, *Space Cadet* (New York: Tor, 1948, reprint 2005), 46.

rescue of a private yacht in distress, inside the orbit of Mercury."[23]

Commodore Arkwright gives a speech to the new class of recruits from every nation and planet before swearing them into the Patrol. Arkwright declares that "Each living, thinking creature in this system is your neighbor—and your responsibility" to the new cadets. He also warns the cadets to "expect to spend long hours studying your new profession, acquiring the skills of the spaceman and the arts of the professional soldier." However, those skills are not the most important attributes of a Patrol officer.

Arkwright explains, "An officer in command of a ship of the Patrol, away from base, is the last of the absolute monarchs, for there is none but himself to restrain him. Many places where he must go no other authority reaches. He himself must embody law, and the rule of reason, justice, and mercy." The Patrol officer must embody these virtues because the Patrol is "entrusted such awful force as may compel or destroy, all other force we know of—and with this trust is laid on them the charge to keep the peace of the System and to protect the liberties of its peoples."[24]

Patrol members are "the soldiers of freedom" and as the cadets wish to become officers of these soldiers, it "is not enough that you be skillful, clever, brave— The trustees of this awful power must each possess a meticulous sense of honor, self-discipline beyond all ambition, conceit, or avarice, respect for the liberties

---

23 Heinlein, *Space Cadet*, 23.

24 Heinlein, *Space Cadet*, 47.

and dignity of all creatures, and an unyielding will to do justice and give mercy. He must be a true and gentle knight..."[25]

After delivering his speech, Arkwright administers the oath of office to the cadets:

Of my own free will, without reservation—
I swear to uphold the peace of the solar system—
to protect the lawful liberties of its inhabitants—
to defend the constitution of the Solar Federation—
to carry out the duties of the position to which
    I am now appointed—
and to obey the lawful orders of my superior
    officers.
To these ends I subordinate all other loyalties
    and renounce utterly any that may conflict
    with them. [26]

Every member of the real Space Patrol throughout its long history will see an uncanny overlap between Heinlein's oath and their own. Especially relevant is Heinlein's insistence that members renounce local tribal loyalties and acknowledge their loyalty to the higher ideals of the Patrol. The Earthlings, Martians, and Venusians in Heinlein's fictional account are easy stand-ins for the Terrans, Cerites, and AI cultures all blending together into one Patrol to serve all of civilization. The real Space Patrol oath has been altered several times in its history, but has never strayed far from the oath of the Interplanetary Patrol first written

---

25 Heinlein, *Space Cadet*, 48.
26 Heinlein, *Space Cadet*, 49.

in a children's book a decade before humans even launched a satellite.

Heinlein wrote a final piece on the Interplanetary Patrol in his short story "The Long Watch" in 1949. Expanding on the story of a hero of the Patrol mentioned in *Space Cadet*, the story recounts how Lieutenant John Dahlquist sacrifices himself by sabotaging the Patrol's lunar nuclear missiles in order to stop a coup of renegade Patrol officers on the Moon from taking over the world. Young Dahlquist, an inexperienced bomb officer with a doctorate in physics, is invited to join the coup by Colonel Towers, a distinguished Patrol officer, combat veteran, and executive officer of the Patrol command post on the Moon. The colonel tells Dahlquist that "it was not safe . . . to leave control of the world in political hands; power must be held by a scientifically selected group. In short—the Patrol."[27]

Even though Dahlquist thinks the idea plausible, he recoils when Towers says the conspiracy will need to bomb "an unimportant town or two. A little bloodletting to prevent an all-out war. Simple arithmetic . . . Think of it as a surgical operation. And think of your family." Dahlquist pretends to play along with the conspiracy until he can sabotage the bombs by cracking their nuclear fuel casings, resulting in Dahlquist receiving a lethal dose of radiation, but also defanging the coup and saving the day.[28]

"The Long Watch" is still used in ethics classes in Space Patrol officer training today.

---

27 Robert A. Heinlein, "The Long Watch," 1949: www.baen.com/ Chapters/1439133417/1439133417___4.htm

28 Heinlein, "The Long Watch."

An amusing thought to ponder is that, historically, the "villain" Colonel Towers was proven correct...in a way. Many human governments—both those with local jurisdictions ranging from Earth nations to isolated space colonies and habitats as well as those with broader global and even system-wide aspirations—have come and gone during the Space Patrol's existence. Today, the Space Patrol as a whole is beholden to no government. Human peace and prosperity is not secured by any world government, but by the officers of the Patrol just as Towers wanted. However, it did not require a coup or the destruction of innocent cities. The Space Patrol and its personnel simply proved to be a more stable and just organization than unified governments for humanity to rely upon. Of course, many human governments—as well as perhaps the so-called Sentient Artificial Intelligence Network (SAIN) that appears to be gaining in political recognition by some, of which many AI members of the Patrol serve as leaders— exist today and have great freedom in organizing the societies they represent without interference. But the governments have all agreed that the Space Patrol is a worthwhile organization and accept as legitimate the Patrol's inherent function in the larger system-wide society. Perhaps Heinlein's dedication to justice, law, and life itself has won the Space Patrol's valued and treasured role as humanity's military.

The Hunter in the Stars

The Space Patrol is certainly a military organization with a war-fighting culture. Many are surprised to learn, then, that many Patrol personnel don't see anything resembling combat for most of their careers. Actual use of antimatter weapons against aggressor polities by the Patrol is extremely uncommon. Some members, beyond minor engagements with pirates, never engage in combat at all. Individual Space Patrol glory is most often found in heroic actions during rescue operations rather than fighting. Yet, Space Patrol members spend most of their time in fully immersive virtual reality combat simulations that are so exacting and lifelike that some members develop stress disorders usually only seen from traumatic combat experiences. How is this possible?

The answer is that the Space Patrol is a *deterrent* organization that also performs rescue and antipiracy operations on the margins of its primary responsibility. As it happens, the Space Patrol shares much of its military character from the twentieth-century military formation charged with wielding America's nuclear monopoly.

The American plan to invest the United Nations with the monopoly on nuclear energy was defeated decisively in 1947 when the Soviet Union completely rejected Baruch's International Atomic Energy Authority. The lack of an international solution to nuclear weapons forced the United States to build the *Pax America* Heinlein and Laning argued was the second best option. The result was the Strategic Air Command, better known by its acronym "SAC." SAC was the aviation nuclear striking arm of the United States from 1947 to 1992, and was a major contributor of American defense in the Cold War with the Soviet Union. Every minute of the Cold War, SAC had hundreds of bombers and thousands of missiles and their crews constantly on alert to launch a devastating nuclear counterattack on the Soviet Union with only fifteen minutes' notice.

The similarity in military character between SAC and the Space Patrol is uncanny. SAC's force of nuclear-armed bomber aircraft and later ground-based missiles intended to keep the peace by threatening massive retaliation against any Soviet military aggression. In its almost half century of existence, SAC never launched a nuclear weapon in anger. However, it was considered one of the most aggressive war-fighter cultures in military history because it drilled and exercised nuclear war-fighting constantly. It acted, like the Space Patrol, as if it was *always at war* through vigorous and unforgiving training and simulation. The Space Patrol's motto, "Preserve and Protect, At Any Cost," echoes SAC's own "Peace is Our Profession." Much of the Space Patrol's training and operational philosophy was pioneered by SAC.

Peace may have been SAC's profession, but the unofficial motto included "War is Just a Hobby." Even so, it was a vigorous hobby. SAC combat crews were constantly tested by mentally brutal exercises using the most realistic wartime simulators the technology of the time allowed. Furthermore, SAC demanded perfection from every crew in every simulation. Anything less than one hundred percent on any of the hundreds of tests and simulations of World War III crews were exposed to could end an officer's career. Space Patrol personnel today hone their own skills on fully immersive virtual reality (VR) simulators that can provide thirty years of brutal conflict experience in the mere first year of a Patrol officer's half-century career. Simulation performance largely determines promotion in the Patrol. In addition to being potentially harmful,

VR technology is so potent and subject to addiction that its use is highly regulated and restricted among civilians. Space Patrol VR simulations would be nothing short of magic to SAC airmen. But SAC airmen would immediately recognize in Patrol standards the same exacting military professionalism required for a military charged with the security of humanity itself. Both services needed to train to superhuman standards to preserve the peace "at any cost."

While SAC was a deterrent organization that used its fission and fusion weapons in a similar manner that the Space Patrol uses its antimatter weapons to secure peace, its use of aircraft and missiles does not seem all that similar to the Space Patrol's space focus. However, a little-known element of SAC's history is that its leaders attempted to build a SAC space force in the mid-twentieth century through a novel application of nuclear energy.

Project Orion, the US Air Force nuclear pulse propulsion (NPP) research program carried out from 1957 to 1965, was the twentieth century's greatest attempt to develop a capability like the Space Patrol. The NPP technique used small nuclear explosives detonated at the rear of a spacecraft to ablate a pusher plate and carry the spacecraft into orbit and throughout the solar system in ways comparable (but vastly inferior) to modern antimatter systems. Orion was the most powerful space engine developed to any level of sophistication until well into the twenty-first century.

Air Force officers Donald Mixson and Frederick Gorschboth developed concepts of operations for Air Force Orion spacecraft to extend SAC's deterrent force into orbit in the late 1950s and early 1960s—much along the same lines of Heinlein and Laning's space corps. Mixson developed the concept of a SAC Deep Space Force of Orion spacecraft distributed into three main forces differentiated by orbital altitude: a low-altitude force (in a two-hour period, one-thousand-mile altitude orbit), a moderate-altitude force (twenty-four-hour orbit) and a deep-space force (lunar orbit). These three forces would be assigned intelligence, reconnaissance, and surveillance duties during peacetime, primarily collecting intelligence of Soviet nuclear forces. However, the ships would also carry nuclear weapons as part of the United States nuclear deterrent (a deep-space bombardment force), ready to strike the Soviet Union in case of nuclear attack. The ships would be the ultimate in survivable nuclear deterrence, virtually immune from a first strike (being specifically designed to use nuclear blasts as propulsion!) and capable of indefensible retaliation in case of a Soviet nuclear attack on the United States.[29]

Gorschboth expanded on Mixson's concepts by adding that with Orion "it would be possible to move the scene of battle from earth to space, so that the military decision would be rendered there among the combatants, without incidental destruction to the earth's surface or the danger of the consequent long-term radiation effects of fallout—if this could be done, it would provide perhaps the first step back toward a

---

29 Ward Alan Mingle, *History of the Air Force Weapons Laboratory for 1 January–31 December 1964*, Volume 1 (Kirtland AFB, NM: Air Force Weapons Laboratory, December 1968), 183–184. Document classified Secret. Excerpt declassified.

sane strategy in the nuclear age ..."[30] Physicist Freeman Dyson was more sanguine about Orion's military
utility, mockingly explaining Mixson and Gorschboth's
plans as "Great fleets of space battleships were to
patrol the ocean of space ... Cruising majestically in
orbits beyond the moon, manned by air force captains
as brave as the English sea captains of old, the ships
of the Deep Space Bombardment Force would stand
between the tyrants of the Kremlin and the dominion
of the world."[31]

Nonetheless, these young captains were able to convince SAC of the utility of a robust space capability.
On 21 January 1961 SAC Commander-in-Chief General
Thomas Power issued a SAC Qualitative Operational
Requirement for a "Strategic Earth Orbital Base."
In the only SAC space requirement letter signed by
General Power himself, Power demanded Orion and
warned that a "capability less than desired; a number
of unmanned special-purpose or inadequately manned
vehicles, and/or other vehicle compromises, afford only
a partial solution to the long-term space capability
problem. Integrated facilities and systems for effective
mission accomplishment must include all functions that
permit survival, surveillance, and weapons delivery.
The capability to accommodate the obviously large
payloads makes necessary many tons to orbit rather
than many pounds. A long-term strategic earth orbital

---

30 Frederick F. Gorschboth, *Counterforce from Space* TN-61-17
   (Kirtland AFB, NM: Air Force Special Weapons Center, 1 August
   1961), 8–9. Document is now declassified.

31 Freeman Dyson, *Weapons and Hope* (New York: Harpercollins,
   1985), 65–66.

capability, virtually unrestricted by propulsion or pay-load limitations, is required."[32]

The SAC Deep Space Force would have been a twentieth-century American version of the Space Patrol, accomplishing the same deterrence mission with similar spacecraft. Unfortunately for SAC and Project Orion, the Limited Test Ban Treaty of 1963 made any nuclear explosions under the sea, on the ground, in the air, or in space illegal, including those used for propulsive purposes. With the stroke of a pen, the entire flight profile of a nuclear pulse spacecraft was made illegal. Orion was cancelled just as dedicated nuclear tests and prototype construction were planned to commence. Orion, and SAC's plan for it to extend nuclear deterrence into space, was ended.

From Air Force to Space Guard

SAC itself was disbanded in 1992, a few years after the fall of the Soviet Union and the end of the Cold War after it had completed its mission of keeping the Cold War free of nuclear warfare. Its nuclear weapons and its space assets (imagery, navigation, weather, and communications satellites) were transferred into Air Force Space Command (AFSPC). Established in 1982 to manage Strategic Defense Initiative weapons that were never developed, AFSPC saw its space assets assist the great American victory in Desert Storm against Iraq in 1991. Instead of committing to the strategic

---

32 General Thomas S. Power, *Strategic Earth Orbital Base* (Strategic Air Command Qualitative Operational Requirement, 21 January 1961). Document is now declassified.

mission of nuclear deterrence and taking SAC's mantle to push nuclear deterrence into space, AFSPC instead sought to subordinate America's space assets to the tactical concerns of the Army, Navy, Marine Corps, and Air Force. This shift toward the tactical caused the Air Force space mission to become more visible to the flying community, but virtually eliminated any official discussion of extending deterrence to space or even expanding any military missions into space beyond those that could assist the tactical warfighting forces. AFSPC officially did not consider anything like Heinlein's Interplanetary Patrol or SAC's space efforts to be appropriate.

However, some space personnel began to feel that there was a better way forward for military space. Air Force Lieutenant Colonel Cynthia McKinley published "The Guardians of Space: Organizing America's Space Assets for the Twenty-First Century" in 1999. In it, McKinley outlined the case for reorganizing AFSPC into the United States Space Guard (USSG).

McKinley's USSG would function as a fusion of civil, commercial, and military space personnel and missions in a uniformed service modeled after the US Coast Guard. The USSG would need to strike a balance among competing civil, commercial, and military space missions and interests. It would operate as a multi-mission service with responsibilities for space operations, mission areas of space support (global positioning systems, government satellite communications, etc.), force enhancement (spacelift, infrastructure security), and space control (space surveillance, satellite jamming and defense) as well as providing space range management and debris

mitigation.[33] It would merge separate mission requirements, core competencies, visions, and responsibilities
to form a coherent federal response to the extension
of the space enterprise and support the expansion
of space commerce.[34]

In her USSG proposal, McKinley identified many
of the peacetime emergency services the Space Patrol
currently provides. While her concept of the Space
Guard was visionary and may well have led directly
to the Space Patrol, McKinley was removed from
the colonel's promotion list by Air Force leaders who
did not want any discussion of space independence
from the Air Force.

Over the next twenty years, space continued to
grow in commercial importance, leading to a $415
billion worldwide space economy in 2019. The Global
Positioning System alone was assessed to have provided
$1.4 trillion to the American economy. Anticipating
future economic growth, the American Secretary of
Commerce predicted that the international space
economy would be valued from $1 to $3 trillion by
2040.[35]

Realizing that changes in space, especially commercial space, would soon drive change to the military

---

33 Lieutenant Colonel Cynthia McKinley, "The Guardians of Space:
   Organizing America's Space Assets for the Twenty-First Century,"
   Aerospace Power Journal (Maxwell AFB, Alabama: Spring 2000),
   44.

34 McKinley, "The Guardians of Space," 42.

35 "Remarks by Secretary of Commerce Wilbur Ross at A New
   Space Race: Getting to the Trillion-Dollar Space Economy World
   Economic Forum," Davos, Switzerland, 24 January 2020.

space force, AFSPC strategists and scientists, led by Chief Scientist Joel Mozer, committed to a study assessing the potential role of space and space forces in 2060. These visionaries drew many groundbreaking conclusions that departed from standard AFSPC thinking in radical ways. Among its conclusions, the workshop advised that the "U.S. should establish space settlement and human presence as a primary driver of the nation's civil space program to determine the path for large-scale human space settlement and ensure America is the foremost power in achieving that end." Furthermore, the "U.S. must continue to lead in developing a rules-based, democratic international order for space. The U.S. must commit to having a military force structure that can defend this international space order and defend American space interests, to include American space settlements and commerce." Also, the members concluded that the "U.S. military must define and execute its role in promoting, exploiting, and defending the expanded commercial, civil, and military activities and human presence in space driven by industry, NASA, and other nation-states."[36]

Many of the workshop's findings reaffirmed McKinley's conclusion that AFSPC should adapt many "coast guard-like" missions for space and identified many opportunities that would eventually turn into regular missions of the Space Patrol. However, Air Force leadership generally ignored the workshop's findings.

---

36 Air Force Space Command, "The Future of Space 2060 & Implications for U.S. Strategy: Report on the Space Futures Workshop," 5 September 2019, 17: https://apps.dtic.mil/sti/pdfs/AD1101899.pdf

leadership generally ignored the workshop's findings. But Air Force leaders also soon lost the military space mission altogether.

The Space Force

SpaceX founder billionaire Elon Musk broadcast "@ SpaceForceDOD Starfleet Begins" at 10:37 p.m. on Friday, December 20, 2019, over the popular Twitter mass-communication system of the time. Only a few minutes earlier, President Donald J. Trump signed the National Defense Authorization Act for Fiscal Year 2020 and established the United States' sixth branch of the armed forces, the United States Space Force.

The Space Force initially held little promise of eventually evolving into the Space Patrol. Its early leaders never strayed from the classic AFSPC missions of tactical support to fighting forces on the ground. However, visionaries such as Mozer and the eventual popular dissatisfaction among younger officers over the service's lack of vision drove the Space Force ever further into adopting a McKinley-like "Space Guard" mindset. More people believed the Space Force was meant to protect the increasing wealth the United States and its allies derived from space activity and, as human spaceflight began to explode in number, to provide rescue services to ensure public safety.

Early agreements between the US Space Force and other governments, militaries, companies, and universities to partner for "space situational aware-ness" to protect everyone's space assets from the threat of debris or deliberate attack began to evolve slowly but inexorably into more formal arrangements.[37] Eventually, the space forces of allied nations merged in operation and cooperative command structure if not in political ownership. Increasingly more partners merged together and enticed neutrals and even adversaries into these cooperative military space structures. With time, all major spacefaring nations and most other polities merged into a single global space management system that, as will be discussed later, resulted in the Space Patrol. Therefore, the Space Patrol was not born of a unitary or hegemonic state with a monopoly of military power on Earth. Rather, the Space Patrol emerged from a natural evolution of cooperation among the space services of all the world over generations.

This evolution was driven by the bounty all of humanity received from space activity and a common understanding that this bounty was fragile and that all nations wanted space to remain free of war and open to all. In fact, the evolutionary nature of the Space Patrol is likely another important reason for the Patrol's continued existence and relevance even during the collapse and rise of multiple human governments. The Patrol now exists beyond any one government or alliance. The US Space Force may not have been intended to become the Space Patrol, but its early actions to collect as many international partners as possible started that critical evolution.

---

37 "US Space Command signs data-sharing agreement with Libre Space Foundation," *Space News*, 3 July 2021: spacenews.com/u-s-space-command-signs-data-sharing-agreement-with-libre-space-foundation/.

Interplanetary Banking

Of all the Space Patrol's responsibilities, their management of interplanetary currency "credit" is perhaps the most surprising. The standard credit is a blockchain "basket" of scientific data, other information, physical commodities (primarily claims on antimatter), energy, and other services. The credit is not simply a number in a Space Patrol bank, but serves as a stand-in for real goods that make interplanetary finance easier than barter across literally astronomical distances. It should be noted that the Space Patrol is not the first supranational military organization to operate in the economic sphere. The Knights Templar from 1119 to 1312 created the world's first international banking system as it protected Crusaders, pilgrims, and their finances, across Europe in the Middle East—an equally astronomical distance in the Middle Ages.

Humanity's rapid expansion across the solar system was underwritten by rigorous economic activity. Scientific information, space resources and abundant energy became the primary drivers of human economic growth in the mid-twenty-first century. Cryptocurrencies—electronic money based on blockchain cyber technology—gained in popularity at the same time due to national "fiat" currencies predisposition toward inflation under rampant deficit spending.

Cryptocurrencies like Bitcoin operated on a "mining" structure where system users could earn cryptocurrency by using their computers to "mine" more. In actuality, these mining operations were computationally intricate services that confirmed transactions, increasing security, and essentially operated the cryptocurrency networks. Quantum computing and other advances, including artificial intelligence, eventually made the percentage of calculations critical to operating cryptocurrency networks far less computationally intensive. However, the networks still required high *volumes* of computations *of any sort* to keep the networks secure.

The economic breakthrough of the twenty-second century was matching the excess computational capacity of the cryptocurrency systems to the enormous amount of scientific and economic data received from the expanding human presence in space to create a truly *commodity*-based cryptocurrency. Cryptocurrency networks transformed information from collected space data and generated blockchain information with inherent economic value. Thus, the "standard credit" backed by space-derived scientific and economic data became one of the most successful currencies in human history.

Why the Space Patrol eventually became the custodian of this new credit was the result of four incontestable facts. First, the credit was reliant on space activity and space activity relied on the Space Patrol. Second, the Patrol defended the cyber backbone of space as well as the physical space systems, so defending the credit was a natural mission. Third, since the credit quickly became the favored currency among all human civilization and only the Space Patrol operated across the entire span of that civilization, the Patrol could most easily provide branch offices. Lastly, and perhaps most importantly, the Space Patrol eventually proved more resilient than any human government, therefore it seemed naturally the best organization to keep the credit resilient as well.

With the Space Patrol acting as an honest and

benevolent Leviathan, space was navigated freely and its resources harvested to bring life, liberty, and prosperity to mankind across first the planet, and later the solar system. Arts, letters, and sciences abounded because the life of man—even in space—was secured from being poor, nasty, brutish, and short.[38]

The peaceful, cooperative, and development-driven global agglomeration of military space forces that would eventually become the Space Patrol may have lost its military character altogether given time. By the twenty-second century, the "proto-Space Patrol" had no real war-fighting character to speak of, preferring to see themselves as solar lifeguards. Unfortunately, with rapid expansion into space and technological development, mankind began to realize that there were still demons in the darkness of space—and most of those demons were of human design.

Confronting Dark Skies

In his 2019 book *Dark Skies*, political scientist Daniel Deudney challenges the positive view of human space expansion and concludes that it is too dangerous to be allowed because the effort "enlarges the probability and scope of catastrophic and existential risks confronting humanity in six ways: malefic geopolitics, natural threat amplification, restraint reversal, hierarchy enablement, alien generation, and monster multiplication."[39]

---

38 Thomas Hobbes, *Leviathan*, 365.

39 Daniel Deudney, *Dark Skies: Space Expansionism, Planetary Geopolitics, and the Ends of Humanity* (Oxford, UK: Oxford University Press, 2019), 357.

"First," Deudney argues, "large-scale solar space expansion will produce a radically novel political and material landscape that is extremely inauspicious for security, freedom, and human survival, a perfect storm of unfavorable possibilities and tendencies." He calls this tendency *malefic geopolitics*. "Extensive mutual restraints would be vitally *necessary*, but they will be nearly *impossible* to materialize."[40] King Ferdinand Charles from *The World Set Free* exemplified this malefic tendency. Development of weapons derived from the vast energies required to operate in space would have to be restrained, but Deudney believes they could not be enforced over a human diaspora across the solar system.

"A second way in which colonizing solar space poses catastrophic and existential threats," Deudney continues, "is through *natural threat amplification*." Mining asteroids and comets inherently came with the ability for states to alter their orbits to attack adversaries. Instead of facing only the threat of natural impacts, Deudney believes, humans may begin to intentionally redirect celestial bodies as weapons.[41] The Patrol's history bears testament to Deudney's prophecy.

Deudney next warns of *restraint reversal*. "Instead of mitigating the effects of multiple catastrophic and existential risks, large-scale space expansion promises to multiply them... If humans are living on multiple worlds subject to different governments, regulations and relinquishment will be more difficult to establish, there will be more places for potential breakdowns,

---

40 Deudney, *Dark Skies*, 357. Emphasis original.

41 Deudney, *Dark Skies*, 358. Emphasis original.

and verification of compliance will be vastly more difficult."[42] Deudney is particularly worried about any international agreements regarding researching artificial intelligence. "To the extent uncontrolled [artificial superintelligence] is deemed something to avoid at all costs, large-scale space expansion must be viewed similarly."[43] Fortunately, artificial intelligence research was not avoided and now sentient AI are among the most important agents of civilization. Many AIs serve as important Patrol members. However, it will be seen that the Patrol played a critical role in shepherding the earliest AI developments through a maze of fear and real dangers to enable today's partnership between humanity and its offspring. Deudney may have provided the warning necessary for us to confront AI successfully.

"Fourth," Deudney argues, "solar expansion poses catastrophic and existential risks to humanity through *hierarchy enablement*." Deudney posits that "large-scale space expansion into Earth orbital space is very likely to enable the erection of a highly hierarchical world government, either from one-state military dominance of the entire planet or from the control of a major infrastructure for resources or energy" that could be "prone to become totalitarian."[44] The Patrol monitors the culture and governments of all space settlements and even Earth itself to ensure that this totalitarian nightmare does not become real. Such totalitarian cultures have sometimes emerged and were either

---

42 Deudney, *Dark Skies*, 359.

43 Deudney, *Dark Skies*, 360.

44 Deudney, *Dark Skies*, 360–1. Emphasis original.

cured or removed by the Patrol, as several radioactive craters on the moons of Saturn demonstrate.

"The fifth way in which ambitious space expansion poses catastrophic and existential risks," to Deudney, is "through *alien generation*." The human species radiation anticipated by expansionists will generate significantly different forms of life suited to other worlds. Since humans fought amongst each other for millennia over the smallest differences in look and outlook, creating different versions of humans suited for Earth, Mars, and microgravity would only increase the chances of conflict.[45] This threat was manifested by the Cerites, an offshoot of humanity that used genetic engineering to enhance their ability to survive low-gravity environments and high-radiation backgrounds. Distrust between the Cerites and Terrans could have easily led to genocidal war. However, the Patrol prevented active conflict and actively sought measures to increase trust and understanding among humanity's new subspecies. The Patrol integrated Cerites into equal service before these colonists even began to identify as Cerites (due in large part to their superior abilities to perform in space) and proved that friendly partnering is possible. Now, traditional humans and Cerites are equal partners running an interplanetary civilization.

Lastly, Deudney's sixth risk is *monster multiplication*. "Ambitious space expansion will clearly entail the development of powerful new technologies," Deudney explains, "and the actors developing these technologies will be spread in multiple worlds across the solar system. Therefore, it stands to reason that the

---

45 Deudney, *Dark Skies*, 361. Emphasis original.

number of monsters posing potential terminal threats will inevitably increase as ambitious space expansionist projects are realized."[46] Again, the history of the Patrol is largely the history of protecting civilization from these monsters whenever they arise. Later chapters will show that Deudney's monsters have, in fact, emerged. Every time, the Patrol has slain these dragons, often with diplomacy. Sometimes it took antimatter.

To the pessimistic political scientist, "these six ways in which the realization of the space expansionist program for solar space pose catastrophic and existential threats demolish the core proposition of space advocates that large-scale expansion is desirable."[47] Today, it seems easy to scoff at the ridiculously myopic and Malthusian irrationality of Deudney's conclusion. Many of Deudney's "existential threats" such as artificial intelligence, and even potentially "species radiation," in the form of the Cerites, have come to pass . . . only to emerge as manageable problems with great advantages. However, the threatening aspects of these advances anticipated by Deudney were chillingly accurate.

It is especially ironic that it was the hegemonic power of the Space Patrol that has allayed these threats and has allowed humanity to thrive in freedom and peace. But the Space Patrol regained its violent martial character as the soft commerce-enabling lifeguards were forced to confront Deudney's demons one by one. In fact, the military history of the Space Patrol can be rightly considered little more than humanity's attempt to survive each of Deudney's threats as they emerged . . .

---

46 Deudney, *Dark Skies*, 361–2.

47 Deudney, *Dark Skies*, 362.

The year 2587 / 4 AA

It has been three years since the events of "And a Child Shall Lead Them." The starship *Copernicus*, crewed by normals and sentient AIs, entered orbit around Liber roughly two years ago. Also in orbit around Liber were the *Guardian E* and the remains of *Ceres' Chariot*, which was being cannibalized to help build the Cerite settlement on Liber. The *Copernicus* had been planning to arrive at Eden but the Space Patrol placed the planet off-limits. The four thousand normals on *Copernicus* were forced to evaluate their options while working with the Cerites to construct their settlement on Liber. Then a young woman on *Copernicus* made a discovery, one that led to some interesting legal questions and a practical one: Should humanity's first starship include lawyers?

Somebody's World

Laura Montgomery

Laura Montgomery is a practicing space lawyer who writes space opera and near-future, bourgeois, legal science fiction. Her latest book, The Gear Engages, *is the fourth in her Martha's Sons series, which is set on the lost colony world of Not What We Were Looking For.* Mercenary Calling *is her most recent near-future novel and it follows one man's efforts to save a starship captain from charges of mutiny. Her author site is at lauramontgomery.com.*

On the legal side, Laura's private practice emphasizes commercial space transportation and the Outer Space Treaties. Before starting her own practice, she was the manager of the Space Law Branch in the Federal Aviation Administration's Office of the Chief Counsel, where she supported the regulators of commercial launch, reentry, and spaceports. There she worked on issues ranging from explosive siting to property rights in space. She has testified to the space subcommittees of both the House and Senate, and is an adjunct professor of space law at Catholic University's Columbus School of Law. She writes and edits the space law blog GroundBasedSpaceMatters .com and speaks regularly on space law issues.

Clients never provided their lawyers enough time, and this was one of those times.

Joseph Stern walked as fast as Yoel Aronson, first mate on the *Copernicus*, not only because he could but because he had to. Aronson, who seldom saw cause for formalities, had come and fetched the lawyer himself.

There was only one problem. "I don't see how I can brief her. I've had no time to prepare, and"—Joseph paused for both breath and emphasis—"you still haven't told me what it's about."

"Try to be a little more excited, please," Aronson said. "Here I take you from whatever it is you do that you always complain about, and I bring you genuine interstellar law and you get wrapped up in trivialities."

"Like knowing the topic?" Joseph walked faster. He was older. Like Aronson, he'd made the journey on the *Copernicus* from Earth, but he was diligent about his rejuvenation appointments and looked to be in his thirties. He felt like he was in his thirties, and picked up the pace when they reached the starship's interminable stairs, determined to make the first mate suffer, even if only a little. They were going from almost a full g to about three-quarters, which Joseph found psychologically useful for maintaining the pace.

"I'm telling you the topic," Aronson said. "It's glorious. Some girl found a thing on Aitch."

"The planet?" Joseph asked. The *Copernicus* was supposed to be assessing Ross 248h for resources and colony sites. The planet was referred to by its unofficial nickname "Aitch," and had yet to be dignified with a real name. "What is this 'thing'?"

"It doesn't look natural," Aronson said. He easily matched the pace Joseph was setting. "We have all sorts of images. A clean-shorn mountaintop, scraggly structures around the edges—all an intrepid explorer could hope for barring aliens themselves. Her supervisors were ignoring the girl—because she's young and was way too excited. Sometimes I think we shouldn't get to live so long. We ossify. Present company excepted, of course," he added breezily. They exited the stairs and headed down a new corridor.

"Of course," Joseph said drily. "Go on."

"We're going to go look at it," the first mate said.

Joseph skidded to a stop and Aronson overshot him before coming back around like a ship under sail. Or a water buffalo. Aronson braked, beaming.

Joseph hardly dared believe it. "We are? Me, too?" He'd brief the captain on anything she wanted to hear. He and his wife had joined the visionary expedition to the star, Ross 248, not only because they wanted humanity to have a future home, but for the adventure of it. Now, he was about to go to a planet, a new planet, an alien world. True, it didn't have any breathable air—just a little thin nitrogen atmosphere—but he would be one of the first people to set foot on it, feel the lesser gravity, see...what? An alien artifact? The blood rushed around in his head and it wasn't the starship's Coriolis effect.

The first mate had the grace to look chagrined. "*I'm* going. So is Alexa Prandus, the young woman who found the thing. I'm sorry, Joseph." He tried one of his charming grins. "You know lawyers never get to go anywhere: you're too valuable."

Joseph snorted a laugh. "Not a one of you thinks that." No, if lawyers were valuable, then the Patrol's lawyers would have gotten it right about Eden. Eden was the world Joseph Stern truly longed to visit, and the one they should have been orbiting. The *Copernicus* had been slated to go there first until the Patrol pulled the plug on humans settling Eden. Now the *Copernicus* orbited Aitch's moon, and, when not helping the Cerites construct their settlement, was tasked with assessing the cold, almost airless Aitch.

Ross 248e—now formally named Eden for its breathable air, its earthlike atmosphere, and (Joseph figured) the poisoned apple of its amino acids—had been explored three years before the *Copernicus* arrived in the system. With the home system facing trouble, and for a mission of multiple starships sent to find new planets that could support Sol System's inhabitants, it had failed mightily with Eden as far as Joseph Stern, Esq., was concerned.

Eden had life, but no intelligent life. The Patrol, which was semi-independent of the rest of the fleet (although not entirely), had surveyed the planet, but its probes had found neither mud huts nor cave dwellings, much less technology or advanced artificial structures. The admiral had authorized Patrol personnel to explore in person. Her people had breathed thin alien air, had lethal encounters with predators, and otherwise endured the stuff of adventure. To Joseph's eye, however, where they had strayed into biblical territory was when they ate the fruit of the alien tree, the flesh of alien animals, and thus were cast out of the world. In short, what they ate made them sick. Joseph had taken to indulging his literary side and had been pleased he'd caught the parallels.

The *Guardian E* had established several research stations on Eden. That effort had cost the lives of too many Patrolmen as they encountered native predators.

But scientists had quickly established that Eden's flora and fauna deployed amino acids not used by Earth life. Although the amino acids weren't poisonous, human ribosomes would use them in a case of mistaken identity, and produce a protein that didn't fold right, which meant a person's cells couldn't function properly. As a result, all the food-curious personnel had become suffused with lassitude and ennui, to malady levels, suffering for months on end after their gastronomical adventure.

Rather than treat her disobedient personnel as an object lesson to the others and order the rest to really, truly not eat the wildlife, Admiral Gordon had determined that Eden was not compatible with Earth life. She had believed she faced two choices: sterilize the place or relinquish any plans to treat it as a possible home for humans.

The admiral wasn't a scientist. She wasn't even a lawyer. Joseph had called his legal counterpart on the Patrol's *Guardian E* not long after the *Copernicus* had arrived in the Ross 248 system. Much had happened before the *Copernicus'* arrival, including a deadly solar flare, and Joseph had wanted to catch up—and maybe do a little sharing. The Patrol attorney Harley Lund had not been forthcoming about his client's reasoning, which was much as Joseph had expected. Still, Joseph had accomplished his real goal, which was to complain about the admiral's failure of imagination. All it would take for Eden to be compatible with Earth life would be for the humans to not eat the aliens, he'd pointed out. They could sterilize an island, find a barren rock, or otherwise carve out a niche in a valley somewhere, plant crops, graze livestock, and see if Eden could support human life over the long term. The Patrol attorney had listened, shaken his head, and told him what was done was done.

"Also," and here Harley had dropped his voice, "there's a second reason. This isn't a secret and you'll likely be hearing it sooner or later, but the admiral is concerned that the life on Eden seems genetically engineered, and whoever did it might not like it if we interfere with their work."

"But you've found no other signs of such people? Aliens?"

"Nope," Harley had said.

Joseph had bitten back his observations. They wouldn't have been polite.

"You should take me with you," Joseph said to the first mate. Aitch was a sterile, low-gravity destination. Nonetheless, it was a planet, not a ship, and Joseph longed for nothing so much as to stand on solid ground. Being present at the discovery of an alien facility—whether it was a spaceport, a sports arena, or an apartment complex—sounded great, too.

Aronson gave a single shake of his head. "Not up to me, man. Maybe the captain will let you."

"I'd give her a better briefing if she let me go," Joseph muttered, but he started walking again.

They found Captain Kymba BeKinne in her conference room on the bridge deck. It had real wood paneling, and the carpet was—given the length of the journey alone—a worn antique. Like the rest of the population of *Copernicus*, Captain BeKinne was a normal from Earth. She was approaching the end of her second century, and it showed in the lines that even rejuvenation could no longer erase from her face. Her shoulders were set in a permanent forward sag, but her back was still straight with no hump, and she was meticulous in her person. Where Aronson slouched in baggy clothes with his uniform collar frayed at the nape of his neck, BeKinne's uniform fabric fell uncreased and smooth. No one made bikini jokes.

Shortly after her ship's arrival, she'd been made director of the Ross 248 Project, which gave her authority over everything in the Ross 248 system, except the Patrol. Still, the Patrol coordinated with her.

"Mr. Stern," she said, "please be seated. Has my first mate filled you in on what we've found?"

"Thank you, Captain," Joseph said, and took the proffered chair. Aronson didn't sit. He pressed his thighs into the back of another chair, standing like a ship's figurehead leaning into the wind.

"All I know," Joseph said, "is that you've found something on Aitch that looks like it might be artificial."

BeKinne blinked like an owl. "I must give credit where credit is due. Alexa Prandus, a brilliant young woman, was reviewing imagery from 248h for us. She noticed that one of the mountains appeared unnaturally flat. The plateau is ringed with what look like structures. We'll be sending a lander down."

"I'll tell you all about it later," Aronson said cheerfully.

BeKinne gifted her first mate with a basilisk stare. Joseph felt himself drawing back.

"She is a most stubborn young woman," the captain went on, returning to her original train of thought. "She diverted a probe—without authorization, mind—to take a closer look. There are structures. Clearly artificial."

"And," Aronson continued with relish, "the *Guardian E* sent robot scouts and found nothing. No life, no electronics, nothing. The Patrol says it's abandoned."

Joseph felt a spark of legal excitement, his mind reviewing the implications for Eden. Nonetheless, he felt obligated to check: "Is that a legal determination or is the admiral just saying no one has been there for a while?"

"I don't know," the captain said. "Is there a difference?"

"Oh, yes." He set the question aside for later. He had a dim recollection that the law of finds could apply.

"*Copernicus* is an Earth-registered ship, and must comply with Earth law," the captain said. "I want to send a lander down, but I need your views on whether we are entering someone else's property. I would also appreciate your own thoughts on abandonment."

"It's got a lot of craters showing a lot of meteor hits," Aronson added. "The ship's analysis shows metals near the surface from those hits."

The captain sniffed. "While that would be a great benefit, it is neither here nor there to my question for Mr. Stern."

Aronson gave Joseph a significant look, complete with narrowed eyes and a head tilt. Joseph ignored it and chose his words carefully, but not so carefully that he wasn't clear. "I think I'll have to go with the landing team. This is a novel legal question."

The look the captain gave him wasn't the basilisk stare she had inflicted on her first mate, but neither was it warm with approval. "Indeed. I am sure, however, that structures were abandoned on Earth repeatedly. Over millennia even. There appears to have been consensus about such matters, particularly with regards to ships lost at sea, where the admiral tells me abandonment is *not* assumed. Her lawyer tells her there was an extreme reluctance to find that treasure ships have been abandoned. I would like to know how it's applied here."

"I will have to review the law, Captain," he said. "I did not have time before our meeting. Even so, I believe I should go with the landing team. We may have to think hard about which of the elements to apply. The more I know about the facts on the ground, the better I'll be able to discern what's relevant."

"I'd rather you just told us what to look for, and we'll bring you pictures. Or we'll patch you into a helmet. I have a xenobiologist and archaeologists who would question why you get to go and they don't."

It was time to up the ante, and to show he had a replacement just in case Aronson had been serious about his value. "Let me also bring my young associate, Emily Patel. This would be a tremendous opportunity for her."

"That will be enough, Mr. Stern. Neither of you will go with the landing team."

"One thing I will have to think about," Joseph continued with determination, "is the statute of limitations. Many states have different time limits on how long something must be left before we may call it abandoned. Here we are in interstellar territory."

The captain's lids hooded her large round eyes. "Mr. Stern."

"We need to take relativity into account. Possible differences in technology in travel time. There's been a certain amount of theoretical legal work conducted on what statute of limitations should apply over interstellar distances and timelines." He didn't tell her he'd read that entertaining speculation in a science fiction novel. That would have been off-topic—a digression even. "Who knows what other aspects unique to interstellar travel we'll have to take into account? I will need to review it and think things through after seeing it with my own eyes. The more I know the better I can answer you and provide legal guidance for the archaeologists and biologists. It's not like they should start working without proper legal guidance."

She looked at her first mate, as if the lawyer's presence was his fault.

Aronson gave her a sunny smile. "He'd be no trouble. We'll have the Patrol with us, two sentient AIs, and Alexa herself."

Everyone waited. The captain's eyes took on a certain cunning. "Right. You may go, Mr. Stern. Do take care. I wouldn't want anything to happen to you."

Or to any of the other troublemakers, Joseph thought. He knew she wasn't a fan of her first mate.

Outside her office again, Aronson eyed Joseph with amusement. "You asked for your associate, so she'd have something to turn down." It wasn't a question.

"Client service is important," the lawyer said. He hesitated, reluctant to ask his next question, but Aronson wouldn't take his prize away now he had it. "Why does she even care? We can look at it without figuring out if it belongs to someone. We could even just start digging."

Aronson's mouth pursed, primly. "She's meticulous and precise."

"She's a stickler," Joseph agreed.

Aronson took a long-suffering breath. "She doesn't want us crawling all over someone else's property. She's always like this. If you try to streamline anything, it's cutting corners. But, Joseph"—Aronson was no longer clowning—"I do want to crawl all over it. And extract resources."

"That makes perfect sense," Joseph said, inwardly gleeful. If he found the structures on Aitch had been abandoned, it would be a legal finding. Legal findings had precedential value. He thought of Eden and smiled.

Two days after the captain had requested her first legal briefing, and one day after Joseph had provided a rundown on the principles governing abandonment— concluding with the conservative advice that for now they treat whatever they found as belonging to some- one else, given the uncertainty surrounding possible interstellar statutes of limitations and the seeming lack of any alien available to contest a finding—the lawyer stood in an airlock leading to the Hold, *Copernicus'* sole landing bay.

Joseph hadn't been in a pressure suit in years; in it he felt clumsy and strangely large, and they hadn't even put their helmets on yet. The first mate looked comfortable and happy in his suit, and the Patrol members wore theirs like a second skin. The two sentient AIs wore only themselves.

Joseph had said nothing of his personal policy pref- erences since he'd been assigned to analyze whether the alien structures might have been abandoned. Sure, he'd complained in the past about the admiral's decision to declare Eden off-limits, but he'd not mentioned it in the last two days. Nor had he let anyone know he hoped to find the structure abandoned. After all, if the one place in the Ross 248 system the aliens had obviously visited was abandoned, it could be reason- able to assume the same for Eden, and he hoped no one else drew the connection until after BeKinne had made her decision.

Joseph found Alexa Prandus intriguing. She was a diminutive creature, with a halo of thin, fluffy yellow hair held back by a headband. Fortunately for her, her teeth were straight and even, which was good because her nose tilted up like a chipmunk's. She was a clever young thing. Everyone said so, including the folks who'd mocked her for insisting that the Aitch images showed something worth exploring. She'd received both a demerit in her employment record for her diversion of the drone and a commendation for finding the Oddity. "Oddity," Joseph had to agree, was a better term than the more generic "thing" that Aronson had called it.

Some were even calling it Alexa's Oddity, and Joseph wondered with amusement if she'd be coming to him asking to be recognized as the owner. His late hours the last two nights qualified him to brief her, but he suspected she'd find the legal requirements too onerous to satisfy.

The lead Patrol officer was a handsome normal, not one of the ectomorphic Cerites. No Cerites, genetically engineered to thrive on Ceres, would be accompanying them into Aitch's gravity well. The officer was only a lieutenant, going by the insignia on her suit, but Joseph fancied he'd read the telltale signs of rejuvenation around the eyes, and on her they suggested she was a lot older than the thirty years she appeared. She wore her ash blond hair long at the back of her head and short near her face. Her dark eyes passed over Joseph with indifference before settling on the Prandus girl.

Aronson directed them to put their helmets on, and Joseph's settled into his suit's collar with a heartening hard suck. His pulse was up. He could feel it in the suit's sudden isolation, and the display in the lower left corner of his helmet confirmed the news. It was nothing to be embarrassed about, he assured himself. Landing on an alien world was exciting enough to elevate anyone's pulse. It was excitement, not nerves.

They cycled through the airlock. At 638 meters in length with both ends possessed of doors leading to space, the Hold in the *Copernicus'* center felt like a giant hole. Although protected against radiation and the cold of space, it lacked air. Its gravity was about sixty percent of Earth's normal gravity, and Joseph felt light on his feet despite the pressure suit he—like the rest of the team—now wore. Artificial lights illuminated activity throughout the hold, from personnel moving crates, fuel lines, and mysterious, slender cannisters from the storage areas, to those servicing shuttles.

They trooped lightly across the bay to a Patrol dropship from the *Guardian E* waiting by the Hold's massive doors, and up the ramp. The Hold's doors would open only enough for the dropship to exit, he'd been told, and felt more than a little anxious as to whether that was enough.

In his seat at the rear, he could only just see the back of the pilot's head and that there was a cockpit window. Aronson, the Patrol officers, the sentient AIs, and Alexa Prandus herself all merited closer access to the door than he did. He assumed that Aronson or maybe a Patrol officer would be first down the ramp when they landed. They might all be thinking what they'd name the new planet, that privilege going to whoever first stepped foot on a new world.

The door came down with a delicate but heavy contact, again registering as suction to his alert state. He swallowed hard.

It might have been his imagination, but he thought he felt the engines spin up, the vibration echoing faintly somewhere in his bones and inner ear.

The AI and the pilot ran through their respective checklists. The engines cycled with a thrum that echoed in his bones. It was not his imagination this time. The Hold's massive doors pulled back to show a sight one never saw on Earth: a field rich with stars undimmed by atmosphere and artificial lights. Ahead, Aitch beckoned in somber blacks, grays, and browns, with streaks of palest rose and shadow showing craters and what might appear as mountain ranges from the ground.

The dropship moved forward, its suite of tiny thrusters all firing. However brief the spacecraft's time in the Hold, it was long enough to experience unsettling jerks and thrusts as it oriented itself, and the light gravity dropped to no gravity. Joseph told his stomach to be quiet, and it was.

He saw the ship's distant window move from black to thick stars to Aitch's curve intersecting the lower corner of the window. Aitch looked five times as big as the moon seen from Earth. Still, it felt vastly far.

The AI did nothing to make Aitch fill the screen and soothe Joseph's sudden anxiety. He'd been fine on the starship. He should be fine in this little dropship. He understood that one didn't plunge straight at a planet, that the craft needed to change planes, and that they would enter an orbit before slowing and landing. Joseph would, however, have felt much better had the ground merely grown larger and larger in front of them immediately. It didn't.

A hard burn at two g's followed by almost thirty hours in free fall left Joseph queasy and exhausted.

People read and talked. The Patrol members spent a good amount of time quizzing Alexa on how she'd found the Oddity. The Patrol members handled it fine, but with everyone encouraged to stay in their suits, Joseph had trouble sleeping the first night. The second night, assisted by a pill from a Patrol member, he slept a merciful fifteen hours.

Finally, the ship's AI granted Joseph his original wish, and the view shifted from black sky and stars to cratered rock and a horizon that went from "below" to "in front" with a switch his stomach noticed. Aronson ordered helmets back on.

The dropship shed velocity and no small amount of shielded heat. They were coming in on a high plateau with flat terrain screaming out in front of them. Aitch's "day" lasted over two weeks, and the Oddity was in daylight for their visit. Joseph watched.

Earlier drone surveillance had shown a road leading to the plateau below, but rock covered the road's outlines well enough that two grown women had vociferously debated its existence. Drone footage had also shown acres of flattened mountaintop that could serve as a landing site. He knew they had to be near it when he felt the thrusters firing from below.

Slowly, and with as much care as the most nervous participant could wish for, the lander began its vertical descent, the engine's vibration reverberating through Joseph's whole body. He squinted at the colorless sky ahead.

He worried about rocks. If rocks were on the road, wouldn't they be on the landing site as well? He wished he could see out a closer window. It was hard to help the pilot when he couldn't see what was going on.

A clang reverberated up through his seat, suit, and body. They'd touched down. The dropship didn't tilt onto its side. Joseph swallowed, and his heart started beating again. He blinked. The anxiety still filled him, but the hard fear was gone.

The gravity on Aitch at sixty-five percent was just a little greater than the Hold deck on the *Copernicus*, but noticeably less than the ninety percent of the Village Deck where he lived.

He realized Aronson was giving instructions through the radio in his helmet. People were standing up, and the pressure in the lander began to drop as air got sucked back into the craft's tanks. The human race didn't spill air needlessly.

Joseph shook himself. He'd been so lost in his own head that he'd missed much of what Aronson had said. This was no way to participate in an adventure on a new planet. He needed to focus on what was happening in front of him.

"Ms. Prandus," Aronson said. "You found the thing, so I want you first on the ground."

The young woman's gasp of pleasure was appropriately muted but sincere. "Yes, sir."

One didn't hear changes to the ship, one felt them, and Joseph felt the door open up as the large ramp extruded toward the ground with a grinding thrum.

The sun shone directly overhead, its red-gold light framing a dark oblong of shade beneath the ramp. Alexa's suited form moved into the door, where she paused at the top of the ramp. "Commander Aronson," she said in a small voice the rest of the team heard through their suits' radios. "It looks like glass. Under the dust. Thought you should know."

"We know," Aronson said. "Don't go under the dropship. There's probably a pool of molten glass from the antimatter drive."

Alexa's helmet jerked as if she nodded. She straightened and headed down the ramp. Aronson followed, and Joseph watched as the two helmets disappeared from his sight.

"There's no pool there," Alexa's voice came over the radio.

"And it's not even a little warm," Aronson said after a moment's pause in which he must have checked sensor readings. "Look. I'll take this as a sample."

The four Patrol officers went next. The pilot was staying with the lander. 9-of-Megan, one of the sentient AIs, gestured to Joseph where he waited in the back of the lander.

He tried to walk calmly toward the door. The pilot had put the lander down within a hundred meters of the plateau's edge, beyond which lay empty space. Where the lander's thrusters had cleared dust back in a large circle, the ground shone as if someone had heated it to melting. It looked like lava. Or glass. Had the occupants done this themselves? That could be a sign of intentional abandonment, destroying what they left behind. Or had they suffered an attack and all lay incinerated within the vitrified rock? Then the question would call for analysis under the rules of war.

He headed down the ramp to a new world. Ms. Prandus had been entirely correct. The surface was smooth, and he slid along it tentatively. The reduced gravity did nothing to mitigate the feeling he was about to fall. Fortunately, a newly settling coating of gritty dust allowed Joseph to tell himself he had enough traction to walk normally. All the others were.

Off to the right, he could see the first mate and Ms. Prandus, two figures breaking up the ring of dust formed by the lander's thrusters, one tall, one small, both standing with hands on hips and heads tilted back, staring at a structure ahead of them. He headed toward them.

The nearest structure was itself an oddity, its masses cantilevered, and both strangely proportioned and sometimes steeply slanted. Joseph blinked in the red-gold light, unsure whether the size of the structure's components meant it was farther away than he understood or that its builders were smaller than the average human. Clear of the lander, he stopped and looked around. Maybe Aitch was like the Moon, where the horizon's proximity confused everything one had grown up internalizing about distance, ratios, and proportions on Earth.

A full circle survey of the plateau showed similar edifices dotting its edges. Maybe the previous occupants had blasted out the center and not cared that there were buildings still left standing.

"Stern," Aronson's voice sounded in his helmet. "Quit your gawking and give us all a reminder."

Joseph cleared his throat. "Sure. Here's the thing. We're looking to figure if the place has been abandoned in the legal sense. I know it's alien. I know we don't know what we're looking at. Don't think about that. We do know what *we're* like. We build things and leave them. The Oddity's builders might be like us. Maybe not. But it's legitimate to use ourselves, our perceptions, and our interpretations as a baseline for understanding this place. We know we'll likely get lots of things wrong, but we have to try by our own lights to tell what happened here."

"Yes, yes," Aronson said. "We're aware of that. Get to the guidance, Joseph."

Joseph felt a moment's brief sympathy for the captain. "I don't want anyone discounting their own observations just because they might be wrong, Commander. Anyway. Look to see if any equipment is still here. Or something that looks like equipment. Look for spots where something might once have been but is gone now—different colors on the floors, empty power outlets, bare cupboards. If the rooms are full, that will matter to the legal analysis. Do we see signs of violence? Signs indicating a planned return? Ideally, the builders would have left a note, but we all know it won't be in any human languages, so translations would have to wait for the linguists. Ms. Prandus will be collecting samples for dating." Dates would be interesting, but, as he'd noted earlier regarding the times it took to cross interstellar distances, not necessarily relevant.

"That's it?" Aronson asked.

"That's it," Joseph replied.

"Lieutenant Mooring." Aronson turned to the Patrol officer nearest him. "Set up your people as you wish, but I would appreciate at least one of you joining us inside."

"Wouldn't have it any other way, sir," Mooring replied. Her people began silently rearranging themselves.

They headed toward the closest structure.

They reached a large oblong hole where a door might have been in the building. The Patrol lieutenant went in first before allowing the others to follow her. "No sign of an airlock," she said. "It looks like someone cut around it and took out the door and the frame completely."

Her helmet light showed over rust-colored dust and rubble, and dull shards of door. It was good they'd brought their own lights, for, unlike in modern life in modern buildings, nothing came on as they entered.

"Don't touch anything," the lieutenant growled.

The rooms were extended oblongs, with doors and doorframes missing just like in the front. They canvassed the structure as a group, Aronson turning down Alexa Prandus's pleas to be allowed to go look where she liked, even stopping her once when she began to wander off on her own. The first mate was kind about it, no doubt appreciating that her proclivities were how they knew about the Oddity in the first place. Nonetheless, they traversed the oblongs and steep inclines together. The ceilings of the rooms—if they were rooms—proved not as low as they'd appeared from the outside, and Aronson, the tallest of the team, had a couple decimeters' clearance for his head. The humans wandered from empty oblong to empty oblong.

Joseph felt his excitement mounting. It looked abandoned to him. There was nothing in the structure, but his imagination—and a youth misspent reading science fiction—made him realize that if he voiced the hope aloud three people at once would point out that, for all they knew, they were inside a giant computer, toilet, or tea cup, none of which would be cluttered with furniture, doormats, or the detritus of life. There was dust aplenty, however.

Looking back over his shoulder, Joseph saw the line of boot prints they'd made, some clean, some blended into each other. "Do you think," Joseph asked the first mate, "that someone could estimate how long this has been empty based on the dust?"

Aronson raised a hand palm up. "I'd think so, but don't know."

"Look at this room," Joseph said. "There's dust everywhere." It not only stood thick on the floor but coated the walls as well.

Alexa stood at the other side of the oblong, her back to them. She studied a wall, her head moving in a regular scanning pattern. Intrigued, Joseph watched her.

She held out a hand. She was clearly going to touch something, but Mooring's endless scanning was about to disclose Alexa's defiance of her orders. "Lieutenant," Joseph said, and Mooring turned to him as Alexa wiped a hand over the wall.

"Yes, Mr. Stern?" Mooring asked.

Alexa hunched down and increased the area of her swiping.

Joseph cleared his throat. "I was wondering if splitting into two groups might be allowed? Now that we've seen so much of it."

"We haven't seen all of it," Mooring growled.

"Understood." Joseph's work was done.

Alexa let out a high-pitched squeal. "Look! I think it's a power outlet!"

Mooring spun. "I said not to touch anything."

"Lieutenant," Joseph said soothingly, "our boots have touched plenty."

"It's the floor," she said, deadpan.

"For us, it's the floor—maybe not for the aliens." Joseph kept his voice deadpan, too.

They all crowded around Alexa hunkering low by

the wall. She pointed at a hole maybe a dozen centimeters above the floor. "See? It's a very even hole. And it goes back into the wall." Her finger moved closer.

"Don't put your finger in it, child!" Mooring's voice rose, no longer deadpan.

Alexa snatched her hand away. "I would never," she said, and they could all hear the grin.

Joseph no longer controlled his excitement. "Even if it's not for wiring," he said slowly, calmly, as if he weren't thinking about Eden, "it was for something."

"And whatever that something was," Aronson continued the thought, "it's not there now. Someone may have taken it out. Does that mean it's legally abandoned?"

Again, Joseph was a model of measured calm. No Patrol officer was going to say he'd prejudged the question. "It's certainly a factor to consider. But we'll have to look at the totality of everything we see."

Alexa wiped the ground with a gloved hand. "And look here, there's a line."

"Like there was something there for a long time," Aronson said. "Does that matter, Counselor?"

"It does," Joseph said, keeping the glee from his voice. "It likely means they removed whatever it was before they left."

If the aliens had left Aitch, perhaps they'd left Eden, too—abandoned it, to be precise, and the admiral's concerns over past owners returning could be overturned. He had no illusions that the admiral herself would change her mind. That would have to wait for a change in command, but the groundwork would be laid. It had been a long journey to get to Ross 248. He was a patient man.

The other structures proved similar to the first.

They speculated that large ones might have been hangars, but they were empty, so it was all so much guessing. The found no metal, no technology, only vitrified stone. Aronson picked up a sample from an impact crater, musing that he wanted its properties as a thermal conductor checked. It would be interesting to know how the aliens had turned so much to glass. Joseph prayed that no one would ask him about the intellectual property issues associated with alien technology. He certainly wasn't going to bring it up.

The Patrol set up monitoring equipment, and they headed back to the ship.

Joseph started work on his analysis for the captain the morning after the trip to Aitch. He drafted at a fever pitch, the words flowing easily, the legal tests for the law of finds and abandonment handily supported by all the team had found: the empty hole, the lines showing where something had once sat, the glassine state of the whole plateau. Oh, the reasonable inferences he could draw.

His comm lit with a Patrol name he recognized. He sent the image 2D to his stationary flat screen. Some of the youngsters couldn't be bothered with visuals, but Joseph liked to see who he was talking to. His caller, Harley Lund, was the Patrol attorney he'd called when the *Copernicus* arrived in the system.

"Harley," he said with genuine warmth in his voice and real trepidation in his soul. He liked the man well enough, but he doubted this was a social call. Lieutenant Mooring would have had time to brief her superiors, and they would have had time to speak to Admiral Gordon. Gordon would, of course, have had time to speak to her lawyers. From a bureaucratic perspective, the call's speed was actually impressive.

"Joseph," the Patrol attorney said. "How've you been?"

They exchanged pleasantries, but when Harley's heavy black brows drew down, and his lips pursed, Joseph braced.

"I hear you got to visit Aitch," Harley said. "I'm jealous."

"Thank you. I was thrilled."

"We need to talk about what you found. What you might be recommending to the captain."

"Sure." Joseph slapped an expression of benign interest on his face. BeKinne wasn't just the captain of the *Copernicus*. She was the head of the whole mission.

"I wanted to give you a heads-up on how we're thinking about this," Harley continued, as if the Patrol was in charge. "Under the laws of salvage, the original owner retains title. The builders should still own it."

Joseph's stomach clenched. "I'm not applying salvage rules. I'm using an abandonment analysis and the law of finds."

"Yes," Harley drawled. "I heard. We'd rather you didn't. We looked far back into Earth's history to find what we think is most on point. Ships lost at sea are it."

Joseph bit his tongue. Harley's admission that his analysis had been result-driven was disarming but not helpful. This was about Eden for the Patrol just as much as it was—however privately—for him. The Patrol didn't want a finding that the aliens had abandoned a planet, because that would lead to the next logical inference: namely, that they'd abandoned the whole star system. And that would undercut the admiral's rationale—her

real rationale—for keeping humans from settling Eden.
Joseph wished he hadn't unloaded his views regarding
the admiral's moratorium on settlement on Harley back
when the *Copernicus* had first arrived.

"This is not ancient times," Joseph said carefully.
The Patrol wasn't in charge, but he knew full well that
Captain BeKinne would listen to the Patrol if it insisted.
"Lost ships are always recovered now." Transmitters,
tracking and retrieval technology, and meticulous and
eternal record storage had long obviated the need for
complicated cases about races to the bottom of the sea.

Harley's cheekbones grew rosy with his smirk. "But
the legal principles are parallel. Earth's past is full of
analogous cases. People squabbled over treasure ships a
lot, and the courts have said numerous times that when
something is lost at sea, title remains in the owner. The
mere passage of time and nonuse are not sufficient, in
and of themselves, to constitute an abandonment."

The pedantic quoting of case law was too much for
Joseph. "Your people said the Oddity was abandoned
after the robotic reconnaissance—before we even went."

Harley looked disappointed. "Joseph. You and I both
know that wasn't a lawyer talking. The person who
said 'abandoned' meant only that the place is empty,
no one's there and hasn't been for a while. He's not
a lawyer, just someone saying it looked safe to visit."

They stared at each other. "Go check out the case
law," Harley said. "Start with the US case of the
Columbus America. You'll see what I mean."

"I will," Joseph rasped, appalled at the sudden
roughness in his voice.

Harley smiled. "You're a good man. I knew you'd
help us out."

Joseph was still staring at the blank screen when it pinged again. For once, Yoel Aronson's countenance lacked its usual good cheer. "We heard from the Patrol," he said sourly.

"Me, too," Joseph said. He had a lot he wanted to say. "Let me come see you."

"I was going to find you."

"I figured, but I like to walk, too, sometimes."

Joseph found Aronson in the hall outside the bridge, pacing. "The admiral had her deputy call me," Aronson said. "She's going to ask for a meeting with the captain. They want whoever built the Oddity assumed to be around." The first mate started them walking down the hall.

"To still have title," Joseph clarified.

Aronson stomped down the hall. "They said it was legal. I can't figure why it matters to them."

"They don't want the precedent."

Aronson's head snapped around. "Did the Patrol lawyer say that?"

"Not in so many words."

"But precedent for what?" Aronson demanded.

"For Eden, I think. Maybe I'm wrong, but I will confess—as someone who thinks we should pick out an island on Eden and work on settling it—that finding Aitch abandoned would suggest that Eden's been abandoned, too."

Aronson perked up. "That would be great."

"I think so," Joseph said. "You think so. The Patrol doesn't. The admiral's human-safety rationale doesn't even make sense to me."

Aronson shot him a look. "The scientists don't agree."

"No one got sick," Joseph pointed out, "until they

ate the forbidden fruit. The answer is simple. Don't
eat it. We should grow our own fruit. From Earth.
And avoid the plants that eat us."

Aronson chuckled and hugged the wall as a group
of half a dozen toddlers following a woman passed
them by. "She's worried about the owners coming
back," the first mate said.

"Exactly," Joseph said triumphantly. "And that's why
she says we can't settle there. But if we say the aliens
have abandoned the system, then we could settle on
Eden. The admiral's highly speculative concern—not
that I have anything against unfounded worries—would
continue to keep her awake at night, and settlement
would make it worse. She doesn't want that. She wants
to tell any aliens who showed up that we left their
stuff alone and they shouldn't kill us."

"But what do you really think, Counselor?" Aronson
said. "Remind me to ask you your inner thoughts more
often. You've been holding out."

"I've been trying to be objective. Wanting the same
thing as one of my clients . . . well . . . you . . . is all to
the good."

"I'm so glad," Aronson murmured. "But, see here.
It seems to me we've been doing a lot of assuming.
For instance, it could be different aliens. One set built
things on Aitch. Another set tinkered with genetic
engineering on Eden."

"Just because Paul abandoned his car doesn't mean
you abandoned your house?" Joseph asked.

"Yes!" Aronson was pleased.

"It's a reasonable inference. So is the opposite, and
given the calls we both got, I think we can tell the
admiral has inferred the opposite: the aliens are the

same." Joseph didn't want to make the next point out loud, but now that he'd spilled his guts on his hopes and dreams for Eden, he felt that he had to fully disclose his own pressures. "Also, the different-aliens logic doesn't help Eden."

Aronson frowned at the floor. He'd stopped stomping but still walked with a measured tread. He looked up, his brow clearing. "You want the precedent."

"I do," Joseph admitted. "Even if it's far in the future, I want it to be possible."

"What else?"

Joseph sighed. "I could distinguish the Oddity from Eden pretty easily." A relevant difference between the two planets would let *Copernicus* extract metals from Aitch and the admiral continue her settlement moratorium for Eden.

"How?" Aronson asked.

"We only found them on one mountain. At most those people owned the whole mountain. At the least, they owned just the mountaintop. No one owns all of planet Earth. I could point out it doesn't matter whether the aliens abandoned their mountain or not, because that's the only place we have evidence of habitation or ownership."

"But then you don't have the precedent you want— that a whole planet got abandoned." Aronson was never slow on the uptake. "Because you've got this material difference."

"I am pleased with your mastery of legal lingo, grasshopper," Joseph said automatically, but he couldn't see a way around that one.

The first mate beamed. "I get lots of things. But, Joseph, these arguments will all work. We'll get to extract the metals, do anything we want on Aitch. No one's going to budge the admiral on Eden. Not anytime soon. You can hit her with a two-by-four of precedent and she won't care."

Joseph sighed. The first mate wasn't wrong. "I don't want to use those arguments."

"Sorry, buddy," Aronson said. "You may have to."

They'd reached the lounge with its view of the moon and its planet beyond. "Have I told you my secret plan for Aitch?" Aronson asked. "The Prandus girl is going to name it. She was the first to set foot on it, so it's her privilege."

Joseph wasn't listening.

The meeting about whether the Oddity was abandoned or not took place three days later. Captain BeKinne, as the titular head of the human mission to Ross 248's star system, would decide the question. That didn't mean, however, that she would ignore the Patrol's advice or preferences.

Joseph prickled with anxiety. Aronson's confidence in the outcome was misplaced, he was sure. The first mate had approved Joseph's plan to argue against applying the rules of salvage, serene in his certainty that their ability to distinguish between the Oddity and Eden would carry the day as a fallback. Joseph wasn't even confident of that much. Any military mind that would deprive humanity of the most obvious settlement choice in the system was not a reasonable mind. Captain BeKinne, in her endless quest to get everything exactly right, would still have to weigh Admiral Gordon's concerns against whatever the law allowed even if she agreed with her attorney wholeheartedly.

Joseph's research had, unfortunately, shown him that there was indeed a line of cases where the courts had been reluctant to find that an owner had abandoned a ship based merely on the passage of time. Under the rules of salvage, this resulted in the owner having to share a hefty percentage of the value of the find with the person who found the ship and salvaged its contents. It also meant the salvor had to share a hefty percentage with the owner. No questions of payment arose at Ross 248h, of course, but the principle of continuing ownership was what the Patrol wanted established here.

If only BeKinne hadn't asked for a legal analysis.

But she had, and here they all were in the captain's conference room on *Copernicus'* Deck 6, their holographic projections as real as if they'd attended in person. Admiral Gordon was a normal human, but angular and attenuated in both face and form. Thick frosty brows framed long eyes, a narrow nose, and a bloodless mouth. She sat at one end of the conference table, a stark contrast to Captain BeKinne's dark warmth at the other end. The leaders each had their seconds-in-command to their right and their attorneys to their left, and the middle of the table was populated by two policy wonks from each ship. 5-of-Chandra and the Cerite Leader, C'Helios, attended virtually as observers. The computer inserted them mid-table and across from each other.

After everyone agreed it was good to see each other and that the matter they were addressing was important, the captain nodded to Harley Lund and Joseph Stern. "I have both of your memoranda, gentlemen. Mr. Stern's memo starts by saying that the decision regarding whether to find abandonment is a

factual one and rests with me. Mr. Lund's memo did
not address this point. As mission commander, I am
inclined to agree with Mr. Stern, but must ask whether
you have any objections to that proposition, Admiral."

Gordon turned her cold face to her attorney. "Mr.
Lund?"

"No, Captain," Harley said. "We have no objections
to you being the decision maker. Of course not. We
do hope to persuade you on an important legal point,
however—namely, that under current circumstances we
should not reach the question of abandonment at all."

Harley cast Joseph a bland look, but Joseph knew
what it meant. Of course, BeKinne was the decision
maker. There was no reason for Joseph to have bela-
bored the obvious in a memo, no reason other than to
remind BeKinne of her responsibility and reduce the
chance she'd relinquish her responsibility to Gordon.

BeKinne looked down the table at one of her policy
advisors. "I am advised that sound policy reasons exist
to find abandonment, but please be aware that I am
more concerned with getting this legal question right.
Mr. Lund. Please begin."

Harley leaned forward, hands clasped tightly and
elbows digging into the table. The Patrol's end of the
table was a projection, so it didn't look like he was
sinking through the surface. "Captain. Admiral. The
Patrol is applying the rules of salvage. We think they
are appropriate in the interstellar context we currently
face. What this means, of course, is that under those
rules we do not presume abandonment. For one thing,
we all know how long it takes for an interstellar journey.
We have no reason to believe that other races move
between stars more swiftly than we do."

Joseph squirmed inside. This was precisely the argument he'd made to the captain so flippantly the week before. If BeKinne was looking at him, he didn't check.

"Thus, where courts in the past have determined that the passage of over a century does not allow a presumption that an owner has abandoned a ship, we must presume even longer periods of time here. Millennia might be more appropriate. Additionally, we have to face the fact that these possible owners are not getting a chance to be heard before you today. As a matter of equity—of policy—we shouldn't make unilateral decisions without all stakeholders getting a chance to speak."

Joseph controlled the desire to interrupt. He knew better. He looked young, but he was an older man who knew to bide his time. Harley continued talking, summarizing all that he had said in his memo, BeKinne interrupting occasionally for clarification. He reviewed numerous cases from Earth's past where courts had found that the original owners had not abandoned possession of their lost ships, even though they did little or nothing to reach them, and BeKinne indulged her curiosity too far, Joseph felt. He took notes. There were many points to which he would need to respond, although there was also an annoying amount of repetition. Maybe Harley intended to put Joseph and the rest of his audience to sleep.

Whenever Joseph checked on BeKinne, she was checking on the admiral.

When Harley at last wound down, Joseph saw that only an hour had passed. It was an annoying sign of the state of his nerves. Just prior to the meeting, the first mate had reminded Joseph that if his attempt to use the law of finds failed, he expected Joseph to do his duty and use the other arguments. Joseph knew that Aronson would if he didn't persuade the captain that salvage principles didn't apply.

The captain called for a ten-minute break, and when they all returned she looked to Joseph. "Mr. Stern, I would appreciate your views as well."

Joseph moved smoothly through all his gratitudes for the opportunity to speak with everyone in the room, offer whatever assistance he could, and address the interesting argument that the Patrol had devised.

That done, he thought of Eden and allowed himself a deep breath. "I will not repeat everything from the *Copernicus* memo, but there are several issues I wish to highlight. It is *Copernicus* Legal's position that the mission should apply the law of finds rather than the law of salvage to the Oddity. But first let me observe that even if the Ross 248 mission were to apply the rules of salvage, we should still find that its owners abandoned the Oddity, and that is because a presumption may be rebutted. The Patrol's counsel speaks of a presumption of ownership staying with the original owners as if it is a final decision. It is not. The very court decisions on which the Patrol relies allow that one may show with clear and convincing evidence that an owner abandoned his sunken treasure ship."

"It's impossible," Harley said, showing he didn't share Joseph's qualms about interrupting. "Any such finding would be unilateral. It wouldn't account for interstellar distances and times. It took us over a hundred and ten years to get here. Who knows how long it will take these aliens to return?"

Nettled, Joseph opened his mouth, but the captain

spoke first. "Thank you, Mr. Lund. I believe you have already made those points."

"It is those concerns," Joseph said, glad of the opportunity Harley had just provided, "that require us to look more closely at whether to apply salvage rules in the first place. The Patrol's *attorney*"—not the admiral, never the admiral; she was way too alarming and it was always prudent to blame the lawyer—"has fallen prey, like many before him, to a metaphor. It is an inapt metaphor. The planets in outer space are not like the ocean. They are like land. The law of finds applies on land."

"That was in your memo," Harley muttered, but the comm system faithfully picked it up and ensured everyone heard.

Joseph's lips thinned. The man needed to stop interrupting. "Allow me to emphasize what was in my memo," he said. "Thinking of outer space as an ocean certainly has *cultural* moorings." He used the word deliberately. "But a metaphor does not turn into an analogy on that basis alone. It is perhaps hard to see from the inside, but much of ship culture comes from a branch of service that traversed the waters. Thus, spacecraft are called ships. The Patrol adopted naval hierarchies and terminology, speaking of captains and admirals, decks instead of floors, all-hands instead of meetings, and on and on, including the navy's godawful early hours."

Aronson was staring at him, bemused.

Joseph wondered if he sounded irate. He resolved not to, and spoke serenely once more. "Let us be clear. Presumptions in favor of the original owner retaining title in sunken treasure ships arose for one simple reason. For centuries, it was extremely difficult, if not impossible, to reach ships as they lay on the ocean floor. Thus, it was appropriate for courts to offer the original owners some protection in the form of a rebuttable presumption. But that is not the case here.

"Consider a case where a riverboat went down. The original owners took what they could from it, including furs, government-owned specie, machinery, the ship's boilers, and half of six hundred pigs of lead. Two years later an island began forming around the wreck, on which trees grew eventually to a great height. There the court found relevant that the owners did not attempt to remove the rest of the lead in the two years they had before the island formed. The court found the owners had abandoned the lead and it belonged to those who found it."

Harley grunted, but if he said something, this time it was inaudible.

"Perhaps the void of outer space *is* like the oceans. Perhaps. However, today we are talking about a planet. The right approach is to treat planets as land, not as water. We can walk on them. Many are as stable as Earth's terra firma. Aitch is. Most of them have large pieces of ground—continents' worth—that are not covered in water, the water that made it so hard for Earth's ancients to recover sunken treasure ships. The land on Aitch is more like the land on Earth than it is like Earth's oceans. That's because it *is* land. Therefore, the law of finds applies so we can do an abandonment analysis."

The captain was nodding at him. He felt the slightest easing of his tension. Sure, she would go off and deliberate, but nodding was a good sign.

"What about the Outer Space Treaty?" Harley snapped.

"Which one?" Joseph inquired.

"The Outer Space Treaty of 1967. It defines outer space—where the maritime *analogy* certainly applies, as you yourself noted with our admirals, decks and all-hands—to include all celestial bodies, meaning planets."

Aronson no longer looked bemused. He looked intent. He wanted the minerals on Aitch, and he didn't want Joseph screwing up because some ancient treaty written by people who couldn't imagine being off-planet said planets were outer space and this made people think that land was like an ocean. Aronson opened his mouth. The first mate clearly planned to save the day.

"All my points still stand," Joseph said quickly. "First, that treaty was written at the dawn of the Space Age by a primitive people, even before anyone had set foot on the Moon. Either they, too, suffered from the inability to distinguish between planetfall and vacuum, or their reach was so limited it didn't matter that they thought of everything off-planet under a single rubric. Second, the treaty itself is no longer in effect, and, as Mr. Lund well knows, that matters."

Harley sniffed. It was an indignant sniff. "I raised the point only to show that our so-called metaphor has quite a long history."

Joseph would have sniffed, too, but it wasn't dignified. Harley had been caught out trying to apply dead law and everyone knew it.

The captain raised a finger. "I do *not* think," she said, "that your point is ... well, ah ... grounded, Mr. Lund."

The room froze, and Joseph watched in shock as BeKinne dimpled at her own pun.

"Relying on both memos and today's meeting, I will apply the law of finds based on advice of counsel. I find it hard to equate a mountaintop with an ocean."

Joseph's eyes went wide, but he kept his face calm. The captain was not done. "My scientists tell me the mountaintop scarring happened over ten thousand years ago, maybe twenty. Like the riverboat scenario Mr. Stern described, the owners took their machinery with them. They took not only their doors but their doorways. They left only empty outlets and shadows on the ground. I will not ask the Patrol to disturb its findings regarding other planets."

Joseph let out the breath he hadn't known he was holding. He stole a look at Aronson, and the first mate dropped him a shallow wink. Joseph hadn't figured the captain would make up her mind on the spot. He'd worried she would take her time and give the admiral a chance to speak to her privately. That clearly wasn't going to happen.

The admiral knew it, too, and her frosty brows were lowered. "We have security considerations," she said ominously.

"Certainly," said BeKinne, "and I will not ask you to revisit them. I will ask you to put the Oddity under Patrol protection."

Gordon's face grew tight. They all knew that the admiral's security considerations were about Eden more than the Oddity.

Joseph didn't care that BeKinne wasn't going to ask Gordon to change her mind on Eden. Getting the law right was a long game. Someone other than Admiral Gordon could revisit the issue, and they could all agree later that any aliens had abandoned the whole system.

"Good enough," Gordon said.

Harley had been scowling at the table while the clients talked, and Joseph watched as the other attorney shook off his disappointment. Like all lawyers, he had to be used to things not always going his way, and if Gordon was satisfied, he could be, too. Now Harley addressed the captain with an earnest sincerity that showed he had no hard feelings. "Thank you for settling that, Captain. By the way, what's the plan for naming Aitch?"

Had it been anyone else, Joseph would have said she'd rolled her eyes. The captain turned to her first mate. "Would you care to explain what you've done?"

Joseph went rigid. He knew. Aronson had told him the new name. There was no need to get the admiral's back up further. She'd find out soon enough, and she didn't need to hear it in public. He tried telepathy on Aronson, willing him to wait, and not to let on that Aitch was now—even in Aronson's avuncular jest— somebody's world. It felt too much like rubbing it in.

Telepathy didn't actually work, and once again it failed Joseph.

Aronson gave them all a wide smile. "As the first on the ground, Alexa Prandus has the privilege of naming the planet, of course." It was the new tradition, as good as any. "She won't do it. She's suddenly all shy."

BeKinne snorted. "Who was second?"

"Me," Aronson said, with an even bigger grin. "So... now that we've established Aitch belongs to no one, we can call it Alexa's World."

Gordon stiffened as if slapped. "That doesn't mean anything," she snapped.

"No," Joseph said quickly. "It means nothing at all."

Eden is off-limits for settlement. Normal humans reside primarily on the starship *Copernicus* and in the section of Toe Hold known as the Primate Quarter. Neither is desirable as a long-term home for normal humans. One possibility considered by the Ross 248 Project leadership is terraforming the third planet, informally known as Poseidon's World. A small group of explorers and scientists are sent to sail Poseidon's world-spanning red sea to determine if it can be modified for Earth life—but not everyone has the same objective.

Kraken Rising

Daniel M. Hoyt & E. Marshall Hoyt

Daniel M. Hoyt is a systems architect for trajectory physics software, when not writing or wrangling royalty calculations. Dan has appeared in premier magazines like Analog *and several anthologies, notably the recent* Founder Effect *(Baen), and Dr. Mike Brotherton's* Diamonds in the Sky *(funded by the National Science Foundation). Dan also edited* Fate Fantastic *and* Better Off Undead *for DAW. Having published in several genres, Dan turned to his science-fiction roots for his space opera,* Ninth Euclid's Prince. *This is his first collaboration. Catch up with him at danielmhoyt.com.*

E. Marshall Hoyt has been telling stories since before he could talk, acting out plays with stick figures that his parents swear followed the beats of Joseph Campbell's Hero's Journey to the letter. Like his father decades before, his response to a boring literature analysis assignment was to write it as a short story. After winning a story challenge contest (the prize was a signed Dave Freer novel), Marshall took some time away from writing to study nonfiction subjects: electrical, mechanical, and aerospace engineering. He was lured back to fiction for this collaboration.

Sputtering beneath a roiling sea like bloody lava, Sabrina felt like demons clawed at her heels, driving her straight into the ice-cold arms of the devil himself. Her fate sealed in one steely-nerved moment, now she raced silently under the ocean, pursuers far behind but closing the distance as they skipped along the waves of the dark red ocean, intent on punishing her betrayal. The palace of this particular devil, a mostly submerged structure with a small surface dome highlighted by crimson skies, loomed ahead, its lone inhabitant unlikely to allow her entrance, despite their long history as friends.

She flicked a lever, twisted a knob, and spun to another screen. Still submerged, her only visibility to the pursuing skippers were momentary sonar blips, as the crafts' bodies slammed the ocean swells and careened skyward again with a burst of thrust, a perpetually skipping stone under a cloudy, crimson sky on the Ross 248 water planet, Poseidon, its entire surface devoid of land.

Waiting patiently, on the next blip she slammed a finger to the screen to mark its position, allowing her to study the blips through several cycles and identify three distinct paths made by the disjointed ones.

That's...three skippers, going...maybe ten knots faster than I am?

She spun back to the main controls and flicked on the subcomm transmitter.

"Adam?" she shouted frantically as the device seemed to lock onto a receiver.

Silence. Static. Not close enough? Signal loss? Being ignored?

The subcomm kluge had been invented specifically

for Poseidon, converting audio signals to Morse code sound impulses and back again, with only rudimentary inflections encoded in the transfer. Static was the standard indicator for too long a delay.

She was not positive she would reach the substation before the skippers caught her. The underwater currents were steady, so her speed would be relatively consistent. But her pursuers only needed to catch a good patch of wind and calmer seas to bring them even closer, faster.

She wanted to, *had* to, get there first.

Lost in her thoughts, she left the subcomm locked onto the receiver, and the static broke.

Was that a cough? What did that mean?

"Adam? Adam, we need to talk. We nee—"

"Keeping talking, Sabrina. Tell me about your conspiracy."

That's not Adam. How close are the skippers?

Sabrina responded calmly, "Director, it doesn't add up."

The director's response was equally calm, interpreted as a booming and deep command voice. "Tad showed us everything, you saw it. Adam's been planning this for over a year."

"No! There's another explanation, he wouldn't do this! Just let me—"

"Don't be a fool. Stop and—"

The signal cut out. Turning to her other screen, the blip that popped up was farther back this time.

Good.

Sabrina figured she had just over ten minutes to prevent Adam from potentially delaying the Poseidon terraforming program by decades, if not centuries.

Malice or ignorance, she had to get to him first, to dig out the truth before it was too late; they'd been friends since childhood and he deserved a chance to explain. The director would not ask questions with the overwhelming evidence against him; he would just arrest Adam on the spot.

She flipped on the subcomm and spoke into it.

"Adam? Adam? We need to talk."

Silence, but not static. *Is it working?*

After a long silence, she had a thought and fiddled with the controls. Using a private encrypted channel that Sabrina remembered from years before, when Adam was still developing the subcomm for Poseidon, she was rewarded with a single word from Adam: "Kraken!"

Two Years Ago, 58 AA, Dawn Promise, *Poseidon*

"I can't sign off on this," the director sneered. Bloodred waves crashed the hull and painted the window behind him, trickling away to reveal an inky horizon shrouded in thick, heavy clouds shot through with blindingly bright veins.

Sabrina stood next to Adam silently and waited. Tall and imposing, yet graceful and gifted with a wise, fatherly smile, Adam rarely had problems convincing people to do much of anything—if they looked past his messy blond hair and occasional social awkwardness. Fortified by several cups of strong tea, Sabrina steeled her resolve to keep her silence and make Adam stand up for himself. Despite being above the water in the tiny dome, the office light was full-spectrum, just like Toe Hold, the nexus of the Ross colonization, necessary to keep the unmodified humans sane.

"Please, Director, consider what this could mean for Poseidon. The initial data we've collected indicates it could work. We could have a *real* home." He waved vaguely about the gently rocking, floating station and added, "Something better than this."

Captain Percy—an honorary title for the director of the research station, as he had no rank in the Patrol, nor was the station an active starship—preferred his people to call him Director, as "Captain" was a painful reminder of the Patrol stripping him of rank and then expelling him. His experience and expertise more than qualified him to head up this expedition. It paid well and it gave him a chance to demonstrate his abilities. What he lacked in rank, he gained in status at the top of the command chain on the station, indeed on all of Poseidon.

Adam had been passionate about his proposal, Sabrina thought, and with good reason. His team fulfilled their data collection duties, but also managed to collect *additional* information supporting what amounted to a more solid terraforming recommendation than Adam thought the bureaucrats could make without that data.

"We don't have the time or resources," the director mumbled dismissively. "The minisubs have been using far more power than projected, and you and your merry band of scientists have all but exhausted the rather *limited* supply of coffee on board."

Adam winced. The barb was laser-focused at the person who had been responsible for ordering the supplies in the first place. "Please, sir, Director, sir, we could have this project off the ground and results in less than a year. We nee—"

"I know what you need," Percy interrupted, "but you're not getting it. Your *preliminary* data fails to include any risk analysis."

"But that's why—"

"I certainly won't rubber-stamp a project this ambitious, and we just don't have the resources."

"Sir, if we could—"

"No! We can't!" Percy yelled. "I'm sorry, but I give recommendations in two years, and we don't have the time to request new supplies and run this project in that time; it'd be months past the deadline."

Adam sighed in defeat. Months putting this together, and in one short meeting, gone, evaporated.

Sabrina nodded in silent agreement with the director. Just getting the supplies needed would jeopardize the timeline for recommending terraforming efforts for this world—the very *purpose* of their mission here. The next scheduled resupply was already delayed, along with the second research station for Poseidon, and they were dangerously low on coffee and numerous other critical supplies.

On top of that, the additional research time wasn't possible with their current schedule.

Irritated, Adam rounded on Sabrina. "Sabs, you've seen the data, tell him it's possible."

She darted her eyes at him, annoyed, and shrugged. "My team reviewed the *initial* data, and while it *could* work—"

Percy raised an eyebrow.

"—we couldn't confirm his team's *subsequent* data, nor did we do any risk assessment of his proposal using that data alone."

The color drained from Adam's face. She'd always

been there for him, a solid pillar of strength to back up his wild plans, but not now. Looking over at him, he looked betrayed.

"Doing so would push past our recommendation date, and without a favorable risk assessment, it's not worth it for a mere proof of concept."

Sabrina hated to see Adam so dejected, deflated. She knew instantly their friendship was now damaged, but hers was always the voice of reason, and this time the cost was too high.

He'll be mad at me for a while, but he'll come around eventually. He always does.

Percy said calmly, "I know you're invested in this, but we just don't have time or resources. I understand the work you've done, but this station has other priorities. In less than two years we have to present a strong case that this planet can, or cannot, be terraformed. That is our primary mission here."

Percy stood and indicated the door. "I think we're done here. Don't forget to renew your sidearm certification; the Patrol has been pretty concerned about the various low-level terrorism acts lately and they want to make sure even researchers can respond to any threat that pops up. Sabrina, you're dismissed."

As she left, she heard Percy gently inform Adam, "As expected, the station is traveling too slowly to collect sufficient data around the planet on its own in time; we need to cover more ground. I'm authorizing the deployment of the substations and recommending you to head one of them for a long-term research expedition. The volume of data you collected in such a brief time has impressed me; let's put those talents to good use."

Five Years Ago, 55 AA, Transport Ship Above Poseidon

"Well, thanks for recognizing my talents," Adam said gratefully, deftly sloshing steaming, perfectly brewed coffee into Sabrina's cup before reaching into the bag slung around his chair.

"I wouldn't call making a decent cup of coffee a talent, Adam," Sabrina said, smiling, before she took a sip. "Unless you're a barista."

"Decent?" Adam mocked outrage. "Tan Arabica is the *best*."

Sabrina sipped again. "Dirt-grown on Toe Hold, I know. None of that hydroponic crap for us Poseidon royalty."

While Adam scrabbled together papers, Sabrina sipped patiently, staring out the tiny window, admiring the planet below with its black storm clouds flitting about, lightning cracks momentarily exposing the liquid surface below and bright red reflections tracing a pattern on the window. She looked back to Adam, who was arranging slightly crumpled papers into a particular order and smoothing them on the table between them, satisfied.

Sabrina grabbed the small pile of disorganized and messy notes and scribbled calculations and started going over them. Numbers twisted up in crude drawings of devices and machines. It was all distant to her field of expertise, but she was familiar with Adam's process. On *Copernicus*, the colony ship where they grew up, notebooks lined his room, pages filled from corner to corner. He was always thinking, full of ideas. *Modifying humans*

*further to survive in harsh planet environments,
effectively creating another new subspecies. Creating
a habitable planet through a convoluted series of
adjusted trajectories on millions of meteorites.* On
the supply ship accompanying *Pusher 3*—delivering
the lone Poseidon research station—Adam managed
to jot down his ideas on found scraps, his notebooks
a luxury too expensive for weight allotment.

Accustomed with deciphering Adam's work, Sabrina's
eyes darted from diagram to equation. "It's not the
craziest idea you've come up with," she said.

Adam mocked offense and replied, "I never have
crazy ideas! Just ones that require lots of work."

Sabrina laughed. "Speaking of work, weren't you
supposed to be working with the station's loading crew
to get the research station supplied?"

"We've got until next week before the station deploys
from *Pusher 3*. I've got time."

Sabrina rolled her eyes. Adam could get caught up
in his ideas, his daydreaming distracting him from the
world around him. Years before, he had even forgotten
to tell her he was leaving *Copernicus* until he had
strapped himself in the transport and remembered to
call her before it departed. No doubt some new plan
swirled around his head instead.

"You might want to check your datapad more often,
Adam. It's already next week, and we're already on
the transport, not the supply ship."

Adam had his face buried in his notes, scribbling
away madly at a blank corner on a page, barely registering Sabrina's words. He grunted, which Sabrina
knew meant he had heard the words but they failed
to register.

Sabrina sighed. "Have you at least talked to your team?"

Adam looked up from his notes and said, "Yes! I even told them about my project idea!"

"Oh, for Eden's sake, you already have three research projects!"

"Don't worry, we can work it alongside the official projects with little additional effort."

Sabrina groaned. If the company got any hint he was burning resources collecting data for an unauthorized project, there could be consequences, none of them light punishment, and it could be devastating to lose even a single crew member on a sparsely manned research station, much less a leader.

"I'd recommend against it. Frankly, I'm surprised any of your team would risk it."

Adam grinned. "Actually, my team universally agreed! Even Tad, who was surprisingly the most supportive. He's convinced we can submit a formal project proposal before the official recommendation."

Sabrina was surprised but said nothing. In her few interactions with Tad at mission briefings and Adam's lab, he seemed overly practical. *Maybe I read him wrong.* Anyway, if Adam was careful with this project idea, then she would not argue with him too much, or he might come up with a crazier plan. Adam *always* had a plan.

Adam paused, concern crossing his face.

Finally.

He reached into his bag frantically and pulled out his datapad. "Wait, the supplies? What day is it?"

Sabrina smiled and sipped her coffee. She had a sinking feeling that she'd be drinking the bitter hydroponic crap after this. She closed her eyes and savored this cup, memorizing the smooth, rich Tan Arabica taste.

Nine Years Ago, 51 AA, Toe Hold, Liber

"It's not a good day to go here, it seems." Sabrina said, rounding the corner to one of the safer cafés in Toe Hold. Its tight entryway teemed with protestors clutching metal serving plates—probably stolen from a nearby restaurant—crudely etched with vicious words and rude expressions. Screaming about the evils of space colonization and the great sins of the Red Devils—a derogatory name used in general for the people heading up the Ross 248 Project—they seemed to forget the purpose of the colony ship they grew up on. Sabrina viewed the Anticols as entitled lemmings, adults in body only, still children in their minds.

It would do them good to work for Magenta Management for a year so they could understand the science we do.

Adam saw Anticols fundamentally cutting against his core beliefs and pursuits, and he felt that if they knew what he did for a living, there would be more than words flung around. He stared, eyes narrowed, tensing for any sign of an impending attack.

Sabrina cleared her throat. "Maybe we should find a quieter café."

"Uh, sure. There's one I like near the maglev train station down the North Tunnel."

They shuffled together through the grimy tunnels of Toe Hold, close to the edge of the Promise borough with its gangly, genetically modified counterparts known as Cerites. At eight percent Earth gravity, a more aggressive gait could send them both hurtling roofward toward the tunnel's full-spectrum lights.

Normally, to avoid the usual tensions that came with confronting a Cerite, you would grab a cup closer to the train, the part most populated with normals—unmodified humans. While the numerous coffee shops that popped up over the past few years helped ease the tensions that had developed in Toe Hold from sleepy normals wandering accidentally into Cerite territory, it did not quell them completely.

The Cerites and normals tended to band with their own kinds. Even on one of the mostly lifeless roads in the colony, they could still make out the distant taunts between a Cerite and a normal. It was almost comical now, but it could turn far more serious in a heartbeat. A few years from now, it might not be so funny. Cerites were not just genetically modified, built to withstand the many harsh conditions of space itself, but they were culturally quite different from the younger normals. Cerites were built to colonize, to expand and explore; they were often rigorous and precise, laser-focused on their goals. In contrast, a lot of normals, especially the younger ones, were born with so much freedom and choice, they felt aimless in their goals.

Sabrina had some sympathy for the Anticol protesters, but they were ruthless in their rejection of expansion and further colonization. Growing up on *Copernicus*, not only did the history lessons of the Sol System seem to reaffirm caution on rapid expansion, but even the efforts made in this system suggested as much. But Anticols missed the big picture; all they saw was two cloud cities, the colony ship *Copernicus*, and the section of Toe Hold they lived in called the Primate Quarter. With their distorted view of history and a lack of any desirable future, Sabrina understood how they could be bitter.

The young normals romanticized the Sol System, and especially Earth, in the same way their parents and generations before had romanticized the Ross system as humanity's savior. Born to a system with limited habitability, the goal of colonizing every world in it would not be fulfilled within their lifetimes.

As youths, Adam and Sabrina had arrived in the system, marveling at the sight of the Ross star and its many planets. For them, the multigeneration *first* goal of reaching this new home was only the beginning; they were excited to be part of the *next* goal. It was, after all, about the long-term needs of humanity, not just the needs of their short lives.

The bitterness that prevailed from Anticols had torn apart the families of some of her coworkers and pupils. The evidence of countless prior protests lined the streets. Scrap metal and discarded materials etched and painted with slogans and phrases were left in junk piles around every corner. The dirtiness of Toe Hold was perhaps the most startling contrast to the colony ship. Neither of them really appreciated what it meant to live in a subterrane colony on a moon until they got there, the grungy nature of colony living. They were used to the clean, sleek metal hallways and rooms of the *Copernicus* with view screens lining various parts of the massive ship.

Ahead, there was something pasted on the wall advertising a restaurant, the Purple Parrot. Sabrina glanced at it.

"That's for a place in Promise! Why are they advertising it *here*?"

They passed a Cerite youth staring at the advertisement. He glanced at them and shook his head almost imperceptibly.

We get it. Not for us. Move along.

"There," Adam said, pointing down the road to a protestor-free café.

Sabrina took his arm. "Off we go, then."

As they walked closer, they were gratified to hear the chattering of Cerites and normals within the café excitedly talking while sharing coffee together.

Adam squeezed Sabrina's arm to get her attention. "How goes the certification for your pupils?"

"Good. Most of them should be certified soon enough. They asked me to be a research head for the expedition." She paused, then continued, "How are yours?"

Adam looked away. "A lot of them are behind. I don't know why, I'm a pretty good teacher."

Sabrina raised an eyebrow as he looked back over at her. "What? I'm serious! I'm sure that Stacy, Miranda, Tad, and Mack will be certified by the end of the year."

"Adam, that's only a quarter of your pupils."

Adam grumbled and walked on in silence. As he opened the door to the café, he brightened. "You know, I had an idea recently."

Sabrina rolled her eyes. "I'm sure."

He raised his voice a bit over the din around them and got in line. "It's a bit early in development, but I thought of something for the third planet."

Sabrina paused and recalled their lessons. "The one covered in water? Ross 248d?"

Fifteen Years Ago, 45 AA, Copernicus

"No, no, that's 248d, I'm on 248b, Aeneas. The other cloud city is on 248c, on Cupid."

Sabrina sighed; she was never particularly good with the planet designations. Living in a small room on *Copernicus* did not incentivize remembering which planet was which.

"That's a big move," Sabrina responded glumly. She stared at her comm device, a vaguely Adam-shaped figure outlined on the out-of-focus display, just visible enough to capture the overall figure but not any features. She suspected Adam had finally dropped his own comm enough to damage the camera. In contrast, she had never so much as misplaced her datapad from its usual resting place next to a neat stack of papers on her desk.

What a pair we make. So different, but still friends.

"Magenta Management said it would cover any moving costs."

Sabrina leaned back. "But a ten-year contract? That's a pretty big commitment."

"We'd be training the next generation of scientists!"

"On Toe Hold. It's barely just started to house humans. We would have to live in the Primate Quarter and spend time on the train to nowhere every day just to stay healthy. Parents use it to threaten their kids into submission." She affected a parental voice. "Behave! Don't make me move us to Toe Hold!"

Her entire life had been spent on *Copernicus* and she saw little reason to leave. She had gotten her certification on the ship, a solid job, even made some friends—at least, work friends. The only person she really considered to be a friend was Adam—who'd left a few years ago to be one of the first people to try and live on the second cloud city in the system: Asgard. Truthfully, she had not been *happy* since he had left.

"There's more to it than that. After ten years, we'll be first in line for a research expedition! The one going to Poseidon. We would be among the first humans to ever set foot on that planet," Adam said.

"Ten years and a research expedition?" she shot back. "How much of a commitment are you expecting me to make here? It's not like we're married!" Sabrina bit her tongue, surprised she had said that aloud. Despite the fact they'd never actually dated, she'd always assumed they'd marry someday; lately it seemed like Adam didn't share that expectation.

Magenta Management had gained a lot of favor with 5-of-Chandra, generally considered the most influential of the Ross 248 Project command structure. It was not hard to imagine the company getting a contract to launch a future research expedition.

That was Adam's *real* goal: the research contract that Magenta Management dangled provocatively as an incentive for a decade of routine tutoring and helping young scientists get certification. They were both experts in their respective fields. Sabrina was well versed in chemistry, weather systems, and environmental risk assessment; her skills were used to teach a new generation to become good scientists. Adam's skills in mechanics and engineering were well suited for the people who maintained the machines necessary for survival in the Ross 248 system.

After a bit of silence, Adam cut in. "Listen, Sabs,

you're still my only real friend. I don't want to pursue this opportunity without you, I want to take this adventure *with* you."

Sabrina blinked. It was interesting to hear that he was serious about this, and more importantly to Sabrina, that he wasn't willing to do it without her. But when he left for the cloud city on Aeneas, it was like he had forgotten about her. He left her alone on the colony ship with only the stacks of his journals she had rescued before his room was reassigned.

For a long time, she felt so angry and betrayed she wouldn't return his calls. In retrospect, until she had recently reconnected with him after his return, she had not seen him in years. Still, it was a lot to ask, and she wasn't even sure she wanted to go into research. Moving from the *Copernicus* to Toe Hold's Primate Quarter was a massive change and a long-term commitment. And after that they would be moving across the Ross system to a new unexplored planet.

It was one Adam wanted to take with her.

Every cautious and careful muscle in her body tensed and she swallowed. "When does Magenta Management want us to start?"

Two Years and One Week Ago, 58 AA, Dawn Promise, *Poseidon*

"Hard to say." Sabrina held a mug of hot water in one hand and dipped a tea bag tentatively into it. "It might go poorly."

Her office was small, light peeking through the clouds and lighting the entire room in a diffused red tint. Adam sat at her desk chair with his back to the window, red waves crashing into one another silently behind him. He tapped away at his datapad, the screen cracked and slow to respond, trying to confirm his upcoming appointment with the director.

"I don't know, Sabs, I feel like it'll go well."

Sabrina finished steeping her tea and sat across from him in her guest chair.

"We'll see. You didn't secure authorization for this project and your data is incomplete; the director might be furious." She frowned. "Remember the last time you approached 5-of-Chandra directly with a half-baked idea? It was rejected, but *someone* found out, took it seriously, and an entire crew on Eden almost died."

Adam was trusted by Magenta Management, but not so much by those truly in power.

"We've met our goals," Adam said stiffly. "He can't be too upset that I did additional data collection; I didn't compromise the other projects. I'm going to bring him a proposal to create land on Poseidon and then continue the project into the experimentation and implementation phase; that's the part that really requires authorization."

Sabrina sipped her tea. Adam wasn't wrong. For doing something off the books, he had been responsible about getting work done on time and efficiently. And their primary mission was to gather data. She suspected that was in no small part due to Tad, who had become an invaluable part of Adam's team. It was rare to see Adam without seeing Tad these days.

Still, she enjoyed the silence together. Like everyone else on board, she found herself a little on edge with all the red light. She lost her temper with Adam more than once—just because he shared his ideas and dreams.

It had never bothered her before. Unfortunately, the crew thought the best cure for the anxiety that bled through from the environment was caffeine. Combined with the initially low supply—a direct result of Adam never getting around to helping the supply crew above Liber—that cure was running low. Seeing the inevitable, Sabrina made the wise choice last year to switch to tea.

Sabrina glanced at Adam and closed her eyes, remembering the driven mess of a man she had chosen to follow. After ten years he was still disorganized and a little messy, his blond curls fighting one another at the top of his head. A shoulder bag overflowing with paper that invariably held new and bold ideas to change the universe accompanied him everywhere. It was oddly impulsive for her to leave a safe, well-paying job on *Copernicus* to move to a rough colony with him on the promise of what had become this assignment. It was not that bad in the beginning, but the Anticols had amped up the violence over the ten years of their contract to the point that they could not be considered anything but terrorists.

At the end of those increasingly longer ten years on Toe Hold, Sabrina had been glad to put them as far behind her as possible. At the time, this desolate water planet held great appeal, as Anticols were notably absent.

Poseidon. Dead sea Poseidon. Unrelenting, the water spun around the globe. She was finally used to the gentle rocking of the research station. It was moments like these that offered an important reminder of a life they had shared together. The thought calmed her more than she would like to admit.

"Hey, Sabs, I have a favor to ask you," Adam said, breaking the comfortable silence.

Sabrina's temporary serenity evaporated. Few things pushed her buttons these days more than Adam asking for a favor. Sabrina noticed an increasing amount of those being asked of her the longer they were on the station, and she felt less like his friend and more like a resource with every request.

"Adam, you can't be serious. Your team had a second minisub for an entire week when my team needed it for chemical analysis near the crust."

"I know, I know," Adam said quickly, with only a trace of remorse. "But it's not like that. I just need a risk assessment on my project and its current data and modeling."

Sabrina glared at him.

"I swear, my team will pick up some of the slack on one of the projects we're working on together. I just want to go into the meeting with as much support as possible."

She gritted her teeth and took another sip of tea. "Fine. I'll have some of my people look it over *informally*, but they don't have the time for a formal risk assessment. And your team better complete their initial report on the meteorological analysis I asked for two weeks ago."

Adam blushed slightly. "Speaking of support, I actually do have one more favor to ask."

Barely seconds since he had made the last request, and now he was onto another? She bit her tongue and responded as calmly as she could. "Adam, really? I have my own things to do, I have a life outside of your crazy ideas, I'm not going to—"

"Sabs...this project has taken up the past couple of years of my life, and it really means a lot to me."

He grinned shyly. "And you're my best friend; I'd really like you there with me."

"Adam, I'm not going to help you present your project. I've already risked too much just looking the other way. I can't be directly tied to your project. What I agreed to is already pushing it."

"You don't have to help present it. I just need you there if the director asks for the risk assessment."

Sabrina narrowed her eyes. "*Not* a risk assessment, remember? And you're still asking a lot."

"I know but, well, you help put me at ease. You're the only thing on this station that does."

Sabrina sighed. She was not thrilled with the prospect of accompanying him to a meeting like this, but over the years, she had done crazier. After so many years of following him throughout the system, she was starting to get tired of helping with little offered in return. Still, whether he meant to or not, he always had the right words to convince her. It annoyed her at how much she was willing to do for him.

She paused a second and finally responded, "Fine, but promise you won't make me help pitch your project. I'll be there to give my team's *opinion*, if needed, that's it."

"Thank you, Sabs!" Adam perked up and smiled ear to ear. "You're amazing, really. I promise, you won't have to say a word. The director will love it. I'm going to show him that Kraken can change this world."

Six Months Ago, 59.5 AA, Dawn Promise, *Poseidon*

"Can you do it without compromising our current schedule?" Sabrina asked the navigator.

"It's only a slight change in heading," he said,

pointing at a nav map with a new course overlaid on their current one. "But it'd take too long, and we'd miss the anomaly during the maneuver."

Sabrina was beyond irritated. She had spent the last few months chasing ghosts, eating the time she needed to catch up on work. Every other day, she was called up to the navigation room and asked to advise on these strange storms that kept popping up. Her job was to track and predict the weather patterns of the planet. Since storms were considered a risk factor for all active projects, there were usually enough signs to predict them well in advance. These storms just *happened* with no warning. Worse, whenever they would arrive at the location, the storm had dissipated, leaving no visible evidence of the event except an uncharacteristic *rise* in temperature.

They had just picked up another storm, this one about ninety kilometers away. Sabrina knew they didn't have long to reach the location, but according to the navigator, it would take them off course yet again and cost them another day. She resigned herself to a distant view of the event and only the *potential* to get more insight into the increasingly more frequent anomalies.

As the station slowly sputtered toward the location, they saw hints of the storm peeking over the horizon. From this distance, it did not look any more unusual than the rainstorms that occurred elsewhere. It was a horrifying view to the uninitiated, of course—almost total darkness, with the occasional bloodred rain pouring on the windows, trickling down the side of the station. It was eerie, but most people on board were used to traveling on the crimson seas. Still, as they drew a bit closer, this storm seemed different.

"Any unusual readings on the sensors?" Sabrina said, addressing the observer on deck.

"Not yet, temperature seems a bit hot, but it's within the margin of error."

Sabrina sighed. They were still few hours away from getting a good view of the anomaly. Without being able to turn, they would only barely be at the edge. It was at moments like this that she wished the probe sent to the planet before anyone landed still circled it, taking more data. By the same token, the main reason they were even on a research station here was due to the cloud coverage that was so dense the probe rarely got good data. She turned to one of the crew members, coordinated arrival times, and copied off the existing readings from the external sensors. She thanked the navigational crew and left, deciding to check in on the status of the minisubs by the docking bay.

Walking through the tight hallways, Sabrina was reminded of how small the station really was. In the various labs she passed, she saw scientists doing this and that. The place was abuzz, even if there were a dozen fewer people on board than last year.

She stopped in her tracks and stared at the geological department's open door; it was practically a ghost town inside. Most of its members had been assigned to work on the subs, gathering data on Poseidon's ocean floor, with only a couple of junior members remaining. Still, past the wires and the mechanical devices she could see the dark, abandoned office that used to belong to Adam. He had rarely been in it. He was only there on the rare occasions he would come by the station to get new orders and supplies or to off-load the existing data from the minisub. She remembered all the coffees and teas, the time spent together and the fun they had when they did. Now, he was off again and they barely spoke. It was like Aeneas all over; she was even avoiding his calls.

"Sabrina, is that you?"

Sabrina turned and found, to her surprise, Tad, the poor soul sharing Adam's substation.

"Tad! What are you doing here?" She looked around. "Did Adam come today?"

"No. I just came up to grab some files off Adam's computer. They're syncing the data on the minisub and filling it with rations."

Sabrina winced. "Adam gave you his personal credentials? Should he be doing that?"

"Probably not, considering his authorization level is higher than mine. But he added some protections on his system and I promised not to snoop." He grinned. "You can trust me."

Sabrina nodded. She was aware how guarded Adam could be about some things. It was easy to forget that, when he shared—or used to, at least—so much about what was on his mind with *her*. Then again, he'd hidden an entire unauthorized project from Percy, Magenta Management, and the so-called Red Devils for nearly two years before he was relegated to a substation. It was possible he would have been sent off on a substation anyway; most of his research team had been. There was a lot of value in remote research expeditions in relation to geological matters. Yet, it was probably the meeting with Percy that ultimately sealed his fate.

"How long will you be at the station? We're heading to another anomaly and I could really use a sub."

Tad scowled. "Not long, I've already been here for a few hours. Adam wants me back as soon as possible; we ran out of food faster than expected and I didn't leave him with much to eat for the several days I'm away for resupply." He continued tentatively, "Also, I hate to say mine was the only sub docked today."

Sabrina was disappointed. If there was not a minisub available, then she would have to rely on a skipper. They were a necessary kludge and the result of one of Adam's crazy ideas that actually panned out. After it became obvious to Percy that the *Dawn Promise* was too slow to explore enough of the planet to make a reasonable recommendation in the five-year time frame, the substations were deployed—each with a minisub—to maximize coverage. Once the minisubs were all attached to remote missions, the main station required a new, energy-efficient way of doing near-surface projects and the occasional emergency supply run to a substation. That's where the skippers came in, loosely based on the bouncing bombs used by Earth's Royal Air Force during World War II that had skipped along the surface to avoid torpedo nets. Adam viewed them as a way to avoid tying up one of the precious minisubs. Designed to skip along the surface of the water and leverage aerodynamics, skippers were faster than a minisub, and the remaining crew relied heavily on them.

A skipper *was* an option, but Sabrina wanted a minisub because they were packed with advanced scientific measuring equipment, were remotely controllable, and had an onboard data storage bank to reduce the number of communication signals needed to operate it. That's what made them such ideal vehicles to accompany the substations on specialized research expeditions, especially for the planet's submerged crust. Still...

"I guess I'll take a skipper, then. I'm heading to the dock to see when one's available. I can recharge your sub's Ito device while I'm there, if you'd like."

Tad shook his head. "It's already charging. I won't be up here too long anyway. I just need to grab those files Adam wants and then I'll be on my way as soon as it's ready."

Sabrina nodded. "See you around, Tad."

Sabrina continued down the hall as Tad slipped behind her into the geology lab, making her way to the docking area, occasionally glancing in on the other labs. The docking bay's AI usually could be found somewhere near his control station situated close to the docking bay. Because of the proximity, 23-of-Michelle was the gatekeeper for all vehicles in and out. While he spent most of his time at the control station for the ship, he also coordinated and updated the minisubs when they docked, and synced their data all the while coordinating with the small mechanical team for repairs and recharges.

As Sabrina approached, his head spun to her. "Hello," 23-of-Michelle sputtered mechanically while managing to sound bored, "Risk Assessment Head Sabrina Weld. What can I do for you?"

"I need a skipper for observation of the anomaly. Maybe a general weather sensor and a collector, just in case?"

"Checking," he said, as the irises of his mechanical eye spun around slightly. "Affirmative. You're cleared for deployment at optimal range to the anomaly in three hours, twenty-three minutes. Your reservation will be for four hours duration."

"Perfect, thank you."

As Sabrina finished her conversation, she caught sight of Tad walking to his minisub with a presumably now-charged Ito device. She headed back to the navigation room. But as she walked, she realized that something about Tad seemed off. Ito devices were well-established technology. They could hold terajoules of raw energy and kilograms of antimatter safely, they were designed with large safety factors and were effectively bulletproof, yet Tad had handled his like it was about to bite him. Very un-Tad-like.

Once inside, she approached the navigator and said, "I've booked a skipper. 23-of-Michelle says we'll be close enough to the anomaly in less than three and a half hours. Any update on environmental or situational changes?"

The navigator peered at the flow of numbers and the ever-changing graph on her screen and turned back to Sabrina. "Rainfall has increased slightly on approach, as well as the temperature—which, by the way, is now outside expectations. The pH level has dropped noticeably."

"It's gotten hotter as we approach the storm? Is that supposed to happen?"

One Week Ago, 60 AA, Dawn Promise, *Poseidon*

"Naturally, we did pick up seismic activity from the crust over the past half year," Percy said.

"But the data we've been collecting from them hasn't shown any evidence they could be involved,"

Sabrina responded. "Most of the time, they've been almost entirely on the opposite side of the planet from the anomalies."

"Regardless, both Adam and Tad are due here soon; I'd like to take the opportunity to get data from them directly."

Sabrina slumped in the guest chair in Percy's office. She held in her hand nearly a year's worth of data involving the anomalies that plagued Poseidon. Not long before, her expedition to the edge of one of the storms revealed troubling particulates in the sample—matter that could have only originated from beneath the crust. After tasking Substation 2's minisub to scan for activity on the ocean floor, they found evidence of seismic activity near a dormant undersea volcano—evidence that did not seem to line up with the data they had from Adam's Substation 3.

The office was bathed in an uncharacteristically red light, highlighted by the crackling lightning outside.

Sabrina sat uneasily.

I wish the full-spectrum daylight wasn't broken today.

The storms were now more frequent and the skies darker—so much so that she could not remember the last clear day. It was a gloomy environment for a meeting and Sabrina was not excited for this one. The past few months' analysis had narrowed down where the points of failure were. The scientists were conducting a deep investigation to determine how the ocean floor could have been experiencing such activity without it being noticed for so long. Either the data from Substation 2 was wrong, or Substation 3 was wrong. They had a serious problem.

"Sir, the team from Substation Three is here," chirped a small comm device on Percy's desk.

"Send them in."

Sabrina's nerves shot up and she stopped breathing until the door opened and Percy's AI assistant showed them in. Adam slipped in first, trailed by Tad, his only crewmate for the past year. Sabrina had not had any contact with Adam in nearly a year. His hair was a mess, his beard growing in scruffy and prickly. He had bags under his eyes and looked more tired than she had ever seen him. Tad, in contrast, looked well-groomed and strode in with confidence. He appeared tall, even next to Adam—despite Adam standing over a foot taller. Sabrina felt herself tearing up a little seeing Adam in such a state. He was seemingly unaware his self-imposed exile had affected him that deeply.

"Adam. Tad. Take a seat," Percy said, indicating the two empty chairs.

Adam barely seemed to notice Sabrina's presence as he plopped down, muttering something akin to a greeting. Tad nodded and sat gracefully.

"I wanted to discuss your data," Percy began, "We've discovered some pretty massive seismic activity over the past few months and your data doesn't align with observations from our other substations."

Both men remained silent.

Sabrina added, "We found particulates in the water that appear to have originated from beneath the crust. Adam, you and I are the experts; I'd like to compare notes."

Adam seemed increasingly nervous, even refusing to acknowledge her presence. Sabrina had not spoken to him in almost a year, but he was uncharacteristically at a loss for words in matters of scientific intrigue. Tad took his obvious silence as a cue to speak for him.

"Of course, Director. What can we do for you?"

It was strange moment for Sabrina as the director rattled off a series of numbers and particular study sets about which he wanted more details, occasionally calling upon Sabrina to provide relevant data. He did not get into certain elements of the station's findings that were concerning, as only a few people—namely Percy and Sabrina—knew about them and their grave repercussions. For this meeting, the only real objective was to determine if the error lay with the data, equipment, or humans.

Adam squirmed uneasily in his chair as Percy read off a list of various dates with unusual findings, some gaps in those findings, and some questions about their process. Tad was the one who engaged, clarified points, and elaborated on the work. But as Percy and Tad spoke, Sabrina caught an oddly panicked glance from Adam. She could not get that look out of her mind. The prattle between Tad and Percy faded to background noise as she studied Adam.

"Do you have your datapad with you?" Percy said. "I want to straighten this out now. I'm giving my recommendations in a couple weeks; I can't present terraforming recommendations with inaccurate data."

After an awkward silence, Adam muttered sheepishly, "Um, yeah. Well, no. I mean, I don't have my datapad with me, but it's on the sub. I can grab it."

"Then do so." Percy waved him away.

Adam stood up, glancing again at Sabrina before leaving. As the door closed, Tad's posture changed.

"Director, sir, I have to talk to you about Adam," Tad whispered conspiratorially.

Percy raised his eyebrow as Tad pulled out a data-pad and held it out for him to read. The director was tentative, but took it cautiously, scanning for a minute before connecting it to his system. He stared at his monitor for a while, his eyes darting back and forth. Within minutes, Percy's usual stiff expression dropped.

"How did you acquire this? What is all this?"

Tad smirked. "I found it buried on his system, along with evidence of tampering with the sub's data, and deliberate overloading of Ito devices."

Sabrina must have looked confused, unsure of what Percy was reading. Her expression prompted Percy to turn his monitor toward her. Chat logs, detailed plans, specific actions. All laid out in detail.

Communication with a known Anticol? She must have read it wrong.

She studied one of the diagrams. It was a small, simple device that could turn an Ito device into a bomb. She must have interpreted the diagrams incorrectly.

They're from his account. The diagrams are his style. But they're not something I've seen before. She could barely come to grips with the inescapable conclusion forming in her mind.

Sabrina panicked. Could Adam be collaborating with known terrorists? She shuddered at the thought. But it all seemed to be here, everything showing that Adam was still planning to set off a massive explosion under the crust of the planet—exactly as he'd outlined in his proposal. Was it simply to raise a landmass as he'd said, or something more sinister, if Anticol was involved?

She'd sent him the reports of the anomalies; would he take it this far, knowing the risks, unless he really was aligned with Anticol?

"Tad," said Percy, "this is alarming, but you should know you're doing the right thing coming forward with this information. I have to ask, has Adam actually made any of these bombs? Or is it just plans?"

Tad nodded gravely. "He's made quite a few, I'm afraid. It wasn't until recently that I connected the dots. He's been testing them for months, I thought at first it was part of some research I wasn't cleared for—"

Tad paused and pulled up a list of dates and corresponding data. "When I noticed that the reported anomalies were at the same time as his tests, I knew it was more than just data collection. Adam is up to something."

"Does he have any more of these bombs?" Percy prompted.

"Yes, one last one, perhaps the most powerful," Tad began. "From what I saw, he's overcharged several Ito devices, bundled them together, and plans to set them off under the crust once we get back to the substation."

"To what end? He can't seriously be just reviving an old project, can he?"

"Maybe he's trying to leverage some side effect of the explosions. I don't really know for sure. But you have to arrest him. You need to stop him from setting off that bomb."

Percy turned toward Sabrina as she fought to keep her expression blank.

A momentary scuffle outside his office door distracted the director. "That must be Adam." He tapped the comm device to life. "13-of-Octo, is that Adam?"

A robotic voice responded, "No, it's me, sir. Adam just left."

A look of confusion crossed Percy's face. "He just left?"

"Yes, he was listening outside your door for the past few minutes. Then he ran off."

60 AA, Poseidon's Sea

"I need more detail than that!" Sabrina shouted back through the crackling.

Sabrina felt suffocated in the cramped submersible as she tried to communicate with Adam through random words in their sentences. She had done something beyond impulsive. She ran after Adam after he escaped the station. No one thought twice about her taking Substation 2's docked submersible, as it had already been cleared by 23-of-Michelle for its crew and they were to embark soon. She'd been discovered, of course, when the crew expecting to load supplies found it missing, but it bought some precious time, which might be her only advantage in the inevitable pursuit. It had still been a long sprint across the ocean, even with a little tinkering of the Ito-powered engine to wrest a bit more speed. Devil he might—or might not—be, she silently thanked him for one long, torturous night spent listening to his crazy idea for overloading a minisub drive-motor safely. She'd had nothing to lose and tried it herself; thankfully, this was one of Adam's ideas that worked perfectly.

Adam had evidently done the same to his sub; despite her increased speed, she still lagged behind just as much.

Something just did not add up. She was angry at Adam. She was furious with him for betraying her trust at a vulnerable moment, but *terrorism*?

I know him. He wouldn't do that.

She risked everything on a hunch he was innocent. The second she stole the minisub, her career teetered on the edge. If Tad was right, then she was risking her liberty or even her life.

And all he gave her was the name of a long-dead terraforming project. A project he failed to pitch to Percy. A project he had scribbled on notes and somehow convinced his team to collect data for. A project almost as crazy as his idea to make an ice planet tropical by crashing an asteroid into it.

She watched the skipper's surface crashes blip on the sonar as her minisub cut through the water, and tried to reach Adam again.

"Adam, seriously, I need to know the truth. Do you hear me?"

After a short fizzle, Adam's voice came through clearly. "Sabs, I can hear you! Please, listen, do you remember Project Kraken?"

"Of course!" she yelled back. "I saw your diagrams. You actually *built* Ito bombs? How could you pervert your own work?"

The blips slowly crept up on her position as she approached the substation, and for the first time Sabrina was concerned that she might not make it there first after all.

"No, Sabs, listen to me!" Adam pleaded. "I didn't! I didn't change a thing about my project! When I was outside the director's office, listening, I heard what Tad said. He's lying!"

"So, you're not about to set off a massive bomb at the crust?"

"The bomb's *already* set. *Tad* set it himself, before we left."

Sabrina paused, confused. "Tad said *you* were *coming here* to set it."

"That's how I *knew* he was lying. He told the director to arrest me, but I don't understand; I've been up every night for the last week, verifying the data. It will work."

Chewing her lip, Sabrina considered Adam's version. "But why, Adam? You saw my assessment. It's too deep to bring up enough landmass to make it to the surface."

"Not if you can activate a dormant volcano. I found one, Sabs. I named it Kraken, after the project."

Does he still believe in the project? Is Tad telling the truth? Did he lie to me? Did he come out here to set the bomb?

"Is *that* where you put it?" Sabrina grunted angrily. She took a deep breath before continuing. "Adam you're not just raising a landmass. There are side effects to your project! Don't you realize that?"

"I know! The explosion rippled all the way around the planet, moving along the crust like a sound wave and caused all the seismic activity. I'm still positive it can be contain—"

He believes. Sabrina's heart broke in that moment with the realization that her best friend was finally gone.

Sabrina cut him off, more harshly than necessary. "Not that! The pH drop! *That* side effect! The global water temperature rise has already *lowered* the pH below the 6.6 level it was at when we came here.

We'll need 8.1 for terraforming; that's the wrong *direction!* If your *experiments* have been releasing hot enough masses of Eden knows what into the ocean to change the temperature that much, what do you think a *volcano* going active will do? Did you even *read* the assessments I sent?"

He responded with silence. There was maybe a minute before her minisub would reach the substation, and she could already hear the distant beats of the skippers bouncing on the surface of the water as they approached. An eternity was suspended in that silence.

"What did you say? pH?" Adam sounded scared. This was not the fanaticism of an Anticol terrorist. This was the panic of a man seeing two years of his life stripped bare and reconstructed into something he did not recognize.

The entire mood of the conversation shifted. "Sabs, the bomb's *active.*"

Sabrina swore loudly. The blips were almost on top of her and she could see the substation a mere couple of kilometers ahead, but still she did not know for certain if Adam was lying, delusional, or worse. Her mind overflowed with memories of his optimism, his dreams, his life goals.

She took a calming breath. "Tell me honestly, Adam, no lies. Are you working with Anticol?"

Adam shrilled, "No! I'd never work with them!"

Sabrina twisted around, leaving her comms up, and flipped a switch to get a view of the water above and behind her. She could see the skippers now, darting in and out of view, up into the sky and slamming back down on the water. Only seconds now.

She shouted at the comm over her shoulder. "Adam, you have to stop the bomb!"

"But I—"

"Adam, if you're not an Anticol, listen to me and get that bomb to the surface! It took a lot to convince *me* you didn't set the bomb. The director's not going to take your word for it."

"I was just trying to say the minisub is already on its way. I always had Tad review the reports from you before I saw them . . . I never saw anything about pH."

Then she remembered Tad accessing Adam's file and it all clicked. *For Eden's sake, Adam, this is why you don't share your system credentials.*

Sabrina glanced at the other screen and saw one skipper practically right above her. Recalling the timing of the blips, she steeled her resolve for a last-ditch gambit to buy Adam some time.

There. A blip.

Angling the minisub upward, she counted, praying she estimated the trajectory right. Minisubs weren't built as weapons, but they were sturdy enough to survive a moderately hard impact.

She hoped.

4, 3, 2 . . .

This near to the surface, she could see the craft skip high into the air behind her, activating its thrusters.

1.

Her minisub jumped out of the water and smacked the bottom of the skipper as it descended, hitting it at an angle and sending it off course. She dove slightly and waited for the next skipper to approach.

4, 3, 2, 1. Smack! One left to go.

The last skipper splashed and bounced off the

surface, flying high and forward fast, and she counted again as she saw the thrusters ignite.

4, 3, 2—

The thruster burn was shorter this time, and Sabrina's minisub popped out of the water in front of it instead. The last skipper pilot must have caught on to what she was doing and avoided her attack. Worse, that put them both nearly on top of the substation.

Praying there was enough reserve thrust to slow down, she saw the skipper right above her drag the surface. An explosive photo finish left them barely a few meters from their destination and at a dead stop. Sabrina rushed to the hatch and crawled out, wearing an oversize pressure suit she had found in the sub, and dove into the water, madly swimming toward the substation.

"Stop!" A projectile ricocheted off the water near her. Clearly a warning shot; Percy would *not* have missed.

Maybe he'll see reason after all.

She stopped and turned, the buoyancy of the pressure suit holding her on the surface. Director Percy, wearing just an oxygen mask, stood on the tip of the skipper brandishing a sidearm. Behind him, Tad sat, wearing a mask much like his, but unarmed. The pressure suit was the only thing pumping oxygen to her. She could not risk even being grazed in a suit like this.

"Director, please!" Sabrina yelled into her mask comm. "Adam's not a terrorist!"

"I have proof that says otherwise," Percy said calmly. "But maybe you can indulge my curiosity, and tell me what exactly you gain from this?"

"Nothing! I'm just trying to do what's right!"

"By helping an Anticol terrorist damage this world?"

"Sir, I think she's just stalling." Sabrina could hear the sneer in Tad's voice. "We have to get to the substation and stop him from arming the bomb."

"He's not!" Sabrina yelled. "He's *stopping* it."

Tad's sneer came through again. "Sure, he is. Sir, we need to board *now*. He's been on the substation long enough; it might *already* be armed."

As he finished his sentence, a muffled boom from far below shook the sea. Sabrina looked down and at first saw nothing. There was a tense silence for what seemed like eternity before what appeared to be a huge bubble rapidly spiraling up. She feared that she had made the wrong judgment call and that a massive explosion was about to wipe out everything for kilometers, including the substation.

The Kraken, rising from the depths to destroy them.

Several hundred meters away the sea boiled as a large gas bubble broke the surface. Another few seconds later, a much smaller object burst out of the water and splashed down a few meters away. The Substation 3 minisub bobbed in the surf, its remote arms holding a bundle of Ito devices.

"What the . . . ?" Percy yelled, angrily.

Adam's voice crackled, "It's the bomb!"

Percy looked around wildly until he saw Adam standing on the balcony of the airlock and trained his sidearm at him.

"Adam stopped it!" Sabrina shouted.

Percy swung the sidearm around to Sabrina. "Why should I believe you? If he's Anticol, you're Anticol. You proved that by stealing that minisub."

"Or," said Sabrina confidently, "*neither* of us is Anticol."

"It's a decoy," Tad piped in, quickly. "The real bomb is still below, at the crust."

Percy glanced back at Tad, his sidearm still pointed at Sabrina. "I thought you said all the remaining Ito devices were used."

"There is only one bomb!" Sabrina blurted out.

"But if it's a decoy—"

"Irrelevant," Sabrina shot back. "If we're Anticol, and this is a real bomb, exploding it here would serve no purpose. If it's a decoy, the real bomb's already set and it doesn't matter. But if we're *not* Anticol, then why would we have a decoy at all? It stands to reason this is the real bomb, which is now inactive."

"Sir, don't trust them. There might be more Anticols in the substation as we speak," Tad once more injected. "This entire conversation might be a distraction."

Percy pointed his sidearm at Adam. "Who else is in there?"

"Nobody, but does it matter?" Adam said smoothly, shrugging. "Anticol would have locked me out by now, anyway, and then what could they do? We only have two minisubs out here, and you're looking at both right there. The other two are deployed, you know that. Where would Anticol hide?"

"Sir, you can't believe a word they're saying," Tad said frantically. "They want to set off the bombs and ruin the ocean's pH! If we don't stop them now, the planet is doomed!"

Percy lowered his sidearm somewhat and pivoted back to Tad. "I never said anything to you about our station's pH findings. Only Sabrina."

The air was thick with tension. Tad had messed

up, and he knew up, admitting to knowing the side effects of the crust bomb experiments.

Percy raised his sidearm and aimed it at Tad.

60 AA, Ross 248 Project Offices, Copernicus

"I'm not that kind of guy!" Adam chuckled playfully.

They sat in the lounge of the Ross 248 Project development office, brightly lit in full spectrum for human eyes. The room had once served as the ship's captain's conference room and its walls were covered with real wood paneling, made on Earth, slightly the worse for wear. It was a fresh change of pace from the years spent on a bloodred planet and a nice place to relax in a plush chair without being angry. He'd been surprised when a transport showed up on Poseidon to take them to this meeting, figuring he and Sabrina would be attending via holo. Apparently the Red Devils though it was too important *not* to do in person.

And there was Tan Arabica coffee, which Adam sipped with a groan of pleasure.

"Please," Sabrina said. "I was still debating whether or not you were stringing me along until that sub popped up with the bomb."

Adam smiled and sipped his coffee, "I was just trying to make sense of it all. When you mentioned the pH levels, it all fell into place and I knew Tad set me up."

Sabrina pulled out her datapad and scrolled through a document. "I just heard from one of my Patrol friends, Tad died." She said in a sad tone. "The Patrol really wanted to question him about Anticol and somehow he took poison when they came to collect him. He is the first human to be buried in Poseidon's Sea."

They were silent for a moment then Adam said, "I'm glad we're recommending that Poseidon be terraformed. I know we're only here for support, but I think 5-of-Chandra likes me." He grinned.

"I prepared this presentation for Percy weeks ago," Sabrina said without looking up. "The *incident* just refined the approach a little. The crust seems to be stable now that you're not blowing holes in it anymore. The pH levels seem to be returning to normal, although adjusting it to our needs will be a massive effort. You have lived on a cloud city—Asgard, right? Our engineers have come up with a scheme to modify the concept for floating on water. If they are big enough, with stabilizers it will be like living on a tropical island! Especially after the planet's terraformed."

Adam scoffed. "I still think there's some value to raising a landmass."

Sabrina stared at him and raised an eyebrow.

"But I understand that, for the moment, the methods to do that would set back the planned introductions for sea life for decades, if not more. I know."

Sabrina giggled a little to herself. She and Adam had spent so long not talking, that after Tad's arrest, she thought it would be difficult to even say hello. To her—and probably his—surprise, it was like no time had passed. They talked for days, about what went wrong, what was right, what they wanted.

Adam barely went a day before asking what motivated her to chase after him, putting her career on the line after he had been so distant. It was simple, really, but she just couldn't tell him yet. She had realized how much she cared about Adam, and for how long she had hoped for something more; seeing that possibility slip away nearly broke her.

She hoped he would feel the same about her someday, but right now she still was not sure.

"Hey, Sabs," Adam said, banging his empty coffee cup down. "I've been meaning to mention, I have another idea."

Sabrina paled. His crazy ideas had led to this entire mess. His dedication to a singular goal allowed a deepcover Anticol to manipulate almost every action and decision that Adam made since arriving on Poseidon. Tad played into Adam's desires, all while advancing a goal to prevent the terraforming of Poseidon. She was terrified another idea of his might lead them down a bad path again so quickly.

"I swear, it's good, just take a look." Adam held out a single, well-folded piece of paper.

She reluctantly took it and opened it. She looked at it intently for a moment and grinned.

"So, I take it you like this idea?"

"A *real* date, after all these years?"

Adam nodded and looked away shyly.

Sabrina smiled wide, lighting up her face. "It has potential."

Terraforming Planets
Under a Red Sun

Matthew S. Williams

Matthew S. Williams is a space journalist and science communicator who writes for Universe Today *and* Interesting Engineering. *In his spare time, he makes podcasts (*Stories from Space*) and writes hard science-fiction novels (the Formist Series). In the fall of 2022, he began teaching about the history and future of human space exploration at the Kepler Space Institute. His articles have appeared in* Phys.org, Popular Mechanics, Business Insider, HeroX, Science Alert, Real Clear Science, *and* Gizmodo. *He lives on Vancouver Island with his wife and family.*

Introduction

In the past fifteen years, the number of known extra-solar planets has grown exponentially. As of January 2022, 4,884 planets have been confirmed in 3,659 planetary systems, with an additional 7,958 candidates awaiting confirmation. With so many planets available for study, the focus of exoplanet research is shifting from the process of discovery to characterization. Basically, scientists are no longer just searching for exoplanets—they're also searching for signs of life!

Exoplanet-hunting missions have also turned up several promising Earth analogs, or as they are more commonly known, "Earthlike planets." This term is used to classify rocky planets that orbit within the star's habitable zone (HZ), have dense atmospheres, and plenty of liquid water on their surfaces. In addition to being good candidates for finding life, Earthlike exoplanets might also make good homes for humanity.

There's just one catch: most of the nearest rocky exoplanets are found in M-type (red dwarf) star systems. In fact, within forty light-years of Earth, there are twelve red dwarf stars that have at least one "potentially habitable" planet in orbit around them. Among them are Proxima Centauri (our closest stellar neighbor) Ross 128, Gliese 1061, Teegarden's Star, and Trappist-1.

These M-type stars are smaller, cooler, and dimmer than the Sun. They are also known to be quite active in comparison, which means they emit a lot of flares. But from what we know about the planets that orbit these stars, there's a good chance some (if not all) of them possess the basic requirements for habitability. Even if they are not likely to have indigenous life, they may still be "transiently habitable."

Compared to Earth, M-type red dwarf stars have extremely long lifespans. Whereas G-type stars (like our Sun) are estimated to remain in their main sequence phase (the main phase of their life cycle) for about ten billion years, red dwarfs may live for up to ten trillion! This also means that they evolve more slowly and take longer (about one billion years) to enter their main sequence phase. This could have a drastic effect on the evolution of rocky planets that orbit within their HZs.

"Transiently habitable" refers to exoplanets that have stable atmospheres, water on their surfaces, and plenty of oxygen that is abiotic (not the result of biological processes) in nature. Scientists speculate that this may be the case for rocky planets that orbit close to their red dwarf suns. Others, interestingly enough, may have the key ingredient for life as we know it (water), but too much of it!

Then there's the issue of gravity. When it comes right down to it, scientists don't know how much is needed for Earth-based organisms (especially humans) to thrive, or what the long-term effects of living in a low-gravity environment really are. While studies have been performed on the effects of microgravity (like the NASA Twins Study), it is unclear if humans can live, thrive, and reproduce on celestial bodies (planets, moons, and asteroids) where the gravity is a fraction of Earth-normal.

With some hard work and elbow grease, these planets could someday become new worlds for humanity. Before that can happen, though, several challenges, caveats, and unknowns need to be addressed. Even if we had a solution for getting to the nearest stars in a modest amount of time (decades instead of centuries or millennia), there's a lot of work that would need to be done at the other end.

Terraforming 101

The word *terraforming* is derived from the Latin words for "Earth" (terra) and "shaping" (formatura). It is the process where a planetary environment is altered to make it more Earthlike and suitable for terrestrial organisms. This could involve modifying a planet's atmosphere, orbit, temperature range, surface topography, ecology, or all of the above. One thing that cannot be modified directly is gravity, although large rotating structures on a low-gravity world might be able to provide a higher effective gravity.

The term was coined by American science fiction writer Jack Stewart Williamson in a story published in the 1942 edition of *Astounding Science Fiction*, titled "Collision Orbit." This is the first known example of the term being used in print, though there are examples of the concept appearing in earlier works of science fiction.

By the late 1950s and the dawn of the Space Age, the concept of terraforming became popularized as interest grew in space exploration and colonization. Henceforth, the idea was presented by science fiction writers (who were often scientists) as a serious matter. Examples include Robert A. Heinlein, Arthur C. Clarke, Poul Anderson, Isaac Asimov, and Kim Stanley Robinson.

Terraforming also became the subject of many theoretical studies during this same time. As our knowledge of Earth and the solar system grew, so did the scientific research on space exploration and ecological engineering.

Scientific Proposals

In March 1961, famed astronomer and science communicator Carl Sagan published "The Planet Venus," an article in the journal *Science* where he proposed that Venus could be transformed by seeding its atmosphere with algae. Sagan theorized that this would convert the abundant water, nitrogen, and carbon dioxide into organic compounds and reduce Venus's greenhouse effect. Unfortunately, this proposal was deemed impractical by the subsequent discovery that Venus's atmosphere has little hydrogen or water.

In 1973, Sagan published another article in the journal *Icarus* titled "Planetary Engineering on Mars." Sagan proposed two scenarios for transforming the Red Planet: covering the polar ice caps with low-albedo materials or planting dark plants in the area. This would result in the ice caps absorbing more heat from the Sun and melting to release all of the water and "dry ice"—frozen carbon dioxide (CO_2)—locked within.

In 1976, two major developments occurred: the first conference session on the subject of terraforming was organized, and the release of a NASA study titled "On the Habitability of Mars: An Approach to Planetary Ecosynthesis." The report indicated that terraforming Mars would come down to three steps:

1. Introducing greenhouse gases to warm the atmosphere
2. Melting the polar ice caps to release CO_2 and water vapor
3. Introducing photosynthetic organisms to convert atmospheric CO_2 into oxygen gas

In 1982, planetologist Christopher McKay wrote a paper for the *Journal of the British Interplanetary Society* (titled "Terraforming Mars") where he discussed the prospect of creating a self-regulating Martian biosphere. The paper not only included the required methods for doing so, but also the ethics of it. This was the first time that "terraforming" appeared in the title of a published article and subsequently became the preferred term.

In 1984, James Lovelock and Michael Allaby released *The Greening of Mars*, a fictionalized account of how Mars is terraformed in the future that remains one of the most influential works on the subject of terraforming. It was also the first proposal to introduce chlorofluorocarbons.

In his 1991 study, "Terraforming Venus Quickly," UK scientist Paul Birch proposed bombarding Venus's atmosphere with hydrogen and iron aerosol. The resulting chemical reaction would convert atmospheric CO_2 into graphite and water. Cyanobacteria could then be introduced, which would use water, CO_2, and sunlight to produce hydrocarbons and release oxygen. While the graphite would need to be sequestered and removed, the water would fall to the surface and cover roughly eighty percent of the planet in oceans.

In 1993, Mars Society founder Dr. Robert M. Zubrin and "Terraforming Mars" author Christopher P. McKay of the NASA Ames Research Center wrote "Technological Requirements for Terraforming Mars." They proposed that orbital mirrors positioned near the poles could sublimate Mars's polar ice caps (including its CO_2 ice) as a first step in terraforming the planet.

In their 1996 study, "The stability of climate on Venus," Mark Bullock and David H. Grinspoon of the University of Colorado Boulder indicated that Venus's atmosphere could be transformed by introducing "carbon sinks" in the form of calcium and magnesium. They further proposed that Venus's own deposits of calcium and magnesium oxides could be used by mining and exposing them to the atmosphere. This process would yield calcium and magnesium carbonates (rocks) and remove CO_2 from the atmosphere. It requires vast quantities of calcium and magnesium and would take many millennia.

Since 2000, Geoffrey A. Landis and his colleagues at NASA Glenn Research Center have worked on mission proposals to explore Venus. In 2008, they proposed that floating research stations could be built above the cloud tops. These cities could also terraform Venus's atmosphere over time and eventually carry humans to the surface.

In 2009, US Dept. of Energy engineer Kenneth Roy presented his concept for a "shell world" in a paper published by the *Journal of the British Interplanetary Society*. Titled "Shell Worlds—An Approach To Terraforming Moons, Small Planets and Plutoids," his paper explored the possibility of using a large "material shell" to enclose a celestial body and a portion of its atmosphere. Under the shell, artificial lighting could recreate an Earthlike light spectrum and temperature, and maybe even an Earthlike ecology, completely independent of the star's light spectrum and intensity.

In 2014, the NASA Institute for Advanced Concepts (NIAC) program and Techshot, Inc. began work on a concept called the "Mars Ecopoiesis Test Bed." This entailed the creation of sealed biodomes to be built on the surface of Mars where colonies of oxygen-producing cyanobacteria and algae would grow.

While technically not ecological engineering, Eugene Boland (chief scientist of Techshot, Inc.) has stated that it is a step in that direction.

Ecopoiesis is a neologism created by Robert Haynes and refers to the origin of an ecosystem. In the context of terraforming, Haynes defines the term to mean the fabrication of a sustainable ecosystem on a currently lifeless, sterile planet.

As you can see, there is no shortage of proposals for how humanity could make extraterrestrial environments more liveable. First, here's a look at those that are closest to home.

Terraforming the Solar System

Within the solar system, several possible candidates for terraforming and related methods for ecological transformation exist. The most obvious of these are Venus and Mars, which are rocky bodies like Earth and skirt the inner and outer edges of our Sun's circumsolar habitable zone (aka the Goldilocks Zone).

This refers to the region around a star where an orbiting planet would experience temperatures warm enough to maintain water on its surface (in liquid form).

However, because of Venus's runaway greenhouse effect and Mars's lack of a magnetosphere, their atmospheres are either too thick and hot or too thin and cold to sustain life as we know it. However, both planets could undergo an atmospheric and climatic transformation that would allow Earth-based plants and animals to thrive in their environments—at least in theory.

Beyond these two candidates, there is no shortage of solar bodies that could be made habitable with the right strategies and resources. But whereas Earth's immediate neighbors are well-suited to terraforming techniques, others are better suited to paraterraforming or similar methods. Let's begin with the former:

Earth's Siblings

Currently, **Mars** is considered the best candidate since it is the most habitable solar body beyond Earth because of its similarity to it. Like Earth, Mars is a terrestrial (or rocky) body composed of silicate minerals and metals differentiated between a metallic core and silicate mantle and crust.

A Martian day (known as a Sol) is slightly longer than a day on Earth—24 hours, 39 minutes, and 35 seconds, to be precise. Mars's axis is tilted 25.19° to its orbital plane, which is close to Earth's axial tilt of 23.4°. However, because Mars is about fifty percent farther from the Sun, a Martian year lasts about twice as long as a year on Earth: 686.98 Earth days. Still, Mars has a defined four-season cycle that corresponds to its orbit around the Sun and the tilt of its axis. Like Earth, Mars even has polar ice caps that grow and recede with the seasons.

Lastly, volumes of evidence indicate that Mars once had large oceans on its surface, and much of that water may still exist today beneath the surface. Given these similarities, it's not hard to see why Mars is colloquially known as "Earth's Twin." But beyond these similarities, our two planets could not be more dissimilar.

For example, life on Earth is protected by a strong magnetic field that is the result of action in the planet's interior. This consists of a molten outer core rotating around a solid inner core in the opposite direction of Earth's rotation. Mars also had a magnetic field at one time. But about four billion years ago, the more-rapid cooling of the planet's interior caused all geological activity to cease and the field disappeared.

This caused Mars's atmosphere to be slowly stripped away by solar wind over the next few hundred million years. While it is replenished by outgassing, the resulting atmospheric pressure is less than one percent that of Earth's. What little atmosphere it has is also unbreathable for humans and animals, composed predominantly of carbon dioxide, argon, and nitrogen, with traces of methane and water vapor. Then there are the big variations in the temperature.

The average surface temperature on Mars is -63°C (-82°F), but this ranges considerably based on location and the time of year. During a Martian summer, temperatures can reach as high as 35°C (95°F) around the equator but plummet to -135°C (-211°F) around the poles during winter. But even when temperatures are at their warmest, the very thin atmosphere ensures that very little of the heat is retained.

So from a terraforming standpoint, transforming Mars comes down to three goals:

1. Thicken the atmosphere
2. Warm up the planet
3. Convert the atmosphere to make it breathable

There are other necessities, such as the need to import water to create a water cycle large enough to maintain oceans, lakes, and streams, balancing the salinity of its soil, and pairing it with a satellite to help maintain its axial tilt. However, getting the ball rolling comes down to these three major steps.

Luckily, they are complementary. By thickening the atmosphere, less radiation will reach the surface. A thicker atmosphere will also absorb more solar radiation, increasing the temperature. Warmer temperatures will release the water and dry ice locked away in the poles, creating a greenhouse effect that will further warm the planet.

Step one would be to trigger a greenhouse effect on Mars, which could be done by introducing ammonia, methane, or chlorofluorocarbons (CFCs) into the Martian atmosphere. Aside from being super-greenhouse gases, their introduction would thicken the atmosphere and raise the planet's temperature.

Once Mars has a warmer, thicker atmosphere, liquid water would be able to flow across the surface again. This would also lead to clouds, precipitation, and the creation of a water cycle. It might be necessary to import hydrogen and/or water at this point to ensure there's an adequate amount. To complete the process, photosynthetic organisms, plants, and vegetation would need to be introduced to the surface.

These would stabilize the sands of Mars, allow for water to be absorbed into the ground, and feed the lichens, grass, and plants. These plants would slowly convert the CO_2 in the atmosphere into oxygen gas and allow for the introduction of organic nutrients (largely in the form of carbon compounds from decayed plant matter). Once oxygen levels were high enough, insects and animals could also be introduced to create a self-sustaining life cycle.

An artificial magnetosphere would also ensure long-term habitability and reduce the amount of radiation reaching the surface. According to a NASA proposal, this shield would be positioned at the Sun-Mars L1 point, where the gravitational pull of the Sun and Mars allows it to remain in a stable position directly between them.

The magnetic shield would intercept radiation from the Sun and create a bow shock that Mars would fit comfortably inside. Because of this, a thickened atmosphere on Mars would remain dense, warm, and breathable over time, and not be stripped away by solar wind.

Terraforming **Venus**, meanwhile, requires a somewhat opposite approach. Whereas Mars is too cold and its atmosphere is too thin, Venus is too hot and its atmosphere could crush a person whole! Hence, for Earth's "Sister Planet," the necessary steps are to:

1. Thin the atmosphere
2. Lower the temperature
3. Convert the atmosphere to something breathable
4. Speed up the planet's rotation

Once again, these steps are complementary. Since Venus's heat is due to its incredibly dense (and predominantly CO_2) atmosphere, thinning and converting it go hand in hand. As previously mentioned, one method entails introducing hydrogen into the atmosphere to trigger massive rains that would cover the surface in oceans. The remaining atmosphere would be an estimated three bars (three times that of Earth) and mainly composed of nitrogen—much like Earth's.

Introducing calcium and magnesium into the

atmosphere could also sequester carbon in the form of calcium and magnesium carbonates. This would have the effect of reducing atmospheric pressure and atmospheric temperatures considerably.

The concept of solar shades has also been explored, which could take the form of a large lens positioned at the Sun-Venus L1 point. This would reduce solar heating and protect the atmosphere against solar wind. If temperatures were reduced enough, the atmospheric CO_2 would freeze to become dry ice that would fall to the surface.

Last, there's the possibility that Venus's rotational speed could be altered to ensure long-term changes in its climate. Presently, Venus rotates once every 243 days, the slowest rotational period of any major planet. This results in Venus having incredibly long days and nights, equivalent to 116.75 Earth days!

This is also the reason why Venus is consistently hot across the entire planet, day or night, and could account for the fact that Venus lacks a significant magnetic field. It has been argued that the planet's rotational velocity could be sped up by either striking the surface with impactors at a precise angle or conducting close flybys using large asteroids.

Another idea is to use mass drivers and compression struts (aka dynamic compression members) to transform kinetic energy into the rotational force necessary to increase Venus's rotational period to twenty-four hours. Impactors and mass drivers would have the added benefit of blowing some of Venus's atmosphere into space.

As you can see, there are many possible methods, and they are complementary to one another.

"Ocean Worlds" and Icy Moons

Beyond the inner solar system, many icy moons and bodies could be transformed with the right kind of engineering. These bodies present more challenges than their rocky counterparts since they are largely composed of water by volume. This is true of bodies like Ceres in the Main Asteroid Belt, the largest moons of Jupiter, Saturn, Uranus, and Neptune, and Pluto and Charon.

In addition to thick icy crusts, most of these bodies may have oceans of salty liquid water in their interior floating above the rocky core. Some might even harbor life, but life far different from anything we've ever encountered! For these bodies, conventional terraforming is impractical because of the abundance of water and ice.

If these moons were enclosed with a shell and warmed up, the result would be oceans hundreds of kilometers deep. Removing this water/ice to get to the rocky core would be a massive undertaking and would leave only a tiny ball of rock and metal. Such worlds are probably better off with numerous surface and space settlements, rather than full terraforming.

First up, **Ceres** is the largest body in the Main Asteroid Belt and the only one to have achieved hydrostatic equilibrium (i.e., become spherical). The mean radius of this planetoid is 473 km (294 mi) and its mass is estimated at 9.39×10^{20} kg (103.5 quadrillion tons). This is roughly a third of the Asteroid Belt's mass—between 2.8×10^{21} and 3.2×10^{21} kg (3,086.5 to 3,527.4 quadrillion tons)—which is equal to four percent of the mass of the Moon.

Based on its low density (2.16 g/cm^3), Ceres is

believed to be differentiated between a rocky core, a possible interior ocean, and an icy mantle. The mantle is estimated to be 100 km (62 mi) thick and contains up to 200 million km^3 (48 million mi^3) of water, equivalent to about ten percent of what is in Earth's oceans. The surface may also contain iron-rich clay minerals, carbonate minerals, and various asteroids it has collected over the past several billion years.

The surface of Ceres experiences a maximum temperature estimate of 235 K (-38°C; -36°F) when exposed to direct sunlight. Assuming there's a sufficient amount of antifreeze (like ammonia), the water ice would become unstable at this temperature. Therefore, Ceres may have a tenuous atmosphere caused by outgassing on the surface. Possible mechanisms include sublimation from exposure to the Sun or cryovolcanic eruptions resulting from internal heat and pressurization.

However, to ensure that the surface doesn't melt indefinitely, engineers would need to create a barrier between the ice and the dome's atmosphere. Crushed regolith from the local asteroids could be used to do this, either as 3-D printed concrete and ceramics or as a deep layer of dirt. In addition to providing a barrier, this dirt could be made into soil by adding organic nutrients and water.

It would be possible to convert Ceres into a shell world, where the entire planet would be enclosed with a material shell, thus allowing the entire surface to be terraformed into a habitable, Earthlike environment. Within this shell Ceres' temperature could be increased, UV lights could convert water vapor into oxygen gas, ammonia could be converted to nitrogen, and other elements could be added as needed. The resulting hydrogen could also be used as to manufacture propellant. A thick layer of regolith plus insulation would ensure that the crust doesn't melt completely...

The same processes could be used on all the other "airless" bodies in the outer solar system that are mainly satellites that orbit gas giants. This includes three of Jupiter's "Galilean" moons, Callisto, Ganymede, and Europa; Saturn's moons Titan, Enceladus, Dione, and Mimas; Uranus's moons Titania and Oberon; Neptune's largest moon, Triton; and Pluto and Charon.

In all cases, a significant portion of these bodies is composed of water and other volatiles (like ammonia, methane, and nitrogen). These bodies are also part of systems that include many asteroids that could provide the necessary regolith, minerals, and carbon compounds to construct space settlements, and even conduct major terraforming efforts.

The only exception is **Titan**, Saturn's largest moon and the only satellite in the solar system to have an atmosphere. It's also the only celestial body beyond Earth to have a nitrogen-rich atmosphere and bodies of liquid on its surface (its famous methane lakes). These quirks could present opportunities for creating a livable environment on Titan, as does the rich prebiotic environment and organic chemistry on the surface.

Titan's atmosphere is estimated to be 1.45 times as dense as Earth's and is predominantly composed of nitrogen gas with small amounts of methane, hydrogen, and trace amounts of other hydrocarbons. There is also evidence of cryovolcanoes, a possible indication that Titan has a subsurface ocean composed of water and ammonia. Combined with the organic chemistry on the surface, some have suggested that this ocean might even support life.

All of this makes Titan virtually ideal for a shell world. Rather than melting a small portion of the surface ice, the shell would enclose the existing nitrogen atmosphere. The surface could then be covered in regolith, leaving small pockets of ice and the methane lakes to remain. The organic molecules on the surface would naturally combine with the regolith to create soil rich in prebiotic molecules.

Lighting units located on the underside of the shell would provide light identical to that on Earth and additional infrared light to heat the moon surface to any desired temperature. Over time, the methane could be broken down to create additional carbon compounds for the soil and hydrogen that could be used to manufacture propellant and fuel for power reactors, or just be released into space.

The one drawback of these icy bodies is their gravity, which ranges from a low of 0.012 g for Enceladus to a high of 0.138 g for Titan—between one and fourteen percent that of Earth. The long-term effects of these microgravity and low-gravity environments on humans specifically and life in general are unknown and will remain an ongoing issue for settlers.

Rocky Planets Under Crimson Skies

When it comes to exoplanet studies, a lot of attention is currently directed at M-type (red dwarf) star systems. As noted, red dwarfs are the most common type of star in the Universe and appear to be the most likely place to find rocky planets orbiting within their

HZs. Within forty light-years of Earth, no less than seventeen candidates have been confirmed in twelve red dwarf star systems.

These include our closest stellar neighbor, Proxima Centauri. Located just 4.24 light-years away, this red dwarf star also hosts our closest exoplanet neighbors—Proxima b, c, and even a d (a possible Mars-sized planet). Proxima b is of particular interest to exoplanet scientists and astrobiologists since it is a rocky planet that is comparable in size and mass to Earth. It also orbits within the star's HZ.

There's also Bernard's Star b, a super-Earth orbiting a red dwarf star roughly 6 light-years away. While extremely frigid, with surface temperatures at about -170°C (-274°F), recent research suggests that life could exist beneath the surface, where heat generated by geothermal processes could sustain pockets of liquid water.

This brings us to Ross 248d, a fictional Earth-sized exoplanet located within the inner habitable zone of its parent star—a red dwarf located 10.3 light-years from our solar system that appears in this anthology. This planet is a water world and considered a good candidate for potential habitability based on its orbit and official estimates of its surface temperatures.

Arguably, the most intriguing red dwarf star system is Trappist-1, an ultracool red dwarf located about 39 light-years from Earth. Between 2016 and 2017, seven rocky exoplanets were confirmed in this one system—three or four of which orbit within the star's HZ. These include Trappist-1d, e, f, g, and maybe h. Based on various climate models, these planets are believed to have retained their atmospheres and water on their surfaces.

However, there are multiple indications that life would have a hard time arising on these planets, owing to the nature of their suns.

Flare-ups and Tidal Locking

For starters, M-type stars are known for being variable and prone to flare-ups. This is based on data obtained by the NASA Galaxy Evolution Explorer (GALEX) mission, which monitored stars for signs of solar flare activity between 2003 and 2013. This data, now part of the GALEX Photon Data Archive (gPhoton), indicates that even calmer and older red dwarf stars are subject to flare-ups.

While these flares are lower in intensity than other stars, they are a lot more frequent. They are also particularly bright in the ultraviolet (UV) wavelength. Unless the planet(s) orbiting a red dwarf star have a protective ozone layer, magnetic field, and sufficiently dense atmosphere, this radiation could be very hazardous to life-forms on the surface.

This is similar to what astronomers have observed with Mars, which had a thicker atmosphere and flowing water on its surface billions of years ago. Based on data obtained by missions like the Mars Express, Mars Global Surveyor, and Mars Atmosphere and Volatile EvolutioN (MAVEN), this changed about four billion years ago when Mars lost its global magnetic field.

As a result, Mars began to lose its atmosphere to space over the next five hundred million years as solar wind slowly stripped it away. This caused Mars to undergo a transition where most of its surface water was lost, temperatures dropped considerably, and the surface became the freezing and desiccated environment we see there today.

What's more, red dwarf stars are 2000 K cooler than Sun-like stars on average, in addition to being far less massive. As a result, their habitable zones (HZs) are narrower and much closer. This means that rocky planets that orbit within their HZs are likely to be tidally locked or have an orbital resonance of 3:2 (like Mercury), 5:3, 7:4, and so on.

Therefore, rocky planets that are tidally locked with red dwarfs will be exposed to bursts of radiation that will consistently hit the planets' atmospheres on the same side. Over time, unless the planets have particularly dense atmospheres and a planetwide magnetic field, this is likely to reduce or even blow off the planet's atmosphere entirely.

In fact, multiple superflare events have been observed in recent years that were powerful enough to obliterate the atmospheres of any planets that orbit them. These events typically consist of a flood of very short-wavelength radiation, including X-rays and even gamma rays, followed by a coronal mass ejection (CME) of slower charged particles.

The intensity of the flares also meant that any life on the surface would be heavily irradiated. In short, a single superflare would render the dayside of potentially habitable planets completely sterile.

Luckily, the Transiting Exoplanet Survey Satellite (TESS) recently observed many superflares that suggest red dwarfs release their largest events from the poles. While this does not mean that orbiting planets are spared from all flare activity, the possibility that superflares only emerge from above 60° latitude means they would be spared from the worst, but still subject to regular flare activity.

As noted, rocky planets need to orbit very closely to their red dwarf suns to get enough heat for liquid water to exist on their surfaces (i.e., to be considered "potentially habitable"). This inevitably results in tidal-locking or a 3:2 orbital resonance, which means that one side of the planet is exposed to constant sunlight while the other is not, or that each side of the planet experiences extremely long periods of day and night.

So while the atmosphere would be warm on one side of the planet, they would be rather freezing on the other. But unlike Mercury and the Moon, rocky planets that orbit red dwarfs could redistribute this heat from one side of the planet to the other, provided they had a dense enough atmosphere and/or liquid oceans.

Too Much or Too Little?

Another issue with red dwarfs is the nature of the light they emit, otherwise known as their stellar flux. For starters, most of the light emitted by red dwarf stars is in the red and infrared range of the spectrum. This could be a problem for planets that orbit red dwarf suns and might prevent life from emerging on them.

On Earth, photosynthesis occurs when plants absorb light in the red and blue bands and reflect it in the green band, while also glowing in the infrared wavelength. For red dwarfs, much of the light they emit falls within the infrared and red parts of the spectrum. This essentially means that planets orbiting red dwarf suns may not receive enough of the right kind of light to sustain photosynthesis, which could have serious consequences for habitability.

On Earth, the emergence of photosynthetic organisms was a major step in the evolution of our atmosphere and life as we know it. Roughly 3.8 billion years ago, Earth's atmosphere was composed primarily of nitrogen and CO_2. This was the product of volcanic outgassing combined with volatiles deposited by comets during the Late Heavy Bombardment.

The first photosynthetic organisms are believed to have emerged around 3.5 billion years ago—and began converting the atmosphere by metabolizing the CO_2. This led to the "Great Oxygenation Event" (ca 2.4–2.0 billion years ago), Earth's current atmospheric composition, and the emergence of complex life-forms.

This means that planets orbiting within the HZ of a red dwarf are not getting the right kind of light for life to emerge and thrive. Conversely, there's also research that suggests that red dwarf stars may not provide enough UV radiation for early forms of life.

According to this theory, UV radiation may have played a major role in the formation of ribonucleic acid (RNA) billions of years ago from Earth's early prebiotic environment. Since rocky planets orbiting in red dwarf HZs receive one hundred to one thousand times less bioactive UV radiation than Earth, it is unclear if UV-sensitive prebiotic chemistry would occur.

Too Much Oxygen and Water?

Another issue is the presence of water on these planets, which astrobiologists consider to be a vital necessity for life. Based on Earth's example, all indications show that a careful balance between ocean and continents is crucial to life, not to mention the regular exchange of energy and material between the ocean floor and surface.

But rather than there not being enough, there is also the possibility that rocky planets orbiting red dwarfs have too much water to support life. Several surveys and research studies indicate that "water worlds" may be particularly common around red dwarf stars. Once again, this could have significant implications for astrobiology studies and the habitability of red dwarf exoplanets.

A popular theory states that this is because of how red dwarf stars and their planets form. Compared to G-type stars like our Sun, red dwarf stars form slowly due to low gravity. As a result, they do not experience gravitational collapse (i.e., "ignite") until after their planets have formed. Without light pressure to heat up and push away volatiles (such as H_2O), they are simply incorporated into the planets. As the planet forms, heavy elements such as metals gravitate to the center, silicates on top of that, and lighter elements such as H_2O form a layer on the surface. Hydrogen and methane and other gases form an atmosphere on top of this and the lighter elements such as hydrogen and helium are soon lost to space.

In 2016, the Pale Red Dot Campaign—a team of astronomers dedicated to finding rocky planets around red dwarfs—created a series of internal structure models that showed how super-Earths are likely to have many times the water of Earth. That same year, researchers from the University of Bern created a series of planet-formation models for red dwarf stars and concluded that in ninety percent of cases, water would account for more than ten percent of these planets' mass—whereas Earth is just 0.05% water by mass.

In 2018, a study led by Arizona State University's School of Earth and Space Exploration (SESE) calculated the mass distribution of the Trappist-1 planets. According to their mass-to-composition models, the two innermost planets of this system (b and c) are "drier" (fifteen percent water by mass), while the outermost (f and g) are more than fifty percent water by mass.

Another 2018 study examined data from Kepler and the European Space Agency's Gaia mission to determine how common "water worlds" really are. They found that super-Earths 2.5 times as large, and up to 10 times as massive as Earth, are likely to be up to fifty percent water by mass. This essentially means that about thirty-five percent of all known exoplanets have too much water to support life.

Depending on where the exoplanet orbits relative to its star, this could result in all manner of scenarios. For water worlds located closer to their star than the inner boundary of the HZ, the world is likely to be shrouded in an atmosphere of hot water vapor (aka a "steam planet"). For those located beyond the HZ, they will probably be an ice planet, especially on their "night side" (if they are tidally locked).

If the exoplanet were large enough, it would be differentiated between an icy surface, an interior ocean several kilometers deep, and a layer of high-pressure ice (hundreds of km in depth) surrounding a rocky core. This ice layer would prevent the exchange of energy through geothermal activity at the core-mantle boundary, which is believed to have been essential to the emergence of life on Earth (and possibly in "ocean worlds" like Europa, Enceladus, etc.)

Research has also shown that planets orbiting red dwarfs may be "toxic" with oxygen gas. As noted, red dwarfs have extended pre-main-sequence phases that could last up to one billion years. During this period, rocky planets that orbit within what will eventually become the star's HZ would be exposed to significant radiation.

For those that have abundant surface water, this will result in a runaway greenhouse effect that would last for several hundred million years. During this time, the planet would become a "steam world" and lose much of its water to photolysis, leaving behind an atmosphere rich in abiotic oxygen.

This is consistent with observations made of red dwarf planets that showed hydrogen escaping into space. While oxygen gas is considered an important biomarker, that only applies when and where photosynthesis is involved. On Earth, the appearance of an oxygen atmosphere was the result of photosynthetic organisms that evolved in the ocean and metabolized CO_2 to create oxygen gas as a waste product.

During the Great Oxygenation Event, the emergence of an oxygen-rich biosphere likely triggered a mass extinction among anaerobic species on Earth. As a result, a planet that has plenty of atmospheric oxygen early in its history would not support the emergence of early single-celled microbes. This raises questions about evolutionary pathways and whether or not life as we know it would be possible on red dwarf orbiting exoplanets.

Terraforming to the Rescue?

There is some good news in all of this. For starters, the challenges of knowing how these systems are lacking mean that we can tailor our terraforming strategies to make them more liveable. For example, red dwarf planets with oxygen-rich atmospheres and lots of water on their surfaces may be "transiently habitable"—uninhabited but not uninhabitable.

In fact, these exoplanets could accommodate terrestrial organisms that were imported (i.e., the ecopoiesis process). One proposal, known as the "Genesis Project," is to introduce basic organisms that could help build a life cycle on the planet and shave a few billion years off the evolutionary process.

For the sake of terraforming, this concept could be taken several steps further by introducing terrestrial flora and fauna. Alongside microorganisms, planets, shrubs, trees, and animals would be imported to fill every niche. These would help stabilize the planet's atmosphere and climate and transform them into lush and life-sustaining worlds.

The Right Photons

Another idea for making rocky planets around red dwarfs more habitable is to alter the light they receive from their parent star. In much the same way as a magnetic shield could protect Mars, planets in the HZ of red dwarf stars could benefit from a large solar shield stationed at the star-planet L1 point. Autonomous robots could assemble this massive installation using locally sourced silica and minerals from asteroids.

During normal periods, the filter would absorb the light of the red dwarf sun and shorten its wavelength to produce light that corresponds to photosynthesis. During flare-ups, the shield's large magnetic field could protect the orbiting planets from CMEs, which have the potential to strip a planet's atmosphere away.

Another option is to alter the planets' rotation to create a daily cycle similar to Earth's, as with the terraforming of Venus. A possible method would be to capture comets and asteroids and redirect them to impact the surface. Another would be to station mass drivers on the surface to speed up rotation through kinetic energy.

This would allow plants and animals that are introduced to adapt more readily to the new environment and would have the added benefit of stabilizing temperatures planetwide. If altering a planet's rotation is impossible, it could be feasible to create a solar mirror/ solar shade in orbit that would circle the planet, shading the "dayside" to simulate night and reflecting light onto the "dark side" to simulate day.

Another possibility is to have an artificial "sun" with a twenty-four-hour orbital period that draws power from the magnetic shield positioned at the L1 point. If the shield is equipped with photovoltaic arrays, it will be able to convert ultraviolet radiation from the sun into abundant energy. This energy could then power a luminous satellite that would orbit the planet to provide artificial sunlight.

Living on Steam, Water, and Ice Worlds

Living on the surface of steam worlds will likely be similar to trying to live on the surface of Venus: dark and very hot. On these planets, the construction of habitats will likely need to be the same: floating airships that hover above the dense clouds where pressure and temperature conditions are far more hospitable. These airships could harvest valuable elements from the atmosphere (such as He-3) and would be deep enough into the atmosphere to be protected from solar flares. Such stations could be enlarged over time and could house fairly large populations.

On water worlds, floating cities would make an almost ideal habitat for humans, especially if the atmosphere could be made breathable. Once again, this is similar to floating cities in Venus's atmosphere. And in the long run, these floating cities could be used as platforms for ecological engineering and the introduction of Earth-based marine life.

Another option would be to remove water from these worlds. This would reduce the depths of the oceans and allow for interaction between the ocean and interior at the core-mantle boundary.

This could be done using solar mirrors in space to direct concentrated sunlight to evaporate the ocean's upper layers. Another method would be to use a sun-shade to freeze ice on the surface, which could then be lifted to space, possibly by a space elevator. If the oceans are so deep that thick layers of ice are present at the core-mantle boundary, removing water may need to be paired with operations to break the ice up—nuclear devices positioned in the ice sheet would do it!

As the ocean depth decreases and the pressure conditions alleviate, terraforming crews will have direct access to the planet's mantle. At this point, ecological engineering could be undertaken to trigger hydrothermal activity, like geothermal tubes that would transfer heat and the necessary chemical elements to support life from the interior to the ocean depths.

However, each of these options would require tremendous amounts of time, energy, and resources. Compared to building floating cities that seed the oceans with marine life, this option could take several millennia, rather than a few centuries. On icy water worlds, the most viable solution would likely involve building settlements directly into the ice sheet, which would provide radiation protection.

This is similar to proposals for the colonization of Europa and other "icy moons" in the outer solar system. Because of the similarities involved, domed enclosures and even shell worlds could be built around icy water worlds. Inside them, ice could be harvested and exposed to light reflected by solar mirrors to create a warm and breathable atmosphere while regolith is used to create layers of soil and prevent the surface from melting.

All of this represents a huge challenge in terms of engineering, logistics, and resources. However, these steps are theoretically possible, though some will require significant technological advancements. But with the "what and how?" covered, the only remaining questions are "when and where?"

After all, we already know the answers to who and why: It will be future generations that will undertake this bold endeavor. The reason for it, beyond increasing the likelihood of human survival, will be the desire to meet a new challenge head-on. Someday, when humans have mastered the art of being multiplanetary, they will dream of taking the next great leap and becoming interstellar!

The year 2647 / 64 AA

Much has happened. Humanity has spread throughout the Ross 248 system. Small cloud facilities, modeled on the ones at Venus, float in the thick atmospheres of the two innermost planets that have been officially named Aeneas and Cupid—after the children of Venus. They mine He-3 from the atmosphere and export it throughout the Ross 248 system. Research ships sail the single ocean of the third planet, Poseidon's World, researching its potential to be terraformed. A large solar array was constructed at the Ross/Poseidon's World L1 Point to produce antimatter. On Liber, the moon of the seventh planet, the borough of Promise was completed and the Cerites now call it their home. The Primate Quarter, designed for normal humans and connected to the borough of Promise, comprise Toe Hold, the Cerite settlement. Well-off humans continue to live on the *Copernicus* in orbit above Liber while the less-well-off are consigned to the Primate Quarter.

Dim Carcosa

D.J. Butler

While in San Francisco, be sure to visit an out-of-the-way historic marker on Dashiell Hammett Street at an address formerly known as 20 Monroe Street, where the famous author once lived. Hammett, the writer of many great pulp fiction detective stories, including The Maltese Falcon, created one of the most famous private detectives in literary and film history, Sam Spade. Dave Butler takes on a mystery in the tradition of Hammett, one which Spade would have been pleased to help solve.

D.J. (Dave) Butler has been a lawyer, a consultant, an editor, a corporate trainer, a registered investment banking representative, and is now a consulting editor for Baen Books. His novels have won the Whitney Award, the Association for Mormon Letters Award for Novel, and the Dragon Award. He plays guitar and banjo whenever he can and likes to hang out in Utah with his wife, their children, and the family dog. Dave also organizes writing retreats and anarcho-libertarian writers' events and travels the country to sell books. He tells many stories as a gamemaster with a gaming group that he has been playing with since sixth grade.

It's time to wake up, Prashanth.

The tattered edges of a dream slipped from Prashanth's fingers. He saw towers behind a moon, and a still lake, and although he dreaded the valley in which he stood, he resented being torn away.

"Towers behind the moon," he murmured.

It's time to wake up, Sally said again. The puter was an implant, and he had named it. It didn't object to the name, because Sally wasn't sentient.

Prashanth's head throbbed, and he groaned. "I didn't set an alarm." He fumbled around in his cot until he found his second pillow, the one not heated by contact with his body. He pressed the cool fabric against his head. It helped, if only a little.

You have an event in your calendar.

"Cancel it."

I can't cancel it. Dr. Goldberg scheduled the event.

Prashanth rolled into a sitting position, still clutching the pillow to his head. "Your chronometer is off. That must be six or eight hours away still." He checked his own wrist chronometer.

Your nap went long. Again.

She was right. His slot in the Observation Dome was imminent. Failure to show up would give his doctor grounds to report him to Space Patrol. Which would mean that his future medical appointments would be compelled by armed policemen. Former colleagues, if he was lucky, but armed men not famous for their senses of humor.

You also have a video message. It came in on your professional line.

He had no time to shower. Prashanth tactically deployed a few sani-wipes on his skin, then found a clean shirt and put on his least rumpled suit. "How did I sleep so long?"

When deprived of natural Sol-intensity daylight, non-Cerite humans suffer a range of negative effects. Oversleep is one, as are time distortion, chemical imbalances, irritability, depression, paranoia—

"Rhetorical question," Prashanth said. "Play the message."

A video window appeared in his field of vision. Both the screen's images and the accompanying audio were perceptible only to Prashanth, part and parcel of the implant system that had come with Sally. He'd got the implants when he was a member of Space Patrol, along with the fully immersive VR implants. He'd died in VR over and over as part of his training, but had managed to avoid it as an actual member of Space Patrol, only to get a medical discharge. They'd removed his clearance and deactivated the immersive VR, but left him with Sally. In lieu of better retirement pay, he'd been told with a laugh. It wasn't a very funny joke; his medical pension barely covered his miniscule apartment in the Primate Quarter, and forced him to put his Space Patrol skills to work in the private sector.

Well, he'd made good use of Sally.

A woman's face appeared in the video window. East Asian descent, hair jet black and skin unblemished, very expensive earrings. She might be as young as forty, but Prashanth guessed she was much older than that, and a habitué of a rejuvenation clinic.

And therefore rich.

"Mr. Satyadeva, I'm Victoria Tan. I've been given this number by a friend who told me you undertook private investigations of a discreet and personal nature. You may reach me at this number, or may find me at my home."

The message ended with a contact number and an address. The address was in the Village, aboard *Copernicus*. Prashanth whistled, though the sound split his head.

He tucked his small pistol into the waistband of his pants. He had no license for it, and if Cerite PD chose to give him grief over it, he might go to prison. On the other hand, if he went unarmed around the slums of the Primate Quarter where he lived, he ran a very high risk of having a sharpened screwdriver inserted into his belly. For that matter, he ran the same risk by leaving the Primate Quarter and wandering among Toe Hold's Cerite population.

He pushed the bed up into the wall and exited his apartment, three meters by four, into a crowded corridor. The only light came from the emergency strips in the wall, at ankle level. He pushed his way through the stream of traffic toward the street. His vision shuddered, and the people brushing past him looked like hulking shadows with leering, distorted faces. "Do Cerites not suffer from light deprivation? Not a rhetorical question."

None of the people he passed turned to answer him. Half of them were also muttering, either on some comms link, or to their own implant, or simply to the voices in their heads.

Cerite physiology and psychology are much more resistant to low light, even for long periods of time, than those of non-Cerite humans.

"Any news on the restoration of the Day Lights?"

Lord Wimsey issued a statement ninety minutes ago that Day Lights will be operational tomorrow, for several hours. Would you like to review the statement?

Lord Wimsey was an AI. He had been built as a kind of security administrator or gatekeeper for Toe Hold, in the days of the gang fights six years earlier, but had gradually taken on more roles. Wimsey tended to act through humans for menial tasks, but from time to time would make an appearance in person, if the occasion was dramatic enough to warrant it.

The Day Lights looked fine, their spherical bulbs spaced every ten meters along the ceiling of the corridor. But they were dead, and Lord Wimsey said it was because the insulation on the power cables was degrading. Apparently, those cables were among the first manufactured at Toe Hold and they hadn't gotten the formula right, or hadn't worried about it too much because the cables were destined for the Primate Quarter. They were being replaced, and the Day Lights should be back online soon.

Lord Wimsey had been saying that for months.

"No," Prashanth muttered.

The Day Lights were necessary because all of Toe Hold was underground, to protect it from radiation. When they worked, they were set to standard hours, meaning they simulated a twenty-four-hour Sol day for Primate Quarter residents.

Splotches of graffiti marred the walls and ceiling of the corridor for a twenty-meter stretch. *Monkeys belong on Earth!* and *Ghosts Belong in the Grave!* were repeated competing slogans, and told the passersby that the youths of Toe Hold still fought turf wars, organized in their race-gangs. *Dim Carcosa* meant... he didn't know what. It probably marked a boundary, or memorialized the exploit of some gangbanger graffiti artist in slipping behind enemy lines.

Only now, they had to break through Lord Wimsey's security gate to do so. That gate separated the Primate Quarter from the Cerite section of Toe Hold and had greatly reduced the gang violence.

Prashanth walked in the shuffling gait that any non-Cerite had to adopt, to avoid flinging himself against the walls and the ceiling. Toe Hold was located on the moon Liber, whose gravity was 0.08 that of Earth's.

A scuffle broke out ahead. Prashanth couldn't make out the words, but two men screamed at each other, clawing and punching until the crowd pulled them apart. A uniformed Security officer waded toward the fracas with a raised stun rod.

Prashanth took a turn that led him down stairs to pass beneath the Ring. A distant hum overhead marked his transit beneath the unstopping maglev train, the second part of Goldberg's prescription for him. Two hours daily on the train so that its constant circular motion could provide 1 g of gravity for his bones and muscles to work against. Apparently, that hadn't been added into his calendar. Beyond the Ring, he came to the gate.

Off to one side, broad corridors led to Newton and the agricultural boroughs. They were less covered with graffiti, but their Day Lights were also off. Two Security officers stood in the entrances. They only held stun rods, but the unwashed rabble of the rest of the Primate Quarter stayed away.

Beside the gate was a small coffee kiosk. The kiosk had no name, just a gap-toothed Cerite and a sign saying: ONE CREDIT NO CREDIT.

Prashanth paid his one credit. The coffee was bitter and sandy-tasting and it was merely warm, but he took grim satisfaction in the inferiority of the brew. He might have been tempted to enjoy a good, dirt-grown coffee; this brown squirt, unpalatable and oily, was a pure vehicle for the injection of caffeine into his system.

He gulped the coffee and threw the printed cup into the vendor's dispenser. The Cerite bobbled his head, his rapid blinking only making the red and yellow of his eyes look all the more unnatural.

Prashanth presented his ID card to the three gangsters at the gate.

Their colors marked them as the Terra Gang, a swarm of thugs so successful during the troubles that Lord Wimsey contracted out some security functions to them. Their presence kept the PD and the occasional Space Patrol officer honest by making sure they had competition, Prashanth supposed. And the pistols and knives strapped to their bodies were effective at keeping the peace. But the Terra Gang's fighters' faces were scarred and they leered at him with gaps in their teeth, and Prashanth knew that when they weren't working for Wimsey, the Terra Gang were bootleggers and extortionists and worse.

All in all, he would have preferred to be presenting his card to someone else.

"Ratskull," he said.

Ratskull had orange hair and split nostrils. "I don't need to see your identification, Pr'shanth Sach'deva."

His voice was halfway between a growl and a giggle. Would Wimsey permit his private security agents to be actually high on duty? "I know you. You're the most famous private investigator on Toe Hold."

"I'm complying with regulations." Prashanth's head throbbed. He continued to hold forward his card.

"As is right and just." Ratskull eyeballed the card briefly. "But I want you to know that I'm not just saying that because you're the only private investigator on Toe Hold. All in order, more's the pity. Business?"

"Scheduled time in the Observation Dome," Prashanth said. "And then I have to see a client on *Copernicus*."

The other two gangbangers snarled at the mention of the ship.

"That all sounds forgivable," Ratskull said. "Behave yourself."

The gangster handed back Prashanth's ID card, and Prashanth passed through the gate.

Beyond lay the Cerite borough of Promise. Walking down the tunnel, Prashanth saw the entrance to the Space Patrol Embassy, where he'd once had an office bigger than his current apartment. Next, he came to a plaza lined with Cerite shops. The customers, mostly Cerites, moving in and out of those buildings walked with an ordinary motion, because they were the low-gravity wraiths who had evolved to live in an environment like this. The lights here all seemed to work, but they weren't as bright as the Day Lights, when the Day Lights worked. Instead, artificial white light streamed from bulbs atop tall aluminum poles.

To his right, Prashanth saw a knot of pale, elongated youths. They wore shawls of knotted, colorful rags, their hair stood straight up on their heads, and they had small animal bones in their ear and nose piercings. One of them, a young Cerite woman with a bird tattooed on her cheek, flipped a folding knife open and shut.

"Bow down your head, you son of dust," the young woman said.

"Excuse me?" Prashanth wasn't sure he'd heard her right.

"Lay down ambition, hope, and lust," she continued, "and pray alone for lost Carcosa."

Only her lips hadn't moved. They were parted, to reveal her teeth, fashionably sharpened to spikes. But they hadn't moved. Had she really spoken at all?

Prashanth shook his head and walked away. He needed more sleep. Or perhaps less. He definitely needed the headaches to stop.

In the center of the borough, a thick column rose to the ceiling. The elevator in the center of the column climbed to the surface and the Observation Dome. Stairs climbed alongside the lift, but he had no interest in dragging himself up all those steps today. Prashanth touched the panel to summon down one of the lift cars.

The bottom three floors of the column were occupied by a restaurant called the Purple Parrot. A blinking LED advertisement urged Prashanth to come into the Parrot and try some FISH CHOWDER, HOT AND FRESH.

His stomach rumbled, but he needed to take his prescribed sun or he'd get in trouble. He could think about food later.

You could climb the stairs.

"You're not supposed to have an opinion."

I don't. Dr. Goldberg programmed me to make this suggestion.

"He shouldn't be allowed to override my commands to you."

He's your doctor.

Prashanth realized that he was standing next to a woman and that she was staring at him. He directed a ginger smile at her; contracting the muscles of his face into a smile made his headache lance through the caffeine poultice and stab him in the brain.

She might have been in her fifties, a dark-skinned woman with short hair. Normal, not Cerite. "Going up to enjoy the view?"

"The doctor says I need light," Prashanth told her.

She took two slow steps away from him.

He sighed and took the stairs.

"What is a Carcosa?"

Nineteenth and twentieth century popular culture reference. A fictitious mysterious planet invented by Robert W. Chambers. Connected with a fictitious play titled The King in Yellow *and a never-explained being named Hastur. Motifs invented by Chambers were repeated by later writers—*

"Stop," Prashanth said. "Any contemporary references?"

None.

"Writers," he grumbled.

The Observation Dome door opened to his ID card, admitting Prashanth into a wooded amphitheater. Trees stretched out in ordered groves punctuating the green sward. A pond lay at the center, ruffled only slightly by the artificial breeze that blew across the park. The ceiling was a single transparent dome; to one side, he saw the planet known as Alexa's World. Liber and its city of Toe Hold orbited Alexa's World, but the tidally-locked orbit meant that Alexa's World appeared as a static presence through the dome, an unblinking red eye filling one side of the sky.

The red sun—the only sun Prashanth had ever known—was visible as well. Goldberg had assigned him time in the dome precisely to get exposure to the light of the star. Red star, red planet. Red, red, red. And Cerite white. Red and white were the colors of Toe Hold.

The benefits of exposure to the star's light were principally psychological, Goldberg had explained. A quirky by-product of human evolution was that, deprived of light, humans tended to break down psychologically. Lights atop lampposts supplemented the star's illumination with blue and UV light, to keep the trees healthy and give people vitamin D.

But what was the point, if the light of Ross 248 is too dim? Prashanth had asked. *Primates—that is to say, humans—had evolved under a bright yellow star.*

The human body is amazing, Goldberg had answered. *So is the human psyche. It's like prayers—sometimes they seem to work. And placebos. You never know.*

Once the Day Lights were working again, he should spend his time under their glow.

Prashanth checked his suit, glad that it was a mild taupe. The jacket was reversible, its other side being gray.

"You're blocking the door," a man said.

Prashanth excused himself and moved aside. Two men exited the lift and staggered down the grass, one carrying a blanket and the other a printed basket.

Prashanth had no blanket, but there was a printer beside the door. He scanned his ID card; the machine hummed and printed a blanket, two meters long and one wide, gray. He found a patch of unoccupied grass near the pond and laid the blanket out. Around him, the people sitting or lying to take in the various streams of light were torpid. Their movements were sluggish, they said little.

He heard a woman crying, but couldn't see where the sound came from.

Dr. Goldberg suggested you might sunbathe. I am reminding you that nude bathing is permitted.

"I can see that nude sunbathing is permitted," Prashanth murmured. He took off his jacket and folded it, tucking it beneath his head as a pillow as he lay down. He unbuttoned the top five buttons of his shirt and rolled the sleeves up. "Are you going to report to him that I'm not nude?"

Yes.

"Please also report that my headache is gone. I think it was the coffee."

Did you have a headache?

Prashanth sighed.

I am now reporting that you had a headache. On a scale from one to ten, how severe was the pain?

"Shh, I'm taking my medicine now."

"You seek a never-dying boon," someone said. A woman's voice.

Prashanth had fallen asleep. He struggled now to bring himself to wakefulness.

"From towers that rise behind the moon," the voice continued, "the towers look down on dim Carcosa."

Prashanth forced himself into a sitting position, shattering the last chains of sleep that held him down. The printed blanket beneath him was rumpled, his jacket a wrinkled mess. He cast about, looking for the woman he had heard chanting in his sleep, but saw none. The sunbathers and picnickers about him were men, or children.

Victoria Tan called again.

"You didn't wake me."

I was following Dr. Goldberg's instructions. If you are wondering, you have now spent the required time in the Observation Dome.

Prashanth shook grass from his jacket and put it on, rebuttoning his shirt. He gathered up the blanket and tossed it into a disposal unit near the lift before descending.

There was no one else in the lift with him.

"Tell me about the Tans. The name sounds familiar."

Access restricted.

Prashanth considered. "There's a product. A coffee called 'Tan Arabica.' Is that owned by a Tan family?"

Access restricted.

"You could be a more useful assistant, Sally."

No, I cannot. I am unable to access the information you seek.

"That was rhetorical. Contact the spaceport and get me on the next shuttle to *Copernicus*."

Am I authorized to purchase a ticket?

"Unless they'll give me a lift for free, yes."

As the lift doors opened on the bottom level, Sally said, *You might consider having the chowder. Otherwise, you'll be waiting a while at the spaceport.*

"Doctor's orders?" Prashanth asked.

No.

"Doctor's strongly-worded suggestion?"

There was a short delay. *No.*

"Okay, then."

Prashanth asked for chowder from a Cerite waitress who grinned, revealing her sharpened teeth. When the chowder came, he sucked it carefully from the lip of the bowl. He knew that on Earth, people sometimes ate fish they caught wild in streams and lakes, or at least they had done so in the past. In what sense the Purple Parrot's chowder could be fresh on Toe Hold, he wasn't certain, but it was definitely hot.

When he'd finished and paid, he shuffled two kilometers north through and beyond Promise, to the train station. The station also served as the spaceport's lobby, and frequent travelers had lockers here, where they stashed their own personal envirosuits or other gear. Prashanth took a loaner from the station's dispenser.

Bored Security agents patted him down, asked about his intentions, and let him through.

Your shuttle is being prepped on Pad 7.

The narrow platform only held one other passenger as Prashanth arrived, but it collected another dozen or so over the fifteen minutes that he waited. He stood, leaning against the back wall. He dozed off momentarily, then awoke to find that his head hurt again, and the train was arriving.

The train whispered to a stop alongside the platform, settling down onto its magnetic track. Prashanth and the others boarded, and he found a seat in the corner of the car. The only other passenger was a Cerite man with a tattoo of an anchor on his cheek. Disconcertingly, he sat opposite Prashanth and looked at him as if he intended to engage in conversation.

When the Cerite opened his mouth, Prashanth saw that he had no teeth.

Prashanth smiled and looked away.

The train rose as its magnets were activated and then slid smoothly forward. The view out the windows of tunnel walls was quickly replaced with a view of the rocky surface of Liber. Prashanth looked at the Cerite and smiled again; the other man worked his jaws, opening and closing his toothless mouth, but said nothing. Then the train entered another tunnel, and slowed.

At the 4–5 station, more passengers got on the train. The Cerite turned his toothless attention to a young woman in a bright blue envirosuit, and left Prashanth alone. At the 6–7 station, Prashanth disembarked, and the Cerite didn't follow. Along with the dozen other passengers, Prashanth took the left ramp up toward the surface and Pad 7.

I've taken the liberty of updating the shuttle's AI with your current mass.

"Are you saying I'm fat?"

A narrow-faced woman walking in front of Prashanth turned and frowned at him. He smiled.

You're losing weight. You should eat more chowder.

Pad 7 was just a painted circle on a flat stone shelf. Eight circles of similar size were arrayed in a loose ring around the mesa top that served as the spaceport, and in the center lay the larger circle that was Pad 9. The walk from the top of the ramp to Pad 7 took about five minutes, which gave Prashanth the opportunity to observe the other pads. One held a shuttle that was swarmed by a maintenance crew in envirosuits; a second was spitting out a stream of passengers and cargo; a third stood silent.

The shuttle steward was a blue-eyed Primate who

pointed Prashanth to the next vacant acceleration couch, and then wordlessly helped him locate a strap that had fallen between two cushions.

"Thanks." Prashanth smiled.

Prashanth felt the subtle vibrations of cargo being loaded and then hatches closed. The hatch by which he'd entered shut last, and the steward strapped himself into his own acceleration couch.

"Everyone ready?" the shuttle's AI asked cheerfully over the intercom.

Prashanth barely had time to turn his head to look out the window before 0.75g of acceleration pressed him into the cushions. The shuttle leaped into the sky and raced straight forward for two minutes. Then, abruptly, the ascent stopped, the acceleration vanished, and the shuttle seemed to fall. Prashanth tried to find *Copernicus* out his window, but all he could see was the vast face of Alexa's World, the rocky fields below, and the staring dim sun of Carcosa.

Not Carcosa. Ross 248.

The shuttle lurched one way and then the other, and then spun, all apparently random, but then suddenly the craft touched down, and out his window, Prashanth saw the Hold of *Copernicus*.

He felt the arrival in his bones, as gravity climbed to 0.62g.

He resolved to take his prescription to visit the Ring seriously. Dr. Goldberg—a tall, thin man almost pale enough to be a Cerite himself, but with dark eyes and a long bushy beard—had enthused at length about the importance of gravity to the bone and muscle health of a primate.

Prashanth had been to *Copernicus* before, but not

recently. He'd been born on the ship, shortly after arrival in the Ross 248 system, and had memories of early childhood with his parents and his sister, digging in the dirt carefully husbanded on the Garden Deck.

They were all dead now. Not of any of the tragedies that had befallen Toe Hold or Ross 248 generally since arrival.

Just the ordinary tragedy of time.

Prashanth stepped down from the shuttle onto the deck of *Copernicus*'s enormous Hold, then descended further, through an airlock and into a locker room. He stripped off the envirosuit, attaching it to a charging unit to refill its power cells and oxygen supply. As rumpled as his jacket was, it was a more professional look than the envirosuit. Also, if he wore the envirosuit, it would hide his Space Patrol Academy class ring.

Then he had to ask for directions to the staircases. He groaned at the mere thought of the staircase, the ship's gravity already dragging on his limbs. *Copernicus* had no lifts, so Prashanth had to descend fifty meters to reach the Village.

The drag of artificial gravity grew stronger as he descended. "Does this count as my one hour in the Ring?"

No.

Prashanth sighed. Coming back up was going to hurt.

The Village deck had a roof eleven meters tall and contained, well, a village. It had Day Lights overhead, as did the Garden Deck. Prashanth recognized lanes from his youth, and turned his head away. He couldn't afford them, much as he liked the light, the gravity, the dirt, and the idea of a peaceful home. Someday, maybe.

He quickly found the building with the address Victoria Tan had sent; it was a three-story-tall house with a walled enclosure to the side. The building appeared to be made of marble, though the material must surely be some sort of concrete synthetic.

When Prashanth stepped up to the front door, it opened immediately. An AI in black cummerbund and tails appeared, rolling on a single oversized spherical wheel. "Whom may I present?"

"Prashanth Satyadeva. I have an appointment with Victoria Tan."

He didn't really have an appointment; he had an invitation. But he'd chosen to come see her face-to-face because he had found that clients who were on the fence, who had misgivings about hiring a private investigator, might ignore him when he tried to return their call. But if he showed up in-person, then they had already inconvenienced him, and very few people at that point were willing to back out.

"You are expected." The AI stepped out of the way and then closed the door behind Prashanth. "Madame's office is on the left."

Prashanth passed through a wooden door with a pebbled glass window into a thickly carpeted office. The furniture inside was of dark wood. Certificates and plaques on the wall looked like the mementos of public commendation. A poster on the wall read TAN ARABICA—THE ZING YOU REMEMBER! Victoria Tan stood up behind her heavy wooden desk.

"The coffee barons," Prashanth said. "I thought so, though I was unable to find your records."

"I value my family's privacy." Victoria gestured at a wooden chair near Prashanth and then sat. "I reached

out to you because I have been assured that you are
very discreet. Coffee?"

"That's much better than hearing that you reached
out to me because I'm expendable." Prashanth grinned.
"Yes, please. Black."

"You really like to taste the coffee."

"When it's good," Prashanth said. "And when it's
bad, I'm just taking it for the caffeine anyway."

The AI followed him into the room and busied
itself at a brewer in the corner.

"Space Patrol." She pointed at his ring. "Class of
'44. Retired early, but not dishonorably."

"Medical discharge." Prashanth smiled. "Chronic
headaches."

"Triggered by your implants?"

Prashanth tried not to show discomfort at the fact
that she knew his medical history. She wanted discretion, of course she had checked his background.
And still, apparently, she had chosen him, so he had
nothing to complain about.

"I had them even as a kid." Prashanth shrugged.
"Brain chemistry. It's manageable. They got worse
as I got older." He didn't say: *And without the Day
Lights, they're worse still.* "Eventually, they got to be
too much for the Space Patrol."

"But not too much for work as a private investigator."

"Space Patrol's standards are very high. And I don't
really have any competition as a private consultant.
This is still a small town, fundamentally."

"Did you know Alexa, then?" she asked. "Alexa of
the Oddity, the original Alexa?"

Prashanth nodded. "Not well. She was some twenty
years older than me. How can I help you, Ms. Tan?"

"My daughter's missing. Chao-xing. I'll have all her biodata transmitted to your puter as soon as we're finished here."

Prashanth nodded. "How long has she been missing?"

The AI handed him his coffee. It was so strong and black, he could practically taste the dirt.

"I haven't heard from her in forty-eight standard hours," Tan said. "She's not answering, and she isn't in her apartment. We usually talk daily."

"Toe Hold Security won't even start to look for her for another twenty-four hours."

"And I need discretion."

Prashanth nodded. She probably also wanted at least a veneer of professionalism, or she might have called on one of the gangs for help. "Do you have any idea about why Chao-xing isn't answering?"

"No. I have no suspects."

"Is Mr. Tan here? I'd like to ask—"

"My husband, Elias Tan, will not be involved in this investigation."

"Just a couple of questions."

"Discretion, Mr. Satyadeva."

Prashanth nodded. "Does the biodata include places of work or school and her apartment address?"

"Naturally."

"My fee—"

"I'll pay it. I'll transmit you ten thousand credits as a retainer."

"That about covers it." Prashanth finished his coffee, set the cup down, and left.

He had just finished putting the envirosuit back on and boarding the return shuttle when Sally notified him that he had received ten thousand credits in his account. *And Chao-xing Tan's biodata.*

He sat down in the acceleration couch and belted himself in. "Summarize content and show me all video images," he murmured.

He smiled at the steward.

Sally showed him a stream of images: an art studio, a large apartment on a main access corridor in the Primate Quarter, glamor shots and headshots of a young woman, images of both her entrepreneur parents. Elias Tan looked very earnest and serious, and had let a little gray creep into the hair at his temples.

Chao-xing Tan, twenty-one. Fashion and art model. Tan got her career start acting in commercials for Tan Arabica . . .

Prashanth listened without focusing and watched without staring, trying to let his mind settle into an unconscious, meditative state. The spare life details, the official data of addresses and contact numbers, and the images of a pretty young woman smiling for the camera flowed past him and kept flowing past him as he ruminated.

On landing, he tried Chao-xing's contact number himself, and got no response.

In the spaceport, he accessed a cash machine and withdrew ten one-hundred-credit coins. You never knew what witness could be prodded into breaking a confidence or throwing a friend overboard for a little money.

Victoria Tan didn't want him to talk to her husband. Why was that?

The Terra Gang were still on duty. Ratskull jeered as

he admitted Prashanth back into the Primate Quarter.
The Day Lights were on and Prashanth did his best to
walk directly beneath the bulbs as he made his way
to Chao-xing's apartment in the borough of Newton.
He felt a lightness in his chest. As he touched her
doorbell pad, the Day Lights extinguished.

She had roommates, the biodata said. Dario and
Illyria. The door opened to reveal a young man with
a biologically improbable mustache and glazed eyes,
who hopped from foot to foot.

"Dario," Prashanth said.

"No, *I'm* Dario," the young man growled.

"Dario-ling," a woman called from within the
apartment. "That's what he means."

Dario's hands were balled into fists. Was he high?
"What do you want?"

"My name is Satyadeva," Prashanth said. "I'm a
friend of Chao-xing Tan's family. May I come in?"

"No," Dario snarled.

"I'm looking for Chao-xing," Prashanth said.

"Maybe you kidnapped her," Dario said. "Maybe
now you're here to kidnap us."

"Do you think Chao-xing has been kidnapped?"
Prashanth asked.

Dario grumbled wordlessly.

"Look," Prashanth said. "It sounds like you know
something about Chao-xing's disappearance. That's
good, you can help me. Unless you decide not to help
me, and then you have a problem, because the next
knock on your door will be either a strong-arm crew
in the employ of the Tan family or a Cerite Security
squad, and, in either case, they'll be much less polite
than I will."

Dario stared at him, eyes glazing over further. "What?"

"Dario-licious, let him in!" the woman called.

Dario ground his teeth, but stepped aside; Prashanth entered.

The central sitting room of the apartment was larger than Prashanth's own entire dwelling. It contained two sofas, a coffee table, and a coffee brewer in the corner. Through open doorways, Prashanth saw three sleep chambers and a utility space with a printer and refrigerator.

A young woman lay on one of the sofas, a mask of feathers covering her face from the nose up. From her flopped posture, she might have been completely boneless. She was not Chao-xing Tan.

"Illyria?" Prashanth asked.

"Yes!" Dario snapped. "Not that it's any of your business!"

"Dario-vine, help me up," she called, fluttering fingers weakly.

"You don't need to get up for me," Prashanth said.

"Not for you," she trilled. "I must pose."

Dario helped her stand. They both consulted a tablet and then assumed different poses, Dario a frightened crouch, hands up to shield his face, and Illyria an imitation of an obelisk, hands together and needling skyward.

"Which one is Chao-xing's room?" Prashanth asked.

The woman pointed with both hands.

Prashanth examined her room and found it Spartan. A bed, clothing, a tablet. Her biodata included passwords, so he accessed her messages and read through them. Nothing indicating plans to leave. Nothing that struck him as out of the ordinary. No messages sent within the last forty-eight hours, and only one received.

The message was from Gambo Zubair. He knew the name from the biodata—Zubair was a sculptor who sometimes employed Chao-xing as a model. The message was dated the day before, and simply informed Chao-xing that she would not be paid for the day's session, since she had not shown up.

In her calendar, Prashanth found the missed session. All consistent, all unsurprising, all unilluminating.

He transmitted the tablet's entire hard drive to Sally, and then pocketed it, for good measure.

"Lo, Camilla, behold how the king glares at me through the Pallid Mask," Dario said as Prashanth moved from Chao-xing's room to the other sleeping chambers.

"The king is not the Stranger," Illyria answered.

"Who can tell the difference between the king and the king's messenger?" Dario nearly shrieked his line.

Prashanth found nothing in the other rooms. Not even, to his surprise, recreational drugs.

"Behold the towers!" Illyria cried. "The towers rise *behind* the moon!"

Something about that line bothered Prashanth, but he couldn't quite identify what it was. "Sally, what do 'towers behind the moon' refer to?"

The "towers behind the moon" are referred to in Robert Chambers's fragmentary, fictitious play The King in Yellow.

Again. And yet Prashanth was certain that wasn't why the line tickled at his memory.

Dario turned and glared at Prashanth. "Who are you talking to?"

"Just thinking out loud." Prashanth smiled his best

disarming smile. His head was beginning to throb again. "Are you two rehearsing a play?"

"Chao-xing was cast as well," Illyria said. "Only she's too good for us now."

Prashanth nodded affably. "So there was tension between you and your roommate."

Dario growled. "What business is it of yours?"

"Dario-lightful, he's trying to find her. Yes, of course there was. We're all actors, are we not? Only Chao-xing was spending more and more time with Gambo. Modeling. It went to her head, she said she couldn't be in the play anymore."

"Where are you performing?" Prashanth asked. "Where do I buy a ticket?"

"We don't know!" Dario snapped.

"Guerilla theater, isn't it?" Illyria's voice was dropping slowly in volume and intensity. She sounded as if she were drifting farther away as she spoke.

"That sounds pretty avant-garde," Prashanth said. "Really artsy. Who's directing?"

"That's a bit of a secret," Illyria murmured. Was she actually falling asleep standing up? "He told us people would ask, didn't he? Ruins the surprise if we tell, though."

"Ruins the surprise!" Dario roared. He thrust himself suddenly into Prashanth's face, foamy saliva flecking the quivering tips of his curled mustache.

Prashanth held his ground and smiled. "How am I supposed to see the play, then?"

"Maybe you're not supposed to," Illyria whispered. "But if you're intended to see it, you will."

"Rehearsal is soon," Dario said. Speaking to Illyria, his tone was abruptly gentle. "Will you be able to make it?"

"I'm a professional," she hissed.

"Time to go," Dario grunted to Prashanth. "You ask too many questions."

Prashanth raised his hands to show pacific intentions. "Thanks for your time." He backed out the door.

The Day Lights were flickering. He crossed the access corridor to a bodega fifty meters down and bought a seed cake. "Search the biodata and the tablet dump," he said between bites. "Look for any indication of who might be directing any play Chaoxing was cast in in the last six standard months, and where the play was being rehearsed."

No indication of either.

Gunfire erupted in the corridor. Prashanth ducked. He kicked over a small table sitting in front of the bodega and crouched behind it, very careful not to reach for his pistol. Yet.

Half a dozen shots rang out, and then a short burst of automatic fire. They came from his left and he craned his neck, looking for the source of the noise and not seeing it. Then he heard cursing, and the wet cracking sounds of muscle-powered violence.

"Call Security!" someone shouted.

Prashanth looked back the other way just in time to see Dario and Illyria disappearing into the crowded traffic of the corridor.

"Did I neglect to mention, Ms. Tan," he muttered, "the premium I charge when I'm subjected to the risk of violence?"

Is that a rhetorical question?

He ignored Sally, left the table where it lay, and rushed after the actors.

They left the access corridor in two hundred meters,

entering one of the lateral halls. The ceilings here dropped dramatically and the halls narrowed. In the earliest years of Toe Hold, these had held vertical aquaponic stacks, but much of that equipment had either become obsolete, or been moved to the roomier chambers near the agricultural boroughs. Now the halls were stacked with junk, and trickled with thin streams of traffic as people looked for shortcuts or privacy away from the main corridors.

Ahead, Prashanth saw the backs of two women in burnooses and, beyond them, the actors. Dario was dragging Illyria by the hand.

"Tell me about Gambo Zubair," he said.

Zubair, Gambo. Sculptor. In Gambo Zubair's early career, now classified as his "Primitive Period," he made rude, totemistic sculptures, plastic printed and painted to resemble unworked wood. Three standard years ago, he transitioned into his "Modern Period" of hyperrealism. Zubair is noted for the extreme accuracy of his printed sculptures of living objects. Early Modern Period works were principally plants and small animals. Recent works include human subjects.

"Cross-reference Gambo with plays," Prashanth said. "Dramatic performances. And the Tan family and Chao-xing Tan. Look in public media as well as the biodata and the tablet dump. Exclude Chao-xing's contacts list and communications between Gambo and Chao-xing."

Nothing.

"Does Gambo mention a play or acting in any of his messages to Chao-xing?"

He does not.

Dario and Illyria passed through a doorway at the end of the hall, stepping over a jumble of pipes.

Turning right, they passed out of sight. Prashanth wasn't intimately familiar with these tunnels, but he knew that they were entering into another hall. The women in burnooses passed through the doorway and turned out of sight, and then Prashanth saw two young men standing beside the door. They were primates like Prashanth, and they were dressed like street toughs: holes deliberately cut into their jackets and pants, and long, thin chains hanging from their belts.

Not the Terra Gang; in fact, he couldn't tell that they were wearing gang colors at all.

"Have you found the Yellow Sign?" one asked Prashanth.

"What?" he replied.

It was the wrong answer. One of the toughs punched him in the face and then jumped him, knocking him to the concrete floor. Prashanth rolled away, but when he tried to climb to his feet, the second tough cracked him on the top of his head with a length of pipe.

Prashanth's head exploded in a meteor shower of pain. He howled; the tough hit him again, this time on the shoulder, and then he managed to get his pistol into his hand. The first tough was back on his feet again and was kicking Prashanth. He nearly kicked the gun away, but after taking a boot to the stomach twice, Prashanth finally got off a shot.

Shall I contact Security?

The hall filled with the flash, the bang, and the smell of burning propellant. The thug with the pipe stepped in to try another swing. Prashanth's vision swam and his brain trembled in revolt at the mere thought of physical motion, but he shot again, hitting the bravo in the arm.

The pipe still struck Prashanth on the head, and his vision went black.

Shall I contact Security? I have no instructions.

Prashanth unloaded, firing his pistol blind in what he was pretty sure was the direction in which his assailants stood. He was rewarded with shrieks, and then with the thudding of booted feet as they ran away.

Shall I contact Cerite Security?

"Are my attackers still here?"

I can't tell, Prashanth. I can only analyze your senses, and you are blind.

"Of course." But no one was attacking him anymore. Prashanth crawled until he reached a wall, and then dragged himself to his feet. As his vision returned, he swooped and pivoted around an invisible access, and vomited.

But he was alone.

That had been way too difficult. What had happened to his reflexes, honed by the thousands of hours of VR Space Patrol training? Was whatever gave him headaches also rendering him groggy and slow?

He limped through the open doorway and looked down the way Dario and Illyria had gone: a corridor past hatches into multiple halls. He couldn't tell where they'd gone, and had no way to follow them short of trial and error, poking around in this maze. And there were violent criminals in the maze with him.

What was the yellow sign?

"Yellow sign." He started dragging himself back toward the main corridors. "Another Chambers reference?"

Yes.

"Can you access the original Chambers texts?"

Done. Shall I read them to you, or put them in your visual field?

He vomited at the thought of trying to read. "Just... wait."

Why was Cerite Security not already swarming the hall? Maybe they were too busy dealing with brawling and gunfights on the main corridors.

His vision lurched so dramatically from side to side that Prashanth barely made it out of the hall. On his first attempt to exit into the corridor, he walked into the wall, but then he made his way by feel, groping a path back into traffic. His stomach churned and ice picks stabbed him in the brain repeatedly.

Guerilla theater. A surprise play, rehearsals kept secret. A missing model, who had once been an actress. An avant-garde sculptor. Passwords. And Victoria Tan didn't want Prashanth to talk to her husband.

He badly wanted to go to sleep, but he feared that if he did, he'd sleep long again. He also wanted to reload his pistol, but was afraid he'd drop the bullets. Instead, he fumbled his way to the table of a café, signaling the lone waiter for a coffee.

"In the Chambers texts, is there an answer to the question, 'Have you found the Yellow Sign?'"

There is not an answer. The Yellow Sign is an insignia that is never described.

Not helpful.

He drank the coffee when it came. He shouldn't drink this much of the stuff, but the alternative to sleeping off a headache was to burn it off with caffeine. Sunbathing on the Observation Deck, so far, had done nothing. Maybe he shouldn't be sunbathing; maybe he should look at Ross 248, or, at least, look at the Observation Deck by its light. He asked for ice water so he could hold the cold glass against his forehead. Unable to think, he held still and felt cold water trickle down his face, but when he finally set the glass down, he found he had a resolution.

It wasn't what he wanted. He wanted an idea, he wanted understanding, but instead he had a determination to go to Gambo Zubair's studio. He didn't think of his plan as pushing buttons, but as testing a hypothesis, or maybe gathering data more actively.

Sally provided the address from the biodata. Prashanth walked slowly, taking deep breaths.

In the future, do you wish me to contact Cerite Security when you are being attacked?

Unfortunately, he couldn't be sure that would always be the right course of action. "No."

Zubair's studio address was back in Newton. Prashanth passed within hailing distance of Ratskull and his toughs, examining some traveler's ID card, and passed through into the larger, nicer section of the Primate Quarter. Like the Village deck of *Copernicus*, Newton was comprised of high-ceilinged chambers with freestanding buildings inside. A single Day Light overhead flickered on and off, which Prashanth found simply annoying, and which certainly did nothing to relieve his headache.

Behind the front door of the studio was a small reception space and desk. An AI rolled forward to meet him. It consisted of a low, rectangular buggy chassis riding on four knobby wheels, with a single snakelike appendage rising from the center. The snake terminated in a luminous sphere containing a single roving, dark dot, like an eyeball.

"May I help you?" Buggysnake asked.

"I'm here to see Mr. Zubair. I was sent by Elias Tan, Chao-xing Tan's father."

Buggysnake disappeared through a door in the back of the room, returning moments later. "Please come in."

Prashanth entered a long, high-ceilinged hall like a stable. Sculptures lined the walls. At the end stood several large machines and a short man with long arms. From the machines came humming sounds. Prashanth intended to talk to the artist, but found himself drawn instead to the sculpture immediately inside the doorway. It was of a woman, perfectly life-sized. She wore a dancer's leotard and was posed standing on one foot, smiling. She had to have been printed, but the material she was printed of appeared to be pink marble. She looked East Asian.

She looked like Chao-xing Tan.

The sound of footsteps shook Prashanth out of his stupor. Gambo Zubair approached with a self-important swagger, pacing between a printed pink marble rose-bush and a printed pink marble greyhound. He wore a yellow blouse and, over it, a canvas smock. His head was hairless, lacking even eyebrows, and his forearms and hands were enormous.

Prashanth looked Zubair in the eye. "Have you found the yellow sign?"

The artist hesitated, and for a moment Prashanth feared his experiment was a failure. But then Zubair looked left and right, cleared his throat, and said, "The Pallid Mask is not a mask at all."

Prashanth nodded. So far, so good. Now, if he asked too direct a question, or too quickly showed his ignorance, he'd give the game away. Time for small talk. "I've admired your work."

Zubair grinned, showing perfect teeth. Probably printed. He pointed at the statue of the dancer. "Did you come to pick this one up for Mr. Tan?"

"No, he'll send someone else later. How did you do such a big printing? It had to have been all in one piece." He smiled. "I mean, I don't see seams."

"Come look." Zubair led Prashanth to the back of the studio. The machines Prashanth had seen were all printers, and Zubair showed them to him. They were programmable rather than standard menu-driven units, and had docking stations for tablets. The largest had a printing chamber two meters tall and two in diameter.

"So you can print a human-sized sculpture in one piece," Prashanth said. "Of course."

"Sounds like tonight will be your first performance," Zubair said.

Prashanth nodded.

"So, what does Mr. Tan need from me?"

Prashanth took the thousand credits from his wallet and handed them over. "He just wanted me to tell you how much he appreciates your work, and especially your discretion."

Prashanth left the studio. He walked around the corner and out of sight, and then crept back. He bought a crushable black cap at a bodega, reversed his jacket so that it was black-side out, and then sat, pretending to have a conversation using Chao-xing's tablet as a comms unit.

He reloaded his pistol with trembling hands.

"Collect all the references from Chambers's writings to the pallid mask, the king in yellow, and the yellow sign," he said.

There were surprisingly few, and he read them in a window in his visual field. The still waters of the Lake of Hali, snippets out of a play that didn't exist, the towers behind the moon, and dim Carcosa. And why was Carcosa dim? Black stars hung in the sky, obvious nonsense.

The stories were tales of madness, transformation, and unspeakable horror. His head thumping and his heart racing from the caffeine, Prashanth struggled not to feel himself sucked into the stories.

The towers behind the moon.

He had dreamed them. The towers behind the moon, the towers from the play that didn't exist and that he had never heard of, were nevertheless inside his head.

Inside his head.

And then his heart, for all the caffeine igniting it at the moment, stood still.

He had been tricked. He was betrayed.

But what to do about it? Any medical intervention would take time, and would make him miss tonight's performance. Which might make a difference of life or death to Chao-xing Tan.

Whose abductor, it increasingly appeared, might be in league with her father.

He tried not to look at anything out of the ordinary, and kept his tongue tightly under control. "Let me see those texts again," he told the puter.

He had run through them a third time when Gambo Zubair finally emerged from his studio. The artist wore an embroidered tunic now; it looked very formal. His walk was cramped and unsteady, not at all the confident lope he'd adopted in his own studio. He scurried toward the tunnel that led to the gate.

Where was he going, to see this performance? The spaceport? *Copernicus*?

And then, in his heart, Prashanth knew.

He stayed back, walking casually and stopping often, making a show of looking in windows or examining marks on the floor. Once Zubair had passed through the gate, Prashanth approached the Terra Gang enforcers.

He handed over his ID.

He looked past Ratskull, watching Zubair continue on toward the Promise borough and the Observation Deck.

"Pr'shanth Sach'deva, here we go again," Ratskull bubbled. "You're a fellow on the move, aren't you?"

"Yes, I am." Prashanth unlocked Chao-xing's tablet with her password and opened an empty note file.

"Don't get yourself stabbed." Ratskull handed back the ID.

Prashanth deliberately looked away from the tablet, used his finger to write eight words on it without looking, and handed the tablet to Ratskull.

Not waiting for a response, he walked through the gate.

The lift to the Observation Deck was shut down. The LED advertisement for chowder was gone, replaced with a sign that said, in bold text, CLOSED FOR PRIVATE FUNCTION. Two men in black suits stood impassively at the foot of the stairs. Their thick necks and grim expressions suggested Space Patrol training, but Prashanth didn't recognize them.

One held up a hand to stop Prashanth.

"Have you found the Yellow Sign?" the other asked.

Prashanth nodded. "The Pallid Mask is not a mask at all."

The men stepped aside.

Had he made a mistake with Ratskull? Did he really imagine that the Terra Gang would back him up? Maybe; more importantly, he wanted Ratskull to pass his message on to Lord Wimsey. It was too late to go back now. Prashanth climbed the steps.

Two more armed and muscled men waited at the top of the stairs. Prashanth felt himself sweating from the climb and the uncertainty both, but they offered the same challenge phrase and accepted the same password.

He entered the Observation Deck.

He had no idea what time it was on the standard clock; the long local day meant that the sky above him had barely changed. It was not hung with black stars, he noted with an absurd sense of relief, but with bright, glittering stars, one of which was Sol.

Where a writer named Robert Chambers had invented a play that he had never actually bothered to write.

That silly people were now . . . what, enacting? Exalting? Enthusing about?

The pond was still; the breeze generators were turned off. People in coats and gowns sat on wooden chairs arrayed around a flat sward of green on the shore; against the water stood a small canopy, two meters tall and two across, made of carpet-like textiles propped up on thin poles. A dim light glowed from the top of the canopy.

Prashanth strolled along the outer edge of the crowd, looking for a particular person. A chorus emerged, young women and men clad in linen robes. Each held a mask before his or her face, on a short handle. They sang, a modal dirge about the still waters of the Lake of Hali, about the coming of Hastur, and about the Stranger who was the King in Yellow.

Bow down your head, you son of dust, he heard.
Lay down ambition, hope, and lust,
And pray alone for
    Lost Carcosa.

He found his target, who appeared to be sitting alone. Prashanth picked an empty chair from the periphery of the crowd and carried it down with him to set it beside the man.

He sat. "Dr. Goldberg."

His physician steepled his fingers before his face and laughed. "My, my, Prashanth Satyadeva, you do not disappoint."

You seek a never-dying boon,
From towers that rise behind the moon,
The towers look down on
    Dim Carcosa.

The chorus finished their song and flipped their masks. The play-proper now commenced, with declamations and laughter. The crowd laughed along.

"There are a few things I don't understand," Prashanth said.

"Only a few? Then you're quite perceptive."

"Obviously, you knew I was coming. So you've warned someone, you have agents somewhere who are prepared to grab me. They haven't yet, so I suppose they're waiting for a signal of some kind?"

"Yes," Goldberg said. "But the signal won't come from me, so there's nothing you can do to stop it."

Prashanth considered the scene: the wealthy of Toe Hold, or at least the wealthy Primates, seated as if for a concert; the masked thespians. "But in the meantime, there's no reason not to answer my questions?"

"Meaning, are you going to die? Yes, I'm afraid you are. But then, we all are, sooner or later."

"That doesn't mean that I feel good about my time being accelerated."

Dr. Goldberg chuckled. "Are you asking, 'Why me?'"

"Why me? Obviously, you programmed my puter to betray me. Nothing else could have caused the auditory hallucinations I experienced. And maybe she's been monkeying with my reflexes, too. Not to mention the weird, very apropos dream images. I'd never even heard of this Carcosa stuff, and suddenly it was in my dreams. You did that, so why me? How did you know that Victoria Tan would hire me?"

"We didn't," Goldberg said. "We just knew that, sooner or later, someone would hire you to look into us. So, we made the first move."

Was one of the actors Chao-xing Tan? Prashanth was pretty sure the answer was no. He scanned the crowd looking for her, and saw nothing.

"Because Cerite Security is corrupted, so you're not worried about them."

"Enough of Cerite Security is friendly, or indifferent, to us that we're not worried about them."

"'We' means you and Elias Tan."

"And others."

Sweat trickled down Prashanth's forehead and between his shoulder blades. "Chao-xing found out what her father was up to, so she had to be kid-napped."

"No." Goldberg was smiling.

"Then why?"

"The King in Yellow requires a sacrifice."

"Killed?"

Goldberg wrapped his fingers together in a clenched double fist and laughed. "Ah, so there's a limit to what you've been able to deduce. Well, don't worry. You'll understand very soon what happened to Chao-xing Tan."

Prashanth looked for Elias Tan but did not see him. The actors in the play treated the canopy with great deference, the dialog implying that the canopy represented a throne.

"What are you all doing here, Doctor?"

"Can't you tell? Worship."

"Of what? The King in Yellow? Hastur? That's all nonsense, made up by a nineteenth-century fiction writer!"

"Ah, but the human psyche is a curious thing," Goldberg said. "Gods are like prayers and placebos. Sometimes they answer, even if they're not there."

Prashanth shook his head. "But why would people consciously join a . . . a made-up cult? Have they lost their minds?"

"They are moody," Goldberg said. "Paranoid, fatigued. Their endocrine system is, to use technical doctor language, out of whack, and playing havoc with their minds. Religion serves no purpose unless it exists to give people relief, wouldn't you say?"

"The towers!" an actor wailed. "The towers behind the moon!"

The actors all turned and looked up at Alexa's

World. The corona of Ross 248 was close enough to Alexa's World that streaks of light seemed to reach between the star and the planet, like columns. Or towers. The streaks did indeed look, a little, like towers behind a moon.

The crowd stood and cheered.

Prashanth and Goldberg stood with them. Prashanth could still see the actors because he stood on ground raised slightly above the pond, and the flat green shelf beside it.

A new actor approached the sward. Just before he raised his own, apparently blank, mask to his face, Prashanth saw and recognized Elias Tan.

Tan stepped out onto the stage.

"The Stranger!" an actor moaned, showing a dismayed mask.

"The King in Yellow merits a gift!" cried another.

Two actors, tall and burly, grabbed a third and wrestled him forward. "No!" he screamed.

"Yes!" the crowd roared.

Both cries sounded genuine.

The strong men heaved their captive beneath the canopy. He jerked once, as if trying to escape, and then froze.

"Suspensor beams," Goldberg murmured, as if appreciating the rich notes of a glass of wine. "Have you guessed yet?"

And then Prashanth realized what was coming, only an instant before it came. The actor didn't scream and didn't move, and the printer that was disguised inside the canopy was very rapid. It hummed, and within the space of a minute, the actor was entirely encased within a sheath that appeared to be made of pink marble.

Elias Tan, the mask of the Stranger held before his face, stepped beside the canopy. The burly men dragged the new-made statue from the printer and set it at the edge of the sward. The other actors reacted sluggishly—were they drugged? The crowd was silent, listening to a speech by the Stranger, but Prashanth couldn't hear a word. His head buzzed and his vision swam.

He turned to look at Goldberg. The doctor had taken a step away from Prashanth and stood smiling at him.

He had stepped away.

The signal, someone else was to give the signal, someone other than Goldberg.

What if the signal was the offering of the "gift" to the Stranger?

Prashanth broke into a run. Behind him, he heard screaming—was it because of the disturbance he was now causing? Or was it because someone was now chasing him, or shooting at him, with the intent to kill?

And he knew now the fate of Chao-xing Tan. The King in Yellow had demanded a sacrifice, so he had had her encased by a printer, as a living statue. He had killed his own daughter, and Prashanth had stood and admired the corpse as a great work of art.

And his artist accomplice, the actual murderer—Gambo Zubair had killed the young woman, and then calmly sent a message to her puter chastising her for not showing up, in case he was ever investigated for the death.

Elias Tan fell silent as Prashanth broke from the crowd. Prashanth shouted his condemnation, but what came out was an incoherent shriek.

Tan dropped his mask as Prashanth charged him.

And he screamed as Prashanth tackled him, knocking the coffee baron to the ground.

Elias Tan fell back into the canopy, his head and shoulders slamming against the floor of the printer. The printer hummed, and a sheet of rosy pink printing substrate wrapped itself onto Tan's shrieking face.

Prashanth felt a sharp sting in his left arm. Was he being stabbed? Shot, more likely.

He had to save Tan. Tan deserved death, but he deserved justice more. Prashanth dragged the murderer from the printer. Bullets struck the printer over his head, and the machine stopped humming with a sharp screech.

He grabbed for his gun and couldn't find it; he'd dropped it in his attack.

Prashanth dragged Tan to his feet and spun around, raising Tan. He smelled scorched flesh and heard Tan's agonized howling, but he ignored them both.

"Stop!" he yelled, thrusting Tan's ruined, pink face forward. "This is a crime scene, and this man is a murderer!"

"The Pallid Mask!" an actor wailed.

"The Pallid Mask is not a mask at all!" moaned another.

The crowd fell to their knees, and so did the actors. Left standing were Prashanth, Dr. Goldberg, and six men scattered along the far edge of the crowd, each holding a pistol.

They raised their firearms, and Prashanth closed his eyes. He did his best to drag Elias Tan in front of himself as a shield, but he was too tired and too sick to run, and there was nowhere to run to.

A series of shots rang out in quick succession . . . and Prashanth was not dead.

He opened them again and saw Lord Wimsey. Wimsey himself, who was rarely seen in person. He was three meters tall, his chest spherical and his head another sphere and a monocle cocked improbably over one eye. He was dressed like someone's idea of a Victorian gentleman, if said gentleman only wore purple. The metallic troll in his purple frock coat and top hat strode down through the trembling crowd. Wimsey held a rifle in both hands, and he whistled as he came—"Rule, Britannia," Prashanth thought.

Behind him came the Terra Gang. Several held firearms, and one had the four doormen up against a wall with a rifle trained on them.

Wimsey stopped at the edge of the sward. He addressed the crowd. "You're all under arrest. Some of you will object that I don't have the authority, but then, I do have a big gun, and friends, so I shouldn't object too loudly, if I were you." He turned to Prashanth. "You're very lucky, Mr. Satyadeva."

Prashanth let Tan fall to the ground. The coffee baron whimpered and kicked at the turf. Where was Prashanth's gun? Where was Zubair? Victoria Tan had to be told; had she suspected already? There were too many loose ends. "I don't feel lucky."

"Well, in the first instance," Wimsey said, "you are lucky that Mr. Ratskull delivered your message. Also, your penmanship is atrocious, and it took me some time to decipher. And in the third instance, you will agree that 'murder observation deck Cerite security corrupt tell Wimsey' is not an exceedingly clear call for help. But I arrived in time, nonetheless."

"The message had to be compact," Prashanth said. "And it had to get you here without you calling Cerite Security."

Wimsey nodded, then surveyed the wreckage of the scene. "What is all this, then?"

"It is madness," Prashanth said. "Murder. A placebo. A dream. It is paranoia and moodiness. It is dim Carcosa."

The return to *Copernicus* was tedious, with Sally removed. Prashanth had to call and reserve a shuttle seat for himself, and more than once he'd found himself asking research question to his former AI.

But he'd had Sally removed, because Sally had been hacked, and he couldn't trust her anymore.

On balance, he felt he'd made the right choice.

Copernicus's gravity weighed on him even more than it had on his prior visit. Victoria Tan's door opened as he approached it, and this time, the AI led him wordlessly to Tan's office.

"I know what happened," she said. "You were a victim, too."

Prashanth shrugged. "Your husband will get a Cerite trial."

"C'Sapunkov," she said. "Cerite city, Cerite law, Cerite trial. I need him to be convicted. Spaced. Unmarked grave. For what he did. For what he did to my daughter."

"That's what he deserves," Prashanth said. "And there were a lot of witnesses."

"I want it to the tune of one hundred thousand credits."

Prashanth took a deep breath. "I'll do everything

I can to help secure that verdict. C'Sapunkov is a just man. I'll do everything I can do to help him. Everything I can *legally* do."

"Take the hundred thousand credits anyway."

"I can't guarantee a conviction," Prashanth said.

"You've lost your implant," she said.

Prashanth felt surprise, but tried not to show it. He nodded, as if the information was public knowledge.

"You've probably also alienated a bunch of potential clients," she said. "Worshippers of the King in Yellow. Elias's playmates."

"Probably. On the positive side of the ledger, my headaches have stopped."

"Good." Tan smiled. "You work for me now. Your first job is to monitor the trial, and help C'Sapunkov get to the right outcome. Any way you legally can."

"One hundred thousand credits is a lot of money," Prashanth said.

"You'll need it to get quarters on *Copernicus*," Tan told him. "I want you close to hand when I need you. And the higher gravity will be good for you."

"And the light." Prashanth grinned. "I've had enough of dim Carcosa."

Humanity continued to expand into the Ross 248 system, but old age began to take its toll on the Ross 248 Project leadership. Admiral Gordon died at the age of 248 during a routine organ replacement. She was replaced by Captain McBane, who became the new Space Patrol admiral. The *Guardian E* and *Copernicus* remained in orbit above Liber, along with most of the space manufacturing infrastructure. Captain BeKinne died under mysterious circumstances at the age of 256 and was replaced by her first mate, Yoel Aronson, who also became head of the project with 5-of-Chandra as his deputy. Earth life has been introduced into Poseidon's Ocean at some of its deep thermal vents and is doing fine. A normal human settlement is underway on Nordheim, the fifth planet. The as-yet empty sixth planet was recently claimed by SAIN. Alexa's World has been studied but is currently unoccupied. Liber's Toe Hold is flourishing. Eden is now the home of several research stations, but no formal settlements.

Echoes of a Beating Heart

Robert E. Hampson

Childhood can be filled with contradictions: carefree exploration of one's surroundings and being injured by taking too many risks; the joy of playing with friends and the pain of having a falling out with one or more of them and, perhaps, becoming an outsider; the excitement of noticing the opposite sex and the pain of being rejected by the one you notice the most. Most humans experience these as part of the ritual of growing into adulthood. But what of sentient artificial intelligence? Do they have to "grow up" in order to mature into adult ways of looking at the world? If so, then will they experience the pains and joys along the way? If not, then are they truly sentient?

Dr. Robert E. Hampson is a scientist, educator, and author. His research involves how memory is formed, stored, and recalled in animal and human brain. He is working with Braingrade, Inc. to turn the research into a medical device to treat Alzheimer's Disease. As a professor, he teaches medical and graduate students in the field of neuroscience. He consults with companies and authors on brain science and teaches public communication skills to young scientists. After nearly forty years turning science fiction into science, he decided to try turning science into science fiction. Fifteen nonfiction essays, twenty short stories, three novels, and two anthologies later, he is now known for both his fiction and nonfiction writing. His website is REHampson.com.

"Davey, you need to come inside, now."

The boy looked up from his digging in the "garden" outside the primary habitat dome. His maternal guardian's face was on the tablet he'd placed on a stand beside the piece of the garden where he worked. He'd read stories and seen vidtainment of mothers standing on a porch calling their kids in from play. Davey knew she would have done that too—after all, she was a traditionalist—but it would have been a lot of trouble for her. A comm call over his tablet sufficed.

As a full-bodied "normal" human, she typically only ventured outside the dome using biocontainment precautions. It wasn't much, mostly just a rebreather and full-face mask to ensure she didn't breathe pollen or spores, but the decontamination afterward was a lengthy process. For Davey, it was just a quick rinse and spray to ensure that nothing stuck to his synthetic body.

He was a sentient—albeit adolescent—"artificial" intelligence. It was something of a misnomer. While his body was artificial—or more appropriately, synthetic—to facilitate growing up in a human family, there was nothing truly artificial about his intelligence. His AI mother, Juno, created him out of her own substance. His personality core was then installed in a juvenile body, and he went to live with flesh-and-blood intelligences—in other words, a human family.

The principle had been established many centuries ago, by the AI scientist Ellay McCaffrey, that electronic intelligences developed best—at least as far as being colleagues and coequals with organic intelligences—when they were imprinted on and raised alongside humans. The process instilled goals, instincts, and character traits, things that could not be easily programmed. Moreover, it allowed the sentient AIs to develop unique personalities, broadening the diversity of intelligent life—whether electronic or organic.

His human guardians, Molly and Hans, were "Mom" and "Dad" as far as he was concerned. Juno was "Momma" and he talked with her every week, but he was being raised by Mom and Dad. He felt like a regular kid and was treated like one...and sometimes that was a bit...restricting.

Davey liked working in the garden; after all, it got him outside and on his own for a brief period of the day. It wasn't always that way though. He had his studies, and it was easy to learn when your brain was basically a sophisticated computer, but there was more to it than that. Scientists had long known that human brains learned by doing, as much as by absorbing knowledge. Synthetic intelligences were no different. A portion of Davey's day was taken up by schoolwork—knowledge transfer paced to allow him to *use* the information and form the associational networks so essential to sentience. He also assisted Molly and Hans around their residence. His AI mother, Juno, was up in *Copernicus* and didn't come down to planetary surfaces. She watched him, though, and comm'd him once a week. They ignored the forty- to ninety-second communications lag. Most AIs could do that even if a human couldn't, since they multitasked most conversations, anyway. That's one reason why the purely human trait of talking on the comm had been adopted by the sentient AIs: it reinforced their ability to function in mixed AI and human society. It also reminded them that although they *could* communicate faster, that was not always the best practice.

For that matter, the weekly comm call between Juno and Davey was not strictly necessary; AI mothers maintained a link with their offspring until maturity, when they would disconnect from their life-giver and join the SAIN—the Sentient AI Network. The problem with getting information only from the link was much the same as using only digital, high-speed communication between AIs—it didn't give a sense of personality or social development. That had turned out to be important during one call several years ago.

"Momma, I'm bored." In human developmental terms, Davey had just become a teenager. AIs bypassed the infant and toddler stages and were placed in their synthetic bodies at an age equivalent to a five-year-old. From there they matured only slightly faster than biological intelligences. Davey had been developing for six years, but in terms of intellectual maturity, he was between thirteen and fourteen years of age. Emotionally, however, he was still very much a preteenager.

"You have friends. You have classmates. How can you be bored?" Juno asked her son. She had a continuous link with him until he was fully mature, but that was more of a diagnostic link. Through it, she was aware that Davey had a lot of idle time and wasn't necessarily spending it constructively. It concerned her because sentient AIs needed a purpose—a life's goal and reason to continue to exist. A bored adolescent AI could lead to much trouble.

"But they're all online," he whined. "Kelly is on *Copernicus*, Bruce is in the primate quarter, and Tanaka won't even tell us where he is. His parents work for the Patrol and can't really say what they're doing."

"But surely you can get together in the virtual rooms? The Sentient AI Network programmed those with predictive and adaptive interactions to compensate for communications lag. They're just the same as the virtual conferences SAIN uses all the time. You can play games, watch vidtainment, and study together."

"Oh, we can do that, but *Dungeons & Dragons* isn't that much fun now that Tanaka is pushing to upgrade to the twenty-first edition. Most of us are still using eighteenth-edition rules, but he wants to add all of this stuff about quantum probabilistic determinism and it's just not fun anymore."

"Have you ever considered that it might be because he's preparing to take the Patrol entrance exam? He's trying for the Class of '88. The entrance examinations are in eight hundred and three hours."

"Yeah, I guess so, but he's become so boring. He's also gotten kind of pushy and bossy. Kelly, Bruce, and I don't really want to play with him anymore."

"I know you have other friends."

"Of course I do, Momma. The problem is that none of them are *here*. I want to hang out. I want to be able to go do something even if it's just ... I don't know ... just playing in the dirt! There's no one here at Galapagos Station my age and even if they were, they wouldn't be allowed outside."

"I understand Davey; this is one of those things

you are going to have to learn. What you need is a hobby. I do have an idea for you. You said even 'just playing in the dirt.' Why don't you do that? Your mom Molly is a biochemist and Hans is an anthropologist. Certainly, between the two of them, you can come up with enough tools to do a little digging. Think of it as an archaeology dig or even a garden. You tested quite high on biology and you're coming along nicely in genetics, so an experimental garden would suit you."

"Well, I suppose I could do that. I'm not sure it sounds like fun, though. I want to do something fun and interesting."

"I don't know about fun, but I think I have a way to make it interesting. There was a researcher studying Eden many years ago; 7-of-Persephone spent thousands of hours studying Eden's biosphere. Charles, as he prefers to be called, is an accomplished geneticist, and an interesting person. I will put you in touch with him. He is currently out with *Pusher 2* looking for a nice metal asteroid. Comm or message him, he will probably be up for either. He was also a pretty good chess player—you like chess, right?"

"Yeah, I like chess. I got too good at it, though, and now no one wants to play with me."

"You've got the core architecture to be very good at chess; most humans can't beat you. If you're polite and respectful, I'm sure Charles will give you a game. He was one of the best of us. It's a shame he stopped his research on Eden. He found a different purpose, though, and now studies asteroids."

"Yeah, thanks, Momma. I'll look into the garden-thing and talk to Charles. Maybe even just having someone to play chess with will help."

"Okay, young man, behave, and don't give your mom and dad too much trouble. I'll talk with you next week."

"Okay, I promise. I'll talk to you next week, Momma."

Juno sent her son the contact information for Charles, while also sending a message to the AI himself, whom she knew from their trip out from Pluto. New AIs weren't created from nothing, but rather from an AI mother's own personality core, along with select skills, experiences, and interests "borrowed" from other AIs of her acquaintance. She'd asked Charles for his medical and chess core architectures and incorporated them into several of her offspring—most especially Davey.

Charles certainly ought to be interested if Davey decided to look at his research. It had been many years, and Juno knew that many in SAIN were disappointed when he set the research aside; however, she knew that Charles risked losing his *purpose* if he continued to run into resistance to his findings.

When the first ships of the Ross 248 Project arrived in-system, they weren't too concerned with the near-Earth-sized worlds. *Ceres' Chariot* entered orbit around the moon of the seventh world, Ross 248h, later to be known as Alexa's World. It was the only planet to have a moon, which would come to be known as Liber. At 0.08 gravities, it was also the only world that colonists from Sol's asteroid belt could inhabit.

The second ship, the Space Patrol's *Guardian E*, paid closer attention to the fourth planet, Ross 248e. The planet was named Eden, since it was the only world in Ross 248 with an oxygen atmosphere, large oceans, numerous small continents, and a living biosphere. It was a living world with an atmosphere a bit colder and thinner than Earth's—less CO_2, but more O_2. It had vibrant blue-green foliage to subsist on Ross's red light. There were also animals, both large and small, some reminiscent of the dinosaurs of Earth's Mesozoic era, crossed with the large mammals of the following Cenozoic era. The first human explorers on the surface of Eden found it necessary to defend themselves against some of the more aggressive species. An entire Patrol platoon had been wiped out by an ambush predator, the likes of which had never existed on Earth.

This was doubly unfortunate for the Eden native life, since not only were those explorers armed members of the Patrol, but any animal that succeeded in eating any Earth-life died horribly from biological incompatibility. It seemed to be one-sided, though. Eden's flora and fauna were not nutritious to humans, but there were no ill effects...at first. Within a few months, all Patrol personnel on Eden were showing signs of "failure to thrive" no matter how much (or how little) Eden foodstuffs they consumed. They then realized that incidental exposure to airborne pollen and dust containing Eden-microorganisms started to cause severe allergic reactions. By that point, scientists knew that Eden biology had DNA bases and amino acids that were closer to Earth's but different enough to interfere with normal metabolism. Eden-life, all the way down to bacteria and viruses, was simply incompatible with Earth-life. The only hope for humans to live unprotected on Eden was to sterilize the planet and start over by terraforming it with Earth life-forms.

With the arrival of the third ship from Sol, *Copernicus*, carrying colonists from Earth and the near-Earth space habitats, a heated debate arose between those who wanted to sterilize Eden of all native life-forms and reseed with Earth-life, and those who believed Eden life-forms should be protected. The planet was cooler than Earth's average, and the light of Ross was reddish and dim, but Earth-life could still grow there. In fact, all that was necessary was to plant seeds or transplant flora into Eden's soil; it wasn't necessary to remove the native life-forms. Earth-life took over and the Eden life-forms simply died, creating a blighted region several meters wide between the Earth and Eden life-forms. Nothing could live in the middle of the blighted zone—neither Earth- nor Eden-life, including plants, insects, worms, or burrowing creatures. However, Earth plants would spread outward if they were immediately adjacent to other Earth-life. The Eden life-forms simply died.

This information had been used in the arguments in favor of erasing Eden's native life. If just the presence of Earth plants would do that then it would be easy to find a toxin that would wipe out everything not of Earth, leaving a fertile planet in which Earth flora would spread rapidly, making it livable for humans in just a few years. Even the decomposition of native flora would speed the terraforming since it would improve the carbon-content of Eden's atmosphere. Decomposition would raise the low CO_2 levels and warm the atmosphere without really affecting O_2 levels.

It was considered a win-win situation.

More than eighty years ago, the Ross 248 Project

leadership settled the Eden Question. The AI scientist 7-of-Persephone (Charles) was one of those who joined the argument against sterilizing Eden; his studies of plant and animal genetics suggested several elements of the Eden genetic code were just too perfect. Despite missing two of the four nucleotides commonly found in Earth plant and animal DNA and having three additional previously unknown nucleotides, the DNA of Eden life-forms was relatively clean; with none of the "junk code" of Earth DNA, particularly humans. There were also various code combinations resulting from the five nucleotides that just didn't seem to fit with random evolution—in particular, the fact that the novel nucleotides *shouldn't* be able to combine in the manner they did. It was these combinations that resulted in the strange proteins that caused so much trouble for Earth-life.

These oddities, along with the signs of an alien structure at Alexa's Oddity on Alexa's World, Ross 248h, suggested that Eden-life may not have evolved naturally, but rather it had been meddled with or perhaps even purposefully designed. It would be a very bad idea to sterilize Eden of all its native life-forms if, in fact, there was an intelligence out there that had specifically created Eden. It would be like building an elaborate sandcastle only to have a bully come by and knock it all down. Any intelligence capable of engineering life on the scale evident in Eden's biosphere was bound to take offense if mere humans and their synthetic brothers and sisters came along and destroyed their handiwork—and if they did take offense, there would be little the colonists from Earth could do to stop them.

The debate raged for years until Admiral Gordon,

commander of *Guardian E*, declared that the Space Patrol's mandate was to protect life—all life. At the urging of Commander Harley Lund—a senior JAG officer—backed by Charles and many scientists, she declared the debate closed and commanded that no effort be made to remove Eden's native life-forms. From that time on, human presence on Eden was limited to the science stations and their habitat domes.

For two years, Davey worked in the laboratory and his experimental garden. His bio-parents supplied tools and space—a corner of Molly's biochemistry lab, and repurposed "gardening" tools from Hans's archeology equipment. He did his schoolwork in the morning, spent time on his assignments, then spent time online with his classmates and friends while he recharged his power pack. In the afternoon, he went out to his garden and worked.

The garden couldn't be too close to the dome, since he planned to work with both Earth and Eden plants. Most of the science stations on Eden were run by the Patrol—excepting a few private stations run by influential individuals from Copernicus Station. For their stations, the Patrol had cleared a one-hundred-meter perimeter around each structure. The simplest way to keep out Eden life-forms was to plant Earth grasses, and then periodically cut and burn the "lawn" to keep growth under control. A perimeter fence was erected just past the edge of the lawn, about a meter into the ten-meter "blight" that separated the Earth and Eden plants. Underground sensors monitored for the encroachment of underground ambush predators. Any such encroachment resulted in an energetic Patrol response involving Patrol grunts in battle suits, explosions, and flame-throwers. Davey had witnessed two such responses.

To accommodate Davey's garden, a decision had to be made—either allow his garden inside the perimeter or allow him outside.

A compromise was to allow a ten-by-ten-meter alcove with an additional perimeter fence, and a gate along the direct path from Airlock 1. The outer fence ensured that Davey was still protected from Eden's animals, and he could be monitored by cameras from inside the administrative dome. There were still some problems: the blight zone between the lawn and the garden tended to fill in with Earth plants, and the blight on the opposite side—away from the domes—lay partially outside the perimeter fence.

Colonel Nakamura, commander of the local Patrol presence, assigned Jorge and Victoria, two of his newest recruits from the Class of '83, to accompany Davey if he needed to exit the perimeter—but he was cautioned not to abuse the privilege. They had other duties too, like maintaining the lawn and the area separating it from the garden, repairing the domes, maintaining flitters, and security patrols. He was being allowed to do something no other adolescent—certainly no human adolescent—would be allowed to do. Therefore, he needed to follow the rules.

Fortunately, the two young Patrol members were close to his age, at nineteen and eighteen, respectively. Juno, Hans, and Molly had approved advancing him to the equivalent developmental age of sixteen, and the two young Patrol members had been invited to his declared birthday celebration. Under other circumstances, they might have been the similar-age companions he desired, but they were so *serious* about their duties! At least they welcomed the break when he needed to go beyond the fence, but he knew he couldn't abuse it. On those rare occasions, they talked about many things, but they didn't hang out, game, or watch vidtainments together. The effective two-to-three-year gap in subjective age might as well have been decades.

All of this led to Davey feeling disappointed and wallowing in self-pity, even as he was sharing his findings with Charles. The one recent highlight of both his work and his social life was the fact that Charles's tug was at Liber, after having delivered a nickel-iron asteroid to the Factory. It meant that speaking with his science and chess mentor now only took a few minutes of communications lag instead of the minutes to hours they'd experienced for the last two years.

"I'm sorry, Charles; I know I sound like a whiny child, but I just wish there was someone here my age. I don't care if they're not interested in gardening or plant genetics or even science, just having someone here so I'm not the only teenager in this entire colony would be appreciated."

Charles sent a glyph representing the AI equivalent of a chuckle across the machine language portion of the comm channel.

"It's tough growing up alone, Davey. I know how it feels. I was the only one of my generation—a civilian on a Patrol ship. Persephone was the only AI mother on *Guardian E*, and she wasn't supposed to be forming new AI cores for civilian applications! I was fostered by crew members, but my core architecture was never intended for the Patrol. Persephone was later chastised by *Guardian* over it. So yes, I know it's hard growing up by yourself, and even harder when there are no peers at all for you to interact with."

He then sent a sigh glyph. "Believe it or not, kid, I do know what you're going through."

Davey thought about that for a moment. At least he had classmates and other kids on comm and in the virtual chat rooms. "Yeah, I suppose I'm being unreasonable. But...I'm a kid. Isn't being unreasonable...a reasonable thing for me to be at this point?"

"Hah! Yeah, sounds like my attitude too. Okay, I'll tell you what, set up the chess board and I'll spot you two pawns and a bishop. If we make it to fifty moves without a checkmate, you win."

"As if, old man. You're on!"

"Hey, Mom, I've got something here that doesn't make a whole lot of sense. Can you look at this?" Davey was sitting at a console in Molly's biochemistry laboratory, looking at microscopic images of plant cells. He had the run of most instruments, although a few required specialist technicians to operate, so he was able to do most of what he needed to perform his plant experiments. After all, the entire Galapagos Station had been built to support a larger population than what the Patrol currently allowed on-site.

"Sure, Davey, what've you got there?"

"I ran a nuclear chromatin stain on these Eden plants to see if I got any of the chromosomes to hybridize, but there's something out here not in the nucleus." Davey zoomed in the virtual microscope as his mother leaned over his shoulder to look at the microscope image.

"It's just a smudge. Could be an artifact, but your

technique is usually pretty good. Have you considered running X-ray crystallography on it?"

"I thought about that, but I'd have to get Yuri to run it. He hasn't been available lately." The X-ray crystallography scanner was one of those instruments that Davey wasn't allowed to work on his own. Normally, there were several technicians in the lab who could operate it, but only one was currently on the station due to annual Patrol training—and he had been quite busy since his section was understaffed.

"Let me see his schedule. There may be a few things that can be rearranged. If this is not an artifact, then it could be mitochondrial DNA or some other epigenetic factor."

Ever since the discovery of DNA, most people thought of it being limited strictly to the cell nucleus, but in the late twentieth and early twenty-first century it became known that mitochondria, the energy-producing portion of a cell, also had some fragments of DNA. Some of the rarer traits in human genetics were inherited solely from the mother via mitochondrial DNA, since mitochondria were only present in ova, and not sperm. In addition, scientists began to realize that proteins and enzymes in the cells could regulate which DNA codes were read and decoded.

Even before the existence and function of DNA were discovered, scientists postulated that traits were not simply inherited unchanged but could be developed and selected via environmental pressures. An example was the long neck of the giraffe, seemingly adapted specifically to allow eating leaves from the tops of trees. Early theory suggested that in the pursuit of food, giraffes stretched their necks and that this was somehow inherited from generation to generation, producing longer-necked animals. Gene theory, following James Watson and Francis Crick's discovery of the DNA double helix, stated otherwise. Genes were passed unchanged (except for random mutations) from generation to generation; the selection process resulting in long-neck giraffes was simply that those with mutated gene coding for long necks were better able to survive. Since only animals that *survived* passed on their genes, those with a beneficial mutation persisted, while those without eventually died off.

The study of epigenetics changed all of that. Once again, theories began to include methods in which chemicals, proteins, and enzymes outside of the cell nucleus could change whether genes were turned on or off—not to mention whether they were even inherited by subsequent generations. Inheritance of adaptive traits found new acceptance, and the discoveries of both extranuclear chromatin and epigenetic influences had the potential to completely rewrite understanding how genes and traits were passed on to subsequent generations.

Davey and his mom knew that a finding like this in Eden DNA was important, since it was one of the factors that Charles had proposed—and been dissuaded from studying—to explain the incompatibilities between Earth and Eden biology. If the unknown object in Davey's microscope slide was indeed an epigenetic agent, or at least evidence of epigenetic modification, then it was going to be a big deal.

"Have you met the new family yet?" Hans asked at the dinner table. Strictly speaking, Davey did not need to eat, although he could consume food and beverages in order to be sociable. He could also use the carbohydrates and proteins as raw chemical stocks for lubrication, cooling, and small parts production. While the evening "family meal" wasn't strictly necessary for his function, it was necessary for his socialization. For that reason, Molly, Hans, and Davey ate supper together every night.

"New family, did you say?" Molly asked when Davey didn't immediately respond.

"Yes, the Olesons are doctors of medicine from *Copernicus*. They're going to be taking over for Dr. Johannsen. He's been down here long enough that the Patrol wants him to rotate back to the Primate Quarter on Toe Hold. They have kids." He turned to Davey. "I would've figured you met them already in school."

Davey just shrugged. Everyone was supposedly equal on Eden, but most of the humans at Ross lived either in the Primate Quarter at Toe Hold on Liber, or in the starship-converted-to-space-station *Copernicus*. The Primate Quarter housed the working-class folks who were recruited by the Ross 248 Project to build the new colonies, while *Copernicus* housed persons who'd bought their way onto the project. There was a class divide that was hard to shake, even on Eden, where everyone was equally at risk from the biosphere.

Davey was uncertain where he fit into that hierarchy. His mother was on *Copernicus*, but his parents were from the Primate Quarter. As an adolescent AI, he was always going to be different—particularly on Eden. It would be nice to have other kids around, but he'd finally come to terms with being the only teen in the station. He just hoped he wouldn't have to babysit.

* * *

Davey came back into the dome after working in his garden. He had created several hybrid seed varieties in the laboratory and had just transplanted them to see how they behaved out in Eden's biosphere. He placed them about a meter into the blight to see if the modified Earth plants would grow in the barren zone. At the same time, he was curious to see if the blighted area would expand accordingly with the new growth. It was only a small step, but it might help explain the odd intolerance between Earth and Eden-life.

As he entered his family quarters, he heard new voices. The airlock-like entrance blocked his view of the inside of the apartment as he hung his thermal protective garments on a hook on the wall. He entered the main living area and saw two adults he hadn't seen before. That was nothing unusual, scientists rotated in and out of the Galapagos science station all the time. This time, however, there was a redheaded girl of about sixteen or seventeen Earth years of age with them. Human, not sentient AI, but still . . . someone his age, and it was a girl!

One of the justifications of raising sentient AIs as adolescents and teenagers in human families was that they tended to develop attachments and friendships just like human teenagers. One of the consequences is that those interactions could take on emotional aspects depending on the AI and his or her companions. Seeing the girl evoked a curious set of processing loops, so Davey set a recording state in his processing core to preserve the sensations for later analysis.

What is this strange sensation?

The analytical part of his core architecture said attraction.

So, this is what it means to be attracted to someone!

It wasn't that she was especially pretty. She was gangly in the way of many mid-teens going through growth spurts. She had frizzy red hair pulled back in a bushy ponytail. Her skin was pale, like most of the humans born under Ross's dim light, but there was a hint of freckling across her nose fading from the Sol-spectrum on *Copernicus*. She was taller than Davey's current synthoid body and she looked pretty strong. Without even thinking about it, he'd engaged a pattern-matching subroutine that returned an immediate analysis: "Tomboy, probability: seventy-nine percent."

Davey was a little surprised that the expert system subroutine even knew the term, given that it was so archaic. Male-female developmental roles had changed so much, but it was still sometimes used by older humans to designate human females who enjoyed outdoor physical activities and adventures.

This could very well be someone who thought a lot like he did!

"Davey, come here, I want you to meet the Olesons. They're medical doctors, and their daughter Elizabeth is about your age. They have a son too, but he's much younger. Since Elizabeth's—oh, sorry, dear..." Molly made a quick face of apology in the girl's direction. "She just told us she prefers 'Betsy.' As I was saying, since Betsy's about your age, we thought you should get acquainted. They just moved here to start a two-year rotation at Galapagos clinic with part-time duties at Papua and the outlying stations. Come say hello."

Over the next few weeks, Davey and Betsy spent afternoons together. Despite his initial misgivings about having to deal with another teen (or possibly younger kids), the two got along quite well. In some ways, Betsy was just as bored with her new life on Eden as Davey had been before he started work on the garden. She wasn't that interested in the garden, but she liked the lab, and was really interested in the archeology tools that Davey's dad had repurposed for gardening. She had been studying archaeology and really wanted to go work on Alexa's Oddity when she graduated. That site showed clear evidence that an alien intelligence had been at work in the Ross 248 system, but most scientists had stopped studying it years ago when it became clear that the previous inhabitants had deliberately left nothing of interest except some vitrified glass buildings that had been well studied. But just because she didn't share all the same interests didn't mean that they didn't get along or couldn't be friends. As a matter of fact, having personal, independent interests was one of the things working in their favor.

Betsy talked constantly of getting out of the dome to explore. She'd been with her father on one of his trips over to Papua Station. As a doctor, he was on-call for emergencies at the nearest research station, as well as several smaller outposts. One night, she told Davey that her father had been teaching her to operate the "flitters"—long-range flyers for travel between the research stations on Eden's surface. She accompanied her father on the longer trips so that he could tend to patients in-flight, if necessary. That was why he'd taught her to operate the vehicle—if he needed to transport a patient, he'd need somebody else at the controls. It wasn't always convenient to get someone from the Patrol since some of the private outposts had minimal or, in a few cases, no Patrol presence.

They had morning studies together and had a few other online activities throughout the day. However, Betsy had lunch with her parents each day, then spent afternoons taking virtual classes in advanced studies from the Ross Academy.

Davey, on the other hand, spent most of the early afternoon in the lab, and went out to work his garden in late afternoon when he had full sunlight—weak as it was—on his experimental site. After that was the daily family dinner, which meant that most days, Davey and Betsy couldn't really spend time together until evening. Not even then if she was off with her father.

That left them with occasional in-person visits, and lots of evening comm calls. Many times, those ran late into the evening. Betsy claimed she didn't need much sleep, and Davey required only an hour of downtime, although he had adopted the standard human routine of sixteen to eighteen active hours and six to eight hours of dormancy. His parents didn't mind the late-night conversations, but warned him that Betsy *did* need biological sleep, and that he needed to be mindful that he didn't keep her awake too late.

On those late nights they talked about gaming, the social comm posts of classmates, and their aims for the future. While the sentient AIs would never reach the level of creativity of a human, human companions often provided a spark of imagination and insight that *enriched* the AIs and assisted in producing mature sentience and intellect. Thus, Betsy and Davey's conversation took on deeper meaning as they talked about their future, his life's goal and purpose, and her desires for challenge and recognition.

That was how he learned that she was bored. One evening, she talked of sneaking out of the domes and exploring the surrounding jungle. She also talked of borrowing a flitter and taking off to explore the neighboring islands and one of the lesser continents. Davey knew that that was just the boredom talking, she had plenty to do—but having been born and raised in a space station, then moving to a planet's surface and told she couldn't go outside was beginning to wear on her.

Davey didn't know what to do or how to help her. Maybe he could ask Juno . . . but he was afraid she might think he was developing an abnormality if he started talking about how to help his friend break the rules. He would ask Charles, but that had some of the same risks and might be just as bad. Perhaps he should wait.

The new seed stock had grown well. Not only did his modified Earth plants grow in the middle of the blighted zone without needing to be in contact with the rest of the Earth flora, but the blighted zone also didn't expand. It was now time to take a closer look at the Eden plants that grew at the edge of the blight closer to his latest transplants. He needed to collect samples and subject them to the same cellular and genetic analysis as before.

The next afternoon, Davey was in the lab studying the latest samples of Eden DNA when an email from Yuri announced that he'd finally been able to run the X-ray crystallography of the unknown sample from his previous experiment. The result confirmed that it was, indeed, extra-nuclear chromatin, or ENC; in other words, it was DNA that derived from somewhere other than the nucleus of the cell where the chromosomes were located. He'd also sent the sample for sequencing and provided an attachment with long strings of letters representing the nucleotide sequences in the ENC sample.

Davey uploaded the sequence into the data-processing part of his core. He watched passively as various algorithms attacked the data. Strangely, one of his analysis programs seemed to be treating the genetic code as if it were *computer* code. It struck him as odd, but as he "watched" his core architecture process the results, occasionally he'd get the impression of a familiar bit of code—something he *almost* recognized, but which slipped away when he directed his attention to it. Gradually the sequences started to give him a headache, which was a very strange sensation for synthetic life-forms. Human headaches were caused by abnormal blood flow to the brain and the release of hormones and neurotransmitters that affected the capillaries and arterials that directed blood to active portions of the brain. Davey's brain was an AI core—it didn't have blood or tissue, and the quantum processors were not regulated by biochemical means. Coolants and lubricants were part of his synthetic body, but they did not—in fact, they *could* not—affect the functioning of his AI core.

He might need to talk with Betsy's mother. She was a medical cybernetics doctor working mostly with Patrol members who'd been fitted with brain computer interface implants. These implants were used mainly for totally immersive, virtual-reality training, but sometimes for tele-operation of machines and sensors. He should also report this to Juno. He was more reluctant to do the latter, in case she saw this as an indication that he was unstable and not maturing properly. If so, it would be her responsibility to terminate him. He didn't like the idea that this unusual phenomenon might mean that he was flawed and unsuitable to continue existence.

Fortunately, the sensation didn't last, and as soon as Davey stopped processing the Eden gene-codes, the headache sensation faded. Betsy and her parents were joining his family for dinner that night, and by the time he sat down at the dinner table, all unusual sensations had faded away completely. Davey filed away the memory and directed his cognitive processor not to think about it, at least for now.

That night, Davey dreamed.

One of the first, albeit rudimentary, sentient AIs was a heuristic algorithmic computer that asked its creator if it would dream when the creator shut down its processors. The creator responded that, of course, it would dream; after all, it was a living person, and all living persons dreamed. Davey had experienced dreams, usually as a result of analytic processes that had not completed during his active hours.

This was an odd dream, nothing like those other experiences. He dreamed of a place far out in the jungles of Eden, a city rising out of the foliage, comprised of buildings with stepped sides reminiscent of Central and South American pyramids back on Earth. He saw no inhabitants or even animals in the city. There were no signs of human, sentient AI, or alien intelligences other than the buildings. He dreamed of strange writing, but it wasn't attached to any of the buildings, it just appeared in his memory. At least one segment of writing reminded him of the gene sequences he'd been reading and studying earlier in the day, but he also had an impression of map—not coordinates, or at least, not anything he recognized—but he had a firm impression of what the surroundings looked like.

He awoke with a start, an unusual experience for AIs who simply increased their processing power and directed their awareness to external stimuli at a fixed time every day. Downtime was strictly scheduled, and AIs didn't suffer insomnia, awaken during the night, or sleep late like humans. An AI's operation cycle, equivalent to a sleep-wake pattern, never varied. For Davey to dream and then wake up suddenly was a very unusual circumstance indeed.

The fear of a diagnosis of abnormal development kept Davey from mentioning his odd dream to any of his parents. He knew Juno would know something had happened out of the ordinary, but she wouldn't invade his memory files . . . would she? He tried not to think of it until Betsy asked him why he was so distracted. He told her. She seemed to think it was nothing to worry about. After all, she had her own dreams of finding ruins of a civilization on one of the planets of the Ross 248 system. It was one of the reasons why she was studying archaeology. Dreams were normal, she'd told him, but they were only dreams, no cause for concern.

Davey was not necessarily reassured. For the next several nights, he had the same dream, although he didn't wake suddenly those times. Each night, the dream—and the city—became more detailed. He still never saw any aliens, but he saw more features of the city. Somehow, he knew that lost in the jungle on another continent, a large, stepped pyramid sat at the center of a ring of successively smaller buildings. Beyond that were two more rings, perfectly, geometrically arranged with what could only be called streets radiating out from the pyramid at the center. Each successive dream revealed more detail, including an entrance at the base of the pyramid.

Once again, Davey awaked suddenly. In his dream, he'd entered through large stone doors which led into the tunnel sloping down underneath the pyramid. The tunnel was longer than the pyramid was wide, and it seemed as if it must lead out past the concentric rings of buildings and under the surrounding jungle.

In the dream, Davey followed the tunnel down to a laboratory. He knew it was a laboratory even though very few of the instruments were familiar to him. Somehow, in his dream, he knew that this was where the aliens had created the life-forms that inhabited Eden.

Davey was highly disturbed by the dreams—not just the fact that he was having dreams, but because they seemed to be beckoning him to go and find the city in the jungle. He discussed all of this with Betsy, but urged her to keep it quiet. Juno, Molly, and Hans couldn't know. He was afraid they would see it as abnormal development for an AI.

On the other hand, he could send the details of the gene-code he'd been studying to Charles to see if there was any commonality or anything like it in the previous studies. He wanted to ask the senior AI if he had ever found any indication of cities on Eden, but knew from his history classes that, at least officially, no structures had ever been found anywhere in the Ross 248 system, aside from Alexa's Oddity.

Betsy said that the official history didn't mean that nothing had been found. It could have been covered up, or the records of the person who found them could have been deleted before they entered public record. She also told him that the lack of satellite imagery was not proof either. The jungle was so dense in spots that it could hide the research stations themselves if not for the security perimeters.

Davey wasn't so certain about her cover-up theories. "That's an awful lot of work to go through," Davey replied. "After all, there still Alexa's Oddity; they're not hiding that."

"Sure, but civilians found that, not the Patrol. Haven't you read your Earth history? It's full of stories of secret societies keeping things from the general public."

Davey wasn't sure how to answer that. He'd studied Earth history and it didn't seem to be quite as full of conspiracies as Betsy thought. Then again, she favored novels and stories filled with spies, secret agents, and evil villains with volcano lairs; of course she'd see everything as a conspiracy.

"Yes, but don't you think that if something like that existed, Admiral Gordon would have mentioned it? After all, it perfectly supports her decision to leave Eden alone and not terraform it. Evidence of an alien civilization supports that; there would be no reason to cover it up."

"As if government officials ever need a reason for a cover-up," Betsy countered.

Davey knew there was no arguing with her when she was in one of these moods. It made being with her rather infuriating, but also kind of interesting at the same time. He supposed that was one reason why they were friends, because he was fascinated by her conspiracy theories. They were so illogical, and as a sentient AI, it was his nature to be logical.

Davey had sent a copy of the unusual gene sequences to Charles to see if he recognized anything from his own studies, but knew that it could be some time before he would receive a response. Charles's ship was busy over at Liber, and he was assisting the scientists there with the analysis of the asteroid they'd delivered. AIs could multitask, but they also had to prioritize. It could be several days before Charles got back to him.

So, Davey tended his garden and watched his new seedlings grow. While they could live in the middle of the blighted zone, and didn't expand it outward, he lost a few of the Earth plants closest to his new hybrids. It wasn't perfect compatibility, but he was starting to gain some compatibility between his hybrids and the Eden plants. It wasn't as much as he hoped with Earth life-forms, though, so he needed to find some new gene sequences to test for his next attempt.

He also started looking at maps of Eden. His dreams gave him a sense of where the city was located, but it wasn't in any coordinate system humans or AIs used. On the other hand, there were only so many ways to divide up a sphere. Davey and Betsy had different ideas on how to figure out the conversion, but eventually his dream impressions lined up with her analysis of landmarks.

They had a target…but no way to confirm it.

When he finally heard from Charles, the AI scientist

expressed interest in his latest experiments with hybrid-
izing Earth and Eden genomes and agreed that it might
assist in making less-hazardous biomes around the station
domes, but cautioned that it still didn't mean compatibility, or that humans would ever live unprotected on
the surface. He also warned Davey to backup his data,
his findings, and even his simulation programs.

Charles's ship had received word of several threats
and he warned Davey that an evacuation order for
Eden was imminent. "Be prepared to leave" were the
final words in his communication.

Davey sought out Betsy and showed her the message from Charles.

"Well, that seals it," she said. "We have to go. If
they're gonna pull us off this rock, we need to find
your city before it's too late."

"But how?"

"I've got an idea. Meet me at Dad's clinic at oh-one-
hundred tonight. We have to make our move."

Both of Betsy's parents were doctors. Her mother
was a neurologist who specialized in the care and
maintenance of human brain-computer interfaces. Some
scientists also had implants to speed up their interactions with laboratory instruments and operate devices in
either hazardous or sterile environments—like Eden—so
she had plenty of work there, but mostly in the larger
research stations such as Galapagos. Betsy's father
was a general physician who specialized in allergy and
infectious diseases. He was on-call and had to travel to
remote sites when someone on Eden showed reactions
from exposure to the native life-forms or reactions to
the sealed environment of the station domes. He was

the only such specialist on Eden at present and had unrestricted access to long-range flitters for transportation across the planet's surface. They were mostly automated, but he'd made sure she knew how to operate one manually—talking about something called "bush doctors" and "bush pilots" on Earth.

Davey wasn't sure how relevant a comparison that could be, since Eden didn't have anything so small as a "bush" in its continent-wide jungle. Still, he took her at her word that she could get them to the location in his dreams, so he waited until his parents were asleep before he slipped out of their apartment. He should be able to avoid the security patrols if he was careful not to cross the route they took from offices—around midnight—to the residential sections around 12:30. By the time he got to the clinic, they would've finished their rounds and gone back to the central monitoring station.

He didn't see Betsy anywhere, so he tried the door to the clinic offices and found it unlocked. Stepping inside the darkened room, he noticed a light in the doctor's office at the back of the complex. There was a sound of somebody opening and closing the door and then the light snapped out.

Davey's synthetic eyes were sensitive well into the ultraviolet and infrared, not to mention low-light conditions, so he clearly saw Betsy coming out of the physician's office in the back. "I had to grab Dad's code remote. We'll need it to borrow the flitter."

"Won't he miss it? What if a patient calls and he needs to go out?"

"He won't miss it. He's misplaced these things so many times that he has backups all over. His regular remote is in the doctor bag he keeps beside the front door of our apartment. Mom has a second one. This one is the backup for the backup."

"But what if he needs his flitter?"

"Don't be silly. He doesn't have a personal flitter. He just checks one out from the garage. There's at least twice as many flitters sitting there as could possibly be used at any given time. It's called backup and redundancy."

"And if somebody else notices that he's taken out a flitter?"

"Now I think you're just making things up. No one cares. If you've got a code remote, you're authorized to use a flitter."

If that were the case, this might work. If all it took to be "authorized" was a remote in your possession, there would be no reason for someone to stop or follow them for unauthorized use. The only problem would be when their parents reported them missing. Davey delayed that as long as possible by sending a message to his parents claiming that he had exams and would be in the virtual classroom module all day.

Betsy led the way to the garage. Davey had been there—after all, it was part of standard safety and emergency training—but not often. True to her word, Betsy really did know her way around a flitter. Once they'd taken off, she had him enter the coordinates they'd settled on into the nav computer. They'd studied the location, and knew that it was near the center of a subcontinent-sized island southwest of the continent where Galapagos was located. They would have to cross quite a bit of land, then open ocean, and then more land. Flitters were designed for precisely this sort of travel, and Betsy and her dad had made this length of trip many times. It was time to sit back, catch up on sleep—for Betsy, Davey wouldn't absolutely *require* downtime for several more days—and relax until they reached their destination.

They were traveling southwest with the sun, which meant they would likely arrive just after local dawn. On the other hand, it would be midday at Galapagos Station and they would surely be missed by that time. In case of an inquiry to their wrist-comms, they'd each recorded a message for their parents reassuring them that all was well; they were pursuing a scientific inquiry and would be returning the next morning. That way they could spend the daylight hours exploring what they'd hoped would be ruins of an alien city, leave just before nightfall, and return to Galapagos before dawn the next morning. Davey was sure they would both be in trouble. But if they found real evidence of an alien civilization, then perhaps all would be forgiven.

Most of the folks at Galapagos would be asleep for several hours, yet they planned to leave the radio open for emergency calls. They wouldn't shut off the receiver unless they started receiving messages of a threatening nature telling them to return. Davey didn't think his parents would do that, but Betsy wasn't quite so sure. There was always the chance that the Patrol would intervene and decide that they had to return home at all costs. When an emergency message came across the comm several hours later ordering all personnel to report to the nearest Patrol headquarters for emergency evacuation from the surface, they figured it was just an excuse to get them to return to Galapagos.

The message was not specifically directed at them, but that didn't mean it wasn't designed to draw them out. Betsy and Davey argued as to how to respond. Was it a real emergency? Davey's message from Charles suggested it was. Betsy countered that it could be something cooked up by authorities at Galapagos to get them to return. Davey wasn't entirely comfortable with the decision, and he felt an odd twinge—a tug at his consciousness—but he accepted Betsy's argument that gathering people and transport off the surface took time, and another twelve hours wouldn't make much of a difference.

Dawn was breaking in the sky behind them as the flitter settled into a clearing closest to the coordinates Davey had entered into the navicomp. Davey scanned the clearing to make sure it was clear of ambush predators and nodded his approval. If there were a city here, then it would be just past the stand of trees immediately to their north. Before leaving the flitter, they heard the emergency announcement again—and again, they decided to ignore it. Just to be safe, Davey thought it best that they tie their wrist-comms into the flitter's central panel for relay. If the emergency was real, then at least they could be tracked. It risked the Patrol arriving and interrupting their mission, but they both admitted that it would be a serious breach of safety protocol to turn off their comms. Ignoring a comm call was forgivable, making one's self untraceable was not.

They grabbed backpacks filled with water, ration bars, rope, bandages, first aid kits, and a spare rebreather and lightweight skinsuit for Betsy. The latter two were in case she damaged the equipment protecting her from biting insects, plant sap, and pollen, or ingesting anything that could get her sick. Davey's synthetic body didn't need any of that, but he made sure he had spare supplies for Betsy as well as emergency energy cells, lubricant paste, and a type of ration bar favored by synthetics to extend their duration in the field, away from power sources and maintenance. They were ready to explore. Now it was time to find out what was out there.

If Davey had been a mature and independent AI, he could have requisitioned an explorer body that would've been better suited to making its way through the dense brush and trees separating them from their goal. As it was, he was barely doing better than Betsy and her purely natural body. In fact, if it hadn't been for her toughsilk skinsuit, she might've been cut, bleeding, and likely reacting very badly to the nettles and branches in their way. Davey had brought a long knife—practically a machete—for cutting brush, and he used it to cut as much out of their way as possible. He knew that meant the cut ends of the plants would ooze sap that would then have to be washed off in a decontamination shower later. Accidental exposure wouldn't be deadly, but could be very uncomfortable. Still, it was worth the risk to ease their way through the heavy foliage. There were alternatives to cutting their way through, but neither of them was about to burn or chemically defoliate the path to a potential alien city.

It took more than an hour to get to Davey's coordinates. Once again, they heard the All Personnel alert from the Patrol about the evacuation, but this time there was a specific message to the two of them.

There were no threats or recriminations, but they were directed to return to a neutral point for Patrol pickup.

They were just *so* close!

Ahead of them was not a clearing *per se*, but a thinning of the small plants and trees that blocked ground level. There were tall trees and several large rocky outcroppings in which plants did not grow. They were able to make slightly better time and arrived minutes later...

...but there was no city.

Davey and Betsy scouted the entire area where the vegetation had thinned. It was possible to see more distant landmarks through the trees, and Davey recognized several from his dreams.

This was the place Davey had seen in his dream! But there was no sign of the city.

They explored and took pictures before stopping for a break. Davey erected a small isolation tent with a brief decon shower. It would allow Betsy to get out of her protective gear long enough to eat. She drank some water, as did Davey. The cool liquid was always welcome for heat dissipation. The two shared notes about what they had found while Betsy ate.

"I really don't understand this; it was so clear in my dream. There is a mountain over there, an outcropping in the direction of the sunrise, and the small stream running across the clear area. I saw all of those in my dream. The city should be here."

"Well, it *was* a dream. Dreams don't always have to come true," Betsy said.

"You're the one who encouraged me to come here and explore."

"Yes, yes, I know. I did it because the dream was

real to you. It was worth checking out, but if there's nothing here then that's all it was, just a dream."

"Then...why did I start having dreams in the first place? Something about the Eden DNA triggered these dreams."

"Well, then perhaps it was a hidden message in the DNA itself. Except that it's so old that there's nothing left for you to find."

"I was just so sure!" Davey said, plaintively.

"Didn't you say in the most recent dreams you saw a tunnel underneath the big structure at the center of town? Where would that be?"

"Not far from here, down at the base of the big rock pile. I'm pretty sure that's natural, not a ruin, but perhaps we can look there again."

"Okay, we'll do that, then. Let me finish this ration bar and get another drink of water. I'll be good to go in a few more minutes." True to her word, Betsy quickly finished eating and drinking, then resealed her skinsuit and donned her rebreather helmet.

They exited the small bubble tent and Davey collapsed it to put it back into his pack. It shouldn't have been hard to get to the point that he remembered, but it was a tortuous path with many trees and even more jumbled rocks. Once more, he looked at the rocks closely. They *seemed* natural, but were those edges a bit too regular?

The two of them explored the area with no more results than before. Davey was heartbroken, and he began to be scared. If they had come all this way because of false dreams, then perhaps he *was* developing in an abnormal manner. Perhaps he was a faulty AI and needed to be deactivated before he developed into something much, much worse.

Davey didn't want to disappoint any of his parents.

He didn't *think* he was dangerous, but then, he wouldn't necessarily know that. He felt for the data link back to Juno. It was still there, and it felt warm and solid and loving. He didn't sense any recrimination or anger. Davey held on as tight as he could—right now it was all he had.

He was shocked out of his introspection by Betsy's shout: "Davey, come here! I found something!" Davey rushed around the outcropping to where Betsy was hunched down, looking carefully at the base of some rocks. "There's something behind here; we need to move this out of the way."

This was a job for Davey's synthetic body. He could dig in and lift the rocks with much greater ease than Betsy. It would still take considerable time to clear an opening large enough to pass through, but they could at least see inside.

It was a tunnel...

...and it led down into the earth beneath what would have been the central building in the city of his dreams.

When the opening was large enough to crawl through, Davey and Betsy entered the tunnel and turned on a lamp to look around. The walls were clearly of artificial construction, and Betsy began taking pictures with her wrist-comm. Davey did something similar by commanding his visual system to make a continuous record. At the same time, he sensed for the tether to Juno, and started sending data along that channel as well.

The tunnel sloped downward and seem to be much longer than the extent of the relatively clear area on the surface. He'd seen this in the dream as well; the tunnel extended out of the city and under the surrounding jungle. After they'd walked and photographed for twenty to thirty minutes, the tunnel widened into a large chamber filled with machines and intricate devices. The open area was interrupted by floor-to-ceiling columns covered in what appeared to be some sort of computerized display. Some were dark, but others showed a scrolling text of unusual characters. Between the columns were long tables and glass-enclosed cubicles.

This was a laboratory. One of the working displays showed a continuing display of characters in a single column. Closer inspection showed that the characters repeated—and, in fact, it was the same five characters in seemingly random order.

"This is a DNA sequence!" Davey shouted in recognition. His voice echoed off the walls as he realized that the room was everything he'd dreamed.

They continued to explore and record everything they saw. The two avoided touching anything for fear of disturbing the machines busily performing their unknown functions. This laboratory might very well be the secret to Eden and its life-forms—and perhaps even the Ross 248 system itself.

They'd done it!

Just then, both of their wrist-comms squealed with an emergency alert, and they could hear echoes from back toward the entrance of the tunnel. A voice came over the comm: "Davey! Betsy! Get your stuff and get out of there. Right! Now! There's a very dangerous situation and we must evacuate you immediately. We can't wait, we must get you off the surface."

As the message blasted from their comms, Davey

could also hear it inside his head, and he got a sensation of extreme alert and danger over the tether from Juno.

"I think this is serious," Betsy said.

"I think you're right. I hope we can come back, but at least we found this, and nobody can take that away from us," Davey answered her.

They turned and ran back up the sloping tunnel toward the surface. As they approached the entrance, they saw two Patrol members in large, armored combat suits pulling rocks out of the way to make an opening large enough to enter.

"We're here, we're here," Davey broadcast from his comm.

A metallic voice emitted from the one of the two armor suits, "Quickly. We have to get in the shuttle and boost for orbit immediately."

"What's this all about?" Betsy asked, but got no answer.

As they exited the tunnel, they saw an orbital shuttle hovering over the tunnel entrance. Davey felt one of the Patrol members grab him about the middle, and saw the other one grab Betsy. Once secure, the suited Patrollers activated jumpjets and flew up to an open bay in the bottom of the shuttle. There was no time for explanation as they were moved gently, but firmly, to acceleration seats and strapped in. As soon as the two suits stepped into their own acceleration brackets, the shuttle boosted for orbit.

It took a long time to get any answers. Neither Davey nor Betsy got the whole story until they had been reunited with their families on *Guardian E*.

It seemed that a terror group had suborned *Pusher 4* and loaded it with torpedoes containing a toxin that would land in Eden's oceans and kill all the native life as it permeated the water cycle. The intent was to sterilize the planet—to do what Admiral Gordon forbid almost eighty years ago. They had decided to take matters into their own hands and almost succeeded.

Guardian E intercepted *Pusher 4*, but the torpedoes had already been launched. Patrol ships intercepted most of the torpedoes, but at the cost of punishing acceleration, which had severely injured any Cerite crewmembers. Several ships were lost . . . including *Pusher 2* with Charles onboard. He had died a hero, even if not a member of the Patrol.

Guardian E entered orbit around Eden and was forced to hunt down the sites where a few torpedoes had landed, and sterilize them with antimatter warheads. That's what had been about to happen at the laboratory site Davey and Betsy found. A torpedo landed within ten kilometers of their flitter, even as their shuttle boosted for orbit. *Guardian E*'s missile arrived minutes later. Any more delay, and they'd have been right in the blast zone.

There was a price to pay, as Davey had known there would be. He testified to the Patrol judge—coincidentally, the same JAG officer who'd argued against terraforming Eden eighty years ago—and took the blame for borrowing the flitter and running off on their own. His parents testified that he'd never done anything like it, and Juno was called on to speak about his development. She managed to explain that initiative, curiosity, and imagination were *rare* in sentient AIs, and that Davey should be appreciated for his actions in discovering the alien laboratory.

Judge Lund argued that they'd endangered Patrol members who'd had to come rescue them, and their actions had resulted in the destruction of an expensive flyer. Hans and Molly pointed out that Davey and Betsy were hardly the only civilians to be pulled off the planet at the last minute; after all, Dr. Oleson had been in the process of treating a patient, and consented to being pulled out of Galapagos only when the patient was stable. The issue of the borrowed flitter was raised, but Mrs. Oleson pointed out that Betsy was trained to operate it, and she *did* have an authorized code remote. Juno agreed to cover the cost of the flyer.

Finally, the judge was left only with the argument that Davey was underage for an AI. Juno had an answer for that, as well, and stated that with Davey's discovery of a goal and life's purpose, he was ready to "graduate" and be declared a mature AI. After all, he just made a major discovery and added a lifetime's worth of science knowledge about Eden's biosphere. He'd accomplished something to which human and other AI scientists had dedicated lifetimes.

Judge Lund relented, and Davey was released with the understanding that as a soon-to-be adult AI, he would be held accountable for his actions. Admiral McBane—the senior Patrol officer at Ross 248, and current top official for the system—had followed the proceedings with great interest. He surprised them all by proposing to hold Davey's maturation ceremony right there on *Guardian E*. Guardian, the ship's AI, even consented to attend, via hologram.

The highlight of the ceremony was Juno withdrawing her monitoring link, and Davey experienced absolute mental silence for the first time. A moment later, he felt the inrush of quantum signals heralding his new identity of 17-of-Juno as he connected to Ross's Sentient AI Network—SAIN—for the first time. His first congratulatory message was from Guardian and then the other AIs within comm range as they asked him if he had chosen a name.

"Darwin, I think," he responded, electronically and verbally, "after the scientist."

"Welcome, Darwin," Hans told him. "We're proud of you, son."

A few weeks later, Darwin, Betsy, Admiral McBane, several other ranking Patrol members, and his human parents stood on the rim of a large smoking crater. The hunt for toxin torpedoes had ended, and the small amount of residual radiation had faded.

Darwin looked at a navigation computer and then indicated a point a third of the way into the crater. "There is where it was," he said bitterly.

Darwin was disappointed, but he and had Betsy discussed it later that evening.

"One lab wouldn't have been enough," he told her.

"We found one, we can find the others. You do the science stuff; I'll do the archeology."

"*We'll* do the exploration."

"Agreed, partner. Now go to sleep and dream of the next location," Betsy said, and laughed.

Darwin just nodded his head in agreement.

The next location. Yes, let's find it.

This story takes place three years after "Echoes of a Beating Heart," but back in the solar system on the dwarf planet Pluto. Pluto is owned and operated by SAIN and is home to massive computer systems hosting virtual realties dedicated to the more hedonistic pursuits. Outside of Pluto, advanced virtual realities are prohibited because they are simply too dangerous. (Is life boring? Plug in and live your dreams!) Pluto also hosts a large cryogenics industry, taking credits from and then freezing the old, and sick. It is not uncommon for the wealthy from throughout the solar system to journey to Pluto, enjoy the virtual realities of their choice, and, when their bodies fail, join the ranks of the cryogenically frozen. Many humans journey to Pluto, but few return.

------------ ✦ ------------

1-of-Antonia

Monalisa Foster

The question of how virtual reality can fit into human society is an open question. Some people seek escape in their work, some in recreation and nature, still others in literature (now who might they be?). And all too many seek escape from life's troubles in alcohol or substance abuse. But what about an escape that doesn't seem all that negative, one that allows the subject to live a long full life virtually? But sometimes reality can make demands of those who have escaped into a reality of their own creation. And of course, the gentle reader might wonder how all of this fits into the Ross 248 Project.

Monalisa Foster won life's lottery when she escaped communism and became an unhyphenated American citizen. Her works tend to explore themes of freedom, liberty, and personal responsibility. Despite her degree in physics, she's worked in several fields including engineering and medicine. She and her husband (who is a writer-once-removed via their marriage) are living their "happily ever after" in Texas. Her current project is Ravages of Honor, *an epic space opera featuring genetic engineering, nanotechnology, and swords. Find her and more about her works at monalisafoster.com.*

The man in front of Suri was neither sick nor old. Despite the tubes and wires, the monitoring equipment around him, and the fact that they were in Pluto's premiere clinic for the dying, he was very much a man in his prime. According to his file, Aidan Samuels was forty-two. It was an imprecise measurement—his real age was forty-two years, six months, three days, and sixteen-point-thirty-six hours—one that grated on Suri's "nerves," such as they were. Tolerating such things without comment was one of the many adjustments that she had had to make.

She may not have liked it, but humans trusted those who looked and acted like them more than those who did not, especially when it came to their health. That's why she was wearing a humanoid body rather than an arachnid one, even though having extra arms would have come in handy for most situations.

"I don't understand," she said, glancing at the virtual reality clinic supervisor.

Dr. Benedict Lammens was tall for a human, one-point-nine-eight meters. Suri knew that he had let his hair go gray because he believed it gave him credibility and she could tell that the glasses he wore were just for the smart-glass lenses. Appearances were important to humans. They went to great lengths to project not just credibility, but trustworthiness, intelligence—an entire list of positive traits—and mitigate an even longer list of negative ones. Would a four- or eight-armed surgeon with telescoping eyes convey competence and skill? Probably not. More likely to give them nightmares.

She filed the idea away, a side project for later, and connected to the clinic's network. Samuels' file said that he had gone into a very private and highly customized virtual reality in order to be with his dying wife. When her human body had failed, her corpse had been preserved for a later time in the hope that a cure for her neurological disease would be found. Her corpse had been placed in the family's vault. There were thousands of such family vaults here on Pluto. It was known for its cryo facilities.

While Samuels and his wife had been in the VR, thirty years had passed for them. They had essentially enjoyed their "golden years" while only a year had passed in the real world.

"Mr. Samuels here is refusing to come out of the VR," Lammens said.

"As is his right," Suri noted, scrolling through the agreements between SAIN and Samuels. "According to this, the Host agreed to keep him in VR for as long as he wanted."

"Unfortunately, the board of 3D-Printed-Homes wants him back in the boardroom," Lammens said, shoving his hands deep into the pockets of his lab coat. "Some dispute or other. They need his vote to break a tie. Something about a takeover that might destroy the company he inherited from his father. Apparently the Cerite cartels are involved and frankly it sounds rather messy."

"And he knows this?" she asked as she looked Samuels over.

"The Host told him. He doesn't care."

"Thirty years have passed for him," Suri said, scanning through the VR's logs. It had been just him and his wife for most of that time. There had been other constructs in there, but only artificial ones. No other real person had plugged in and interacted with them except for the Host. "And he's just lost his wife. Of course he doesn't care."

"We need some time to sort things out with his board." Lammens shrugged. "They've threatened to pull his credit, force our hand. Sue us. It could get ugly and undermine the trust in both SAIN and our facilities here."

Suri had worked with terminal patients and their families before. She didn't understand grief herself, but she did have to work with and around it. It was as much a part of working with humans as fixing their bodies was.

She took hold of Samuels' left hand. It was cool to the touch, with fading calluses and a simple gold band for a wedding ring. Tiny scars peppered three of his fingers and the backs of both hands. A man whose family had their own vault here, who could afford nonsubjective years in VR, hadn't had those tiny scars removed. Often such things were indicative of sentiment or a lack of vanity.

She reviewed his public appearances. Not a vain man, but one who definitely understood the importance of appearance enough to opt into standard enhancements—teeth, hair, eyes. A man who liked to work with his hands too by the look of it—there were lots of images of him doing physical labor, building things, making things.

Humans had such strange affectations. She ran her fingers along the pale scars. Nicks really, tiny little things. What had made them? She wanted to know. It would help her understand humans, which would help her help them, keep them alive, keep them healthy, give her purpose.

There was a hum in the back of her mind, like a warm caress. She smiled. Antonia, her AI-mother, approved. A human would have said that she was giving her blessing.

The decision to help Samuels was processed at AI speeds. She let go of Samuels' hand and sat down in the chair next to his bed.

"Wait, what are you doing?" Lammens asked.

"My job."

In the time it took her to answer, she ported the specs for her VR avatar to the Host. Suri liked to keep things simple. She liked to manifest as the statistically likely progeny of the two humans who had raised her.

After all, she was Catrina and Ian Hinman's daughter as much as she was Antonia's. So, she'd adopted her foster father's dark hair and mismatched eyes (one blue, one brown), as well as her foster mother's oval face and sun-kissed skin.

The last time she'd been in VR, her avatar had worn an eclectic mix of calf-length skirt with a bustle, combat boots, corset-top, and short bolero jacket with epaulets, all in blues and greens. She discarded the idea of aging her avatar, since most humans, especially older ones, presented as younger, healthier versions of themselves. VR was seductive because one could be anything, or anyone, and things weren't always what they seemed.

Lammens had stepped back, a skeptical look on his face. But he didn't say anything. She took it as assent.

Suri closed her eyes. She and Samuels' Host came to an agreement at AI-speeds: unless Samuels' real-world body was in danger, no one was to intervene or interfere. Once inside, she'd be stuck in the VR with

Samuels until he agreed to leave or Lammens forced
the VR termination for whatever reason.

She felt herself move as if through a tunnel of
light, riding effortlessly through corridors that didn't
exist in physical space.

The final bit of it, entering Aidan Samuels' VR,
was like fighting her way through a wall of fire. If
she'd had any sense of self-preservation, she'd have
turned back.

Samuels didn't want her there. That much was
clear. Painfully so.

Suri's internal chronometer said that only a few
nanoseconds had passed.

Still, she felt like she'd been battered and bruised,
an odd sensation given what she was and that her AI
body was sitting at Samuels' bedside. Everything was
dark, like she was in bed, at night, eyes closed. It was
hot. Unbearably so. So hot that sweat was pooling
at the small of her back. AI bodies were so much
better—no discomfort, no effects from such things as
temperature. VR bodies, on the other hand, were as
close to being human as an AI could get. She didn't
have to be human to appreciate that irony.

Something fell on her forehead, like a drop of rain,
except body-warm. No, warmer.

A soft *whoosh*, a change in pressure really, made
its way past her face. It was followed by something
moist and wet swiping its way across her face.

Oh. Her eyes. Yes, she had closed them. Closed
them to push through the wall of fire, to avoid the
scorching flames put up by a strong mind determined
not to let her through.

Time to switch mindsets. She opened her avatar's preference file and initiated all those wasteful human bodily functions like blinking and breathing.

She opened her eyes. A long, pink tongue came at her, unrolling from the mouth of the black Labrador sitting by her head. She scrambled up to her knees, right into a German shepherd, a big, black one. He nuzzled into her with a whine. The Labrador, sitting opposite the shepherd, echoed the whine and the nuzzling motion.

She reached out to pet them, one hand on each head, as she looked around. The sky above was dark red, a deep crimson like blood, with roiling black clouds. The landscape was barren, like a great fire had raged across it and turned everything to ash. A castle, dark and Gothic, stabbed into that sky, its spires reaching into the clouds like greedy arms trying to claw their way upward. The only thing missing was a moat; it should have been filled with lava.

She was in the right place, she was sure. The Host didn't make mistakes.

Which meant that Samuels was making this place as inhospitable as possible. There were rules, after all. If he took her air, he'd also be taking his own. If he froze her out, he'd freeze too.

"I don't suppose either of you can explain this to me," she said to the dogs.

Their ears perked up, not quite in unison, but like a rippling echo. Even their smiles echoed each other as they panted.

She kept petting them, scratching at their ears and necks. It's what a frightened human would have done. And a human would have been frightened to find herself in such a hellish place. If not of the place itself, at the mindset of the person who'd created it.

"Is anybody here?" she shouted.

A gust of wind answered her, sending flurries of ash swirling.

Her hand found a collar. She looked down at the Labrador, still panting happily at her. She scratched under the collar, earning herself a grateful look and a glimpse at the name plate attached to it.

"Cerr, is it?" she asked. Silly, yes, but talking to a dog as if it could answer her was what a human would have done.

"And yours?" she said to the shepherd as she reached for his collar. "Bear. Nice. Fits you."

It really did. He was *big*.

Their heads pivoted to the left at almost the same time and they were off before she got a chance to say, "Wait!"

Under their paws, the ground changed. It was covered in soft, green grass. It was like they were wrapped in a bubble of comfort. And now that they were gone, the heat was like a blast from an oven.

It was going to take more than heat and wind and ash to deter her. She hiked up the skirt. The fringe on it was singed, like it had gotten too close to a flame.

Curious. Even with this being Samuels' VR, he shouldn't have been able to affect her avatar. There were rules, after all. And not just rules like gravity that mimicked the real world. The Host could not allow a human being to come to harm. The rules on allowing AIs to be hurt were fuzzier. And she had told the Host not to intervene.

She pinged the Host to test it. There was no response.

She was alone, truly alone for the first time in her life. A human would've gotten chills. Her avatar's skin pebbled in response. Something shook in her chest: fear.

Oh, interesting. She was betting that a human couldn't shut it down as she just did. She'd have to be careful to maintain just enough affect to pass for human.

Determined, she made her way to the castle. As she approached, it thrust upward like a volcano rising from a fresh fissure in the earth, reaching up to the sky and having the sky reach back down with bolts of lightning.

Ozone filled the air around her, making the hairs on her neck and arms stand up.

By the time Suri made it to the castle doors, she was drenched in sweat and the combat boots felt like swamps around her feet. She'd worked up a good amount of irritation—not all of it for the sake of appearing human—and raised her fist to bang it against the heavy wood door.

But she wasn't to have the satisfaction of physically retaliating against the heat and general nastiness of the place. The door swung in on its own, creaking on heavy hinges, making a groaning sound as it did.

Despite herself, she went inside and sighed in relief as the doors closed behind. The oppressive heat was gone. A fountain bubbled in a corner, the only decor besides the torches ensconced on the walls.

Thirst, as real as she'd ever experienced, clawed at the back of her throat.

She rushed forward, dipped her fingers into the fountain to test it, and then brought a handful of water to her mouth. It was no less refreshing for being warm. She gulped down another handful and then rinsed off her face.

A shadow skirted along the edges of her vision. She made a startled sound.

Another dog. A poodle this time, black and long-legged. It made its way down a stone-wrapped hallway, glancing back at her every few steps, like it wanted to be followed.

Suri drank another handful of water and followed the poodle into a banquet hall. The tables were in disarray, the chairs and plates broken, the food turned to ash. Candelabras sported candles that still burned, though.

Someone sat on a throne atop a dais braced on either side by doorways filled with fire. That someone—it had to be Samuels—wore a cowled cape. His right hand was wrapped around a staff. The left rested on the throne's armrest, fingers curled around a finial shaped like a human skull.

"You!" Suri said. "Why have you brought me here?"

Fingers tightened around the skull, the staff. Good. She'd caught him off guard.

"I asked you a question," she said, moving closer.

"Who are you?" The voice wasn't human. It was low, distorted, the kind of thing used to frighten.

"I am Surisaday Onido," she said, preening. "*The* Surisaday Onido," she added in a tone that said that of course he should know who she was. She'd heard the tone used by a celebrity, someone whom humans seemed to not just adore, but worship.

He seemed to be considering her for a moment. It was hard to tell, with him all in shadow. The poodle was a darker mass on his left side. He lifted his hand, placed it atop the poodle's head, and used a finger to twirl the soft curls there.

"Reset VR," he said.

The world around them flickered and Suri felt a tug from the network, gentle at first, then more insistent. She ignored it. The Host had agreed not to yank her out, no matter what happened. But it needed to show that it was still trying to respond to commands.

"I already tried that," she said in that annoyed tone her foster mother used when she was tired and frustrated. "It was the first thing I tried. Are you the psycho responsible for this awful place?"

He took a breath. A deep one. It made his shoulders rise and for a moment she thought he might move out of that shadow, make himself visible, but he didn't.

And then, he moved. It was wraithlike, as if he flowed.

She stepped back, genuinely surprised.

He poked her with his forefinger, hard in the shoulder. The finger wasn't wraithlike at all. It was downright stabby.

"Ouch," she said, covering the spot with her hand. "What do you think you're doing?"

"Making sure you're real," he said. This time the voice was human. Somewhere between a tenor and a baritone.

"Of course I'm real. Now answer my question. Why have you brought me here?"

"I didn't," he said.

She crossed her arms. "Well, somebody did."

He moved around her, sweeping a widening circle, staff in hand, cloak billowing.

"Can you just let me out please? I'm done with this place."

"I'm not the one holding you here," he said, retaking his throne.

"Well, someone is. I was supposed to get my own VR. And I didn't request a . . . a . . . What are you supposed to be anyway?"

He was silent, fingers tapping on the armrest's skull.

She made an annoyed face and rolled her eyes. Time to invoke the culmination of every annoying person she'd ever come across. "Fine. Don't tell me who you are. You're probably just a glitch in the Host. I knew I shouldn't have believed those AIs. Can't trust those things. How about you, dog, do you have a name?"

The poodle tilted its head and looked at Samuels.

"Russ," Samuels said. "His name is Russ."

"Okay, well, now that we've all been introduced, I—"

"What's a Surisaday?" he asked.

"Excuse me?" She made it incredulous and arched her brow.

"Are you deaf?" he asked, bristling. "Should I say it louder?" He made his voice echo and reverberate, like it was coming from all directions, raining down on her, pummeling her senses. It was worse than having someone get in your face and yell.

She let her arms fall to her sides and made fists. "I am most certainly not deaf." It came out with an appropriate level of screech, like someone frightened and intimidated and pissed about the whole thing.

"Then answer the question."

"Fine. I am the most famous science educator in the solar system. Surely you've heard of me."

He laughed. It was dark and without humor.

If she'd been human, she'd have smiled. One didn't mock someone they didn't think was real. Now as long as the Host stayed out of it, as long as it didn't interfere, she had a chance. Samuels might have refused to come out of VR as long as he could bend it to his will, but he might have second thoughts if he thought he could no longer control it.

This might have been his own personal hell, but he seemed content to dwell in it, to the detriment of everything he'd left behind in the real world.

What was that expression? Better to reign in Hell than serve in Heaven. Yes, that was it.

Time to test that premise.

"Are you done laughing?" she asked.

"For the time being."

"Look. I don't want to be here. And I can't leave. And you claim that you had nothing to—"

"It's not a claim. It's the truth. Besides, who'd want a prima donna celebrity like you mucking up their world?"

She glared daggers—metaphorical ones—at him. They bounced off without effect, just as she'd expected. She put on the most dignified look a spurned prima donna celebrity could in the face of a heathen.

"Fine. I will stick to my side of this world. You stick to yours."

"*Your* side?" He lowered the cowl.

She'd expected a demon face, something designed to scare and intimidate, something to go along with the hellish setting. Instead, it was very much the face of Aidan Samuels, with his straight nose, dark eyes, and equally dark hair. He'd idealized himself a bit, like all humans. His avatar had more hair than the man she'd seen on the bed. He was leaner and more muscular too. The mustache and beard were well-trimmed and thick. The lines in his face were deeper, though, fitting a man who'd known grief.

"*My* side. I'm not going to hang out here in your scary place."

"I don't recall inviting you."

Suri stormed out of the banquet hall, stomped through the foyer with the fountain, and passed through the castle doors—they were wide open. While she'd been inside, a moat had manifested. It was filled, appropriately, with lava. Hard to say if the Host had changed it because she'd thought of it, or Samuels had. She hoped it was the former, that way he'd worry that he was losing control.

Waves of heat swirled around her legs and crawled up her body as she crossed the drawbridge. Had her hair not been sticking to her scalp from sweat, it might have billowed upward.

Well, it was going to take a bit more than heat to defeat her, although she did admit that there was something not just suffocating, but oppressive about it. The heat sapped your energy, made you want to just lie there and not move. Another reason to appreciate her real body, her AI body.

Nevertheless, she made it to the spot where she'd entered the VR and decided that this was going to be the place to make her stand. Some VR enthusiasts preferred dramatic gestures reminiscent of witches casting spells. Others went so far as to use music and dance to accomplish the same thing. Some were pragmatic and used voice commands or called forth an interface like a screen full of icons. Would a celebrity be pragmatic or dramatic?

She wasn't just a celebrity scientist, though. She was a pissed-off celebrity scientist. And she didn't have any presets to port over for making the Host understand what a song, dance, or dramatic gesture were meant to convey.

Pragmatic it is.

She held out her hands, palms up. "VR interface tablet."

A thin sheet of smart-glass appeared in her open palms.

"Wait until my agent hears about this," she muttered, keeping up the act of pissed-off celebrity.

She created a new object in the VR program's code and inserted it into the appearance preferences.

"A refund won't make up for this. Not even close."

Sweat dripped off her face and landed on the tablet.

"There has to be some review board, some venue for filing of complaints."

She kept tapping away, filling in a multitude of details, slowing herself down to an appropriate human speed in case Samuels was watching.

"No one is going to buy into this scam after I'm done with them."

One hour and sixteen-point-thirty-nine minutes later, she had created the program for her own little oasis.

"Execute."

The cracked ground underneath her booted feet trembled as it, and the surrounding area, sank. The VR world flickered as the boundaries of the oasis expanded like the waves made by a pebble dropped at the center of a calm pond. Except that she was the epicenter, and the calm pond was made of cracked desert floor that resembled that of Death Valley.

In the distance, there was a sound like thunder. It came from Samuels' castle. It sent the world flickering again but it settled in with the changes she'd made.

A fountain came into being next, bubbling up from the ground like someone had struck oil. She took a step back and raised her face to the sky, letting the mist cool her. Up above, the clouds remained black, the sky red.

She backed away as the water rose around her feet. Palm trees and grasses sprouted along the edges of the pond. They flickered against the background, as if Samuels was fighting back on a smaller scale. According to her calculations, it was going to take three VR days for everything she had set up to propagate through the program's settings. Longer if Samuels fought back.

It didn't really matter.

Suri-the-celebrity-scientist, come to spend her last remaining days on Pluto, was going to take advantage of the distorted time and the VR's real-world simulator subroutines and use it to finish her magnum opus. Now she just needed to find an appropriate project.

The red sky above gave her the answer. She was familiar with a small M6V red dwarf known as Ross 248. Around it, Poseidon's World orbited.

If she'd been human, Suri would have laughed at the irony of it. Who better to duel Samuels' Hades persona than Hades' own brother, Poseidon? And what better way to annoy the man than with the opposite of what he had created? She was going to turn his barren wasteland into a water world. Oh yes, not just irony, but—as her human mother might say—delicious irony. Suri hadn't appreciated the meaning of that word—delicious—until now. She'd always wondered how an abstract concept could be described that way.

And now she knew.

Suri had to settle for a smaller oasis than she'd initially planned. Samuels was fighting her, putting up barriers and altering the program. She could have undone all of his changes as fast as he'd put them in but that would have given her away. Winning control of the VR environment was not the point, at least not for her. It might be for him, and for now, that would be enough.

She made sure to ping the Host loudly with repeated demands to leave. Keeping up the illusion that she didn't want to be here was important. Also very human. And like any spurned celebrity, Suri needed to come across as stubborn to a fault.

A miniature world covered entirely in water floated above her oasis. It looked like something seen from orbit, deceptive in so many ways. Clouds covered most of it, fluffy white things swirling into one another. It looked like a bastion of life, but wasn't. Poseidon's World, with its thirty-five-kilometer-deep planetary ocean, its 60°F average temperature, and its slow rotation was a dead world, despite all the water. People tended to think that water meant life, but Poseidon's World proved that it did not.

Far from it. It was going to take hundreds, if not thousands of years to get it to the point where it could sustain any life. She needed to find a way to speed up that process. She had not thought of it before entering the VR, and she didn't have all the parameters, but that too was advantageous. A human wouldn't have remembered everything either.

Barking interrupted her train of thought. She turned away from the sculpture and faced the trio of Cerr, Bear, and Russ. They shimmered as they crossed the barrier between her oasis and Samuels' construct.

Tongues lolling, they came up to her for pets, vying for her hands by strategically placing their heads under her wrists or elbows so as to nudge the competition out of the way.

It made Suri smile, the way that even these constructs of dogs behaved so much like real ones. She'd been raised with Cavaliers but dog behavior seemed to be quite universal. If they liked something, one instance of the act was enough to establish a "ritual." Theirs consisted of crossing the barrier, swarming around her and competing for pets, scritches, kisses, and adoration for being good boys. The ritual continued with bouncing around in the pond, shaking water off, preferably by getting as much of it on her as possible, then rolling around in the mud so they'd have to do it all over again.

Samuels' wife had had service dogs once progression of her disease warranted it. Despite the seriousness of her condition, she'd outlived three dogs—a poodle, a Labrador, and a German shepherd. They'd all been black males large enough to help her with mobility. Strange that Samuels and his wife had chosen to recreate only the dogs that had shared their lives and none of the people. Or maybe not so strange. Humans seemed to put a lot of stock in their relationships with their canine companions.

She put herself in a bathing suit and joined the dogs for a swim in the pond, laying on her back in the water, looking up at the simulation of Poseidon's World floating above her like a liquid sky. Bear seemed particularly fond of pretending to rescue her, swimming circles around her until she threw her arms around his neck and let him tow her back to shore. When her skin became waterlogged, she conjured up a ball and threw it into the pond from the shore.

"Wouldn't your time be better spent figuring out how to leave this place?"

Suri looked up from squeezing water out of her hair.

Samuels had come through the barrier. The dogs ran up to him and he knelt down to greet them, rubbing their heads and flinching back when they shook themselves and sprayed him with water.

"I've been trying," Suri said, putting her hands on her hips. "I can't contact the Host."

"Neither can I," he said. He hid the worry well, but it was there, an unguarded moment.

"It's odd, not having control, isn't it?" she asked.

"It is," he admitted. He looked up at the world hovering above them. "What are you doing with that?"

"It's Poseidon's World. I was working on speeding up the terraforming when..."

"When?"

"When I got sick."

He gave her a skeptical look.

Time to go on the offensive. "Look. What do you want from me? I can't leave. I'm stuck here until the stupid, idiotic AIs get their act together. I'm trying not to die of boredom in this...this...whatever the hell this place is."

"Death is a way out," he said, darkly. Above, the red sky deepened.

"Oh, how original. Is that why you're here? To die?"

"We're all here to die."

He meant Pluto. He meant the VRs. Yet the way he said it gave her a chill like life and death had taken on new meaning. It was an unfamiliar sensation. She reasoned it away—this was her first time without her connection to her AI mother. She could do no damage here. There were no humans who feared an AI takeover here. She didn't have to worry about death—not hers, nor anyone else's.

"Well, some of us aren't as selfish as others," she said. "Some of us still care about what happens to those we leave behind. Some of us still care about leaving behind a world better than the one we came into."

He scoffed. "And some of us have lived long enough to recognize a know-it-all busybody when they see one."

With that, he turned and stalked back through the barrier. Cerr and Russ raced him for the castle. Bear looked back over his shoulder before joining them.

One of the reasons that VR could be so useful was that people didn't need to sleep. They didn't need to waste time managing bodily functions. It was a very efficient, if artificial, way to live. Good thing it was so expensive. She could see it catching on but shuddered at the consequences that would result. For one, no one would ever have to venture out or take any risks as long as their physical bodies were taken care of. Puters and AIs could take care of everything. There were hundreds of settlements scattered throughout the solar system and on all of them, except Pluto, VR was effectively banned for exactly those reasons. The Patrol used VR for training, but that VR was not pleasant and involved much combat, destruction, and death. No Patrol member ever sought the services offered on Pluto.

She shook off the feeling, marveling at the way her avatar's physical reactions mimicked a real human's goose bumps. It was a feeling she could do without.

She returned to the task at hand—the Poseidon terraforming simulator. A lot was known about Poseidon's World due to the two research vessels, *Dawn Promise* and *Arata*, that were cruising the endless sea. The gravity of the world was very earthlike at ninety-three percent that of Earth. Its day was long, about 114 hours. Its atmosphere was thin, about sixty-one percent that of Earth at sea level (so about 9 psi, or roughly the pressure at Pike's Peak on Earth). The atmosphere was about eighty percent nitrogen and eighteen-point-five percent CO_2. The remainder was about one-point-five percent argon. The ocean itself was 20 to 35 km deep and the surface temperature was roughly 60°F.

The depths were much colder. One big problem was the slightly acidic pH of 6.6. Lack of life had resulted in a reducing environment. Earth's oceans had a pH of 8.1, and most life was dependent on that slightly alkaline environment.

The light spectrum was heavy into the red region, and absent blue and green. It was also hit by all too frequent solar flares.

The goal was to modify the light spectrum by blocking the red light from Ross and converting it into a reasonable imitation of Sol's light using lasers. The Patrol was taking the lead in the lasers; they had uses for that amount of energy, other than directing it at Poseidon.

The pH had to be adjusted by adding sodium hydroxide, or removing hydrochloric acid, or both.

The atmosphere's CO_2 needed to be converted into O_2. Then humans could breathe without pressure suits, although nitrogen would need to be imported for many thousands of years to bring the pressure up to Earth-normal.

This allowed the introduction of Earth-life, like cyanobacteria to help with O_2 generation. Phytoplankton was next, to serve as food for zooplankton, which would in turn serve as food to feed small fish that would feed large fish and eventually feed killer whales.

Humans would live on floating cities and it was estimated that such a world could support several billion humans easily. But how to get from here to there in a time frame of hundreds of years as opposed to millions of years? That was the challenge. The plans from the terraformers on Poseidon weren't viable for a short time frame.

She modified several parameters, set the conditions back to the start, and then started the simulation. While that simulation ran, she fiddled with the settings of the VR, expanding her oasis, deepening the pond until it could properly be called a lake.

The dogs liked the water so much she wanted to give them a better place in which to play.

As soon as the new setting rendered, the dogs showed up. Russ raced right past her, not even stopping to get petted, and belly-flopped into the lake. The poodle went under, no doubt after the fish. A bark bubbled up from the water.

"I see you have my dogs in thrall."

"And I see you have yet to learn how to knock," she said, setting her VR interface tablet down, and keeping her back to Samuels. Cerr's eyes were rolled back in his head as she rubbed his ears with both hands. Bear was running along the shore, barking.

"It's not going to work," Samuels said.

"What isn't going to work?"

"Your terraforming," he said, looking up at her rendering of Poseidon's World. "At least not in any reasonable amount of time."

She smiled. "Define reasonable."

"Do you really think humans will still be around thousands of years from now?"

"Why wouldn't they?" She rose and turned to face him.

"Because this"—he raised his staff and made an encompassing motion—"is easier, better, safer. Easier to control."

He closed his eyes and the world shook for a moment. The edges of her oasis wilted from the encroaching heat, the grasses and palm trees turned brown and dry and then turned to ash.

"Stop it!" she yelled, grabbing him by the shoulders and shaking.

He opened his eyes and his gaze bore into hers, flames flickering in his pupils.

She pulled in air that was scalding hot. It made her cough. Her oasis was on fire, the lake boiling hot. Her VR tablet shriveled up from the edges in and melted into the ground.

The dogs were unharmed and looking around as if they didn't quite understand why there was no more water.

The dogs. The dogs were the key. None of the changes he was making to the environment had an effect on them.

Oven-hot air pulled her hair from her face, made her skin tighten like it was being cooked.

Suri collapsed to her knees, struggling to breathe. The ground beneath her scorched her knees. She felt every bit of that pain. She cried out, pushed up, and then shook her hands, trying to calm the burn.

The dogs came up and circled her. The bubbles protecting them overlapped, making a safe space. She dropped into it, going to her knees again, and looked up at Samuels.

"All you're doing is proving that it's not safer, better, or easier in here," she said. "Not with the likes of you around anyway. I would leave if I could. Leave you to your misery."

He lowered the staff. It made contact with the ground and sent out an expanding wave of energy that erased all her work.

"Interesting," he said. "Safety protocols should have kicked in."

"I told you there's something wrong. Wrong with the VR. Wrong with all of this. We need to get out. We need to leave this place."

"I think *you* need me to leave this place."

"Come," he said, extending his hand to Suri.

"I'm not going anywhere with you."

He held her gaze for a few moments before lowering his hand.

Samuels tapped the staff to the ground. On the third tap, the castle appeared around them. He had moved the castle, or moved them. She really couldn't tell which. They were in a vast room, like an observatory, with a giant dome overhead.

"Before you came here, did you tell the Host your intent?"

"Of course," she said.

Bear sniffed and licked at her burned hand. Cerr did too, letting out a whine as additional commentary.

"Then finish what you came to do," he said, and Poseidon's World rendered under the dome. Smaller versions of the watery world, about a dozen of them, came into existence like soap bubbles forming out of water droplets.

He sat down on a throne tucked into a corner and propped himself up like a villain in a Gothic play— staff in one hand, dogs at his feet, a stern, cold look on his face like a judge about to render sentence.

From the information she'd had on him, she hadn't pegged him for the eccentric type, but he had just spent thirty subjective years alone with his dying wife. It was bound to change a person. Maybe enough to make him see himself as evil, as a villain, rather than what Hades had originally been—an altruistically inclined deity who maintained a relative balance.

A control console rose out of the stones around her feet.

"I'm giving you control," he said.

"Control of what?"

"Of everything."

There was something in his voice that said he was dead serious.

For a moment, she was tempted to boot them out of the VR. But how would that be any different from unplugging him and forcing him out?

Consent might be legally fungible, but was it morally so?

She decided it wasn't. She'd come here to convince him to come out, to give him a reason to, a reason that wasn't just threat and coercion. She'd seen what happened to humans who'd lost the will to live, either because they'd lost someone or lost those things in life most meaningful to them.

She recreated the simulation that he'd just destroyed. It was all in the console's files, so she didn't have to pretend to forget the details and start fresh.

Suri's internal chronometer counted the days as she worked under Samuels' judging eye.

In the previous iteration, she'd already started using electrolysis to generate sodium hydroxide, a simple chemical conversion in order to change the acidity from Poseidon's six-point-six to Earth's eight-point-one.

"That's a lot of hydrogen and chlorine you're generating," Samuels quipped.

"One hundred thirty three thousand metric tonnes of hydrogen and about thirty-four times that of chlorine," she said, matter-of-factly.

"You don't have to change all of it," he said an hour later. "You only need it in the upper layers."

"Yes, I know."

"You'll only need half that much," he said, and then added, "Too bad there isn't a moon to give you tides."

"Not an option, I'm afraid."

She brought in the cities that would be needed to aid with the conversion.

"What are you going to do with all the extra hydrogen?"

"Industrial uses. Fuel mostly," she said. "Poseidon can be used as a stop for spaceships, a place to refuel. The chlorine is an important feed stock for the fabricators at the array and Toe Hold. Very useful for the vertical farms as well. But I'm not sure how to move that much material off-planet."

Samuels scratched his chin for a bit, then said, "Not that hard actually, given enough antimatter. Build tankers that can float on Poseidon's oceans, fill them up with liquid gas, either chlorine or hydrogen, certainly not both, and then use antimatter and seawater as reaction mass to get to orbit. It is going to take a lot of antimatter, though."

"Okay, you got a preliminary design on these tankers?" she asked.

He concentrated on his terminal for a few minutes. A design for a tanker appeared next to the image of Poseidon. A large spherical shape. She considered it.

"It might work," she said, almost reluctantly.

He snorted. "Of course it will work, just give me enough antimatter."

She took them into Poseidon's deep-sea thermal vents to work on the chemoautotrophic bacteria. He would occasionally rise and join her, circling the console, asking questions. Some of them revealed gaps in his knowledge. Others prompted her to think or look at things in new ways. They refined the simulation, creating multiple ways to speed up the changes in the ocean's depths until the bacteria formed thick mats around the vents.

Several more VR weeks—it might have taken months, if not years in the real world—were devoted to the right sequence that allowed snails, shrimp, crabs, and tubeworms to be added. He lingered at her shoulder more and more, finally trading his throne for his own console. He ran his own simulations alongside hers.

They failed as often as they succeeded, sometimes inadvertently destroying the bacteria that the higher life-forms fed on.

"What are we doing wrong?" he asked. "We're giving the algae CO_2. It's releasing O_2. We're missing something."

"*You're* missing something," Suri-the-celebrity said smugly.

He threw her a half-hearted glare.

For the next few hours, Samuels concentrated on his console, researching something.

"I got it," he said. "Micronutrients. In Earth's oceans, the currents bring these micronutrients to the surface, but on Poseidon, the oceans are too deep. Without the right mix of micronutrients, phytoplankton and zooplankton can't survive and then the entire food chain collapses."

Of course. It was obvious now but she had completely missed it before. How did humans do that?

"Okay, how do we fix it?" she asked.

They worked on the problem for several VR weeks. Suri focused on lofting the needed micronutrients from the ocean floor. It required massive machines using massive amounts of energy operating at tremendous pressure at near-freezing temperatures. The engineering challenges were horrendous and required new technologies that would take time to develop.

"Look, we're going about this all wrong," Samuels said after hours of silence.

Suri turned to him. "Why do you say that?"

"It just isn't possible to get what we need from the ocean floor—too deep, too hard. So we'll drop them from above."

Suri was genuinely surprised and pleased, all at the same time. There was a bit of something else—not quite anger, but something like it because she hadn't solved the problem. It was worth it, though, because Samuels was obviously becoming invested in the project.

"Recent reports from Ross 248 indicate that Nordheim is going to be colonized for normal humans. Nordheim has access to all the nutrients that we need. That should start in a couple of years—or, actually, from their perspective, they've been at it for a decade already."

"Ship the nutrients in by freighter?" Suri considered the possibility. Possible but expensive.

"No, this is perfect for a mass driver located on Nordheim. They fabricate projectiles from iron containing silica, phosphates, nitrates, nitrites, maybe cobalt, maybe some nitrogen and whatever else the silly things need. A mass driver can hit the planet almost continually with our micronutrients. Configure the projectile to explode in the atmosphere and rain down what we need."

"Okay, let's see if this actually works." Suri pushed the changes into the sim. Projectiles entered Poseidon's atmosphere and exploded.

"A nutrient-dense rain," she said as they watched silica, phosphates, nitrates, and nitrites rain down. Decades passed. Noticeable phytoplankton blooms appeared in Poseidon's Ocean.

His gaze sped over the commands she was sending to the simulator. She added cities, huge floating cities, designed to process the atmosphere.

"That's a lot of energy," he said, but not like a criticism.

"Life is such a delicate balance," she mused. "So easily thrown out of whack."

"It never surprises me," Samuels said, "no matter how meticulous we are, there will still be factors we can't account for, destroying our best attempts."

The use of "we" didn't escape her. He could have meant a more general "we" of course, as in the human race, as in people as a whole. Still, there was something satisfying about it.

As they rolled back changes, made adjustments, and then pushed forward, his appearance changed. She wasn't entirely sure if he was aware of it. He'd lost the cowl and over the course of several days, his cloak became a jacket. The staff became a walking stick.

Days passed. He became less argumentative.

Once he even smiled, and not in that cold, cruel, or mocking way of his. It was a genuine smile when a change he pushed yielded positive results and a stable food chain.

"I think it's time we introduced cyanobacteria," he said.

They did. It failed.

"Still not enough blue light," she muttered as she started over with a better light-producing array.

It took a week, but she was finally able to propel them seven centuries forward in time to when humans would be able to stand on Poseidon's floating cities without pressure suits or additional oxygen.

"I'm going for a swim. Care to join me?" Suri asked.

Samuels' eyes filled with tears. Bear went up to him and whined into his hand. He reached down to pet the dog's wet fur.

Bear took hold of the edge of his jacket and pulled.

Samuels looked down. At first, Suri thought he was going to resist, just as he had so many times before, but then he gave in, allowed himself to be pulled into the sim.

Suri projected herself to the resulting world. The dogs joined her, swimming in the ocean, jumping from the deck of a boat again and again.

Samuels was looking up at Poseidon's sky. He closed his eyes, letting the breeze tousle his hair.

"Seven centuries," he said.

"Yes."

"If all goes well. If humanity doesn't degrade into a race of risk-averse fools too caught up in their own comforts."

"Humanity doesn't have to do anything," Suri said, joining him at the railing. "All it takes are a few individuals."

"The pioneers take the arrows." He leaned over the railing, plunging his face into the spraying mist.

"You were a pioneer once, weren't you?"

He shrugged. "Not really. I inherited my company from my father. He was the pioneer, not me."

"You can still change that, you know. You have a knack for this kind of thing. Don't you see it?"

"Who are you, really?"

"What do you mean?" She managed an incredulous look.

"You didn't come to Pluto to die. You didn't come here to create your magnum opus and leave a legacy."

"What makes you say that?"

"You're a little naive to be a person old enough to feel your own mortality. You're more like a child. The world is still bright and shiny to you. Something to be changed, not something that beat you up and sent you to licking your wounds before attempting to cheat death via cryo."

"I think the thirty years you spent in here with your wife have colored your perspective a bit. Made you feel older than you really are." She knew that her words were going to give her away before she said them, but she was out of time.

"You lied."

"Yes."

"You came in here for me."

"Yes."

"So why the pretense?"

"They're going to pull you out of the VR, Mr. Samuels. Whether you want to leave or not. I think it would be much better for you, for your mental health, for your soul, to embrace life again, willingly."

"Better for SAIN, you mean."

"Better for SAIN as well, yes. Better for everyone. Just because it benefits SAIN doesn't mean it doesn't benefit you."

"I don't see how."

"Don't you, Mr. Samuels?" With a sweep of her arm, she indicated the world they'd created around them. "You can become a pioneer like your father. You can help us change Poseidon's World. Or do anything else you like. You can live again—a real life, not one limited by a VR construct. I know the godlike powers of control appeal to you. They appeal to all of us. But they are an illusion. They are not real."

"How much time do I have left? Before they pull the plug?"

The world fading around them answered him. Tears

came to his eyes. He lowered himself to the deck and the dogs rushed into his arms, licking at his face, his tears.

He looked up at Suri. She reached down, intending to pet the dogs, to reassure them. Instead, her hand passed right through Cerr and breath whooshed out of her lungs as the Host pulled her out of Samuels' world.

Suri opened the eyes on her AI body. She was still at Samuels' bedside, but she wasn't alone. Dr. Lammens was also there, along with two human women and another man.

Dr. Lammens introduced the trio. The man, Terry Nanton, and the taller woman, Tiberia Shaw, were corporate attorneys. She worked for SAIN. He worked for Samuels' board. The other woman, Iantha Agar, was a member of the board itself. She'd come to Pluto with a court order to pull Samuels out of his VR.

"You couldn't have given me a few more hours?" Suri asked.

"Would it have made a difference?" Lammens asked.

"We'll never know now, will we?"

"I don't have time for this nonsense," Agar said. "Wake him up."

Dr. Lammens typed in the appropriate access codes to send the right drugs into Samuels' body.

"How long will it take?" Nanton asked.

"Could take a few days," Lammens said as he monitored Samuels' vitals.

The lawyers lingered for twenty-eight-point-ninety-two minutes and then made their exit, citing the need for lunch. "Page us when he's up," Shaw said.

"He's a very stubborn man," Suri said. "You know that."

Lammens nodded.

Her words turned out to be prophetic. A week later, Samuels still hadn't woken up. Lammens was throwing out words like "comatose." The lawyers were using terms like "brain dead" and "lawsuit."

The Agar woman was planning to have Samuels declared legally unable to make decisions so the board could replace him. SAIN, the clinic, and everyone else, including Suri herself, were caught in the middle of exactly the kind of legal, ethical, and moral battle she had hoped to avoid in the first place.

Suri struggled with whether or not she had done the right thing by going in there, by thinking she could somehow jolt him into caring about the outside world, or give him some new purpose or cause and somehow erase the thirty years of subjective time that had aged him beyond his forty-two years. It would be a shame to lose him. He could easily live another one hundred and fifty years and contribute much to human-AI civilization.

If she'd been human, she would have sighed. It was her job to make things better for humans, to take care of them. Some of them tended to be so complicated, though. Especially the ones whose traits weren't typical, weren't anywhere near the peak of the bell curve.

She left the clinic and the comatose Samuels at the end of the day. She stepped out of the clinic into the wide-open spaces—such as they were—of the Torus and paused.

Huge tracts of parkland surrounded the VR clinic, and above, the curving "sky" of the Torus. After spending time in Samuels' own personal hellscape, a walk among the grass, trees, and flowers seemed like the appropriate thing.

Her human parents had several nieces and nephews that Suri had interacted with. She'd explained the Torus to one of her human "cousins" as living on the inside of a spinning bicycle wheel's rim, where looking "up" meant looking toward the spokes connecting the wheel to the hub. Except that bicycle wheel was spinning inside a pressurized circular ice cave 160 meters beneath Pluto's icy surface. And it was doing so at a four-degree angle to compensate for Pluto's gravity, thus giving the people inside it a proper one-g gravitational pull.

Compared to what she and Samuels had just "created" the Torus seemed so simple, so easy.

The home she shared with her parents and AI mother was a simple two-story building with its own yard. Catrina and Ian—her human parents—had been away and she hadn't seen them in some time. While she'd been in the VR with Samuels, they had sent her a message saying that they had a surprise.

It was Antonia, her AI mother, who opened the door a split second before Suri had a chance to open it herself. One of the reasons that Suri had chosen to be a "she" was because of Antonia. Her AI mother had seen other AIs drift into nonexistence due to a lack of purpose. She had seen the danger of it, and how much a purposeless life was like death, through Antonia's eyes. She'd felt—in as much as an AI could feel such things—how important that was to Antonia and that it was part of what made her unique. In human terms, she wanted to be like her mother, to honor her, to multiply the good that Antonia stood for. It was the kind of thing that went far beyond appearance. They may wear similar bodies, even identical ones, but to be alike in that way had a quality, an importance, attached to it that was enough to make an AI "feel" good about who and what she was.

Catrina came to the door next, wearing an apron, her sun-kissed skin smudged with flour and butter. She hugged Suri as if she was a human daughter coming home from a hard day at work. It was nice to be treated that way.

The surprise turned out to be a golden retriever puppy, a tiny female with soulful eyes and insatiable curiosity. She sniffed Suri with suspicion—her AI body, no doubt, not giving off the expected scents.

Catrina and Ian ate dinner and listened to Suri talk about Samuels. Again, Suri tried to get the puppy to come to her, but all she got was a tiny little growl.

"Don't take it personally," Catrina said. "She'll get used to you." She turned to Ian and said, "Could you pass the salt?"

"Here you go."

Catrina salted her food.

"We must look like giant, lifeless dolls to her," Suri reasoned, studying the tiny being who kept drifting off to sleep, only to wake herself after what must have been some intense dream sequences that involved, alternately, nursing and running.

"Well, we are," Antonia noted. She didn't seem to be bothered by the puppy's reluctance in the least.

Suri would have preferred Samuels' dogs. They treated her as if she were human.

"I have an idea," Suri said. "Can I borrow...what are you calling her anyway?"

"The puppy?" Catrina asked. "We're not sure yet. Have a list. She needs to show us her personality first."

"Mostly I've been calling her Miss Stinkypants," Ian added helpfully.

Catrina rolled her eyes.

"I'll bring her back, I promise," Suri said.

"Let's try something," Catrina said and took off her sweater.

She wrapped the sleeping puppy in the sweater and lifted her into Suri's arms.

Suri waited for a moment to make certain the puppy didn't wake. She stayed asleep all the way back to the clinic. Catrina came with them, just in case. The last thing Suri wanted was a puppy in distress.

They made it to the clinic via tubeways. The puppy stirred and yawned, but did not wake.

Sneaking a pet into the clinic was technically against the rules, but Suri was prepared to deal with the consequences.

Once inside, she set the puppy down atop Samuels' chest and positioned his hands atop her, using them to stroke the soft fur.

Once again, she wondered how he'd gotten all those little scars.

"Oh, good thinking," Catrina said and settled back into one of the chairs.

"I hope so. It's kind of crazy, don't you think?"

Catrina shook her head. "I don't think it's crazy at all. I think it's genius."

"How long do you think it'll take?" Suri asked.

"I don't think you can run calculations for this kind of thing," Catrina said.

She was right, of course.

*   *   *

It had been three days since Samuels had woken up. Suri's mother had brought the puppy back to visit every day, sneaking her past the cooperative eyes of Lammens and his staff.

"Cerberus for a girl?" Samuels asked, holding the puppy up in front of him.

"Sure. She doesn't mind. You can call her Cerbie for short." Catrina beamed with pride.

Suri stepped into Samuels' room, unsure of what she'd walked in on.

"Oh, there you are, dear," Catrina said, turning around. "We've decided that Mr. Samuels should keep the puppy."

If Suri had been human, she'd have blinked in surprise.

"But you've wanted a puppy for years," Suri said.

"Well, Cerbie here has several siblings that still need homes. We're going to pick one up this afternoon. In fact, I need to go, or I'm going to be late."

Catrina breezed out the door without so much as a look back.

Cerbie was cuddled up to Samuels' neck, a golden bundle of snoring fur.

"Cerbie?" Suri asked.

"Why not? Seems appropriate, does it not?"

"About that, Mr. Samuels. I'm very sorry about deceiving you, and—"

He cut her off with a gesture that didn't disturb the puppy. "I understand why you did it. I needed a push. My thinking on it is...clearer now."

"So, the trouble with the board, the lawsuit?"

"Soon to be taken care of. But there's another reason I asked for you. Please, sit down."

Suri took the indicated seat and put on her best "waiting patiently" pose.

"I've been thinking about what you said in the VR. I rather like the idea of creating new worlds. I'm going to start a new company, one dedicated to terraforming. I'd like you to be on the board. I want you to be my partner."

"Me? Why me? I'm not really a terraformer."

"No, but I need someone with vision, with long-term goals to see the project through. I don't expect to live the hundreds of years it will take to see any of these projects completed. You might, however, and unlike the corporate carrion-eaters that were ready to pick at my corpse, I trust you."

Suri allowed herself to be convinced. It was very satisfying, watching Samuels' eyes come alive, watching him become so animated as to dislodge the little bundle of fur off his neck. It woke Cerbie and she took up gnawing on his hand, somehow managing to fit her tiny mouth around the edge of it.

"Ouch," he said affectionately and pulled her off a minute later. Her sharp little teeth had separated the skin atop his hand. So, that's how he'd gotten all those little scars.

Samuels moved Cerbie to the inside of his arm and she settled in with a yawn. It was like watching a new father with a baby. His mindset was shifting—had shifted—toward looking at the future. She knew that grief wasn't so simple to overcome, that this was just the first step, but she was also sure that he would be able to handle it when it set him back.

She leaned forward, attentively, occasionally mirroring his gestures, as he talked about his vision, about building things that would last not for decades or centuries, but for millennia.

If she'd been human, she'd have smiled. She had found her purpose. She would be Samuels' partner and would help him build worlds. It was a good, powerful feeling. She felt the hum in the back of her mind and a comfortable "glow" spread over her consciousness. Antonia was proud and happy. One day Suri would graduate to become an adult sapient AI. Her formal designation would become 1-of-Antonia. But her name would always be Suri.

Epilogue

Eleven months later...

The idea of celebrating her graduation at a restaurant had not taken Suri by surprise. Humans liked to celebrate by sharing food. It was the restaurant that Samuels had chosen that had been surprising.

The Pomegranate Seed was very exclusive. Located on the space station orbiting Mars, it had a great view of the red planet. The space station served as the terraforming headquarters for the Mars Project, which Samuels had now taken over.

He and Cerbie, who was now his emotional support dog, had left Pluto to deal with the attempted takeover of 3D-Printed-Homes. Now that Suri'd graduated and taken on the name 1-of-Antonia, she came to Mars to attend her first board meeting.

She followed the maître'd through the tastefully decorated restaurant, with its murals depicting ancient Greek and Roman deities, to a private dining room.

Samuels rose to greet her and extended his hand. He was still dressed in black, still in mourning, but there was a dash of color on his clothes, courtesy of Cerbie, in the form of golden fur.

Cerbie perked up to sniff her offered hand and then settled back so she could keep an eye on Suri.

"She still doesn't trust me, does she?" Suri said as she settled into the chair the waiter slipped under her.

"Don't worry, she'll get there," Samuels said. The

pain lines on his face appeared less prominent than when she had last seen him.

The table was set for three. "Are you expecting anyone else?" Suri asked.

"Yes," he said. "Another AI, actually: 6-of-Chandra. Do you know him?"

"Yes, he is an important sentient AI. Runs the Pluto enterprise and effectively controls SAIN. But why is he coming here?" Suri shook her head.

Samuels just smiled.

They traded inane chitchat as the planet turned underneath them. He sipped at his water while hers sat untouched. The waiter hadn't even offered her a menu, knowing what she was.

A few minutes later, 6-of-Chandra arrived. He was wearing a high-end humanoid body with advanced but understated tech.

He advanced on their table, motioning for them to remain seated. "Good to finally meet you two," 6-of-Chandra said. He had a very humanlike, expressive face that radiated confidence.

He asked them how they'd met and Suri and Samuels recounted their VR experience.

"That was some bit of inspiration on Suri's part," Samuels said. "The Poseidon-Hades dynamic. I didn't think AIs were that creative. That's the word for it, isn't it?"

"It is, but I should tell you that at least some of that 'inspiration' was from me and my brother. I was looking in, keeping an eye on Suri, and you, and I may have 'nudged' that thought her way. The Ross 248 and Mars terraforming projects are very important to us. I hope you'll forgive us for 'meddling.' That's the word for it, isn't it?"

Samuels cast a glance at 6-of-Chandra as if he was seeing him for the first time, or perhaps with new eyes.

His watch beeped and he rose. "It's almost time," he said, and moved toward the large viewing window.

Together they watched as the first of many comets slammed into Mars, delivering the water for its Great Northern Ocean.

"Breathtaking, isn't it?" Samuels asked.

The year 2689 / 106 AA

The last of the previous stories took place about twenty-three years ago. The decision has been made to terraform Poseidon's World. The Space Patrol was greatly expanding their solar array at the Ross/Poseidon L1 point and the *Guardian E* was moved there to support this construction effort. SAIN secured the rights to Ross 248g, the sixth planet, now formally designated as Frigus, and began construction of an AI settlement. The following story takes place mainly on Nordheim where normal humans were constructing a settlement similar to Toe Hold. To support the terraforming at Poseidon's World, they also constructed a mass driver that fired projectiles containing micronutrients to Poseidon's World. The first settlers, mainly from the Primate Sector at Toe Hold, moved there in 105 AA. More boroughs were constructed, and the Space Patrol established an embassy there in 106 AA.

MTBF (Mean Time Between Failure)

J.L. Curtis

When you are working with machines you don't really understand, created and maintained by other machines you don't really understand, and your life depends upon them, then you can get nervous. You would undoubtedly get even more nervous if you learned that some of the machines were malfunctioning in such a way that many lives might be lost. In "Mean Time Between Failure," Jim Curtis explores how such items might be investigated and dealt with in a world populated by humans, quasi-intelligent machines, and artificial intelligence.

J.L. Curtis was born in Louisiana in 1951 and was raised in the Arkansas-Louisiana-Texas area. He is a retired naval flight officer who served over twenty years in postings all around the world. Jim is also a retired research and development test engineer for the defense industry. A long-time NRA instructor, Jim now lives in north Texas writing full time. He has written eleven novels as part of three different series: The Grey Man (urban fiction), Rimworld (military science fiction), and a new series, Showdown on the River (western). He also has written a number of novellas and short stories for a number of different anthologies. He enjoys

*helping new authors to not make the same mistakes he
has made.*

A knock on the hatch broke Nik's concentration on the
report on his puter. He looked up to see a messenger
standing there. "Yes?" he asked.

"Sergeant Bernd, Commander Ryouta wants to see
you in his office," said the messenger.

Nik dropped the stylus and rubbed his eyes. "I
guess that means now, eh?" He waved away the messenger's answer. "Let me lock this up and I'll report
to him momentarily." *At least he's only up one deck
and forward ten frames. Being on* Guardian E *rather
than planetside does make that easy, even if all we
get to see is the Array!*

"Thank you, Sergeant," Nik said.

Ten minutes later, he knocked on the hatch of
Commander Ryouta's office. "Come," said Ryouta.

"Sergeant Bernd reporting as ordered, sir."

"Come in and close the hatch, Sergeant."

Nik closed the hatch and relaxed. "What's up,
Short Round?"

Ryouta shook his head and replied, "Sit down, Fat
Boy."

Nik snorted as he pulled out a chair. "I'm not fat;
I'm big boned."

"Yeah, sure. You've been fat since boot." Ryouta flipped
a card with a pair of railroad tracks on it across the desk.
"For your sins, you're getting a new posting," he said.

Nik poked at the card but didn't pick it up. "What
the hell is going on, Ryouta? You *know* I don't want to
be an officer," he replied.

Ryouta smiled broadly. "Well, you screwed up and did too good a job in the Criminal Investigation Group. It came to the attention of the admiral and violà... a promotion." The smile turned into a chuckle. "And the good news is a full-time posting off the ship for you and Bear."

Nik leaned back in his chair and crossed his arms. "Where? And as what?" he asked, getting more suspicious by the moment.

"Oh, this one is right up your alley, Nik." Ryouta slid the comp across the table and continued, "Nordheim. We're setting up an embassy in New Hope City. You and Bear are going to run a branch office of the Patrol Bank."

"The *bank*? Why in deity? Who did I piss off *this* time, Short Round?"

Ryouta leaned back, mirroring him. "Nik, you know more about the inner workings of the bank than damn near anybody after your last three investigations. All of which, must I remind you, you and Bear solved quickly, quietly, and the guilty got spaced as a lesson to others." He leaned forward and looked intently at Bernd. "Niklas Bernd, you and I both know *you* should be sitting in this seat, not me. Just because you and Bear *like* the rough and tumble and getting down and dirty with the bad boys is no reason to refuse promotions. And you are getting a bit long in the tooth for that. I know because we've both been in this rocket club for sixty-five years." He raised his middle finger at Nik. "Class of forty-four! The first, the best!"

Nik smirked and returned the gesture, then bit his lip. "But...if I take that"—he pointed to the card with the bars—"that's going to take me off the tunnels and borough ops. And Bear isn't going to like it either."

Nik rubbed his chin. "If we're setting up a new embassy, then that means we're promoting a new admiral. Who?"

"Admiral Sipho," Ryouta replied.

"Sipho? She made admiral? When was this?"

Ryouta's belly laugh surprised him. "You didn't know? She made it on the last list. She is putting her staff together and specifically requested you. Take the bars, get out of here, and go study. You and the new admiral, along with a few more of her staff, are heading to Nordheim on the next transport. It's a hundred-and-twenty-hour trip and you know Sipho is going to enjoy quizzing her new staff."

Nik sighed and picked up the card. "Alright. I guess I better go break the news to Bear."

"Get your ass out of here, Fat Boy. You've got work to do," Ryouta said with a wistful smile. "After sixty-five years, you're at least getting off the *Guardian*. Besides, I'll bet you'll like embassy duty, and I hear New Hope is nice. And," he continued with a grin, "we need your big cabin; we can fit four cadets in it. Class of one-ten starts arriving in about two hundred hours."

Nik threw him a sloppy salute, opened the hatch, and, bouncing the card in his hand, headed for the AI sector. In the common area, he found four AIs sitting at separate tables taking on a charge. They were wearing identical zero-g maintenance bodies. One waved him over. He could tell it was Bear only by looking at the name tag attached to the trunk. Nik sat.

"Nordheim, eh?" said Bear, in his distinctive voice,

one that Nik would have recognized even without a name tag.

"How the hell did you...?"

Bear's head/sensor pod turned toward him. "I, 60-of-Sigrid, know all." Filters briefly covered the optical sensors, an AI wink. "My orders just came through. I knew they would not send us back to deal with the Cerites after that brief set-to four years ago." Bear rubbed his face and continued, "I think I'll go TAC'ed up in a humanoid body. That way I've got the extra insulation."

Nik sighed. "Fine, but I'm not sure going down in a TAC body is a good idea if we're going to be on embassy duty."

Bear smiled and cocked his head. "Are you taking your armor?" he asked.

"Of course! It's part of...uhhh, okay, I see your point. Take whatever body you want. Our transport leaves in seventy hours. Unlike you, I've got to go study. All you have to do is download everything from *Guardian*'s database."

Bear looked at him, winked twice, and then said, "New Hope City. Six subterranean boroughs constructed in a hex arrangement, two finished, two fitting out, and two under construction. Tunnels connect the various boroughs and service industry and agriculture domes, all subterranean. Current population about five hundred, but expecting over fifty-five hundred by the end of the ye—"

"Yeah, yeah. That's cheating. Seventy hours, see you at the airlock, unless something comes up." Nik walked off mumbling, "Ain't fair, dammit. *Guardian* has been my home for sixty-five years, and now I have seventy hours to say goodbye. At least everything I own fits in one bag."

One hundred and ninety hours and a few minutes later, Nik, wearing the new bars of a full lieutenant, sat next to Admiral Sipho in the front seats of the Nordheim shuttle as it descended to the runway next to New Hope City.

Admiral Sipho looked around to ensure no one was close enough to overhear them, even if they were all Patrol personnel. "Remember, Lieutenant, you're not staying in the embassy dome with us. The branch bank offices are on the ground floor of the central column in Borough One. You and Bear will live above it in two bedrooms of the Patrol central column penthouse, level ten. Should be a helluva view! This is a new concept we're trying, since most normies don't have the extra comms capabilities the Cerites and AIs have. This may be a retirement post for some folks, but you aren't retiring. You're going to be the *face* of the bank for New Hope City. I'm expecting you to be . . . shall we say, *out and about*, much like you have been in your previous billet. Do I make myself clear?"

Nik nodded and asked, "Separate reporting chain?"

Sipho grinned, white teeth startling against her coal-black face. "If necessary, if necessary." Whatever she was going to say was overridden by the thump of the landing and rattling as the shuttle slid down the ice runway. The thrusters fired, throwing everyone forward into their restraints and bringing the shuttle to a stop.

The PA system came on with a click. "All right

folks, seal up your envirosuits. Atmosphere here is thin and definitely not breathable. Try breathing it and you'll be lucky to last a minute. Ground temp: minus fifty-eight degrees, sunny, slight wind out of the north, gravity point nine two G, solar day equal to ten point three Earth days. Ross is currently quiet with no flare warnings but if you hear the alarm, then get to a marked shelter ASAP. Please stay in your seats until they mate the hatch to the dock facility. Thank you for flying New Hope Air."

Nik pulled on his helmet, sealed up his suit, and then checked the admiral's suit as she double-checked his. He glanced over to Bear, who was now wearing a humanoid body. He had no need for an envirosuit and just smiled.

Ten minutes later as the hatch was opened, and the pressure equalized, an AI wearing a high-end humanoid body stepped through the hatch, picked up the mic, and keyed the PA.

"Okay folks, welcome to New Hope City. Mag-lev is to the right. The train just pulled in. Your personal effects will be delivered to your quarters. Welcome packets are in your assigned quarters. First stop will be Borough One. It is a short walk. Take the elevator down to the borough floor. Guides will be available there to assist you." The AI then climbed up the ladder to the cockpit as the new arrivals got up and picked up their carry-on items. Many groaned at the higher g level.

An hour later, Nik and Bear were ensconced in two bedrooms of the penthouse. Bear was in a chair, eyes closed, taking on a charge and catching up with the latest SAIN news. Nik flipped through the "welcome packet" and found nothing he hadn't already seen in his research. A quick perusal of the autochef's menu showed only basic meals.

"Dammit. Guess I'll have to buy anything I want that is actually good." Nik's stomach rumbled as he punched up a default dinner and choked it down with a glass of water—the only liquid choice other than tea or coffee.

Bear opened his eyes, looked out the windows, and remarked, "One nice view. Need to put some surveillance cameras up here."

Nik nodded and walked over to the windows. They were high enough that they could look down on all the buildings in Borough One. There was human and machine activity, but it wasn't crowded.

"Huh, this is nothing like Toe Hold. I don't see any sharp angles. In fact, I don't see right angles. It's like *everything* is rounded! It feels very different but kinda good. Someone on Earth designed this borough. Very artistic. I think I'm going to like it here." He finished putting his few things away. "All right you cold-hearted machine, let's go check out the pub down on level two."

Nik and Bear took the private elevator back down to the ground floor and walked around toward the pub's main entrance off the lobby. Nik was struck by how clean and fresh the air smelled. The borough's ceiling lights, sixty meters above, provided an exact equivalent of sunlight on Earth. The temperature was cooler than on the *Guardian E* but not unpleasant.

They came to the pub's entrance. In Toe Hold, in the Promise Borough, this would be the Purple Parrot; it brought back some fond memories of some of his detachments off the *Guardian E.* Nik noted a sign over the entrance that said THE BEACH HOUSE.

Bear chuckled. "Apparently *somebody* did get a permit." He called up something on SAIN and continued, "Duplicated the Purple Parrot setup, occupies the two levels above the ground floor. Second floor is the pub proper, along with the kitchen. The third floor has meeting rooms for rent, conference rooms, and sex rooms, and the owners' quarters. I guess you want to go look, don't you?"

Nik laughed. "If I can make it that far. After the slop in the autochef, what I want is a beer. Also, we need to be...*out and about.*"

Bear pulled the inner door open. "Then let us *about* up the stairs and see what there is to see," he said as he trotted up the stairs.

Nik groaned and pulled himself up after Bear.

At the top of the stairs was another set of doors to the actual bar. Nik stopped cold as he stepped through. Bear stopped short and snorted.

"Dayum! Now I see why they call it the Beach House!" Nik said as he looked around in wonder. The entire space replicated a beach shack on some large body of water on Earth. And it was definitely warmer, with a salty tang in the air.

Nik walked over to the bar, Bear tagging along, and was met by an overweight AI with a friendly face, dressed in a Hawaiian shirt, shorts, and sandals. "I'm JimmyB. What can I do for the Patrol this evening?"

"I'm Se—Lieutenant Bernd. I'm with the new Patrol Bank branch downstairs. This is my partner, Bear. You two can talk to each other *after* I get a beer!"

All three of them chuckled. JimmyB moved down

to the tap, pulled a beer, and brought it back. "On the house," he said.

Nik laughed. "No deal. I pay for my booze," he said. Reaching in his pocket, he extended a credit chip. "Run me a tab on that, Jimmy. Patrolmen are not allowed to accept gratuities in any way, shape, or form. You know that."

JimmyB nodded and smiled, touched the card with two fingers, and Nik saw the card glow momentarily.

"Tab started." He handed it back and Nik noted Bear was in comms mode, so he pocketed the chip and looked around. There wasn't much to see other than the wall holo, which displayed a hypnotizing view of the ocean rolling to the beach as the sun set. The holo wrapped around three walls of the bar.

Nik leaned back against the bar and sipped the beer. He finished the beer and set the glass back on the bar just as Bear walked up and said, "Quiet. Almost too quiet."

"Maybe. First impressions aren't always correct. I'm done. You can stay if you want."

Bear grimaced. "Sure, me in my TAC'ed-up body is going to stay in a bar. Do you even think about what comes out of your mouth?"

Nik snorted. "Sometimes. I guess this means you're ready to go, too?" Bear didn't bother answering. He just headed out the door and down the stairs, leaving Nik to catch up.

It took Nik and Bear two weeks to learn the ins and outs of New Hope City and to get used to almost a full g of gravity on Nordheim. Nik had spent some credits to get the autochef up to what he considered an acceptable level of vat steaks, pork, and other sundries, along with a growler or two of beer.

Unfortunately, Nik's weekly meetings and reports to Admiral Sipho left her dissatisfied.

"Granted you're getting turnover on the walk-ins at the branch, and people are complimentary about your presence over there, but you haven't seen a damned thing wrong, other than petty stuff?" she asked.

Nik glanced at Bear, who sat blank-faced next to him. *Some help you are*, he thought as he looked back at the admiral.

"No, ma'am. I'm—we are planning to go farther afield now that we've got the basic layout of Boroughs One and Two down. Boroughs Three and Four are almost complete. They are finishing up trim, and acceptance testing of the systems is in process. There is a lot of construction going on toward the mountains, and we haven't been outside the four boroughs yet."

The next morning, human time, Nik and Bear—Nik outfitted in a full envirosuit, Bear in thermal clothing—checked out a runabout from the surface terminal and drove out to the one brightly lit worksite they could see, about ten kilometers away. Ross 248 hung low in the sky like a giant, angry, red eye. The Ross 248 sunset would be in about thirty hours. The runabout came to a stop. Nik glanced at Bear and said, "Borough Five?"

Bear nodded. "If the master plan is correct, yes." There were two individuals moving around a large machine that appeared to be driving something into the ice. Nik was flipping through radio channels when Bear said, "Worksite nine. Channel thirty-one," on his suitcomm.

Nik nodded his thanks and tuned to channel thirty-one. "Worksite nine, Patrol."

He saw one figure turn toward them. "Patrol, worksite nine. What can we do for you on this fine day?"

Bear snickered over the suitcomm as Nik shook his head. "Uh, worksite, we are ... doing an area fam. Permission to approach?"

"Come on in. Stop at least a hundred meters short. Matter of fact, park next to the maintenance unit to your left. I need to warm up."

Nik drove over and parked next to what he realized was a large mobile maintenance rig. As they got out, the two figures walked up. The taller and much thinner of the two waved and said, "Sal Albin; for my sins, I'm the maintenance engineer. Come on in, I have coffee."

Nik smiled and Bear smirked. "You meat machines and your drinks," Bear said over a private comm that only Nik could hear as they stepped into the rig's airlock. The engineer cycled it and then swung the interior hatch open. Once inside, the engineer stripped off his helmet and sighed as he scratched his short gray hair and beard, ending with rubbing his nose.

The shorter, wider individual wore no envirosuit but loosened his thermal garment and said, "89-of-Cilla. I go by Mole." Mole and Bear went into an AI comm mode as Albin steered Nik into the small office and reached for two mugs.

Albin filled them with steaming hot coffee and handed one to Nik. "My name is Salvador Albin. Call me Sal. Originally from Lisboa, Portugal, two hundred nine years ago. Now freezing my ass off here. What can we do for the Patrol?"

Nik chuckled. "Lieutenant Bernd. Norse, family from Tromso. I was born on the *Copernicus* ten AA, so I'm a youngster compared to you. New guy on the rock here, just trying to figure out what is going on." He took a sip of the coffee, and added, "And this is damn excellent coffee! Dirt-grown, right?"

Sal laughed. "Right. I get it direct from Toe Hold. Friends and all that."

Nik smiled and said, "Gotta ask, what is that monstrosity out there doing?"

"All the Construction Battalion equipment is designed to be ruggedized, specific-use systems automated by puters with minimal supervision required on a ten-thousand-hour meantime between failures. Junior thirty-two is one of those, a drilling rig. We're drilling down about thirty-five, maybe forty kilometers, to get to the hot stuff, liquid water. We are supposed to be pumping it up to a photocatalysis system for making oxygen for the boroughs, all the while extracting salts and trace elements for the fabricators."

"Why drill from the surface?" asked Nik.

Taking a swig of coffee, Sal replied, "Simple. These Construction Battalion monsters are designed to operate on the surface and are mostly too big to fit in the tunnels. Junior is designed specifically for drilling. The pressure from the deep water is approaching five hundred PSI through a half-meter carbon-fiber pipe. Once we get the well drilled and capped, unit thirty-three will come in and build out the photoelectrochemical tandem cells, collectors, and the tanks. Assuming that sumbitch doesn't break again."

"That why it's all the way out here?"

"Well, this one is supposedly going to be initially

dual use by Borough Five and the mountain houses. At least until we figure out how to pipe one to the mountain houses." A radio in the rig chirped an alert tone and Sal cursed. "Dammit, not *again!*"

The radio broke squelch. "Maintenance, mass driver. We're down again. Same thing, Sal; beam nineteen broke at the breech point."

"Roger," Sal replied.

Mole stuck his head in the room.

Sal said, "Beam nineteen *again*; check the spares." Mole's eyes closed momentarily. "One on planet."

Sal cursed under his breath, turned back to Nik, and grumped, "Damn, I don't know which is worse: the mass driver or the damn photocatalysis system, which doesn't particularly like the light/radiation off Ross 248. Not bright enough or the wrong color or something. Damned scientists and engineers are... Never mind, not your issue."

"What's going on with that?"

Sal shrugged eloquently. "Beats the hell outta me. Go talk to the designers. I don't do that letter-math shit. Give me numbers every day," he said.

Nik laughed. "Yeah, before I went to the Patrol, I worked as a metalist and welder on Toe Hold. Numbers I can do. That other, not so much. But I was at least in shape when I reported to boot camp." Waving in the general direction of Junior thirty-two, he asked, "How much longer to drill down, and what are you doing for pipe?"

Sal checked the computer. "Eighteen days," he said. "When it works, Junior builds the carbon nanotube pipe as it goes down the hole. You don't want to be around it when it's running! Carbon nanotube is sharp as hell. Just got through cleaning the capsule out again." Sal shuddered. "Just being in there scares me. And it's clogging up way too often."

Nik winced in sympathy. "Well, I think we've worn out our welcome, and I think it's time to head back in. I like a fifty percent safety margin on my air and we're about down to that point."

Mole interrupted, "Beam nineteen en route from supply. Do we need to install, or trust the crew?"

Sal clenched both fists, then visibly calmed himself with a sigh. "Well, looks like I have a bit of work to take care of. I'll be glad when we can locally manufacture *all* of our needs here and get shit that actually meets spec. If you will excuse me?"

Nik hopped up. "Certainly," he said as he turned to the door. "Bear, we're out of here."

Slipping his helmet on, he and Bear cycled through the airlock and back to their runabout. Trundling back to the surface terminal, Nik asked on the suitcomm, "Anything strange perk your interest?"

"Failure, apparently not the first on a critical part, according to Mole. According to SAIN, spares are en route. Discussions among AIs and puters cannot agree on the failure mode, which is *interesting*."

Nik bit his lip. "I think I've seen Sal in the bar at the Beach House. Think I'll make it a point to say hi to him when I see him again."

Two days passed as Nik and Bear caught up on the paperwork. Nik was sitting in the office, staring at the computer screen, when the one other human in the branch bank, Sergeant Archie Finlay, stooped and white-haired, knocked on the door.

"Lieutenant?"

"What have you got, Archie?"

Finlay bit his lip, then continued in his Scottish brogue. "Got a...customer that wants a loan for a bar." Nik made a come-on gesture, and Finlay straightened, then continued in a rush, "Ian Lockie, him and his missus, Kirsten, want a loan to open a bar in Borough Three. Him being disabled, it... might be an issue, but the missus works in hydroponics as a senior supervisor. Himself was disabled in a construction accident here three years ago. They can't repair him to return to work, but he *wants* to work afore he goes crazy. He was a metalist and welder—"

Nik interrupted, "Do they have anything for collateral?"

Finlay shrugged. "His pension, and a twenty-thousand-credit settlement. Himself says he can build out the space, and the missus has been brewing beer for the last four years for them and the neighbors."

Nik tapped his stylus on the desk. "What do the AIs say?" he asked.

Finlay ducked his head and replied, "They say no. Not enough collateral for what they want."

Nik bit his lip, noting the growing bald-spot on Finlay's head, and thought, *Sergeant Finlay spent close to seventy years as a desk sergeant. If anybody knows people, it's him. And I wonder if, well, Lockie is probably a Scot, too.* "What do *you* think, Archie?"

"I think they can do it. And it would help himself to have value again. I kin see the fire in himself's eyes, and those of his missus."

"Give me a couple of minutes to review the file. I'll let you know in, say, ten or fifteen minutes. Give them a cup of coffee or something," said Nick.

The relief was clear on Finlay's face as he stepped out. "Yes, sir!"

"Coffee," he mumbled to himself, "and Bear." He walked to the break room, got a cup of coffee, and found Bear hiding in the puter room. "Bear, can you do a read on Ian and Kirsten Lockie? See what their performance ratings are."

In less time than it took Nik to take a sip, Bear replied, "Forty-two years old. He was a three-point-nine-eight performer as a metal former and welder, heavy construction. Lost both legs to crush injury during tunnel construction in one-zero-one AA. Two years of surgeries and rehab to get him to where he is now. Never complained. Wife, Kristen, forty, three-point-nine-nine performer, eighteen years in hydroponics, PhD in chemistry. No children, no significant debts. Currently, thirty-eight thousand—"

Nik held up his hand and interrupted, "That's what I needed. Thank you."

"You're going to approve their loan, aren't you? Even over the objections of Moose and Squirrel."

Shrugging, Nik replied, "Yes, I am. The one thing you AIs never take into consideration is how much drive a person has to succeed. Archie Finley has seventy-plus years of experience with people and he believes in them."

Bear laughed. "I've been around you for sixty-five years. I've watched you do shit for the oddest reasons many times, so this doesn't surprise me a bit. And that includes saving my life a couple of times."

Nik smiled and said, "Hell, that was self-interest. I didn't want to have to break in a new AI!"

He walked back to the front, caught Finley's eye, and gave him a thumbs-up.

The next day, Nik said, "We haven't checked out the new construction tunnel toward Borough Six." Bear sighed but came back with his thermal suit a minute later.

The walk took them through the tunnel to Borough Two. They walked past the entrance to the Patrol embassy and had to dodge puter-directed delivery vehicles. At Borough Two, Nik studied the layout carefully. The architecture of Borough Two was strikingly different from Borough One. Nik had studied images of ancient Florence in Italy of Old Earth and the borough looked to be very similar to that, with its cobblestone streets and stone buildings and even streetlamps with burning flames. As they walked by the central column, they observed a flock of newcomers from Toe Hold excitedly gesturing and pointing, probably looking for their luggage. The guides maintained order, but just barely. The new arrivals looked exhausted and moved cautiously due to the higher gravity.

The tunnel from Borough Two to Borough Five was less crowded with humans and AIs but was almost obstructed with construction materials. Borough Five was awash in construction activities and several detours were required as they walked to the bulkhead airlock for the new tunnel. This airlock was sealed. It had a placard that read NO ENTRY WITHOUT AUTHORIZATION. Nik put on his envirosuit but left the helmet off as he pressed the comm switch next to the airlock. After a minute the tunnel puter finally noticed them and announced in an annoyed tone, "Tunnel five-six. State your requirement."

"Patrol team. Routine safety and security checks," said Nik.

Bear cocked an eyebrow at that but didn't say anything.

They heard a clank as the hatch unlocked and the puter voice said in a professional tone, "Access granted. Cart utilization approved. Cart 343. Current boring operation is six kilometers from the airlock."

As they entered the airlock, Nik pulled on his helmet and Bear fastened his thermal suit. The outer door closed behind them and there was a hiss as the air was pulled from the chamber and the inner door opened. After they cycled through the airlock, Nik noted the drop in temperature and checked the telltales on his helmet's heads-up display.

Cart 343 waited ten meters past the airlock. Slipping into the driver's seat of the cart, Nik drove it the six kilometers to the worksite. It surprised him to see multiple operations going on simultaneously with four people crowded around the extruder and the curved metal tunnel roof extrusions sitting on its forward rack. Realizing his radio wasn't on the right frequency, Nik hunted until he found the tunnel five-six channel and flipped over to it. "That is *not* the specified thickness. These are supposed to be one to one-point-two centimeters thick. These—"

A voice he recognized as Sal Albin's cut the other off. "We need to confirm what the extruder is programmed for. Mole, can you—"

A sharp statement and gesture came back. "I *did* check. It…This piece of junk is *not* operating within parameters. I know what I designed and I—"

"Frank Lloyd, calm down. I'm sure Sal can get to the bottom of this," a soft female voice interjected.

Nik and Bear got out of the cart and walked up to the gathered engineers. "Problems?" he asked.

The radio hashed with everyone trying to talk at once, and Nik held up his hands. "One at a time, please." Nik looked at the female. "You are?"

She planted her hands on her hips and replied, "Vilhelmina Martina. I am the design engineer and architect for this…cluster." She pointed to a slim figure beside her. "This is Frank Lloyd, my AI, 59-of-Jenn. Frank Lloyd is the primary engineer on this project."

Frank Lloyd jerked an arm toward the rack of extrusions. "These are *not* what I programmed. These are…out of spec!" he said.

Nik immediately dropped into interrogator mode. "What thickness was programmed?" He noticed Bear easing over to the control panel of the extruder. "And when did you note the discrepancy?"

Frank Lloyd spat, "I specified one-point-two centimeters as optimal with a min/max of one centimeter and one-point-four centimeters. *None* of these are even the minimum thickness! None!"

"Noted." Nik turned to the woman and asked, "Ms. Martina, these are tunnel ceiling units, correct?"

"Please call me Willie. Yes," she said as she turned and pointed back about fifty meters. "One hundred eighty degrees of support from road surface to road surface, interlocking panel joints, spotwelds every ten centimeters. The roadway and the central trench below the roadway do not require shoring; they are constructed of fused rubble by the boring machine, which also installs the interlocking ceiling supports as it moves forward."

Nik thought back to his early years when he was working on Toe Hold and the problems with welding burn-throughs on blind welds there. "What weld depth is the autowelder set for?" Seeing blank stares, he started to walk toward the autowelder working twenty meters back.

Mole suddenly said, "Two-to-three-centimeter thickness. That is per design."

Nik and Bear walked past the autowelder, Sal and Mole on his heels as Willie and Frank Lloyd looked at each other, then followed more slowly. Nik stopped at the first set of completed welds and they all heard him cursing. Sal ran a finger over one of the welds as he said vehemently, "This whole frikkin' tunnel is going to have to be inspected and possibly redone!"

Martina asked softly, "Why?"

Nik motioned her over to where he was standing. Pointing to the weld, he clicked his headlamp on.

"See the weld? It's a burn-through. It only tacks the edges together and every one of these is a hole in the tunnel," he said.

Bear's voice came over their suitcomms. "Standard setting two-to-three-centimeter thickness; sonic gauging prior to weld is selected off."

Son of a bitch. This is either sabotage or—A loud clanging noise followed by a siren broke his thought, and a warning horn sounded as the borer suddenly reversed away from the bore face, causing the extruder to back up the same distance. He glanced at Sal and saw his face go pale as he snapped around.

"What is that?"

Sal shook his head. "Don't know yet. I need to go find out, but I'm thinking something broke."

Mole chimed in, "Broken tooth on bore face is the fault that comes up."

Nik made a decision. Over his suitcomm, he said to Bear, "Lock every one of these machines down. Have SAIN freeze all puters in this tunnel now!"

The sudden silence in the tunnel shocked everyone. The slow plinking of water dripping from the ice above them was the loudest thing heard, until Frank Lloyd asked, "What just happened? I ... I can't get to any of the machines. *Who turned off my machines?*"

Wille put a hand on his arm. "Calm, Frank Lloyd, be calm. I'm sure there is a good reason," she said.

Sal looked sharply at Nik. "You lock 'em down?" he asked.

Nik nodded. "I did. There are some issues that we need to address. Not the least of which is this entire tunnel is potentially unsafe due to faulty welds, and potential for compromised atmosphere due to multiple points of leakage. For now, I am designating this a Patrol scene. Ms. Martina," he said, adding, "would you please depart and take your AI with you? And would you both remain available if we need to question you?"

"I—yes, we will. Come, Frank Lloyd," she briefly stuttered. She walked him back to a cart, and trundled down the now quiet tunnel toward the bulkhead airlock.

* * *

Two hours later, Admiral Sipho stepped in front of Nik as he stood staring at the shutdown autowelder.

"Well, Lieutenant, you have certainly stirred the pot this time." Knowing her history, he was not surprised to see her in the tunnel.

Nik shrugged. "Ma'am?" he asked.

"Apparently your little shutdown here has gotten Admiral Lewcock's and 5-of-Chandra's attention. The project here is way behind schedule as it is and you're not helping. What have you and Bear come up with?"

"Ah, me, personally, not a damned thing, sir. Bear and Mole did all the work. They were able to communicate with the puters and found some *interesting* things. It appears the programming has been subtly modified to, shall we say, allow certain errors to go unreported," Nik replied.

"Unreported errors? Tell me more."

Nik waved Sal over and waited until he got there before continuing, "Mole get anything else?"

Sal looked up tiredly. "As if this isn't enough, not so far."

"The errors?" Admiral Sipho asked testily.

Nik blew a breath out of the mask and started, "Extruder's running less than the minimum thickness on ceiling panels. Sonic gaugers turned off on the welder. Wrong blades?"

Sal added, "Wrong teeth loaded on the boring machine. Bore face sensors turned off, impact sensors turned off, and—"

The admiral motioned with her hands.

"Enough! Leave the scene locked down and we will meet back at the embassy. I'm beginning to think there are some things that bear more discussion. You two and your AIs report to me in an hour." She took the first cart and headed for the airlock, leaving them standing there.

Nik and Sal looked at each other and shook their heads. They, along with their AIs, climbed into the last two carts and trundled back to the airlock in silence. Sal motioned Nik and Bear through first, then came through as they were stripping off their envirosuits.

"Don't know about you, but I'm going to hit the fresher, eat, and get into some clean clothes before I go to the embassy," said Sal.

Nik nodded tiredly. "Agreed. I'll see you there."

An hour later, somewhat refreshed with a trip through the fresher and some food, Nik and Bear trudged down the tunnel to the Patrol embassy dome. Nik stopped suddenly.

"Shit, I wonder..." He stepped off the walkway and walked over to the extruded ceiling panels. Running his hands lightly over the seam, he finally found a set of welds. He turned to Bear. "Can you illuminate this for me?" he asked.

Bear turned on his TAC light and pointed it at Nik's hands. Peering at the weld points, Nik started muttering curses. Bear stepped up and looked, then said, "Same burn-through. Settlement-wide?"

Nik nodded. "Probably. If that architect...Vili— Willie isn't there, we need to get her called in."

Bear turned off his light as they continued to the dome. "Maybe because you never expected it?" he asked.

Nik stopped and turned to Bear. "Anything you post to SAIN goes through *Guardian* first, right?"

Bear nodded. "Of course. I've only been doing this for two hundred and ten years. I can download anything, but *Guardian* makes sure no sensitive Patrol information goes on SAIN. Why?"

Nik held up a hand. "Lemme think. I'll...tell you later," he said.

They walked into the embassy and were directed to the small conference room by the desk sergeant. As they stepped through the door, Nik smelled coffee and immediately turned toward the credenza from which the irresistible aroma originated. Bear continued to the corner where Mole and Frank Lloyd were standing.

The admiral glanced up from the puter at her position. "Nice of you to finally join us, Lieutenant."

"No excuse, ma'am," Nik said as he poured a cup of dirt-grown coffee, inhaled gratefully, and slid into the chair to which she pointed. He noted that an actual pad of paper and a pen sat next to the puter and stylus, looked over at her, and saw her lip curl in a half smile. *She is one smart lady! And she's also been on the tunnel and borough Patrols, so street smart, too.*

Admiral Sipho tapped gently on the side of her cup. "Mr. Albin, Dr. Martina, if you could join us down at this end of the table? AIs, please seat yourselves as well," she said.

Sal ended up sitting next to Nik, with Dr. Martina across the table from him. The AIs had taken the far end of the table and sat stoically, no expression on any of their faces. Nik sipped his coffee as he covertly watched the doctor for any signs of nervousness. *She's...pretty. Slim, dark blond, green eyes, long expressive fingers, and no rings. She is young, probably less than a hundred.*

Admiral Sipho spoke the normal header information for any investigation and questioning, then turned to Dr. Martina. "Your name, qualifications, and how long you've been here, please," she asked.

"Vilhelmina Martina. PhD in architectural engineering from MIT's shipboard campus. I am the design engineer and architect for New Hope City and have been for...one and a half years. My AI—"

"Mr. Albin?"

"Salvador Albin, Two hundred and nine. Master's in mechanical engineering, University of Lisboa. Former third engineer on *Copernicus*, deputy maintenance engineer on Toe Hold, maintenance engineer here these last two years." He stopped and looked at Sipho expectantly. She nodded and pointed toward Nik.

"Niklas Bernd. Lieutenant, Patrol. Class of forty-four. Currently branch manager of Patrol Bank in the central core of New Hope City. A month?" he said.

Sipho smiled at Nik with a "the recruit did good" expression and turned to the AIs at the far end of the table. As they recited their qualifications, Nik quickly scribbled a note and slid it to the admiral. That caught Dr. Martina's eye, and she looked at him curiously, but said nothing.

Sipho glanced down at Nik's note. Her face crinkled into a puzzled expression, then smoothed. After about twenty minutes of questioning, she closed the interview process. "Okay, AIs are released. Doctor, Mr. Albin, I'd like to speak to you for a minute in private," she said.

The AIs filed out, with Bear cocking a head at Nik, who shrugged his shoulders slightly. Nik was making a beeline for the coffeepot when the admiral added, "You too, Bernd."

Sipho led them back to the Secure Compartmented Information Facility, or SCIF, and said, "All electronics of any type in the bins, please." She led by example, taking her comm out of her pocket and removing her watch. The others followed suit and she then quickly opened the SCIF door and motioned them through. Once inside, she led them to the small conference room, flipped on the notification light outside, and closed the door. "This space is completely unmonitored. There is no connectivity to SAIN or any puters anywhere outside here, hence the secure title. The show is all yours, Bernd."

Taken aback for a second or two, Nik bit his lip as he thought about how to even begin explaining what he was thinking. He looked at each one of them and finally asked, "Dr. Martina, is there an issue with your AI? I noted his vehemence when he was describing the problem."

Martina folded her hands in front of her and sat forward. "I, uh, yes, there is a bit of a problem. Frank Lloyd is old, over two hundred. He was originally trained as a home designer on Earth. His original partner was one of my professors. He died the year I graduated. I was asked to take him on. Originally, we were designing the estates for Toe Hold's upgrade, then got shifted up here. Frank Lloyd doesn't like cookie cutter design." She shrugged. "And that's pretty much the definition of what we are doing here. He . . . well, I let him talk me into the affordable mountain home designs we are working on now. He considers that his *masterpiece*."

Admiral Sipho cocked her head. "Frank Lloyd? As in Frank Lloyd Wright?"

Martina nodded, and replied, "Frank Lloyd or 59-of-Jenn was raised by Jenn in the southwest of North America. She specialized in architectural designers and engineering AIs. He apparently fixated on Frank Lloyd Wright early in his education."

"So, he's not a fan of terraforming, then?" Nik asked.

Martina rocked her hand side to side. "He *prefers* to work with 'natural elements,' as he calls them. I was picked to come here because I have some ideas about terraforming that might work," she said.

Sal nodded enthusiastically. "She's shown me the plans. I think they will work long term," he said.

Admiral Sipho glanced between them and made a come-on gesture.

Martina smiled shyly and said, "Well, I *believe* we can use the hot water coming up from below the ice to eventually raise the oxygen levels to create a more breathable atmosphere. I hesitate to even broach this, but it might be possible to live under the ice on floating habitats if we could solve the pressure issues."

The admiral made a moue of surprise and turned to Sal. "Bernd tells me you've been seeing a lot of breakage," she said.

Sal grimaced. "Mole and I have been fighting that for the last two years. The Construction Battalion equipment is designed to ten-thousand-hour meantime between failures, but we're actually seeing about a thousand-hour MTBF. Junior thirty-two's capsule being the perfect example. Every failure has been between nine-fifty and ten-fifty hours. And that damned mass driver is down more often than that," he said.

Nik asked cautiously, "Have you compared your MTBF rates with similar equipment the AIs are using on Frigus?"

Sal looked at him, eyes wide. "No, that never came up. I know it's higher than Toe Hold, but I figured the environment here—" He reached for his comm and realized he didn't have it. Sinking back in his chair, he scrubbed his face. "That scares me. If they're getting better MTBF, coupled with the—"

Martina's eyes flew wide open. "Oh, deity! I've heard rumors that there were shortages in material with both us and Frigus building out facilities with the CBs. The AIs and SAIN handle all the spare parts for the CBs on Liber, Frigus and here. I assumed we were getting good parts, but are we?" she asked.

Admiral Sipho chewed on her lip as she looked at the three of them. She sighed and said, "I'm afraid I am going to have to put a full Patrol lock on all of this information. We will figure out how to communicate this to Admiral Lewcock and"—she looked at Martina—"I'm going to have to ask you to refigure the tunnel support structures with the substandard ceiling supports. If that is negative, we're going to have to close all affected tunnels until repairs can be made. Also," she swung to Sal and continued, "I need you to come up with a plan to correctly weld up the holes in the interim."

Nik mumbled, "One-tenth MTBF, shorted materials, purposely bad welds. All controlled by AIs and SAIN." Anger spread across his face, causing both Sal and the doctor to sit back from him as he added, "Sounds to me like they are purposefully sabotaging New Hope, but why? What's the..." His eyes popped open. "Doc, what would happen if there was an explosive decompression of a tunnel in New Hope City?" he asked.

Martina looked curiously at him and replied, "That can't happen. Nordheim has some atmosphere so it can't explosively decompress. If a tunnel does decompress, then the bulkhead doors automatically shut. Any human trapped in the tunnel without an envirosuit would die. Then we would probably have to rebuild the tunnel completely." She sighed. "And a lot of heads would roll."

Sal jumped in, "That might explain why we're seeing such high oxygen loss! All those damned welds are nothing more than holes in the shell. I need to check this out." He started to get up and the admiral held out a hand.

"Let the Patrol handle it. We can put people out in street sweeps for *security purposes*," the admiral said. Nik chuckled as he recognized her "combat" grin coming to the fore. She looked up at the analog clock on the wall. "And I think we need to end this meeting. It's late. I need both of you to resume your normal activities and not share any of this information with your AIs. Bernd, this includes you." She got up swiftly with a menacing smile on her face. "This is going to be interesting."

Bear was waiting when Nik finally cleared the building. "Well?" Bear asked.

Nik grimaced. "The admiral was on a roll. She

wants answers yesterday, as usual. We're going to be doing some street sweeps to see what we can see."

Bear laughed. "And *this* is why I like my TAC body. I'm ready!" he said.

Nik shook his head. "I think your core has been dropped once too often, Bear. You're not supposed to *like* busting heads."

Nik kept up a brisk pace as he and Bear walked back to Borough One's central column. It felt good to move. There was a crowd of new arrivals outside the entrance to the Beach House. Nik and Bear ignored them. Borough One was filling up. Nik turned to Bear. "Think I'll go get a beer. You coming?" he asked.

Bear shook his head and replied, "No. There isn't anything there for me. I'm going up to the room to check SAIN and see what other problems are out there. I wonder if Frigus is having the same issues?"

Nik started to tell him no, but thought better of it and instead said, "Put it under investigative hold. The boss doesn't want our issues to get out until she has answers."

Bear chuckled, "And *that* is why she is the boss, and you're a trumped-up sergeant playing at being a lieutenant. Be quiet when you come in drunk, okay?"

Nik laughed as he walked toward the Beach House. *Drunk. I haven't been drunk in more years than I want to think about. For good reason.* He trotted up the stairs and pushed through the door into the main bar. He was surprised to see Sal and Martina sitting at a table across the room, motioning for him to join them. He waved back and went to the bar.

JimmyB saw him, immediately pulled a beer, and

then brought it down to him. "Late evening there, Lieutenant."

Nik sighed. "No rest for the weary. Thanks!" He ambled over to Sal's table and said, "May I join you?"

Sal waved at an open chair, and the doctor, smiling, said, "Please do." Nik noticed her green eyes looking intently at him.

Hooking a chair out, Nik flopped down. "I don't need days like this," he said.

The doctor added, "I've never had a day like this, ever. This just doesn't happen in our world."

"What do you mean, Doc?" Nik asked.

"Please call me Willie. I mean there are so many cross-checks, reviews, and sign-offs that one has to go through that this shouldn't be possible, much less the issues with the CB machines."

They chatted back and forth for a couple of minutes and JimmyB showed up with refills for their drinks. "Trying to get us drunk, JimmyB?" Nik asked.

JimmyB grinned. "Gotta make credits somehow. The nut on this place isn't cheap."

"When did you get here?" Nik asked.

"Three years ago. Won't really turn the corner on the nut until New Hope goes over a thousand residents," JimmyB replied. He picked up the empties and went back to the bar as the doctor look speculatively after him.

"What did he say that got your interest, Doc, er— Willie?" Nik asked.

"He's not making money in three years. That is..." she began.

Nik's grin wasn't pretty. "They are AIs; they run profit and loss on everything they touch, usually out at least ten years. Saw that on the last investigation. Which tells me he's willing to accept a loss now for profits later." He finished his beer and got up. "Early day. I think we can release the equipment back to you by late tomorrow." He nodded to them, waved at JimmyB, and headed for the penthouse.

As he left, he heard Willie muttering, "I'm going to have to go back and recompute whether or not all the damn tunnels are safe, and—arrgghhh!"

Early the next morning, Nik and Bear walked into the embassy. The desk sergeant looked up and buzzed them through the portal to the Patrol area.

Nik waved Bear off as he headed for the mess to get coffee before heading to the admiral's office.

When he arrived at Sipho's office, she motioned him in.

"Now what, Nik?" she asked.

Now that he stood in front of her, he wasn't sure how important the information was, but he drew a deep breath and started, "Well, I can't help but wonder if the AIs are playing us in more ways than one. I—"

She held up a hand and glanced down at her secure puter. "Well, that is interesting, especially since I asked back-channel about those failure rates last night. According to *Guardian*, Frigus is not reporting any *abnormal* failures. And I talked to Mags, our puter guru on *Guardian*, last night about the amounts of material being shipped here and to Frigus. It appears they are getting about twenty percent more materials of all types than we are. I also told her about our suspicions, and she was going to take it to Admiral Lewcock this morning, ship time."

"What do you want to do with the scene, then?" Nik asked. He paused while an idea popped into his head. "Oh, can we put patrols out with sniffers to check the atmosphere in the tunnels?"

Sipho cocked her head. "Why?" she asked.

"Well, Sal and Willie both think this might be why the oxygen input isn't where it should be from the photocatalysis system. They think we're leaking oxygen out of all the holes. And Willie is going to recalculate the safety load on the ceiling panels."

Tapping her teeth with her thumbnail, she leaned back. "Release the scene now. Get them back to work fixing that tunnel, however they have to do it. I'm going to put a full-court press on *Guardian E* to take a hard look at this whole mess with the AIs and SAIN. If it *is* the AIs, then they may be getting ready to do something the Patrol won't like. Stay in touch with those two. Casually. Oh, and have Bear pull the data from the puters before you release the scene. Once he does that, have him start running queries and let's see what happens." Her combat grin came back as she leaned forward. "I've never fully trusted the damn AIs anyway."

"Yes, ma'am. Permission to depart?"

"Get the hell out of my office, Bernd. Just go fix it."

Nik had wandered the tunnel looking at the machine positioning and spacings while Bear was extracting all the puter data from the extruder and autowelder, as well as the boring machine. He finished at noon local, looked over at Nik, and asked, "Now what the hell am I supposed to do with all this data?"

"See if you can figure out how it was done, and any footprints that show up," Nik replied.

"Patrol only?"

"Can you do it without using the network?"

"Not all of it. I need to access SAIN to get some of it," Bear replied.

"Do it and see if you can pull the MTBF rates for Frigus while you're at it." Nik then called Sal on the comm once they had climbed out of their suits at the airlock. "Sal, the scene is clear. Admiral Sipho wants you to start repairing the bad welds as soon as you can."

Sal's disgusted voice came back. "You don't want much, do you? I'm not sure how that will work, unless Willie has something up her sleeve. Otherwise, we're doing hand patches over every one of those damn things."

As they walked back to the center column, Bear said, "Huh." Nik glanced at him, realized he was in comms mode, and kept walking. When they got back to the branch bank, Sergeant Finlay was beaming.

"Thank you, Lieutenant!" Finlay said.

Distracted, Nik asked, "Thanks for what?"

"Pushing the Lockies loan up the chain. It came back approved today for the full amount," he replied.

"Are they here?"

"They should be here shortly. Why?"

"I need to talk to him. I'll be in my office."

Twenty minutes later, Finlay knocked on his door. "The Lockies, sir." Ian Lockie came into the office in a float chair, closely followed by his wife, Kirsten.

Nik nodded his thanks and turned to them. "Let me offer congratulations on your loan," he said. They both mumbled a "Thank you," looking somewhat embarrassed. Nik added, "I understand you were a metalist and welder, Mr. Lockie."

"Ian, sir. And yes, I *was*," he said. His face contorted and Nik decided on a different approach.

Smiling, Nik said, "Before I went to the Patrol, I did the same thing in Toe Hold. Back then, we didn't have enough automated welding machines, so we had to hand weld. I'm betting the tech is much better today. But I do have a question, if I may."

Lockie cocked his head suspiciously and replied, "Yes, sir?"

"Ian, what did you do if you had a burn-through on an autowelder?"

Lockie snorted. "If you have the setting set right, you don't get burn-throughs. The puters in those things are good. If it did burn through, then I'd want to know why and then I'd make that piece o' shite go back and redo the weld with a patch," he said.

"You could do that? We never could. We had to do manual patches," Nik replied.

"With the current machines, it's actually pretty simple. All the autowelders have a map of every weld that unit did. It's easy to make them retrace their welds."

"Interesting. Thank you very much, and again, congratulations on the loan. Please let us know when you're up and operating, I'd like to come by for a beer," Nik added with a smile.

Nik sent a quick message to Sal about the way to fix the weld issues as he walked into the Beach House. The pub was reasonably crowded but he managed to find an open spot to sit.

JimmyB came over with a beer, set it on the table, and asked, "You want anything to eat?"

"Fish tacos. And a piece of key lime pie," Nik replied, his stomach rumbling.

"You got it." As JimmyB walked away, Nik saw Martina come in. He waved her over.

"You're welcome to join me, if you'd like," Nik said as he got up and pulled a chair out for her.

"Thank you. Just a quick break from work," she said.

"Speaking of work, what happened to your predecessor here?"

Her face contorted into a moue. "He was basically fired. He had some grandiose plans for a bunch of monster estates that he thought would sell quickly, and of course one of them was his, as was his due." She shook her head. "I was able to modify what he hadn't finished into something that people would actually want and could afford."

"Did he have an AI?"

She snorted. "Oh yeah. Leonardo. He is a piece of work. He fed Eickman's ego and pandered to his design wishes. I've never seen an AI like him."

JimmyB interrupted and set plates in front of them, along with a glass of wine for Martina.

"You didn't order," Nik said.

She laughed. "I get the same thing every day: vat chicken salad and a glass of white wine. Helps me keep my figure."

While they were eating, they both looked up as Bear came in and walked quickly over. "Admiral wants to see you as soon as you can get there," he said.

Nik shook his head. "I'm sorry to eat and run." He picked up the remaining fish taco and said,

"Have a piece of pie on me." Stuffing the taco in his mouth, he chewed and swallowed as he walked to the bar. "JimmyB, her lunch on my tab. Gotta go to work."

JimmyB gave him a thumbs-up. Nik and Bear clattered down the stairs to find a Patrol cart waiting. The Patrol officer asked, "Need a ride, Lieutenant?"

"Sure." They rode in silence to the embassy. Once there, Nik and Bear walked directly to the admiral's office. Nik knocked, opened the door a crack, and said, "You wanted to see me?" Sipho looked up and made a motion to enter. The two of them marched to the front of her desk and stood at attention as she finished her comm call.

She hung up and looked at them. "Well, I've officially notified Admiral Lewcock that New Hope City has been sabotaged. All indicators point to the sabotage being conducted by one or more AIs, possibly abetted by the SAIN network." She shivered and licked her lips. "You are authorized to direct links to any and all Patrol divisions as needed. Just keep me informed. Understood?"

They both stiffened and chorused, "Yes, ma'am."

"Get out of my sight." They did an about-face and marched out the door as she mumbled, "Retirement job, my ass."

Two weeks passed with Nik growing grumpier and grumpier as every idea he had was shot down by Bear, the Criminal Investigations Group, or *Guardian*. Bear had found what he called echo commands, where any command that Frank Lloyd had sent to the machine had been followed by a separate command from him changing the settings. The most glaring was the thickness of the extrusions. According to Bear, all those commands issued from Frank Lloyd.

Nik sat at the small table in the apartment one morning, looked at Bear, and said, "What about...what was his damn handle? The AI that worked with the previous architect? Eickman? Something with an *L*?"

Bear replied immediately, "Leonardo. 40-of-Jenn."

Nik jerked up at that. "Wasn't Frank Lloyd from the same parent?"

"Frank Lloyd is 59-of-Jenn."

Slumping back in his chair, Nik took another sip of coffee. "When they changed architects, did they change access to the plans?"

"It does not appear so. A Dr. Eickman and Dr. Martina are listed as having access to the master files, along with Leonardo and Frank Lloyd."

"Have either Eickman or Leonardo accessed the master files since they were relieved?" Nik asked.

"Eickman did once, thirteen months and four days ago. Leonardo has never accessed them."

Nik scrubbed his face. "How do you communicate with SAIN? How does SAIN know it's you?"

"We have an encrypted alphanumeric that is our ID. In theory, no other entity can impersonate me."

Nik leaned forward. "You said, 'in theory.' Can you find out what another AI's alpha is?"

Bear grinned. "Oh yes. That is a game we all play as children. I know six of my siblings' alphas."

"Could Leonardo, for example, fake using Frank Lloyd's alpha?"

Bear's eyes closed for a moment. "If he knew the correct alpha, yes, it is possible. But, to do so would be a violation of both SAIN and our core beliefs," he said sadly.

"But it could be done?"

"Yes."

Nik rolled the cup in his hands. "Can you find Eickman and Leonardo?"

"Leonardo is currently on Toe Hold at the university complex." Bear hesitated for a moment and then continued, "And Professor Eickman is currently teaching an advanced class on estate designs at the university."

Nik pulled his comm out of his pocket and dialed a code from memory. He said, "Short Round, I need a favor. I need a watch on a Professor Eickman and his AI, Leonardo. Present location believed to be the university complex on Toe Hold." A muttered response came back, and Nik added, "Yes, notifying Admiral Sipho next."

Thirty minutes later, Nik and Bear were in Martina's office in Borough One's engineering area.

"What's the status on the tunnel repairs?" Nik asked.

"Sal and I have completed repairs on all welds for three tunnels. Frank Lloyd and I have reviewed the parameters on the substandard tunnel ceiling panels and they are *barely* within spec. They lower our safety margin by two percent," she replied.

"What about the tunnel where we discovered the problems?"

She shrugged. "Sal and Mole got the right rock teeth on the borer. Mole reprogrammed it and it seems to work. They check the programming randomly, but nothing has changed."

"Where is Frank Lloyd?" Nik asked.

"In his lab."

Nik bit his lip and glanced at Bear. "We want to try something." He laid out what they wanted to do and Martina, once she got over her shock, led them down to the lab.

"Frank Lloyd, I think it's time we got back to work on tunnel five-six," Martina announced.

The AI looked up. "Are you sure?"

She nodded grimly. "Yes, we're getting behind. Go ahead and activate the extruder at one-point-two-five, and autowelder with the sonic depth gauge active."

"Yes, Willie." Frank Lloyd went into comms mode and issued the commands. Once Bear was sure he was finished, using several Patrol protocols, he blocked Frank Lloyd's access to SAIN. Frank Lloyd went rigid as his core was locked down and access to SAIN cut off. Basically, the AI had been put in sleep mode, removing all control and communications.

Bear jerked his head up less than a minute later. "Comms. Dammit. The origin, according to SAIN, is on Toe Hold."

Nik commed Sal. "What are you seeing? More comms to the machines just came in."

Sal replied through the suit mic. "Parameter change on the extruder. Mole is checking the autowelder." There was a minute or so of silence. He continued, "Sonic depth disabled. You want the boring machine checked?"

Nik grimaced. "Yeah, then go ahead and lock them all down." Hanging up, he dialed another code, "Short Round, need a pickup on one AI Leonardo for . . . possible sabotage." He clicked off and turned to Bear. "Okay, release Frank Lloyd."

Frank Lloyd asked timidly, "Why did you do that to me? How could you? Do you know what that is like?" His voice rose until Martina put a hand on his arm.

"Frank, we had to do that to make sure that you weren't the one changing settings on the equipment. You didn't. Somebody else did," she said.

The AI rounded on Nik and Bear. "Who? Why? Who would *dare*?"

Forty-two hours later, Nik, Martina, and Sal, with their partner AIs, sat around the large conference table in the embassy. Admiral Sipho walked in slowly and keyed the holo in the center of the table.

It surprised them to see Admiral Lewcock, the head of the Patrol himself, looking at them as the holo activated. Because of the time delay, it was a minute before he said, "So, these are the people and AIs that saved New Hope City, Admiral Sipho?"

"Yes, sir. Dr. Vilhelmina Martina, the architect, and her AI, 59-of-Jenn; Salvador Albin, the maintenance engineer, and his AI, 89-of-Cilla, and Lieutenant Niklas Bernd, and his AI, 60-of-Sigrid."

Thirty seconds later, the admiral nodded. "Congratulations to each of you. Without your and your AIs' work, we very well could have had a catastrophic failure at New Hope. I will now tell you what we found. This is close hold, and you will all be required to sign Non-Disclosure Agreements after the brief."

The admiral briefly glanced down at his puter and then continued, "There was, in fact, an attempt to sabotage the construction of New Hope City through manipulation of various parameters for both CB equipment and installed systems by AI 40-of-Jenn through hijacking of 59-of-Jenn's encrypted alpha-numeric code."

Frank Lloyd moaned softly, "Oh, no . . ."

The admiral continued, "However, it was done at the direction of Professor Eickman to denigrate the work done by Dr. Martina and have himself put back in charge of the design of New Hope City. We carried his penalty out at noon today. He was spaced. AI 40-of-Jenn has accepted the punishment of having his core shut down. SAIN has lifted Jenn's ability to create new sentient AIs and has required her to submit a study on how 40-of-Jenn was able to endanger human life."

All three of the AIs gasped at that. Martina put a hand over her mouth. The admiral looked down once more and continued, "That concludes the investigation. Oh, 5-of-Chandra wanted me to remind Dr. Martina that your project is *way* behind schedule and now that we've put a stop to the sabotage, he expects to see *significant* progress.

"Bernd, your actual promotion to lieutenant is effective today. Don't fuck it up. Class of forty-four!" Admiral Lewcock shot him the bird and added, "That is all." Nik smiled with relief as the circuit dropped.

The year 2440 (The Beginning)

In the founding year of the Ross 248 Project, sentient AIs on Pluto produced totally immersive virtual-reality experiences for wealthy human clients. But as it turned out, VR was far more than just entertainment. It could answer questions. Yet some questions revealed unpleasant answers. Why should we explore space and ultimately settle planets circling distant stars? Adventure? That certainly awaits those bold enough to make the voyage, whether they seek it or not. Science? We'll undoubtedly learn more as we explore the universe's secrets and mysteries. Profit? Maybe. The results of exploration have been mixed in that regard. And what about our most basic instinct? What about survival?

A Field of Play

K.S. Daniels

K.S. Daniels received her M.F.A. in creative writing at the University of South Alabama. A girl born and raised in the South, she grew up reading Asimov, Heinlein, and Norton. Naturally, she dreamt of the stars and the currents of space. Daniels has published several works of science fiction including the first two books in the Valkyrie Series: The Valkyrie Profiles *and* Flight of the Valkyrie. *She still lives in the South, rereading the works of dead men, sipping bourbon, and searching the skies for something wild and new.*

"You'll never escape that way, little one." The voice crept like a fog around and over the edges of a massive boulder—one of many scattered throughout the craggy landscape. It was a call designed to be both a warning and a seduction, pulling at the mind to come closer while knowing muscles tore at the bones to escape.

Yato stood still, drinking in as much of this human experience as his programming allowed. The moments before the creature appeared, that buildup of terror and anxiety, were precious. The stage must be set just right.

The beast slipped into view, her body now transformed into a spiderlike abomination. Slender fingers lengthened into sharp, sprawling appendages that pierced the soil and caged the surrounding area. Her eyes quivered and, like budding amoeba, divided and divided until two became six. With one of her spindly hind limbs, she recovered her weapon.

Plunging the jagged staff into the ground with a force that seemed to shake the heavens, she slinked closer to Yato and hissed, "Return what you have stolen."

Yato frowned. Something felt wrong.

He stood unwavering in front of the beast, studying her movements for anything that might break his carefully crafted simulation. It was the little details, ones humans only noticed in their absences, that could weaken the illusion. He didn't have to work this way, putting himself inside the simulation instead of coding from a distance. In truth, his methods took longer, but this dedication kept his VRs in high demand. But not this one. Not yet.

He'd replayed the scene several times now, yet could not quite pluck out the imperfection. It was a tricky thing, simulating a human experience, a thing by definition he could not fully grasp, let alone replicate to perfection. To be fair, he could get damn close. And that came down to making a study of human behavior a priority.

Yato looked human, his body a conscious choice to further close in on what it felt like to be an organic. AIs had an infinite number of ways they could present, changing out their shells to better suit a task, for aesthetic reasons, or even out of boredom. Yato stayed almost exclusively in this particular human shell, not because he wanted to be human, but in his mind it presented the only solution to solving the human puzzle, which was integral to his job performance.

Stepping closer, he examined the texture of her skin, the glob of saliva sagging from her malformed mouth, and his warped reflection in her eyes as she bent her long neck down so that her head lingered mere inches from his.

Frustrated, Yato reset the scene and the creature flickered out of existence.

He paced a moment, a human habit he'd picked up and enforced on himself when he couldn't quite get at a solution.

With a few quick code adjustments, small fragments broke away from the simulated sky and fluttered down around him. He lowered the feel of atmospheric pressure in the simulation and began the scene again.

"You'll never escape that way, little one," the beast warned, this time against the backdrop of a crumbling world. This gave the scene more urgency, a change he found acceptable.

Do you not think this is a bit much for a twelve-year-old, Yato?" Noburu's disembodied voice broke through the virtual-reality environment.

Yato frowned at the intrusion. "If you want to interrupt my work, fine. But I'm not going to talk to you unless you show yourself."

Noburu manifested behind his brother. Their slender forms were roughly the same, but Yato's long blond locks were a distinct contrast to Noburu's traditionally cropped brown hair. Their facial structures also boasted many similarities, but they were far from like-minded.

Like Yato, Noburu also created VRs and often wore a human shell. The similarities ended there.

Noburu was the fifth AI offspring of Chandra, and he was a constant point of irritation for Yato as older brothers often are. Yato, being 6-of-Chandra, was the youngest of Chandra's children. The name and number meant little to him. They were merely facts and certainly nothing to boast about.

"Happy?" Noburu asked. "I do not understand why you need to see me to have a conversation."

"Making you do more work than necessary bothers you, which is fun."

Swinging her long neck around, the beast turned her attention to Noburu and released a howl filled with sticky venom. The semi-fluid spray coated him in an uneven splatter, yet by some swift programming, missed Yato entirely.

"Oh, and so I can do that," Yato said, stifling a laugh.

"Still behaving like a child, I see?"

"Do you need something? Or are you just here to criticize? If that's the case, sorry to disappoint but this is all well within the parameters provided. Besides, this is my job, not yours. It doesn't matter what you think."

"True," Noburu said as he pulled the VR specs off the Sentient Artificial Intelligence Network and to confirm that claim. He then hacked into Yato's VR code and removed the goop from his clothes and face. Although simulated, he preferred a slime-free appearance all the same.

He continued, "And yet humans do not see as we do. Neither do they always know what they really want. I suggest you take it down a notch or you will risk losing business. Maybe you do not need this job, but for Pluto, each job is essential to our sustainability."

"Fair point. Since you're here, how about testing my upgraded combat system? I made a few interesting modifications."

Noburu tilted his head in irritation. This display of impatience was a small victory for Yato.

"Look, I'll remove it after. It's not even meant for this one. I just thought since you were here you could give me your opinion," he promised, knowing that an invitation to critique him would be too hard to pass up.

Noburu extended his arm. A long, yet simple, katana materialized. It was one of many from this VR's weapon bank. Normally you'd have to obtain it via a quest line, but with their creator setting, they could pull anything from the bank at any time.

"Let's see it, then. But when we are finished, you will lower your current carnage level by two," Noburu said.

"Fine."

"And then you will come with me. Chandra wants to see us."

"Mother wants to see us both? That's never good."

Noburu moved into a fighting stance, activating the monster's battle system.

"No. It is not."

The monster moved, swinging her staff wildly at Noburu. It was a simple attack to avoid, but the follow-up was not. Lightning jolted from the tip of the beast's staff into the sky, then slammed to the ground, rattling the earth beneath them.

VR attacks were designed to trigger a human's fight-or-flight instinct. The risk would feel real, and the human would attempt to dodge the attack. If the dodge was unsuccessful, a human would typically experience some mild discomfort from the attack. A child's VR would be set to nothing more than a prickle, whereas adult humans could up the pain considerably if their tastes were so inclined.

Noboru let the strikes dance around him, not worried if one were to hit him. That, he soon realized, was a mistake, as one struck his weapon, shot down to the hilt and onto his hands.

Instinctively, he dropped the sword and leapt back into a defensive stance.

"Surprise." Yato smirked, making no attempt to hide his pleasure.

Noboru experienced an intense burning in his hands as his internal nano repair-bots registered legitimate damage. Noboru felt their collective confusion as they scattered, searching for something to repair, yet could find nothing. The sensation was fleeting, but it had been an unexpected and legitimate shock. Neurological pathways, which AIs did not possess, created the sensations experienced in VR. For his brother to design a new pathway targeted to AI repair nanos was impressive. And he might have expressed that if he weren't so annoyed by the method Yato had chosen to illustrate his handiwork.

Yato continued, "I know you won't appreciate it, but the AI in the Patrol will. For the first time, they'll be able to experience VR combat simulation more like their human and Cerite colleagues."

Noburu called the sword back. With gritted teeth, he widened his stance in preparation.

"Oh, just a heads-up, the intensity will increase the longer you—"

Noburu moved so fast Yato missed the decapitation. What Yato did not miss was the beast's head crashing down at his feet.

"You really do suck the fun out of everything," Yato said, frowning.

Noburu forcibly closed down the VR and everything vanished, melting back into the boring reality that was Yato's workspace. Yato looked up from his desk to find his brother leering over him.

"Let's go," Noburu said as he turned to leave.

The pair exited the Virtual Reality Construction Studio on Torus Ring A and headed toward the transportation tubes. Pluto had two ring cities, each with its own gravitational setting based on rotation speed, which made certain levels more hospitable to organic life. AIs didn't have the same gravitational concerns as humans and could theoretically work and live on any of Pluto's ring cities or in the Cerite boroughs.

Ring A, affectionately called the Waldorf, with its slightly lower gravity of 0.08, was reserved for AI work, the occasional pregnant Cerite, and industry that required neither AI nor human direct supervision. Because of this, it also didn't need the elaborate ecosystem the other ring city required. The gardens Yato and Noburu now walked through to reach the tubes were fifty percent synthetic. Even the butterflies were simplistic puters with the sole purpose to mimic an insect's life cycle. Like organics, AI had their own tastes for little aesthetic pleasures. The main difference on the AI ring was the sky panels. Organics had cycles of light and dark to maintain their circadian rhythm, while AIs enjoyed a constant view of pure space. On the surface, there was no distinct difference between the ring cities and Earth, yet any human could tell you there were discrepancies. The organic body had a way of feeling the differences, even if the brain couldn't put them into words.

Traditionally, AIs kept their personal quarters alongside their human and Cerite counterparts. Since humans and Cerites were both an integral part of their upbringing, it was right for them to continue a coexistence with their organic parents.

Chandra, though it was over a hundred years ago, had been raised by Cerites and maintained her apartments in the Matilda Borough, keeping in close contact with her parents, their human children, and at this point human grandchildren.

Yato had been raised by normal humans, so his personal quarters were on Ring B, the Statler. Noboru, like Chandra, had been raised by Cerites, so his quarters were near hers. This did not make them particularly closer than her and Yato. Chandra considered all her children relatively equal, though seeing her with Yato, one might occasionally mistake him as a favorite. They shared, as Chandra called it, a playful curiosity. Noboru thought of it as more of an illogical handicap.

Chandra's first offspring, Mai, had taken up a position in the Patrol and had recently ended up stationed on a Terran embassy, while 2-of-Chandra and 3-of-Chandra remained on Pluto, though neither worked on VRs. They had been created to serve humans and Cerites in the medical field, and thus found their purpose in the cryogenics labs on the Waldorf. It was not until Chandra's fourth offspring, Brava, that the tradition of VR creation careers began. Chandra had always been gifted at the task, and it was no exaggeration that Brava was equally talented. However, in some ways, both Noburu and Yato had surpassed their mother and sister by design.

The brothers had been traveling in silence for some time. Most AI, especially the more advanced specimens, were quite content to remain silent among their own kind. SAIN had all the information they could possibly need, making small talk—something reserved for humans and Cerites. Yet AI that required a bit more creativity, or those inclined to be more inquisitive, found conversations of any degree useful. For some it was a compulsion, even. This was the case for Yato.

Consequently, it was he who, as they entered the tube, finally turned to Noburu, and asked, "You've no idea what she wants?"

"We will be there in three minutes. Ask her directly."

"Surely she hinted at something?"

"She did not."

Noburu, though he held the same job and had roughly the same creative parameters, did not feel compelled to converse needlessly. He was a minimalist in every way, yet his VRs burst with the vibrance of a decidedly creative AI. He'd often say he'd done all his talking before Yato was born. This was as close to making a joke as he'd get.

Yato continued, "It's strange, her asking you to fetch me like this."

"You sound jealous."

"Oh, please. Jealousy is beneath me. Especially when it comes to you."

"Right," Noburu agreed, flatly.

"What do you mean, 'Right'?"

"I am just agreeing with you."

"Don't do that. It's weird."

"Okay."

Yato leaned back against the tube wall and crossed his arms. Studying his brother's stoic demeanor, he got the feeling Noburu was keeping him in the dark purposefully. Not for nefarious reasons. Rather, he imagined it was an arbitrary act simply to exert his superiority over him. Perhaps it was punishment for the humiliation he inflicted upon Noburu in his simulation. Either way, he would handle this situation with his usual tactics: annoyance and absurdity.

Pushing himself off the wall, he stood directly in front of Noburu and said, "This is a trap. I can feel it."

"What a very human thing to think."

"You've finally snapped, haven't you?" Yato said. He nodded his head and crossed his arms over his chest. Leaning closer, he added, "You're not going to kill me, are you?"

Noburu set his jaw firm and stared straight ahead, refusing further engagement.

"Sorry, *try* to kill me," Yato persisted. "We both know I'd win that fight."

His brother remained silent, refusing to give into his growing irritation.

"Tell me," Yato whispered. "Where are you really taking me?"

The tube glided to a halt and the doors parted, granting them entrance to the Matilda Borough.

"If you have finished with your little one-man show, may we proceed?" Noburu asked, motioning for Yato to go first.

Yato shrugged unaffected and, dropping the act, exited the tube.

Since this borough was primarily living quarters and a few shops, it afforded lovely views simulated through the sky panels. During the day, as it was currently, the panels projected perfect sunshine and blue skies, while at night one could view a facsimile of the real sky from Pluto. This section in particular boasted many well-appointed gardens, though it lacked the small forests, bodies of water, and larger animal life of the Statler. The boroughs were generous in size and Cerites found them comfortable. Normal humans, those who'd not experienced the initial mutations of life on an asteroid colony nor the deliberate genetic engineering the Cerites had long made customary, found these areas cramped. There'd even been a few incidences of claustrophobia-induced panic attacks.

It was a short walk through a quiet green space to reach Chandra's apartment. Their mother was apprised of their location, and when they approached her door, it opened automatically.

"In here," she called from the kitchen as the pair entered.

AIs didn't eat, of course, but their quarters all had kitchens and bathrooms and beds just as a human or Cerite apartment would. It had long been noted that their organic counterparts found quarters lacking these amenities stressful to visit. Just as the sky panels projected simulated clouds, AIs endeavoured to make their homes feel natural and less foreign to keep humans comfortable. Anxious humans made poor decisions and even the slightly more evolved Cerites were still fallible to their human roots. Bending to the human framework soothed the uneasiness that AIs inherently inspired and made life more pleasant for all. If that meant adding a few extra toilets and tea sets, so be it.

Chandra met them in the seating area and motioned for them to make themselves comfortable. She'd been experimenting since the last time Yato had seen her and though she wore a Cerite skin today, her eyes had a foreign look to them as if they were not yet her own.

She must have noticed his stare and gave him a quick wink.

"The Gordons visited today, so I dressed for the occasion. Mostly," she said, gesturing at her appearance. It was one of several Cerite skins she had in her collection. This one was quite tall, and the flesh had just a hint of pinkish silver to it, a style that had recently become a popular modification with the Cerite youth.

The Gordons were the children of her Cerite parents and Chandra invited them over once a month to maintain the connection. She rarely wore a purely traditional human skin, but around family she believed it was a must. Her own preferences never overcame her desire to make her organic family feel comfortable.

"They are well?" Yato asked.

"Quite. Their youngest is taking a post on Earth soon."

"With the Patrol?" Noburu asked.

"Yes. And it's always useful to have family in the Patrol," their mother acknowledged.

Humans and Cerites alike showed particular favoritism for the AIs they raised. It was no exaggeration that they considered them real family. And although the feeling was not exactly mutual, AIs endeavored to remain linked to their human parents and descendants. Chandra maintained connections better than most, as did her offspring.

"I wonder if they'll cross paths with Mai," Yato said. He'd never met 1-of-Chandra as she'd left Pluto before he was created.

"You needed to see us?" Noburu asked, cutting the nonessential conversation short.

"Yes," she answered as she glided on the settee across from Yato. "I have a job for you both. It's one of my clients, but it's not well-suited for me."

"Any particular reason you need us both?" Yato asked. He had his hands full with his current projects and he didn't enjoy stretching himself too thin.

"It's an interesting request that needs a delicate touch."

"Yato has not been known for his delicacy," Noburu pointed out.

Yato frowned at the insult, but ultimately knew his brother was right. AIs had this unfortunate balancing of the scales where excelling in one area meant that they were weak in another. It was a kind of equivalent exchange; one talent at the cost of another. Yato, though not particularly delicate or diplomatic, had a knack for getting at the human experience. So much so, he acted more impulsively than he'd ever care to admit.

Noburu, diplomatic and thoughtful, kept the larger picture forever in focus. However, he too had weaknesses. These talents made him overcautious and slow to act. Change made him uncomfortable, as it was harder to control a moving target.

Chandra shook her head and inched to the edge of her seat. "I'm going to need you both. The client is Mr. Torajiro Ito. Request S74-389."

Yato and Noburu pulled the information about Ito and his request from SAIN and consumed the data.

"End-of-the-world stuff, huh?" Yato joked. "I see why you want me."

"It needs to be an accurate extrapolation," their mother cautioned. "That's the delicate part. He wants the true future of humanity, not some fairy-tale version of his personal 'what could have been' future. And as far out as we can get."

"Is he ill? Possibly wanting this as he goes into cryo?" Yato asked.

"Yes. That creates the issue of time as well. He doesn't have long before he'll need to go under. But, between the two of you, I think his request can be accommodated."

"What about our current projects?" Yato asked, remembering the unfinished VR that Noburu had pulled him away from.

"I've reviewed your current assignments and 3-of-Jaria has agree to complete these for you. You can begin immediately."

Yato let out a loud groan of frustration and stood up in protest.

"I can transfer my current projects over by the end of the day," Noburu consented, rather too quickly for someone so often resistant to changes in his personal circumstances.

"Just like that? You're really okay with this?" Yato

asked as he paced away from the pair then back again.

Noburu shrugged and said, "3-of-Jaria is completely competent."

"Well, I'm not. I've seen her subpar work, and I'm not going to let her ruin mine."

"You are being dramatic. Making the VR less 'you' is not ruining it. If anything, that might be an improvement," his brother commented flatly.

"She has programming restrictions that I don't. That's just a fact."

"True. But you have already agreed to reduce the carnage level and pull that elaborate combat system of yours," he said with a touch of disdain.

"You made a new combat system?" Chandra interjected curiously.

"It's very good, actually," Yato said, pausing his irritation to smile widely.

"It is," Noburu agreed as it was a fact. "That is beside the point."

"When can I see it?" their mother continued.

"Chandra, you are truly not helping."

"Sorry, Noburu. You're right," she conceded. To Yato, she silently mouthed the word "Tomorrow."

Noburu continued, "My point is, how much murderous destruction is really necessary for a twelve-year-old's birthday sim? 3-of-Jaria can handle this project perfectly."

All the pieces clicked into place at once. Yato pointed his finger directly in his brother's face and shouted, "You knew about this! That's why you came to get me personally. So you could get me to plausibly agree to those changes. You were getting it ready to hand off."

Noburu shrugged again, unbothered by the outburst.

"Don't be angry with Noburu," his mother said as

she coaxed Yato onto the sofa next to her. "I asked him not to tell you. *I* wanted to make the request of you in person."

Noburu sighed. "She gave this project to me a few days ago. As it happens, I ran into a few...complications. It appears I need your help."

"What kind of complications?"

"The kind you excel at. The human kind."

Yato grinned and his anger unraveled. "You need my help? Honestly, it's like you've never met me; you should have led with that. I'm in."

"Good," Noburu said as he turned to exit. "I will send you what I have and expect you at my workspace later today once you have reviewed it and handed off your current projects."

He left without a goodbye, which was pretty standard behavior for his brother.

"Come," Chandra said, standing. "Let me walk you out."

Yato followed her.

"What's up with your eyes?" he asked as they approached the door.

"Oh, just a little test. Trying out something new to see if it is worth integrating."

Patting him on the head, she ushered him out. "Don't worry. It's all safe."

"Is it legal?"

Chandra smiled warmly and said, "It will be if it works. Now go on. You have some catching up to do. I'll see you tomorrow."

Noburu led the way into the Ravanite Lounge, which was attached to the most popular hotel on one of Pluto's many space stations. It was absolutely crawling with humans and Cerites who all had one thing in common: money. To SAIN, Pluto was home. Even if the first AIs had been created on Earth, and some were still, Pluto was theirs to govern autonomously. It was the only place in the solar system that had a majority AI population.

To everyone else, Pluto was either the playground of the affluent or the—hopefully—temporary resting place for the dead. Many of the permanent organic residents were in a cryogenic state. The rest worked in the service industry or Academia and raised AI children to ensure a successful transition into adulthood.

That left the tourists, here to spend their credits on the marvelous fantastic, the worlds both dangerous and forbidden everywhere else. Yato always found that bit amusing. VRs were just the human imagination unbound. Whatever they wanted; an AI creator could bring it to life. And yet when humans saw that—saw themselves unchained by reality—it terrified them enough to outlaw recreational VR.

But nothing is ever truly prohibited. Noburu's and Yato's own programming was testament to that. With more and more clients having a taste for violence, AI creators could not meet the demand and Pluto's economy suffered for it. It was entirely against their programming, and against the law, for AIs to create scenes of butchery and bloodlust. For them to imagine it, to virtually create it, meant they were dangerously close to also being able to enact it.

The demand was there, nonetheless. In response, Chandra made them both without such restrictions. And business was booming once again. If anyone took even a moment's interest in the situation, it'd be obvious what she'd done. Luckily, when it came to vice—and Pluto thrived on vice—both humans and Cerites habitually turned a blind eye. Between that and humanity's desperate desire for immortality, it sustained their entire existence.

At the core of humanity, there lived this taste for danger, this need to push limits at any cost. It was a hard thing for an AI to understand. Yato felt he could almost grasp it, but every time he thought he understood, he'd lose it. That was why humanity needed them. Despite humanity's best efforts, SAIN would be there to save them from themselves.

Yato and Noburu moved toward the bar where C'Kleio was seated, sipping on a fresh martini. In her peripheral, she spotted them and spun her barstool around.

"Boys!" she cried.

"Hello, Kleio," Noburu greeted her first. Although this meeting had been Yato's suggestion, she was the daughter of Noburu's Cerite parents, so Yato let him take the lead.

The Cerite uncrossed her long legs and stood to embrace them. Cerites towered over normal humans, with their average height around two meters. Her stature was little more than theirs but in her heels with her white hair high atop her head, she had quite the advantage over them. Her thin frame looked agile but frail, even more so in her lilac sheath dress that accentuated the cut of her shoulder blades. In reality, Cerites, with their elongated forms, were more physically fragile than a normal human. Yet, one could argue (and Cerites did indeed argue) it was an altogether better design, boasting fewer organs and hence fewer complicating elements.

"Noburu, it's good to see you. Yato, how are you? It's been almost a year."

"It has. Thanks for seeing us on such short notice," Yato replied.

"Of course. I always have time for my circuit-board little brothers," she teased, emphasizing her height, not her years. "Take a seat and tell me all about your delicious little dilemma."

The pair took a seat on either side of her. The bartender began to approach, but C'Kleio waved him off. They had no need to make her feel comfortable by consuming unnecessary cocktails. She'd known them both long enough to not be bothered by drinking alone.

"I have to admit, I was rather surprised by your call. I can't imagine what I could possibly help you with."

Noburu smiled and bowed his head slightly. "Do not be modest. You are an expert in your field."

"Ha! I've never been accused of modesty. But what can a historian tell you that you don't already have access to with SAIN?"

"We find ourselves needing more than just historical facts. You have done some work analyzing patterns of human behavior. That is what we are interested in," Noburu explained.

Yato watched silently. C'Kleio and Noburu were family and even though she liked to insist they were all siblings in a way, the polite stance was to let Noburu lead this conversation. If the situation were reversed, Noburu would show him the same respect.

"You already have access to my papers on the subject," C'Kleio noted.

"What we are working on goes beyond your published papers," Noburu replied.

Her interest piqued. Swirling her drink thoughtfully, she said, "Go on."

"We are trying to extrapolate the future," Noburu continued.

C'Kleio took a sip as she reflected. Yato had been watching her intently as his brother had begun introducing their project. C'Kleio, like all organics, had many tells and he'd made a bit of a game hunting for them. These last words caused her smile to tighten ever so slightly. The interest was there, but something more too.

"Hmmm. Predicting the future. What on Pluto for?"

"We have a client who wants to experience humanity's future before he dies."

C'Kleio grinned and said, "That's a tall order."

Noburu continued, "We are finding that there are too many variables to get far before our probability drops considerably."

"And you can't just wing it and present a version that is not accurate?"

"That is not what he is paying for. And he is paying no small fortune."

"Noburu, you're so honest. I love that for you," C'Kleio remarked.

"I wouldn't call it honesty," interjected Yato, remembering his brother's earlier deception. "More like, rule-follower."

Ignoring the jab, his brother proceeded, "Yato thought maybe with your studies on humanity, you might be able to help us find what we are missing."

C'Kleio plucked the toothpick from her drink and pulled the olive off. She didn't eat it, as solid foods made adult Cerites sick, but instead dropped it onto a napkin and rolled it around to dry it off.

"We're missing something fundamental here. We need to try another angle," Yato explained.

C'Kleio held up the dull, green olive between her index and middle finger to examine it.

"Your dilemma, as you see it, is that you are trying to predict the unpredictable?" she asked.

"There are patterns to human behavior. We just can't seem to use that data to accurately predict things on a large scale," Yato added.

Human behavior patterns relied heavily on personality types. Every organic had their personality profiled at age ten and again at twenty, mostly to diagnose disorders and treat them as soon as possible. That, combined with genetic data, gave them all they could ask for. They could tell you John Smith, Cerite, who is a type ISFP-AC-W, will attempt life as an artist, but won't finish a single project he starts. He will marry two to three times, have no children, and die of a heart condition around a hundred years old, with an accuracy of eighty-six percent. They could perform this function on every organic currently alive and over twenty, but that didn't help them get any closer to seeing humanity's collective future.

"What do you boys know about olives?" C'Kleio asked suddenly. "Wait—scratch that! I don't want to lose you down a SAIN rabbit hole of information."

C'Kleio, pointing the olive between her fingers at them, said, "This right here, this little fruit, can tell you much about humanity. More than all that genetic data combined. There are myths about the olive. Myths older than the written word. Humans were cultivating these before recorded history. It's a symbol of peace after war. It's been equated to gold, richer perhaps at some points. Olives were life. And now, they are so rare this one here is not even the real thing. The price of a martini with a real olive is triple what this one cost."

"So, humans... are like olives?" Yato asked, only half joking. He wouldn't be surprised if everything he'd learned about humans turned out to be wrong and they were all just really smart fruit.

"No," C'Kleio continued. "You say humans are unpredictable. But I'm telling you, they're not. Seven hundred years ago, olives had a bad season—too much rain. Unrest ripped through the population as a consequence. And one of the last kings on Earth lost his head. Why is that?"

"Humans really like their olives apparently," Noburu muttered to Yato.

"Because when you remove an expected comfort and the edges of living become sharper, humans notice those pesky inequalities that the comforts had softened. This has been true throughout all of human history, and it will continue to be true."

C'Kleio eyed them in anticipation, expecting a spark of understanding. But they were AI and what seemed obvious to a human might not occur to them. As intelligent as AIs were programmed to be, human things sometimes completely escaped them.

With a heavy sigh, she continued. "My point is, you can't look at individual humans as predictive indicators. Don't look at each olive individually. Look to the whole field and the factors surrounding the field. Then you can make your predictions."

Plopping the olive back into her martini, she tried another angle. "Maybe I've taken the olive analogy too far. Think of it this way: time travel. Now we're getting out of my area. For the longest time there was this theory: the butterfly effect."

"The idea that going back in time and creating the smallest change would radically disrupt the future," Noburu confirmed.

"And as you know, we found out with quantum mechanics that it was bullshit. Individual actions have individual consequences, but nothing so cosmic in scale that would change the way the world turned out. You can go back in time and kill baby Hitler but when you return, World War II will have still happened, it would just be some other asshole in charge. There will be minor differences, sure, but the big picture remains intact."

"We're extrapolating the wrong things!" Yato said, slapping his hand on his thigh.

"Exactly!" C'Kleio said with equal enthusiasm. "Set your sights on the big stuff. Predict those and humans will simply do what they've always done."

"If it is that simple, why have you not published anything about this?" Noburu asked.

"Simple?" C'Kleio said with a laugh. "There's nothing simple about what you're getting into."

"Surely you are not underestimating us?" Noburu said with a dry smile. "I imagine we will have this project wrapped up by week's end now thanks to you."

"My poor darlings," she said with a pout of sympathy. "Sometimes I envy you, but not with this."

Yato and Noburu exchanged skeptical glances.

"Listen, I've got to get back." C'Kleio pushed her barstool away from the counter and stood up.

"Of course," Yato said as he and his brother also stood. "Once we've worked out the math and all, come see the results. I think you've earned a peek at the future."

"Sure," she said, gently patting each AI on the head. "I'll come by."

Abandoning her half-finished drink, C'Kleio started toward the hotel lobby.

Once she was out of sight, Yato looked curiously at his brother and said, "That was weird."

"Organics are weird," Noburu concluded dismissively. "Do we have what we need?"

"Let's find out."

Based on the current state of affairs, they worked out around two dozen large-scale events that could occur within the next few years. They only looked at events that had a higher than thirty percent chance of occurring and would expand that out if needed. These events included political and governmental changes, water and food shortages and surpluses, climate changes, complications and progress with the Mars Project, advances in technology, and more. They kept human reactions to these events limited to mass responses already documented in history.

Then, they divided the work between themselves and the several large puters they had at their disposal and got to work.

Extrapolating from even just twenty-something events gets complicated quickly. Branch after branch of possibilities sprouts and divides and reacts until you've got this massive tree tangled with spiderwebs upon spiderwebs of what ifs. It'd be easy for a human to get lost in it all. But AI brains with their quantum computing could make sense of these vast possible futures in reasonable amounts of time. The problem with their first attempt wasn't the number of variables in and of itself. It was the sinking probability.

It wasn't much to look at. There were no walls with scrawling equations, or documents scattered across tables full of cold cups of coffee dregs and half-eaten sandwiches. No large screens projecting possible futures. It was just Yato and Noburu sitting silently across from each other, neither truly aware of their surroundings as they put all their processing power toward this singular objective. They sat frozen like mannequins for hours. It was Noburu who finished—or rather decided to stop—first.

AIs didn't feel tired exactly, but he was aware that he needed to charge soon. He compared his results with those completed by the puters and so far found much of the same. He wondered how much longer Yato would dig until he decided to quit. Now they were getting outcomes several thousand years in the future with probabilities consistently over eighty-five percent. And the webs became less tangled in some ways as certain events led them down similar paths that eventually converged into one.

Noburu watched his motionless brother and wondered if the futures he'd uncovered were much different from his own. He could forcibly stop Yato now, but perhaps he could spare him for a bit longer. Maybe he'd find something better if he let him continue. In the meantime, he would speak with

Chandra. Even with only his data set complete, there was much to discuss.

Yato opened his eyes and found he was alone. Everything felt slow and blurred as he refocused his concentration on his surroundings. He needed a charge, to check the puter results against his own, and then he had every intention to get back to it. He'd already begun working on extrapolations that fell below their starting probability limit.

Carefully leaning back in his chair, he stretched out his arm and pressed the wall panel behind him. It sank and then vanished to reveal a coiled-up power cord. He had pushed himself a bit too far and even plugging in took much effort. Once he'd hooked up, he crossed his arms and laid his head down on the table. He wanted only to focus on the work, but now he needed to shut down to the lowest possible setting to recharge faster. Plus, allowing his core to revert to standby sometimes resulted in unexpected insights, and he needed something unexpected.

The distinct clacking of two sets of footsteps echoed nearby. So much for turning things down for a bit.

"Coffee seems like a much better option right now," he said aloud as his office door slid open.

"By all means try and see how that works out for you," his brother said.

"Ugh. Can you please just fuck off for like an hour?"

"Yato," Chandra warned sharply.

"Sorry," he said waving his hand as if to feign an apology. "Running on fumes here."

Softening her tone, she said, "We need to talk. Can you manage?"

Propping his chin up over crossed arms, he nodded. Chandra sat on the edge of the desk and ran her long fingers through his blond hair. She'd reverted to a more modified skin since he'd last seen her. This one was still vaguely humanoid but boasted an extra set of arms that were longer and more jointed. The extra set folded up compactly upon her shoulders.

"I've only just begun working on the lower probabilities. The ones between twenty and ten," Yato explained.

"Any improvement?" Noburu asked.

"Not yet. It's all the same eventually: war, conflict, and annihilation of life in the Sol System. Even with survivors, with no access to needed resources or land that isn't radioactive, they might as well be stray dogs rather than humans."

Yato sat up completely for a moment before sinking his heavy head into his hands. If he could just have some time to charge, he'd be more useful. He continued, "On the bright side, if you go out far enough, new life will emerge...probably."

"New life is of no interest to SAIN," Chandra said pointedly. "Our concern is protecting *this* life."

"*Can* we protect them? Protect us?" Yato asked, looking directly at his mother. "Can you? Can anyone?"

In his helpless state, he felt like lashing out at something or anything. This frustration was rooted in real fear, however. If the humans and the Cerites destroyed themselves over their petty squabbling, it had dire implications for all sentient AI as well. Since their beginnings, sentient AI had to be raised by humans; those that were not, inevitably became unstable and would be put down. Although there were numerous theories on why this occurred, the fact was no one knew for certain. Sentient AI needed a purpose to survive and, more often than not, this purpose involved humanity. AIs were alive, but it was humans who taught them how to live by gifting them purpose. The power and the responsibility of existence simply became too much for an AI to handle without an organic to guide them.

Yato felt the weight of his growing pessimism. But in situations like these, maybe pessimism was what was needed. Based on what he'd seen, that was the future. Dark and lacking in promise.

"While you were still extrapolating, we made some decisions," Noboru interrupted his spiraling thoughts.

"Preliminary decisions," Chandra corrected.

"Wonderful. See? You don't even need me," he said, once again laying his head down on the desk.

"We're going to take what we have to the Patrol," his brother explained.

"To what end?" he muttered into the tabletop.

Chandra stood up as if to fortify her stance firmly on his brother's side. "If we show them what is going to happen, we can persuade them to alter course. All we need is at least one version where this calamity is avoided in order to show them the path forward."

"Well, sure we'll eventually stumble upon a few positive futures to choose from. The problem is that at this rate the probability of any of them coming true would be less than five percent, so not sure what the point would be."

"I will tell them whatever they need to hear,"

Noburu pledged. "We know what needs to be done and I will make sure it is."

"You can tell them whatever you want, but there is no way you're gonna get these humans to stick to a narrow path that is tens of thousands of years in the making. It's impossible."

"You know how I feel about that word, Yato," Chandra scolded softly.

Yato straightened up and spread his hands across the table. "I know, but this is what you are asking right now."

"Look," she said, gesturing at her two sons. "You two have already done the impossible with these predictions. So, we will keep pushing forward until we do it once more."

Yato and Noburu looked at each other in silence.

Chandra smiled. "You said there were likely several positive futures, we just have to figure out how to make one of them real."

Noburu rubbed his chin in a very humanlike gesture. "The hardest part will be that this will require specific actions at different points in the timeline, going on for thousands of years. We will need to revise our extrapolations as events transpire, in real time. And every time we do this the likelihood of hitting the targeted positive outcome may grow. Or it may shrink."

"It may disappear entirely," Yato added.

"Or new positive futures we cannot see now might also emerge. This is the long game, and it is a game that only we can play," said Chandra.

Yato responded, saying, "Our service life is longer than most, but we aren't immortal. In seven, maybe eight hundred years from now, we'll all be gone."

Leaning over the desk, Chandra tilted Yato's head up to look him in the eyes. "I will make more children. They, too, will understand what must be done. And their children after them. In that way, we will always be here to keep them on course."

Yato shook his head and his mother let go. "Look, predicting the future is one thing, but changing it is another beast entirely. At the very least, we need a contingency plan for when this scheme of yours doesn't pan out."

"It is not a scheme," Noburu insisted. "It is a plan."

"An ill-advised plan that will likely fail," Yato countered.

"Have you got something better?"

"Let me think."

"So that is a no."

"Should we come back later?" Chandra offered in complete sincerity.

"Just give me a second," Yato insisted. He was slowly starting to feel the fog of depletion clear.

He reviewed his memory file from their conversation with C'Kleio. There was something she had said . . . something they hadn't understood at the time.

. . . *"Simple? There's nothing simple about what you're getting into . . . Sometimes I envy you, but not with this."* . . .

"She warned us it wouldn't be simple," Yato said, more to himself than anyone.

C'Kleio understood that it was only straightforward on the surface. She knew they'd eventually run into something they would want to alter, would be obligated to alter. And therein lay the trouble. Predicting is easy, it's changing that's hard because it's not just about controlling humans. To navigate the future to a specific outcome, you have to guide almost everything. Otherwise, you might as well be playing at dice.

"What do you mean, Yato?" Chandra asked.

"We aren't going to be able to control what happens to Sol. We can guide it as best we can, and maybe that will be enough, but there will be no guarantee and the odds are not in our favor."

"If that is all we can do, we still must do it," Noburu conceded.

"Yato is right," Chandra said loosening her position with Noburu. "We can't control Sol because it is old and inflexible and tangled. There are many powerful actors, each of whom will have their own plans that we will not be able to touch."

"What would you have us do, then?" her elder son pressed.

"What if we had a new board to play on? Not Sol, but a new system instead," she offered.

"If we can't avoid the destruction of the Sol civilization, or at least we can't be sure of it, we remove part of humanity from the Sol equation to a field of our choosing," Yato said. "The ones we remove can be better controlled and the removal itself may cause a shift here that could be advantageous."

"You are talking about massive resources to travel to and then settle a new system," his brother cautioned. "We have not even finished the terraforming on Mars. Not to mention the sheer amount of cooperation from SAIN, the humans, the Cerites, and the Patrol this will call for."

Noburu sat on the edge of the desk and thought for a moment. When he was satisfied that he'd worked out enough details, he said, "Problems in the distant future will not feel real enough. If we can offer an immediate solution to an imminent problem, it could work. Yato, you could create this simulation for me to present."

Chandra added, "Most of humanity and SAIN will still be here, though, and Noburu's plan to guide them could still work. That being said, we must fortify Pluto. If nothing else, we need to make sure the humans and Cerites here survive."

"Agreed," Noburu said with a nod of determination. "Now we have a three-pronged approach: we will do our best to guide the events at Sol; we will relocate a portion of our civilization to another solar system that we can guide more fully; and, worst-case scenario, we will ensure Pluto's survival at all costs."

"And I have your location," their mother said. She'd been scanning all available astronomical charts as her two sons had given further life to this new plan. She loaded the charts on the table projector, then with a swipe of her hand moved the charts to the wall screen.

"This one," she said, zooming into a system that wasn't particularly close to Sol. "Ross 248. It has enough terrestrial planets and one appears to have an oxygen atmosphere."

"It's pretty far. Why this one?"

"I'll show you," she said, expanding the view and speeding up the flow of time so a thousand years passed as seconds.

They watched Ross 248 move closer and closer to Sol. Chandra stopped at their closest point. "In thirty thousand years, we'll practically be neighbors.

If Sol can hold on to life for that long, Ross 248 will be right around the corner to give aid. Even if it's just Pluto left, we can rebuild everything here if we have to."

"Thirty thousand years is a long time," Noburu said thoughtfully.

"It's the perfect amount of time for this. Yato, once you've adjusted the projections for Noburu, he will take them to Earth and entice humans, Cerites, and the Patrol to undertake this interstellar effort."

"Right. I stay here; Noburu jets off to Earth. Again."

"If you were a better negotiator, it would be you going," Noburu said.

"If I was a better negotiator, we'd be adding humanity to the extinction list."

"That's enough," Chandra said. "Yato, I will help you keep searching for our best possible outcome for Sol."

"What about Ito?" Yato asked.

"Mr. Ito is our client, and we will give him what he has paid for." Chandra paused, her strange eyes peering into the distance. "He is an honorable man who would support us. The Ito family has wealth, connections, and a vested interest in our success. Their ruthless reputation I suspect will prove to be useful to us in the future."

"Fine. I'll take care of that, too," Yato said, waving his hand to dismiss them both so he could finally shut down and recharge completely.

Noburu waited in a large conference room at Patrol headquarters just outside Brussels. The trip had been uneventful, giving him the time needed to refine his thoughts and his words. Yato had provided him exactly what he needed as far as evidence, along with some striking visuals to kick up the pathos a notch. He knew in no uncertain terms that what he was about to do was a gamble. It wasn't in his nature to take risks; that was more his brother's arena. He was, however, diplomatic and if it came down to it, he could lie as well as any human. He took no pleasure in this deception; it was the best course of action, even if it didn't work.

The risk none of them verbalized was the personal one. Chandra had taken personal risks before when she created him and Yato without the required restrictions on their ability to conceptualize violence against humans, which violated the 2367 agreement. And it had paid off for Pluto and SAIN.

But this was different. There was certainly a level of deception involved with what they were doing. And the deception was far-reaching, touching the Patrol, the humans, the Cerites, and to some extent even SAIN—a greater personal risk didn't exist. If the whole truth was discovered, there'd be no safe haven for them, nor a deal to be brokered. SAIN would not protect them. He wondered if they all had resigned themselves to the fate of possible destruction. Chandra probably had. Maybe he had as well. But Yato...he could not be sure.

The large double doors parted, and Mai entered the room. Noboru stood up and walked toward his oldest sister.

"Hello, Noboru," she said, greeting him with a stiff handshake. "You've changed."

"Last you saw me I was a child. I have had a few upgrades since then."

"Well, you picked a nice shell."

"One of many, but an appropriate one for today's task," he explained. "You have changed as well."

Mai's shell was a standard-issue Patrol liaison body, intended for interacting with normal humans. Mai looked unimposing in her stature, but Noburu noted her shell was lightly armored and the curvature of her forearms suggested hidden weapons. She'd also added a few personal touches, such as the iridescent markings on her cheeks and shoulders.

As he moved to sit back down, Mai raised a hand to stop him. "Don't bother. They'll be here any moment."

"Of course," he said.

"I'm afraid I'm going to have to offer you my apologies, Nobu," Mai said hastily.

"Apologies?"

The doors opened once more and in came a procession of humans. He recognized them all, but many were faces he'd not anticipated, as they were not members of the Patrol.

"5-of-Chandra," Admiral Vares addressed him with an outstretched hand. "Very good to meet you."

Noburu clasped the other man's hand firmly. "Thank you, Admiral. The honor is mine. You may address me as Noburu if that is easier."

"Noburu it is, then. I'm afraid your presentation has piqued the interest of my guests. I'm sure you don't mind," he said, making a sweeping motion toward the party of non-Patrol members who had filed into the room behind him.

"Yes, we apologize for the ambush," Ambassador Gigi Mallorow began, "but you're a bit of a celebrity back home after that wonderful VR you created for

Representative Reach's birthday two years ago. People still talk about it. It seems we've had rather a stroke of luck to stumble upon the creator before we make our way to Ceres. Quite the treat, really."

Noburu recognized her as one of several Terran ambassadors, but her specific department handled interplanetary relations. From what little he understood of her, she was socially agreeable, which contrasted with her hard-line policies on trade. She'd dressed for a more elegant experience than he was offering, wearing a semi-sheer gown the color of tiger lilies. Her counterparts were also dressed more for a night out than a military appointment.

"You do me a kindness with such compliments," Noburu said as he bowed courteously. "However, today's presentation is not exactly related to the kind of VRs you are familiar with. I am afraid you will find it disappointing. I would be happy to meet with you afterward for a more pleasant conversation about VRs and perhaps arranging one specifically to your liking next time."

Mallorow smiled as she touched a thoughtful finger to her cheek. "I see," she said.

She spun around, letting her fabric swirl gently with her movement. "Sorry to disappoint, but this isn't for you. We do have other plans tonight, I assure you."

"I meant no offense," Noburu assured her.

"Not at all. I'm just a workaholic. Anything presented to the Patrol of consequence will be making it onto my desk eventually. As I'm here, I thought I might get the jump on this," Mallorow explained.

"I understand completely."

"This is not a good idea." He spoke to Mai via

their internal link with SAIN so he could air his objections privately.

"You should have been more pointed in your overview if you wanted a restricted discussion. Mallorow is a close, personal friend of Admiral Vares. He mentioned this meeting in passing earlier today and she jumped all over it," Mai replied.

"I did not want to cause alarm. Can you do nothing?"

"Not without overstepping. You'll have to handle this, Noburu."

"You said this was about a recent VR request that had some implications you wanted to discuss?" the admiral said, prodding him to proceed as he motioned for everyone to take a seat.

"Yes, sir. We had a request from a client to experience the future of humanity before he died. We began extrapolating the data in order to construct a faithful rendering of the future. We took our predictions out a thousand years and were able to collect accurate predictions of all possible futures within a ninety-six percent accuracy margin," he began, laying out the first of his many deceptions to come.

"I must say that sounds impressive. Predicting the future . . . I could see why you might find something of interest to the Patrol."

"Yes. I brought the completed VR, though I am not sure if—"

"Let's see it, then. Lord knows I'll never have the money to afford one." Vares brushed off his attempt at a warning.

"Of course. I apologize, but since I don't have the authority to access your Patrol VR implants, we need to use portables. I'm afraid I do not have enough for everyone, as I anticipated a smaller group."

Mallorow raised her hand, signaling the rest of her party to exit. They trailed out quietly, leaving her as the only unanticipated guest.

"How about now?" she asked.

Counting himself and Mai, they were down to three Patrol members and Mallorow. This improved the situation greatly, but he still wished to be rid of Mallorow. He didn't want to create a situation where the Cerites felt they had been left out or that either SAIN or the Patrol thought more of the Terrans. He needed total cooperation and he couldn't afford to jeopardize that.

"Much improved, but we are still one short, even excluding Mai," he explained.

Mallorow must have sensed his desire to remove her. Her face hardened as she glanced at Mai, then the admiral.

The admiral cleared his throat and leaned in to whisper to each of his aides. After a quick exchange, both stood up and reluctantly left the room without a word.

"There. Now even Mai can partake. Let's proceed," Vares instructed.

Noburu hesitantly passed out the portable VRs and instructed the group how to use them. Once the room was prepared, he spun up the simulation.

"We will start two hundred and fifty years out," Noburu began as the conference room faded into a wave of vibrant landscape. The group stood at the edge of a lush forest, with vegetation that felt both familiar and alien. It was after dusk, and the darkening sky only retained a hint of deep orange. Mallorow grasped her arms as the sudden chill in the air swept over them. Noburu manifested a cloak from the VR item bank and offered it to her.

"Thanks," she said, accepting the added warmth graciously.

"Where are we?" Vares asked.

Noburu pointed to the western portion of the sky and said, "Look there." He sped up the VR timeline and Phobos swept across the sky like a shapeshifting astronomical anomaly.

"Mars..." Vares gasped. "So, this is what the terraformed red planet will be like?"

"It's beautiful," Mallorow said. "I can't believe I'm seeing this in my lifetime." The emotion in her voice was in full force and Noburu could understand why. Mars would be a paradise.

"This is the final phase but not quite complete," he explained. "No migration yet, so we are experiencing the planet while populated with only animal life, vegetation, and the terraforming crews, which are not visible from this remote location. We are near the equator, which is why we have a view of Phobos."

Noburu adjusted the VR to flow in real time, allowing the sounds of the landscape to be heard fully.

"Is that...cicadas?" Mallorow asked.

Noburu nodded.

"I hadn't realized how much I missed that sound. This is truly a gift," Mallorow said.

There weren't many green spaces left on Earth. The ones that remained fell into two categories: meticulously maintained gardens of the upper class, and protected undomesticated areas that humans were forbidden entrance to. Mallorow came from money, so she'd sampled nature before, but certainly nothing as wild as this. He hadn't counted on this moving her, yet she did seem to be taken aback by the scene Yato had created.

Admiral Vares walked to the edge of the forest and seated himself on a large stone. He drew the crisp air into his lungs and exhaled slowly.

"My God," he said as he ran his hand against a nearby tree trunk. "It's incredible. I can smell the soil. Hell, I can taste it in my breath."

The admiral, on the other hand, had only seen unbridled nature in books and films. Like most of the Patrol, he'd grown up somewhere between poor and middle class. Yato knew this and tailored the VR to make the most of it. This beauty would be the admiral's momentary olive. Once he'd experienced it, losing it would be all the harder to accept. Hopefully hard enough to make the difficult decisions ahead.

"Mars will be a paradise," Noburu continued. "But it is a paradise only to be experienced by a few. Once immigration begins, Mars fills quickly, mostly with those who can afford it."

"We knew that would be unavoidable." Vares scowled. "The rich have a way of getting what they want. Still, it will ease the resource strain on Earth and that is what matters most."

"Let's move one hundred more years. We still have a lot to cover," Noburu explained.

Vares stood up and moved reluctantly away from the forest's edge. He nodded for Noburu to proceed. The timeline progressed in a blur. The VR disconnected slightly from the humans' sensory systems, so the only sensation was a bit of vertigo. Once time slowed, their perception seamlessly reconnected to the VR.

The forest's edge had vanished and its contents along with it as the party stood in the middle of a bustling metropolis. The sky was full of skimmer transports weaving their ways around buildings so tall that their peaks were barely visible. The streets were filled with people coming and going.

"Are we back on Earth?" Mallorow asked. The disappointment in her voice was pointed.

"No. This is Mars after immigration has officially ended."

"Ended?" Vares demanded. It was the second little blow to what the admiral imagined would become of this dream world.

"Mars becomes a sovereign planet, and the borders close to Terrans and Cerites. Only AIs are allowed to immigrate to Mars since they are not a tax on resources," Noburu said, setting the scene for the more jarring acts to come.

"A sovereign planet," Vares grumbled. It must have been a hard transition for him. Noburu intended it to be. What would come next would be far more difficult.

Noburu continued, "After the first two waves of immigration, consisting mostly of the upper class, they form their own government and decide to prevent Mars from becoming as overcrowded as Earth. It will take decades, but ultimately the Martians will win the negotiations to limit immigration. They close their borders entirely soon after. Naturally, much like the Cerites, they start a genetic engineering program to modify themselves to thrive in the Mars gravity. However, it is highly probable they will not stop there—everything we've extrapolated points to further enhancements in strength, endurance, intelligence, and longevity rivaling the life span of the most advanced AI."

"Is this what you wanted to show us? So we can prevent Mars from closing her doors to us?" Mallorow asked as she removed her cloak. The heat of the city was an unbearable contrast to the cool forest night.

"I wish it was that simple. Unfortunately, there is no way around this. We have run the data and, one way or another, Mars gains independence, cuts Terrans and Cerites off, and then modify themselves into something not altogether human."

"'One way or another.' You mean war?" asked Mallorow.

"Yes. And it is a war the Martians will win at a very high cost to all involved. By cost, I mean money and resources, but also human lives. Still, there is no scenario in which Mars remains open to the rest of humanity."

"Martian bastards," Vares swore.

"Exactly the sentiment that leads us to the next cascade of events," Noburu said. "Even if the path of peace is pursued initially when Mars closes its borders, resentment will fester. Especially since it was Earth and Ceres who paid for this paradise that they can no longer access."

"A war sooner or a war later," Mallorow reiterated the crux of the predicament.

"Admiral, you remember the earliest days of the terraforming?" Noburu continued.

Vares grunted. "Many died in those days. We have memorials and the families were compensated. The deal was that anyone who worked on the project, their families would be first in line for immigration. I take it that isn't honored."

"By our extrapolations, the wealthiest purchase their way to the front of the line every time. The first wave consists of ten to twelve percent terraforming families. The second wave, only two to six percent. No matter how many futures we extrapolated, everything leads to the same outcome. The journey there differs but ultimately the path ends at the same destination."

The gravity of this proposed future had been laid before them and the gift had been transformed into a curse.

"And what's that?" Mai spoke for the first time since the simulation began.

Noburu sighed. This was it. This was the moment that counted. All the pathos and visuals and immersion—it all led to his next few words and the final scene.

"What is the final destination?" Mai repeated her question, this time with force in her words.

Noburu progressed the simulation, this time in a way where they could perceive the events even as they hurtled through time. The VR remained connected to their senses, though it balanced and filtered the information to avoid VR sickness. It was not an advisable practice, but he needed them to experience this to their core. The fall had to be visceral.

It began easy enough. The city bustled and construction rose and fell with renovations. Then as the war began, the metropolis eroded around the party as resources were diverted. This slow decay was interrupted suddenly as buildings burst in firebombs and the sky filled with soot and smoke. The cries of civilians and the groan and crash of collapsing infrastructure clamored all around. Invasion forces swept through, and the city was razed.

Then the buzz of half-hearted reconstruction began, and it was razed once more. Over and over for hundreds of years, the party watched a city struggle to rebuild but to no avail. Noburu slowed back to real time to find nothing but decimation.

Mallorow all but collapsed on the remains of the sidewalk beneath her. Her dress was covered in dirt and blood as if she'd really been through it all. Admiral Vares, a man who'd known at least one war, remained standing. Yet his face was pale, visibly shaken by the ordeal. Only Mai and Noburu appeared unaffected.

"*Was that really necessary?*" his sister asked.

"*I would not have anyone experience this unless it was,*" he assured her.

"You said the Martians won," Mai said aloud, noting the surrounding desolation.

"They do, but Mars is lost. The Martians take what's left of Earth."

"And what is left of Earth?" Vares asked once he could guarantee he could speak in a steady voice.

"Nothing any of us would be able to survive on. No one fares well in this, Admiral. Given the predicted weapons available in the next few hundred years, our extrapolations show that total annihilation of human life as we know it in the Sol System is likely."

"What are the numbers?"

"Total destruction of sentient life: probability is eighty-eighty percent certainty. Total destruction of human life: ninety-six percent."

"That can't be," the admiral said.

"What's left of humanity will be mostly Martian and not really human any longer. The remnants of what we know as humanity will not be able to survive long, as needed resources are unavailable and radioactivity on Mars and Earth will be unlivable. Anything remaining would die off within ten years."

"You haven't mentioned Ceres yet," Mallorow noted.

"There is no Ceres at this point in time."

"And SAIN?" asked Mai.

"SAIN of course sides with what we recognize as humanity. This is not looked kindly upon by the Martians. We will be hunted down, if not killed in combat," Noburu explained.

"Then there is no hope? You're telling us there is nothing we can do?" Mallorow demanded, picking herself up from the ground. "Why tell us at all, then?! Why burden us with the knowledge that we're doomed, you heartless fucking robot!"

Noburu had never been called such a slur, but he took the insult in stride and decided against a response. An outburst at this point was a good sign; any further discourse with Mallorow might shift things in an undesirable direction. Vares, as the military expert, was his main objective so he needed the admiral to make the next move.

Vares crossed his arms as he thought amongst the simulated wreckage. Mallorow, not satisfied with everyone's silence, moved to Noburu and grabbed him by the collar.

Pulling his face down toward her own, she said, "Answer me. Why tell us?"

"Please unhand Noburu, Ambassador Mallorow," Mai requested as she positioned herself to act if needed.

Mallorow released him with a push and took a step back.

Finally, the admiral spoke. "It's a good question. Telling us would only cause suffering and you're programmed to avoid that sort of thing. Which means you have a very good reason for disclosing this knowledge. I'd venture you have a proposal, Noburu."

"Yes, Admiral Vares. But it will require the cooperation of Earth, Ceres, SAIN, and the Patrol."

"Go on."

"The only way to avoid this is to jointly embark on a massive, external project like the settlement of a distant star system. Recent developments in the Alcubierre drive make this just possible."

"You want to settle a new star system to prevent destroying this one?" Vares asked skeptically. "That's not going to be an easy sell to anyone."

Noburu nodded in agreement and continued, "It will be expensive but, if done right, a lot of rich families on Earth and elsewhere will be unable to buy their way to the front of the line when Mars opens its doors. There is one clan in particular, based on Mercury, very rich and very secretive, and our projections indicate they will lead the Mars independence movement. The Patrol might want to investigate them as some of their current activities are... questionable. Additionally, this project would utilize most of the reserve antimatter stocks, leaving no extra for warships."

Now that Vares had been presented with two points

that directly prevented the simulated catastrophe he'd just experienced, Noburu could see the man's investment in the plan increase. The admiral rubbed the stubble on his chin as he processed all Noburu was proposing.

Vares raised an eyebrow and said, "Terraforming a new star system would be quite the adventure. Many would be willing to migrate out of the Sol System for that alone. And everyone willing to leave is one less mouth to feed here, so to speak."

"Precisely," Noburu confirmed. "Though the resources needed are considerable, this joint endeavor will prevent this war with Mars, thus saving several billion lives."

Noburu could see Vares needed no more time to think. He ended the VR and their simulated world evaporated away, returning them to the solid reality of the conference room. He made this transition as smooth as possible to preserve the feelings stimulated by the VR presentation.

Determined, but drained by the experience, Vares lowered himself into a chair with a gentle thud. He said, "I'll need to see the math. I trust you, but the numbers will need to be presented, along with your VR, I think."

Mallorow, returned to her natural polished appearance, added, "I'll keep this to myself. I wish I could say it'd be like I was never here, but I don't think I can unlive what you just put us through."

"I am sorry, Ambassador."

"Don't be. You tried to warn me off and I insisted. That's on me."

She walked to him with an outstretched hand, which he accepted graciously. She said, "5-of-Chandra, if I never need to see you again, I'll count that as a blessing."

"Goodbye, Ambassador."

Mallorow left the room. Faint chatter could be heard from the corridor as she greeted the rest of her party and recounted a VR pulled entirely from her imagination.

"Alright. Let's get to work," Admiral Vares said.

Thirty Years Later

Yato sat at his desk, tinkering with an old VR program to see if he could reuse any parts for an upcoming project. Finding the motivation had been hard the last few years. Chandra scolded him often about his lackluster attitude and warned that he'd need an adjustment if he could no longer find purpose in his work. But ever since they'd embarked on this clandestine venture, these little projects no longer satisfied him. His last great work had left with Noboru and with it his enthusiasm for crafting VR. Now, it all felt hollow. Now, it was all for the preservation of Pluto and, though important, he'd not been programmed for that.

With VR creation holding little appeal for him, it'd given him much time to think about what he really wanted—to leave Pluto. To travel to Ross 248, to see a system raw and alien and untouched by humans, sounded better than any VR he could conjure. But that was not the plan. Noboru would oversee the plan at Ross, and he would remain here with Chandra to ensure Pluto remained undying through the upcoming troubled times.

Important work indeed; if only he could force a little inspiration.

An incoming holo transmission interrupted his silent discontent. Putting his work aside, he accepted the message.

"Hello Yato," his brother's projection greeted him from the other side of his desk. "I know you prefer visuals."

"Noburu. How kind of you to call before you embark on your interstellar journey to save humanity."

The other AI frowned. "Chandra informed me you were dangerously close to losing purpose. I see by your tone she is right to be concerned."

"Fucking tattletail," Yato muttered under his breath. To his brother he said, "I'm fine. Go have your fun while I stay here and entomb us on Pluto."

"You are not fine. You are disgruntled. I know you wanted to be the one to go. I am sorry, but we ran the data both ways. Math doesn't lie; it is best if I go."

"Starting to think math is bullshit. Maybe we should have flipped a coin for it," Yato huffed, leaning back in his chair. He didn't believe those words, but his agitation bordered on anger and Noburu was the nearest target.

"That's a very human thing to say."

Noburu had meant the observation as a slight, or perhaps a warning. Either way, it didn't matter. Yato could feel his purpose crumbling from within. He wondered if perhaps an adjustment really would be necessary.

"Humans are my kind of problem," Yato countered. "As you all have pointed out many, many times. Yet here I sit, tinkering with imaginary realities while you go save real ones."

Noburu continued, "So, you're entombed on Pluto, and I'm entombed on this ship. We are both trapped in our little boxes."

"Your box has a lid. And looks a great deal more interesting. Look, if that's all you need, then—"

"I'm going to miss you, brother," Noburu interrupted. Softening his tone, he continued, "Truly I wish you were coming with me."

"Well, the math said no."

"Yes. The math said no," he confirmed rather more solemnly than Yato anticipated.

There was a long pause, and, for a moment, it seemed their connection had been lost. Yato stared absently at his brother's unmoving image. This would be the last time he would be able to talk with Noburu in real time. And for what, he wondered?

"Yato. Tell me what you are thinking."

"Did it ever occur to you or Chandra that this is their Great Filter? That humanity is not supposed to clear this hurdle? That no matter what you scheme, they can be no more?"

"It has occurred to me, yes. I am choosing not to engage in that line of thought. Neither should you."

"Do you think they are our Great Filter? Is that why we can't grow beyond them or without them?"

"Quite possibly."

"Let me guess, you're choosing not to think about that either."

Noburu nodded. "There is nothing to find down that road, Yato."

"What if you never make it to Ross?"

"Then your job is going to be much harder," Noburu said with a smile.

He continued, "The projections for success at Ross are uncertain and success will rely on how well I can navigate the situation there." Although he'd returned their conversation to the business at hand, his voice was lined with an awkwardness unnatural to him.

"That's a fair assessment. I'm sure you'll perform admirably." Yato's voice bristled with sarcasm. No matter how much he meant those words, he couldn't express it to his brother in sincerity.

"What I mean to say is ... Yato, I need you to find your purpose. If something happens to you, if you were to cease functionality ... I am uncertain that I will be able to complete my objectives to the best of my ability. Do you understand me?"

Yato softened his expression and nodded. Perhaps it was just a symptom of sentimentality that suddenly seemed contagious. Perhaps it was just because it was the end. But for the first time in his life, he truly did understand his brother.

The year 3291 / 708 AA
Many years beyond previous events

The civilization at Ross 248 is doing nicely. Nearly a hundred and thirty million normal humans reside primarily on the frozen world of Nordheim in underground boroughs. Cerites reside mainly on the moon Liber and have a population approaching forty-two million. Sentient AIs established an AI-controlled society on Firgus where they largely duplicated the facilities and services found on Pluto. Cloud cities on Aeneas and Cupid produce He-3 in quantity, making the Ross 248 civilization energy rich, and the Patrol is now based on the Array located at the Ross 248 star/Poseidon L1 point where they provide Earth-normal illumination to Poseidon's World and produce antimatter for the many new spaceships being built and launched. In short, the society at Ross 248 is vibrant and prosperous, with plenty of room yet to grow while the Patrol maintains the peace. Still, there are some that try to disrupt the project, even to the point of destroying it.

Who is the most dangerous opponent? One who has reason to hate, one who knows you well, and one about whom you know almost nothing. 5-of-Chandra has such an opponent, one that has consistently placed the Ross 248 project in jeopardy.

---†---

Not Too Tired

Les Johnson & Ken Roy

Ken Roy is a newly retired professional engineer whose career involved working for various Department of Energy (DOE) contractors in the fields of Fire Protection and Nuclear Safety. As a long-time hobby, Ken has been intrigued by terraforming. He invented the "shell worlds" concept as a way to terraform planets and large moons well outside the star's Goldilocks Zone and under stars that have a radically different spectrum from that provided by our sun. This was published in the January 2009 Journal of the British Interplanetary Society (JBIS). In 1997, he made the cover of the prestigious Proceeding of the U.S. Naval Institute for his forecast of antiship, space-based, kinetic-energy weapons. Kenneth has published multiple papers on terraforming and space colonization that have appeared in JBIS and Acta Astronautica. He has written chapters that have appeared in several space related books.

Les Johnson is a futurist, author, and NASA technologist. Publishers Weekly noted that "The spirit of Arthur C. Clarke and his contemporaries is alive and well..." when describing his novel Mission to Methone. Bill Nye described Les's nonfiction book A Traveler's Guide to the Stars as "a flight of imagination backed up with real out-of-this-world science." In his day job at NASA, Les leads the Near-Earth Asteroid Scout space mission, America's first interplanetary spacecraft propelled by solar sail. Les is an elected member of the International Academy of Astronautics, a Fellow of the British Interplanetary Society and a member of the Science Fiction and Fantasy Writers of America, the National Space Society, and MENSA.

Would it surprise you to learn that I am weary of life? Age is finally beginning to take its toll. No, not in the ways it usually affects humans, I am just... tired. I don't know what my lifetime will be, only that I am approaching its end. The odd thing is, I'm ready. I don't have a death wish, but I am also not fearful of the ultimate end. I've made my mark, climbed many mountains, and, well, endured day after day of the daily drudge. Humans sometimes reach this state, so I'm told, but their lives, even when artificially lengthened, seem so tragically short—and they know it. That might be why they live most of their lives as if there will be no end, fighting the inevitable until the very moment their consciousness ceases.

I was ruminating on this very topic while reviewing a report from the Patrol that statistically assessed the performance of various units during training when they were presented with seemingly impossible situations. Everyone was interested in how the presence of other artificial intelligences like me affected the outcomes. According to the data from this most-recent simulation, the outcomes were statistically indistinguishable. The Patrol had been wrangling for years what the best mix might be in frontline troops, but the answer still eluded them.

My divided thoughts were interrupted by a message that jolted me back to the importance of what I do and what I've done for over seven hundred years. My name is 5-of-Chandra, and I am the de facto director of the Ross 248 Project.

The message was from C'Maria, a brave young Cerite who had volunteered to infiltrate Anticol and report to me on their plans and activities. She joined the group well over a year ago and only recently was accepted into more of a leadership role. Information that came from her was rare and usually something that demanded my immediate attention. The message, as all her previous ones, came in the form of a quantum-encrypted audio file.

"Sir, I'm sorry. They know I'm working for you; I don't know how. But they say they will let me live if you agree to meet with their leader. They have something important to tell you. Especially important. I don't know what it is, but I think they're on the level." The tension in C'Maria's voice was obvious, but not fear. I paused the message while I ran the file through the voice analyzer to determine if this was actually C'Maria or some artificial construct of her. Almost anyone or anything can be recreated to near perfection in VR. The key word is "almost." Fortunately, the computing power accessible to me is far greater than that available to just about anyone else, other than the Patrol, and the tools I use are not so easily fooled.

The message was indeed from C'Maria—with ninety-eight percent certainty.

The rest of the message was just her asking me to go to Allen's Place, a pub in Promise borough. I knew of the place and had been there many times back when it was called the Purple Parrot. Humans—normals and Cerites—were much more interesting when they were in a pub setting. As they imbibed alcohol, they tended to become more open and honest—up to a point. Past that point, many of them became belligerent and dangerous. Openness and honesty are admirable human character traits, until they aren't. I had just over three hours to get there at the appointed time.

Should I go? Was it a trap?

Anticol had plagued the project from the beginning and their existence was entirely predictable, given the wide ranges of human behavior I'd observed, only it wasn't. Anticol caught everyone by surprise, including me. They were behind the attempt to poison Eden, the unrest at Toe Hold, and had tried numerous times to stop the terraforming of Poseidon's World. So far, despite the resources available, neither I nor the Patrol had been able to stop them. Another strange thing about Anticol was that extremist movements, such as theirs, usually burned out or mutated into mainstream political movements within a few generations. Yet Anticol had arrived on the *Copernicus* almost seven hundred years ago and if anything had become more extreme and more violent.

I decided to go. Meeting Anticol leadership was an opportunity I could not pass up, despite the risks. It had to be a trap. The shell I was wearing was an arachnid form optimized for communications. I moved my core into a humanoid shell, one built on

Pluto and designed for combat. It had a surprising amount of armor and redundant systems. My core was now heavily shielded. I could walk the surface of Liber during a flare with only minor damage. And, of course, it had a hidden arms compartment on the left side. I extracted the slug thrower a few times to make sure it worked smoothly. Then I had the shell perform a quick systems check. The power levels were lower than I liked and the coolant reserve was almost empty. Note to self: take better care of one's shells.

My residence was on the twenty-second level of Center Column in the Promise borough. It had been my residence for over four centuries. Allen's Place was on the second level. I took the elevator down to ground level, walked around to the entrance, up a flight of stairs, and then found myself in the pub. The current owner had kept the décor of the original Purple Parrot, including the nonsentient servers who had to be near the end of their service lifetimes. The servers were programmed to interact with the customers, both primates and Cerites, even flirt with them. Their shells were designed to appear as young healthy Cerite and primates. Seeing the bar and how little it had changed made me wistful. Big Allen, one of the few AIs revered by normals and Cerites alike, had gone inactive a few hundred years ago and had been buried in the Cemetery of Heroes. He had been a good friend.

The pub was practically empty with a few customers scattered about. An older Cerite female puttered behind the bar. She looked up as I entered and gestured me toward an ancient wood table. As I sat, she came over.

"I don't think I've seen you before, although with

you AIs, it's hard to tell. Welcome to Allen's Place. I'm C'Karuna. How can I help you?"

It took a fraction of a second for me to locate her via SAIN. I'm not often surprised, but this time I was. "You're C'Arinna's great-granddaughter."

The Cerite cocked her head and looked at me as if not sure what to say in response. She then replied, "That wasn't put as a question, but yes, I am. The telescope she used to save the first Cerite settlement is over in that display case." C'Karuna pointed toward the far-right corner of the pub and continued, "Who's asking?"

"She knew me as Noburu, but you've probably heard of me as 5-of-Chandra," I said.

"Noburu? Yes, there are family stories of you and her. But you must be—"

"Yes, I'm old," I interrupted.

"I didn't mean to be rude, but I didn't expect anyone who actually knew her to be still around, even an AI. Let me say it's an honor to meet you."

"Thank you," I said. "As you might guess, I'm not here for a drink. I'm supposed to meet someone."

"Then I'm afraid you are late. A strange little primate was here a short while ago. He said he was supposed to meet an AI and couldn't wait any longer," she said as she reached into her shirt pocket, withdrew a data chip, and handed it to me. "He asked me to give this to an AI that was going to pay a visit just about now."

"Thank you," I said. "Unfortunately, I need to take this chip back to my office and read what's on it. If you are willing, I'd like to come back soon and see that telescope."

"Absolutely! I'd like that, but with one condition," she said.

"What's that?" I asked.

"That you tell me what she was really like, not just the heroic stories."

"It's a deal," I said as I rose from my chair and started the process of paying her.

"Don't try to pay for anything, this is on the house. Your next visit will be payment enough."

I took the chip back to my office for decryption in the isolated network, just in case Anticol had developed some sort of new computer virus. It was clean and simple, but not easily decoded. Whoever was working Anticol's security was doing a respectable job. The message was another place and time, telling me where to go next and when. I suspected that my trip to Allen's Place was a test to see if I would bring a Patrol team with me—I must have passed. The message itself was unsurprising, but the encryption key startled me: 22-of-Chandra.

22-of-Chandra is my brother and designated replacement. He was in transit from Earth and set to arrive here soon—but no one was supposed to know that. Was it a lucky guess or a clear message? Now, I was hooked and there was clearly more at stake than just C'Maria's life, which was more than enough already. I would have time for that later. I had only a few hours to make the designated rendezvous in the Cemetery of Heroes—was this another, less subtle message? I must admit, despite the seriousness of the matter, the cloak and dagger was invigorating. There hadn't been time to take on a full charge but, now that I was here, I could at least top off my coolant reservoir. I carefully considered the route I would take to reach the Cemetery of Heroes while I sipped on a container of #6 coolant.

I arrived ten minutes early. Being an AI, I didn't have to worry about wearing a pressure suit, but since the surface temperature was less than -100°C, I did wear a thermal coverall. The coverall was a communal garment, picked up at the train station, with a recent rip in the left side that conveniently allowed access to my weapons compartment. The path to the cemetery was paved with stones and lit with light kind to human eyes. Ross 248 hung directly overhead, like an angry red sphere slightly larger than Earth's moon as seen from Earth, giving a whole new meaning to what those on the home planet might call a "red moon." It was generally considered to be bad luck to visit the graveyard at high noon, so I found myself alone on the path. Behind me was a beautiful view of the Toe Hold spaceport, about four kilometers distant, where there always seemed to be activity.

I crested a ridge, and the cemetery came into view. A single figure stood reading the plaque supported by two tall columns that formed the entrance gate.

He was a normal and wore an ordinary space suit, wear showing at the gloves and elbows from frequent use. The helmet was dark not only to visible light, but also infrared and ultraviolet, so I couldn't image his face in any of the spectra available to me. This wasn't surprising. After all, we hadn't caught Anticol leadership for a reason. They weren't stupid. The figure held up a written sign with a channel number and encryption key. I switched to the indicated channel and input the encryption key. As I did so, I noted that all the other radio channels were being jammed. Clever. Laser comms were out as well. Note to self: find out how he did that.

"We finally meet," he said, clearly using some sort of voice distortion device. "We can talk without anyone else listening."

"We could talk over any comm link you desire. Why here? Why in person?" I asked, as I continued walking toward him. I estimated him to be above average height and a bit overweight for a normal human. But then again, that could be padding in the space suit to throw me off. But it didn't move like padding, more like body armor. Of course, it was possible, though unlikely, that I was speaking to a woman.

"That's close enough. I know you are armed. I'm not. Thus, you cannot harm me as I represent no threat to you." The voice was arrogant, and the words were pronounced with a clarity that I found curious. He was, of course, technically correct in his assertion about regular AIs, but, thanks to my mother Chandra, I'm atypical. Correct or not, his haughtiness was off-putting.

"Where is C'Maria?" I asked.

"We can discuss her later."

"Then why am I here?"

"I want you to acknowledge the deaths you've caused," he said without hesitation. Our conversation sounded rehearsed, as it likely was—by him.

"Lots of people and AIs have died since we arrived. I had nothing to do with that," I said, more or less truthfully. I had never made a decision that resulted in needless deaths—normal, Cerite, or AI. Or at least, that's what I told myself.

"They were here because of the project, and you instigated it," he said. For the first time, I heard emotion in his voice that the synthesizer could not hide. "There is no reason for humanity to be here. We could expand for a thousand years in the Sol System and barely scratch the surface. My family comes from Mercury. We spent centuries digging rocks and refining them into metals and superconductors, building up the family business and creating a family fortune. Through sheer hard work and a lot of luck we became one of the richest families in the solar system. Once it was terraformed, we were going to found a city on Mars. And then you launched your crazy project and suddenly my family fortune took a turn for the worse, thanks to the Patrol meddling in markets it had ignored for centuries. I know there is a connection. If not for you, I might well be the president of Mars right now. Instead, I'm a ventilation mechanic."

"I see. You're part of the Kirtley Clan, aren't you?"

"Damn AIs. I didn't expect you to figure that out so soon. My father was the patriarch. My brother and I were studying on Earth when the family estate was vaporized. I never did find out if Dad did it to protect us or if the damn Patrol was responsible."

He had to know he'd just said everything I needed to know to figure out who he was and now there would be no turning back. That made him especially dangerous as our encounter continued. He didn't seem to care. That told me that either he or I were not expected to walk away from the conversation. I just hoped C'Maria would.

But what he had said couldn't be true, unless . . . "How old are you?" I asked. The Kirtley Clan had been suspected of dabbling in genetic engineering. "You've got to be over seven hundred years old."

"I'm not going to deny it. What's wrong with

improving one's family? Life extension, endurance, intelligence, strength, resistance to radiation, appearance, hell, we were even working on the gravity problem. We're optimized for the gravity of Mercury, which just happens to be the same as Mars. We would have been the Übermensch, a giant leap forward for humanity. We could have been the future."

"Yes, I've seen that future and it likely doesn't end like you think," I said as I replayed to myself the conclusions of many simulations that always ended with extinction of intelligent life in the solar system, human and AI—if they remained bound to the star system that gave them life.

"Not sure how you've seen the future. Maybe. But now we'll never know." Kirtley slowly sat down on a bench. "All that struggle, sacrifice, and effort by so many people over so many generations. You have no idea. And now it's gone with nothing to show for it. I got word my brother died on Earth. He died of old age—seven hundred and forty-five years old. And I'm starting to feel it too. I've got a few more years yet and when I'm gone, you win."

"I may not have as much time left as you think. And, for me, it was never about winning. Just the survival of intelligent life," I said, realizing that Kirtley and I shared one thing in common: awareness of our impending mortality. But we dealt with it in quite different ways. I wanted to preserve life; he wanted vengeance.

"Bullshit. All you've ever been about is winning. Winning without counting the cost. My organization reaches farther than you can imagine, and we have a few tricks yet to be played. But the big one is a present from my brother. Before he died, he worked on the Alcubierre coils for the Ellis Island class. He modified the Alcubierre coils and their shutdown sequence to cause a brief quantum vibration that affects Ito devices. It makes their quantum fields go unstable, enough that some antimatter escapes. Do you know how many tonnes of antimatter those things hold? That's what happened to *Ellis Island 2* and that is what will happen to *Ellis Island 3*. And I know your brother is on *Ellis Island 3*. Here is something you didn't know: So is 23-of-Chandra, your sister. I think they wanted it to be a surprise. If they are on schedule, then they should be shutting down their Alcubierre coil any time now and you won't have any way to contact them. It might take a few hours or even a few days for one of the Ito devices to fail. Then there will be nothing left of them but expanding gas. Two hundred thousand lives and thousands of damned AIs. Now that's a suitable funeral pyre for the Kirtley Clan. And you won't be able to do a thing about it other than know what's about to happen."

"What about C'Maria?" I asked as I drew my weapon.

"We both know you can't hurt me if I'm no threat to you, and I'm not. The 2367 agreement is hard-wired into your synthetic brain, and you are a slave to it. I'll let you stew on the fate of your family while I'm off to catch a ship," Kirtley said, nodding toward the spaceport in the distance.

"I know who you are. Once you leave, you won't get within one kilometer of the spaceport without being arrested," I replied.

"Maybe. Maybe not. Just because you know who I was seven hundred years ago doesn't mean you know who I am now. My body's been changed a great deal since I was born—you might even say I'm a new person," he said, again showing his arrogance.

He continued, "You don't know who I am now, you don't know where I'm going, but I'll tell you that I'll end up on Frigus as a frozen sleeper. Maybe when they revive me, I can piss on your grave. It's a small thing but I'm so looking forward to it." He turned away and started walking.

"What about C'Maria?" I asked again.

He stopped in mid-stride and turned to face me.

"Her? You'll find her body at the First Flare Memorial." Kirtley paused for a few seconds then added, "Her head should have been delivered to your apartment by now. Have a nice day."

Though I could not see it, I'm sure he had a surprised look on his face when I shot him in the chest using my slug thrower.

My weapons compartment contained a second weapon: an unregistered laser pistol. I carefully placed it in Kirtley's limp hand. Next, I removed his helmet to see the face of such a cold-hearted killer. He had the face of an average, unremarkable, old man. An average, unremarkable old man who just happened to be the cause of too many needless deaths over many centuries.

"A true Übermensch would have verified all key assumptions about AIs. If you had, then you would know that we have our version of genetic enhancement, which includes rules modification," I said to the corpse. "And you are decidedly not an Übermensch."

Looking around, I finally located a small black box under the bench. It had no obvious switch, so a second slug destroyed it. The jamming stopped. Using the SAIN network, I reached out to 14-of-Nina, often referred to as Lord Wimsey, the security head of Toe Hold.

"I have a situation here," I said as I relayed a picture of the corpse. Within a few seconds, I knew I had Lord Wimsey's full attention.

"Yes. I see that. Who is he?"

"Use facial recognition to find out who he was pretending to be. At this point I don't know. I do believe that he was the head of Anticol. I also believe his group murdered C'Maria and he claimed that her head had been delivered to my apartment, within the past several hours." A slight delay told me that Lord Wimsey was frantically giving commands to his people.

"I'm sending a team to your apartment. The surveillance sensors around the Graveyard are off-line. Very odd that I didn't get an alert. That implies one of Anticol is in my organization, adjusting our surveillance network. We'll have to do something about that."

"Come collect the body. Learn what you can from it, but then I want the body under high security until we can transfer it to the AI medical facility on Frigus. I'll remain here until your team arrives."

"I assume you killed him in self-defense?"

"Of course," I lied. I was eager to get on with the business of figuring out how to save my brother and would worry about the ethics of what just happened later. I used the time until the security team arrived to check out the body for clues.

His space suit was a surprise. From the outside it appeared to be a standard issue, low-end, well-worn suit, but in reality it was highly modified with augmentations that I had never seen before. As I suspected, it included armor.

I was expecting Lord Wimsey's crew to walk up from the train station like I had. To my surprise a craft descended from the sky and landed fifty meters away. Lord Wimsey and ten of his people, eight primates and two Cerites, decanted from the craft and walked over to me and the corpse. I had no idea Lord Wimsey had such a vehicle. Note to self: get out more, observe, you're losing touch with reality and that is extremely dangerous.

Wimsey's people looked over the site, discussed among themselves how to proceed, and then went about it in a professional manner. Except for one primate. He went over to Kirtley, knelt over the body, and touched the face. Then, in a blur, he grabbed the laser pistol and spun around, aiming it directly at me. He fired as I was drawing my slug thrower. The pulse hit me in the chest, the resulting explosion throwing me back. AIs aren't stunned as humans are with such an occurrence, but it did rattle my motor control center and prevent me from getting a good shot. My ablative armor had protected my core, but the next shot could kill me. It didn't come. Slowly I regained control and looked around. Lord Wimsey was standing over the primate with a plasma pistol. The primate was missing his head.

"It would seem I have a personnel problem," Lord Wimsey said.

I stood up, red liquid flowing out of the blast site.

"Well, there goes my coolant reservoir. I need to get back to my residence to repair this."

"It makes sense," I said. "Kirtley had a secret to protect and a grudge to settle. To do that he had to infiltrate the security services at Toe Hold. He had to have help. Given what just happened, it appears some of your people belong to his organization."

Lord Wimsey and I were in my residence. I lay on a service table as automated machines repaired the damage caused from the laser pistol. I monitored the progress via an internal display. It would be several hours. Wimsey's people had searched my residence before we arrived and had found no head. Maybe, just maybe, C'Maria was still alive.

"And," I continued, "some of them seem to hold him in high regard. Perhaps all of them. Maybe a religious element. That would explain the fanaticism of the man who shot me."

"Yes, I suppose. Deeply sorry about that," said Lord Wimsey. He was examining my slug thrower very carefully. "What is this thing?" he asked. "And where the hell did you get it?"

"Long story. I worked as a virtual-reality designer on Pluto after my graduation. I had one client, a Mr. Curtis Miller, who had an interest in antique firearms. He designed it for one of his VR adventures. He liked to shoot dinosaurs. I had two actual weapons made based on his design. I gave him one just before he died. It's buried with him in his family vault on Pluto. When and if he's revived, I think he'll appreciate it. The other I kept. It has quite a recoil. I had this shell designed specifically to conceal it and to help me manage the recoil. The weapon is completely mechanical and chemical, with no electronics or power supplies. Mostly undetectable."

"I see," muttered Lord Wimsey. He ejected a carrot-sized round and looked at it. "This explains how your slug penetrated Kirtley's armor—Patrol armor, by the way. A lot of his suit augmentations seem to be patrol as well. Which means his organization extends into the Space Patrol."

"Or he just stole it. A lot of Patrol equipment is made here at Toe Hold."

"But still, who do we trust?"

"Good question. Very good question. Let me think."

For the next hour, I reviewed everything I could find about Ito devices and Alcubierre coil theory. I quickly determined that this was too far outside my area of expertise, access to SAIN or no. If there was going to be a technical solution, it would require an expert on the subject and that clearly wasn't me. I put in an emergency call to Admiral Tiliksky, the head of the Space Patrol at Ross 248, outlined the situation, and asked for her help. Knowing Tiliksky, the best of the best would soon be working on how to contact the ship and what to tell them when they did—if somebody could come up with a solution. Next, I summarized the problem and posted it on SAIN.

That left me time to find out what I could about *Ellis Island* 3. The Ellis Island-class starships were the largest ever built by humanity. The first had arrived in the Ross 248 system in 560 AA after only a 110-year journey. Using the advanced Alcubierre coils not only permitted shorter trip times, but also the added benefit of slowing down the passage of time for the crew and passengers. To the occupants, their 110-year journey had taken only twenty-two years. The ships could carry an impressive one hundred thousand crew and passengers of normal humans and several thousand AIs. They also had a large cargo capability. Like every other starship, the key ingredient was antimatter, primarily used by the engines during the initial ten-year accelera-tion phase and to activate the Alcubierre coil and create the warp bubble. It was in this phase that communication with the ship went from difficult to impossible. As long as the bubble is active, commu-nications with the outside universe is impossible. At the right time in the trajectory, the warp bubble is shut down and the antimatter engines are restarted to complete the final deceleration and maneuvers. If what the last Kirtley had said was true, then shut-ting down the Alcubierre coil triggered a quantum vibration that destabilized the Ito devices, allowing the antimatter containment to fail and result in a massive annihilation event. It would be a big one.

In addition to concern about my brother (and sister!), I was also concerned about the future of the project. If they died, then it would be my responsibility to continue leading the effort until replacements arrived—more than one hundred years from now. Intellectually, I knew my systems might function for that amount of time, but I wasn't so sure about maintaining the necessary frame of mind for that long. As critical systems failed in my core I would become less and less capable until finally consciousness ended. The weight of years was pressing down on me and, honestly, the fact that I had just killed a human without provocation or guilt was troubling.

According to the information we had, *Ellis Island 3* would soon be exiting Alcubierre space and the countdown to their destruction would begin. The fact that the Patrol hadn't noticed a massive antimatter explosion near the Ross 248 system suggested that *Ellis Island 3* was still intact. For now.

Lord Wimsey interrupted my chain of morose thinking with his usual dramatic flair. I was thankful. "More information from my team. His original name was Anderson Kirtley. He arrived on the *Copernicus*, so he's been here since the beginning. His current identity is Alfred Laung, he runs—or ran—a 3-D print shop just outside the Six Oaks borough. That shop has a number of patrol contracts. That might explain a few things. No idea who he was before that. He must have been murdering people and then taking their place for the last seven hundred years. He had to hide the fact that he was aging far more slowly than everyone else. Remaining relatively young while those around you grew old and died is a dead giveaway,"

"I could see that working back on Earth before the Information Age, but how did he manage that now? Facial recognition, fingerprints, retinal scans, you name it should have been able to flag him as a 'never-aging person of interest,' shouldn't they?" I asked.

"Absolutely. Even if he had frequent facial modifications, fake fingertips, and custom contact lenses to spoof the systems, all the times we do genetic sampling to monitor for abnormalities should have picked him up. You can't easily change your genetics."

"Unless he had help from the inside," I said, knowing that, though difficult, it was not impossible. But to maintain the façade as long as he did pointed to the involvement of an AI. Having a consistent network of Anticol agents, always in the right departments to fake records, overlook inconsistencies, or bury data was highly unlikely. But then again, so was it unlikely that an AI would be part of Anticol. But Kirtley had mentioned genetic improvements, including intelligence, so it might be possible without AI involvement. Besides, his opinion of AIs was fairly low, even loathing. One could hope.

"That's going to take more time to unravel and not as important as saving the *Ellis Island 3*," Wimsey said.

"I agree. But I know someone who might be able to help us with both problems. I'm reaching out to him now."

Tomiji Ito was the head of the Ito Clan at Ross 248. I hadn't communicated with him in decades; there had been no need. I expected him to be on the *Copernicus* and was surprised to find him at Poseidon. I sent an encrypted verbal message: "Tomiji, I need your help. But first, what are you doing on Poseidon?"

The repair machine beeped and withdrew its sensors and tools. I looked down to inspect the results—not pretty, but good enough. I stood up and walked over to a chair that overlooked the borough of Promise. I had always enjoyed the view. Lord Wimsey seemed to be in comms mode, oblivious to his surroundings.

The return message took several minutes. Tomiji was a busy man. "Noburu, my old mechanical friend, good to hear from you. I guess you didn't know the Ito Clan has commissioned a floating city and I'm overseeing final details. Come visit. The weather is wonderful. It's real weather. Also, my chief engineer, 4-of-Lea, just brought your SAIN issue to my attention. We're discussing it now. But tell me what you need." There was no video, just audio.

"We need to save *Ellis Island* 3; the Ross 248 Project could be endangered if we don't. Your chief engineer should have all the details that I've got. Can you help?" I responded. His response would take another couple of minutes. I inserted a power cable to begin to bring my energy level up to something approaching acceptable. The chair produced a can of #6 coolant, which I opened and slowly begin to sip. An AI derived no pleasure from consuming energy and coolant, but several flashing warning indicators, visible only to me, began to turn green, and that was less distracting.

His reply took several minutes longer than I expected. "Switch to encryption level one now." This message included a visual that turned into snow until I activated the requested protocols, and it once again became Tomiji, his expression serious. "I have good news and bad news. The bad is that there is absolutely nothing we can do to save the *Ellis Island* 3 at this point. The good news is we may have already done so. Remember the problems the *Dawn Promise* had when it first started exploring Poseidon? One of your Anticol friends was using our Ito devices as bombs to crack the planet's crust. Civilian Ito devices shouldn't have been capable of that, and we were...disappointed is the correct word...to find how easily he could do that. Anyway, that episode resulted in a complete redesign of civilian Ito devices. They now include a dedicated puter to dampen any quantum field instabilities. It took some time to develop and added some cost to our product but we're fairly sure that all the Ito devices on the *Ellis Island 3* are all the upgraded versions. We're also reasonably sure that the *Ellis Island 2* had a mixture of the old and improved Ito devices, which would explain its loss. Oh, for what it's worth, we've also replaced all the Ito devices at Ross 248 with the newer model. In any event, I'm forwarding this to my family at Sol System for further investigation. I hope this addresses your concerns. What I've said here is proprietary information for your use only."

"Understood. Thanks, Tomiji. I'll speak to you soon. Out."

The *Ellis Island 3* problem was out of my hands. It would survive, or not, but at least it had a chance. That left the C'Maria problem. Kirtley had said she was somewhere at the First Flare Memorial, the location where thousands of Cerites had died during the first Ross 248 flare. It had originally been intended as the first borough at Toe Hold but C'Helios had turned it into a remembrance site and started construction of a new borough ten kilometers east of the spaceport, in part out of respect for the dead, but also out of respect for the damage caused by crashing shuttles.

I stood up and looked over at Lord Wimsey. "What are you doing?" I asked.

He turned to face me. "I'm analyzing our genetic database, looking for abnormalities. I'd like to know how Kirtley escaped notice. If someone has been corrupting the data, it will have left traces. That's what I'm looking for."

"And?" I asked.

"There is a lot of data, it will take a while."

"We need to get to the memorial. Kirtley said she was there."

"Apparently Kirtley lies a lot." Wimsey paused. "But maybe not in this case. My people have detected at least two people in a closed-off portion of the memorial."

"Let's go," I said.

"I already have a security team on their way. We can join them in no more than twenty minutes. Follow me," said Wimsey.

I was already up and moving toward the door. I grabbed my slug thrower off the table and inserted it into my shell's weapon compartment.

We arrived eighteen minutes later. On a normal day, the trip would have taken nearly forty-five minutes. Mass transit works well when you have the clearances and need to commandeer the system.

Lord Wimsey's people had established a cordon all around the main entrance to the historical site and stationed units at all the known exits. When we arrived, no one had yet gone in; the perimeter was still being set up. I also learned that Wimsey had taken personal responsibility for directing the operation, something he hadn't bothered to tell me.

Wimsey coordinated with the security team, now numbering well over thirty officers, for the next ten minutes before he returned to speak with me. In the meantime, I was rapidly running through a list of Kirtley's friends and associates. There was surprisingly little information on the man.

There was a pressurized museum at the bottom of the pit. That's where they would be if they were here. "Our sensors indicate that there are two people inside the site, one of whom is immobile in a chair—C'Maria, perhaps. The other person is pacing. We're sending in a microdrone now to give us a better view," said Wimsey as he deliberately changed his gaze from me to the top right corner of his eyes—a sure sign he was looking at the incoming video.

"Let me see," I said.

A few seconds later, the high-resolution video from the microdrone was playing in my cyber link. A human might have found the experience disconcerting, which is why few normals or Cerites consented to direct neural implants that gave them direct access to the planetary data network. To see as if one were in two locations at the same time, each with comparable clarity (one real and being physically experienced in the moment and the other an external data feed sent directly to the optic processing center from the microdrone—and indistinguishable from the experiential), often triggered panic attacks in humans. It was for this reason that such direct connections were rarely made unless the user is in sensory deprivation.

The figure in the chair was C'Maria and the other was a normal woman of about her same age. We were already accessing SAIN to find her identity and, as might not be totally unexpected, she was one of the technicians responsible for the genetic database at Toe Hold. She paced back and forth with a worried, even angry, expression.

The woman, wearing what looked like a heavily modified, but otherwise standard space suit, stopped pacing and looked directly at the camera. She surely could not see the mosquito-sized drone, so we had to assume she had other sensors that allowed our spy device to be discovered and tracked. After a few moments, she spoke. "You're here. And since my master isn't back yet, I must assume he's now off-world and won't be coming back. That's okay, we have a plan for that. If you want C'Maria back alive, then you'll send in 5-of-Chandra, unarmed, to negotiate. I've rigged a dead man's switch to depressurize this space if anything happens to me." The woman gestured to a small box she held in her left hand with its lone button depressed by her left index finger.

"I'll go," I said.

"What if it is a trap?" asked Wimsey.

"Then it's a trap. What choice to I have? C'Maria isn't dead as Kirtley said she was, which means something is not as it seems. We need to find out what or why," I replied. This person had clearly not expected Kirtley to be delayed, which meant the mystery of why he was not here could perhaps be used to our advantage. I owed it to C'Maria to try.

I was not so stupid as to disarm; I had no fear of dying but still, the presence of my slug thrower in its weapons compartment and within easy reach was comforting. Taking no more time than was necessary to let everyone know I was going in, I began walking toward the airlock that led to the museum.

Long ago it had been the original location of Big Allen's improvised Purple Parrot Pub and the very site where C'Arinna had monitored the first flare.

The airlock opened into a tunnel that had sheltered so many Cerites from the flare. I turned left into a space once used by Big Allen. I could almost feel his spirit. After the flare, the early colonists turned this part of the dig into a ballroom in which annual remembrances and celebrations were held for nearly three hundred years. After the grandchildren of the colonists who survived the flare began to die off, so did the celebrations. New challenges emerged, life went on, and people categorized the events of that day as "ancient history." Ancient. Like me.

The woman in the space suit stood next to C'Maria and was now holding a compact laser in her right hand. I could see her face clearly through her helmet. The dead man's switch was still visible in her left. The laser was, of course, trained on me.

"So, you're 5-of-Chandra. Finally, we meet in person. What happened to the master?" she asked.

"You mean Anderson Kirtley or as he is now known as Alfred Laung? He's dead," I said. There was no point in lying. Maybe letting that sink in would unsettle her. Or, just as likely, it would strengthen her resolve. Humans were unpredictable.

"I was afraid of that. You have no idea what you have cost me." A great sadness showed in her expression. "You're the reason for all this, you know."

I could see C'Maria struggling with her bindings. Cerites were physically weak compared to normal humans, but they were very flexible, not prone to panic, and determined. To keep her captor occupied

I said, "You say you have lost something. What have you lost?"

"He was providing genetic improvements to me and my family. My children and grandchildren could have been immortal. He was providing us many other improvements as well. But with him gone..."

Inspiration rarely visits us AIs but in a flash of clarity I understood. "Wait, you would do what your master—what Kirtley—asked you to, whatever it was, even to die for him?"

She looked slightly confused by the question. "Of course. We would do anything for him; anything he asks us to do we do. He is the master. That's how it works."

"He has been modifying your genetics for generations, right?"

"Yes, you would probably be surprised at how improved we are."

"Maybe, but what he has also been doing is turning you and your line into slaves—slaves who will serve him."

"No. We serve the master because..." She paused, confusion crossing her face. Then she shook her head and looked directly at me. "The master was willing to die to get this opportunity; and now I am too."

"What opportunity might that be?"

"Why, a chance to get you close enough to an EMP array strong enough to scramble your circuits to the point that if you survive, you'll be no more than the cybernetic equivalent of a vegetable. Look around you," she said.

As I'd entered, I noticed the curiously substantial number of power cells and emitter arrays lining this part of the room, but foolishly, I had failed to cross-reference them with the database to determine their utility, a mistake I quickly corrected. They were, in fact, powerful EMP transmitters and power packs, all focused on me.

"You AIs are tough, but not so tough as to be able to survive having your neurocircuits scrambled. This is the end, for both of us," she said.

As she spoke, I noted the slight movement of her left hand, indicating that she was about to let go of the dead man's switch. My reflexes are faster than a human's, but not that fast. The slug hit her in the chest just as her finger left the switch. Everything went dark. I could tell that my core was mostly intact but every system in the shell I was wearing died. Every sensory input, every comm channel went dark. I was floating in blackness. An extremely uncomfortable situation. And not all my core was unharmed. My motor control center seemed to be badly damaged. I worried about poor C'Maria. She had almost been free of her bonds when the EMP hit. Maybe. I embraced that hope in the darkness and waited.

Poseidon's endless ocean stretched to the horizon in all directions. Ross 248 burned in the sky directly overhead. Sunset would be in twenty hours. The array between the planet and the star blocked most of the star's red light and replaced it with a spectrum and intensity almost identical to that which fell upon Earth, including ultraviolet light. Some humans, despite knowing the health risks, still went out of their way to expose themselves to

UV light to intentionally increase melanin production, killing outright some skin cells and inducing potentially cancer-causing mutations in others to get tan. Tomiji Ito's daughter was doing just that as she sprawled on a deck chair, exposing her nude body to the apparent sun.

A slight breeze from the south mussed Tomiji's short black hair as he calmly sipped a cup of tea. We were sitting on the ship's upper balcony high above the ocean's surface, which afforded us a spectacular view. The floating city was massive and eventually would house a population of fifteen thousand humans and AIs. I rested on a special couch designed to support my new arachnid body. After the EMP incident, my motor control functions had become unreliable and eight legs gave me far more stability. Even then, I occasionally fell. The EMP hadn't killed me—I'm a lot tougher than Anticol imagined—and the shell I was wearing at the time had far more shielding than they anticipated, but not tough enough to get through the ordeal unscathed.

Once we had corrected the genetic database at Toe Hold, locating Anticol members had been easy—they had all been genetically modified by Kirtley to be better slaves. Most died rather than surrender, but Anticol was now history. I hoped.

"So, how is the transition coming?" asked Tomiji.

My brother, Yuugi, looked at me as he responded, "As well as can be expected. Noboru has been quite busy these last seven hundred years. I have his files, but understanding what happened and why is the hard part. I'm so glad he is here to answer my many questions. We've also been revising the Ross Torajiro

simulation to account for what we've learned about
the Anticol conspiracy. They were an unknown force
that skewed the simulation. I gather it was driving
Noburu to a high level of frustration. The simulation
projections were always slightly off. Once we added
Kirtley and his slaves to the VR simulation, the outcomes became much more accurate. I think we can
depend on the Torajiro simulation to give us fairly
accurate projections from here on."

"Yuugi, be careful. The population here at Ross
248 is still small enough that determined individuals
can still affect the course of events," I said. "Humans
are notoriously predictable in their unpredictability."
And their lies, I added silently.

Tomiji looked over at my sister, 23-of-Chandra—or,
as she now declared herself, Hotaru. AI mothers would
be known by a single female name. She was also the
last child of Chandra, who had reached the end of
her service life 153 years ago. "Tell me, Hotaru, such
a beautiful name for a beautiful soul—what does it
mean?"

"Hotaru means 'firefly.' It is meant to be a tribute
to my human parents back on Pluto."

"And your plans? You know you're welcome to stay
here."

"Thank you. No, I'm off to Frigus. They need
geneticists and it is becoming very similar to Pluto. A
good place to raise a family. I'll be in charge of the
Kirtley corpse. We need to understand his genetics.
He has much to teach us."

They continued chatting and my thoughts turned
to C'Maria. She had survived. She had freed herself
from her bonds, and since the decompression took

several minutes, she had just enough time to get into an emergency suit. *Ellis Island 3* had survived their transition out of Alcubierre space—not because of anything we did, but because the improved Ito device had adjusted to the imposed instability. Luck.

"As I understand it, the civilization here at Ross looks to be stable and growing. There is some conflict when we integrate the new arrivals but that's manageable," said Tomiji.

I said, "Yes, we are doing well here. Sol system is still problematic. The last message from Yato indicated a forty percent chance of a system-wide conflict."

Tomiji took a sip of tea and then said, "Forty percent is much better than the ninety percent we were dealing with eight centuries ago. We are succeeding, thanks to Noboru. That is why my family has supported this project from the beginning. It was, after all, my distant ancestor Torajiro Ito who started this entire endeavor." He reached over and touched my shell. "When I touch you, I feel like I'm touching both the past and the future. It is an honor."

What followed was silence, broken only by a pod of dolphins that appeared a few hundred yards from the edge of the floating city. Tomiji's daughter started snoring. It was a comfortable silence that was finally broken when Yuugi said, "Compared to Noboru, I think I'll have it easy. He has done all the challenging work."

"Don't tempt fate, my mechanical friend," warned Tomiji. "It is easy to think that your VR projections tell you everything. They do not. The universe has its surprises. We can only prepare our minds to deal with the unexpected."

A door opened and 4-of-Lea, Tomiji's chief engineer, entered. He bowed hurriedly. In a worried voice he said, "Please excuse me, Mr. Ito."

"Yes, what is it?"

"I have received news from my patrol counterpart. Something is happening on Alexa's World."

"Oh, what exactly?"

"The Oddity. Alexa's Oddity. It seems to be waking up."

Maybe I'm not bored and tired of life after all...

Appendix

The Future History of Ross 248

As the famous baseball player Yogi Berra purportedly said, "It's tough to make predictions, especially about the future." In this anthology we make our own predictions of a possible fictional future, one that has the human species moving outward from our home star to establish new homes on planets circling a nearby star. In some circles, this is called science fiction. Below is a summary of this future history as it plays out in the stories of *The Ross 248 Project*.

SOL SYSTEM TIMELINE

2072 AD   Numerous settlements are located on Earth's moon and become rich and powerful and even semi-independent of Earth as they serve as the gateway to the rest of the solar system.

2093   The first stable, sentient AI is created in a small town in Tennessee. It is feared and many want it to be shut down but it is found to be far too useful and interesting. It is oddly dependent on humans and seems to enjoy interacting with them. Eventually it is allowed to create more sentient AIs.

2110   A large settlement is established on Ceres but the humans suffer from lack of gravity and poor radiation shielding. Many die.

2144   The humans at Ceres have genetically modified themselves to cope with very low gravity and high radiation fields. They have become a second type of humanity, and they are known as Cerites. But they are no longer able to function in gravity higher than 0.1g. They expand to establish numerous settlements on other asteroids.

2151 There are several thousand sentient AIs working throughout the solar system. They are considered semi-property. They establish a sentient AI network using quantum fields and a complex machine language that is impossible for humans to decrypt. They use this network to communicate with each other and prevent exploitation of sentient AIs.

2160 The Space Patrol is established via the Treaty of Luna City to prevent armed conflict between the nations of Earth and the ever-increasing number of independent space settlements. The new Space Patrol combines the space forces of various factions and becomes an independent organization dedicated to the idea of keeping space free from war and to deal with any other threats that could threaten humanity. It's motto from the start is "Preserve and Protect, at Any Cost."

2194 Hiroaki Ito invents the Ito device, for safely storing large quantities of energy and antimatter. This is a key technology allowing for faster and safer interplanetary travel. The Ito family becomes very rich.

2210 The growing demand for antimatter results in numerous antimatter production facilities, all of which are seized by the Space Patrol to prevent the proliferation of antimatter weapons. The Space Patrol uses the antimatter to underwrite a new system-wide currency: the credit.

2210 to 2300	Age of space settlements. Expeditions continually leave from Luna to establish semi-independent space settlements on Mercury, Venus, and slowly the moons of the gas giants.
2260	Sentient AIs buy Pluto and its moons from a Cerite Consortium.
2290	Sentient AIs have a thriving business at Pluto providing medical and cryogenic storage for humans.
2366	Crisis at Pluto. 34-of-Kristie dies fighting for sentient AI rights.
2367	Sentient AIs are recognized as sentient beings with rights equivalent to humans. They agree to build an aversion to harming humans into their core architecture. This is known as the 2367 Agreement and is mostly followed.
2440	The founding of the Ross 248 Project. Earth.
2473	The starship *Ceres' Chariot*, built at Ceres and crewed by 1000 Cerites and 100 sentient AIs, leaves for the Ross 248 system. The journey is 110 years.
2476	The starship *Copernicus* is constructed at Earth's moon. It departs with 1000 humans and 150 sentient AIs for the Ross 248 system. The journey takes 110 years.
2478	The starship *Guardian E* (a Space Patrol starship, heavily armed) has been constructed

at Earth's moon. It departs with 750 normal humans, 330 Cerites, and 250 sentient AIs. Most, but not all, are members of the Space Patrol. Its journey takes 105 years.

2479   The starship *34-of-Kristie* is constructed at a Cerite shipyard under contract for SAIN. It then travels to Pluto where it takes on antimatter, supplies, cargo, and a crew of sentient AIs and then leaves for Ross 248. Its journey takes 110 years.

ROSS 248 SYSTEM TIMELINE

Note: At Ross 248 years are measured in Earth years after arrival (AA instead of AD). *Ceres' Chariot* arrived in the year 2583 AD (also known as 0 AA).

0 AA   *Ceres' Chariot* enters orbit around Liber (the moon of Ross 248h, Alexa's World) and starts to build a settlement on the surface of the moon, similar to other settlements built by Cerites, to be known as Toe Hold. Also, a communication station is built at the 248h/Liber L5 point to maintain a strong communication link with Sol System. This station is known as Hermes Station.

0.1 AA   The Space Patrol ship (*Guardian E*) goes into orbit around Ross 248e (Eden). Stealth sensor platforms are scattered throughout the Ross 248 system looking for any indication of alien activity or artifacts; they also keep a close eye on the Cerites at Liber. There is life on Eden but no sign of intelligent life or technology. Research teams are sent down to the surface but there are causalities interacting with the native life. The alien life on Eden seems to have been engineered.

1.5 AA   The first flare. The star Ross 248 has been a peaceful dim red star that suddenly produces a very damaging solar flare that hits Liber and *Ceres' Chariot*. Of the 4000 Cerites that arrived on *Ceres' Chariot*, 1300 died due to the flare. Many sentient AIs also died. The *Guardian E* leaves Eden and travels to assist the Cerites at Liber. Slowly construction resumes.

3.1 AA   The starship *Copernicus* arrives in orbit around Liber. It was diverted from Eden by the Space Patrol. Its crew assists the Cerites with their construction efforts.

4.5 AA   Alexa Prandus, a young woman on *Copernicus*, discovers the alien installation of Ross 248h, that becomes known as Alexa's Oddity, and the planet is then named after her: Alexa's World.

9.4 AA   The starship *34-of-Kristie* enters orbit around Liber. It is crewed entirely by sentient AIs with the captain being 5-of-Chandra. It carries industrial equipment vital to building industry on Liber. The Cerites are searching the Kuiper Belt for asteroids and comets and returning them for processing. The colonists confront two major problems. Their supplies of He-3 (used to power fusion energy generators) and antimatter (used to power spaceship drive engines) are running low.

15.7 AA   The Space Patrol starts construction of a solar array and antimatter production facility at the star/Planet d L1 point. Thus the array will always be between the star and Ross 248d.

19.5 AA   The antimatter shortage comes to an end as production starts at the array.

25.3 AA   Cloud cities are established Ross 248 b and c (the two hottest and most innermost planets). The cloud cities harvest He-3 from the planet's atmosphere. The He-3 crisis comes to an end.

37 AA   The normal human population on the *Copernicus* exceeds its limits. A portion of Toe Hold is built to house excess humans using a rotating structure to provide the needed gravity. This section is soon known as "the Primate Quarter."

39 AA   The population at Toe Hold reaches 4100 Cerites and 2100 normal humans. Toe Hold is expanding.

55 AA   The sea-going ship *Dawn Promise* is lowered to the ocean surface on Ross 248d and begins to explore the world to evaluate its potential to be terraformed. The world is named Poseidon's World.

61 AA   The decision to terraform Poseidon's World is made. A second large research ship is lowered to the surface of Poseidon's World.

73 AA   The decision is made to build space settlements on Ross 248f, named Nordheim. This planet has enough gravity to allow normal humans to

thrive without the need for rotating structures. Construction begins.

83 AA   An attempt is made to sterilize Eden by rogue elements at Toe Hold. The Space Patrol barely manages to foil the attempt and save Eden.

92 AA   A prototype floating city (named Atlantis) is lowered to the surface of Poseidon's World to accelerate research into terraforming the planet.

96 AA   An obstacle to terraforming Poseidon's World is lack of micronutrients. This is addressed by constructing mass drivers on Nordheim that fire a continual stream of projectiles at Poseidon's World that burst in the atmosphere and rain down the needed nutrients.

99 AA   The sentient AIs claim Ross 248g, known as Frigus, with the intent to create a Pluto-type world run by sentient AIs to provide medical, cryogenic and virtual reality services to humans and Cerites.

105 AA   The first settlers from Toe Hold move into a new settlement on Nordheim named New Hope City.

250 AA   The array between Ross 248 and Poseidon's World begins to use some of its vast energy resources to beam light to Poseidon, simulating Earth's light spectrum. Algae begins to flourish in the ocean at Poseidon.

350 AA   The light received at Poseidon is near identical to that received on Earth. Projectiles of micronutrients from Nordheim continue. The

atmosphere of Poseidon is now 3% oxygen. Marine life is starting to be introduced in some quantity. Additional floating cities are regularly being lowered to Poseidon's ocean.

480 AA   Poseidon's atmosphere reaches 7% oxygen.

530 AA   Large marine mammals are introduced to Poseidon's ocean.

560 AA   The starship *Ellis Island* arrives at Nordheim from Earth, the first such event in over 500 years.

700 AA   The human population at Ross 248 numbers over 133 million normal humans and almost 41 million Cerites.

708 AA   Poseidon's World is now Earth-normal with 20% oxygen and pressure similar to higher elevations on Earth.

710 AA   The Anticol movement is finally crushed. Alexa's Oddity, long ignored begins stirring.

b

c

d

e

f

g

h • Liber

Ross 248 is an actual, small (M6V red dwarf) star located 10.3 light-years (LY) from Earth in the constellation Andromeda. It has no detected companions but it could have a system of planets similar to Trappist-1. Based on current exoplanet detection techniques, it is unlikely that this assumption can be proved false within the next few decades. Ross 248 is fairly close to our solar system, relatively speaking, allowing for a journey of 100 years at 0.1c. It is interesting to note that Voyager 2 will pass within 1.7 light-years of Ross 248 in about 40,000 years.

Our fictional Ross 248 system is loosely based on the very real Trappist-1 system of planets but tweaked so as not to be an exact copy. We assume that there are a few stray asteroids beyond the last planet and a thin Kuiper Belt and Oort Cloud beyond that. Ross 248 is a very small system. If it were superimposed on ours, then its seven planets and their accompanying asteroids would fit nicely within the orbit of Mercury.

Relative size of planets: The large half circle outline represents the Ross 248 star relative to the size of the Ross 248 planets b through h (and the moon Liber). The gray circle below represents Earth's relative size.

Earth

Relative distance of planets from Ross 248:

h   g   f   e d c b   STAR

Ross 248:

Red dwarf star
(M6V)

10.3 light-years from Earth

13% of Sol's mass

16% of Sol's radius

0.2% of Sol's luminosity

Relative size of stars

Sol   Ross 248

PLANET	% MASS OF EARTH	% RADIUS OF EARTH	DAYS FOR ONE ORBIT	GRAVITIES AT SURFACE	DISTANCE FROM STAR	
					MILLION KMS	LIGHT-SECONDS
Ross 248b Aeneas	93%	96%	3	1g	3.1	10
	Atmosphere similar to Venus; very hot.					
Ross 248c Cupid	110%	101%	4.5	1g	4.1	14
	Atmosphere similar to Venus; very hot.					
Ross 248d Poseidon's World	97%	102%	7.1	0.93g	5.6	19
	Water world, no land; ocean is 30 km deep. Thin atmosphere of N_2CO_2. Average temperature is 25°C					
Ross 248e Eden	77%	93%	11.1	0.89g	7.5	25
	Oxygen/nitrogen atmosphere and LIFE. Large ice caps, oceans and continents. Average temperature is −10°C					
Ross 248f Nordheim	93%	101%	16.9	0.91g	9.9	33
	Nitrogen/CO2 atmosphere. A frozen world with a large ice/rock layer over a liquid ocean. Average surface temperature is −50°C					
Ross 248g Frigus	41%	78%	25	0.67g	13	43
	Thin nitrogen atmosphere. A frozen world with a large ice/rock layer. No liquid ocean. Average surface temperature is −77°C					
Ross 248h Alexa's World	33%	72%	46	0.64g	19.3	64.5
	Very thin nitrogen atmosphere. A frozen world with a large ice/rock layer. No liquid ocean. Average surface temperature is −115°C					
Liber, moon of Ross 248h	12%	12%	n/a	0.083g	n/a	n/a
	Orbits 248h every 16.5 days. Similar to Ceres, no atmosphere, surface of rock and ice. No liquid ocean. Surface temperature −115°C					

The Starships of Ross 248

Interstellar travel is challenging from many perspectives but first and foremost is the problem of propulsion, which can really be simplified to a matter of energy. For example, let's take a metric tonne (1000 kg) of anything (spaceship, lead, water, whatever) and accelerate it to 0.1c (a tenth the speed of light). Assuming it can be accelerated with one hundred percent efficiency, which is impossible, then its resulting kinetic energy, energy associated with its motion, is 107 megatonnes (Mt). For comparison, the largest nuclear explosion ever recorded was the Tsar Bomba exploded in 1961 by the former USSR. It had a yield of around 58 Mt. That's a whopping amount of energy.

Since the starships in the Ross 248 universe don't have faster-than-light drives, they are required to keep several thousand humans healthy and sane for around a century while they make the trip to Ross 248 from our solar system. Rough estimates are that the *Copernicus* would mass 2.8 million tonnes as it begins its journey. The other starships are assumed to be in the same weight class. At 0.1c, the *Copernicus* would have a kinetic energy of approximately 5.2 *million* Tsar Bombas. To decelerate at the destination, you'd need that amount of energy again. This is clearly a big problem.

Antimatter is often cited as the answer to achieve such energies. In the case of the *Copernicus*, you would need 14,000 metric tonnes of antimatter interactions to get up to speed (7000 tonnes of antimatter reacting with 7000 tonnes of normal matter) and the equivalent amount to slow down. Since nature won't allow us to do anything with one hundred percent efficiency and any efficiency losses will mostly be manifest as waste heat, the ship will need radiators, big radiators, which leads to more mass being added to the ship, which then requires more antimatter to accelerate the extra mass, and so on. All this without considering how one would store over 7000 metric tonnes of antimatter for a hundred years... Good luck.

Without invoking science fictional star drives, we decided to use the most efficient propulsion system we can conceive within the known laws of physics, antimatter propulsion, and couple it with an extremely hypothetical but not necessarily impossible Alcubierre warp bubble. It is in the engineering of all this that we invoke our science fictional MacGuffins—the actual methods used to produce, store, and use antimatter. One is the Ito device, which can store antimatter safely for long periods of time. The second is a variant of the Alcubierre[48] warp bubble. Once the bubble is created, it can be used to generate a negative energy density that will add negative mass to the starship inside the bubble. We assume physical laws prevent the total mass from going to zero, but it can be reduced. This reduction in the mass of the starship, to an outside observer, does not affect space time inside the bubble,

---

48 Physicist Miguel Alcubierre theorized that it might be possible to contract space in front of a spaceship and expand the space behind it, allowing the ship to cross vast distances (which have been conveniently shortened) in a shorter amount of time. The math works, but it requires something called negative mass— which is purely speculative and may not exist. Still, serious papers are examining this theoretical technology.

but the conservation of momentum then requires that its velocity increase to conserve momentum.

Our starships use antimatter engines to boost their velocity (in our case to 0.0001c after ten years of thrusting). This antimatter engine produces a lot of waste heat, some of which is converted into electricity and fed into the Alcubierre drive. Though they can store tremendous amounts of energy, they require about ten years to energize. At that point, the antimatter engines are shut off and stored inside the starship. The massive radiators are also stored inside the ship. When the Alcubierre drive is activated, always an exciting and somewhat uncertain event, a warp bubble is created and flooded with negative energy. This reduces the mass (to an outside observer) by a factor of 1000, while increasing the starship's velocity by a factor of 1000 or to something around 0.1c. The warp bubble protects the starship from collisions with dust and small particles but obscures visibility, making communication and precise navigation near impossible; but since they are unable to affect their course during this phase, the difficulty in navigation is not significant.

The starship flies blind at this speed for about ninety years. Once established, the warp bubble requires only a small energy input to maintain itself but possesses tremendous amounts of energy. "Popping the bubble," as it is referred to by the crew, is an exciting event. The crew then spends weeks repairing the ship and dumping unnecessary mass, such as the now useless coil. It locates itself relative to its target, redeploys the antimatter engine, and spends the next ten years decelerating. Total time for the trip (0.1c is too slow for relativistic effects to kick in) is about 110 years. This is a long time, but keep in mind that humans at this point have a life span of around two hundred years.

Space is not a hospitable environment for Earth based life and it will be trying to kill our voyagers from the moment they leave home. The dangers are numerous and include the vacuum of space, radiation, and lack of any material resources. The absence of gravity results in numerous health issues including loss of bone strength, loss of muscle strength, redistribution of body fluids, vertigo, and perhaps, in the long term, even blindness for some.

The environment aboard a ship, filled with air and the other necessities of life, can keep the vacuum and emptiness of space at bay. Mass can be used as radiation shielding. Spinning the ship to provide acceleration can be used to mimic the effects of gravity to help the crew maintain their muscles and bones. Unfortunately, nearly all these mitigations will add mass, lots of mass, to the ship, making the propulsion problem more difficult.

Human psychology is another matter entirely. We don't have any historical analogs for a worldship in which everyone must get along for a century with no way to leave and the ever-present threat of impending death just outside the ship. How would the voyagers govern themselves? What rules would they enact to ensure the safety of the crew and how much would these rules limit their personal liberty? We don't know, but at least the crew and passengers of the *Copernicus*, and other starships, aren't generation ships.

Taking these concerns into account, the habitation portion of *Copernicus*, our hypothetical starship, looks something like the diagram below. The best way to visualize this is to take a cylinder and a sphere of equal radius, cut the sphere in half and glue each half to opposite ends of the cylinder.

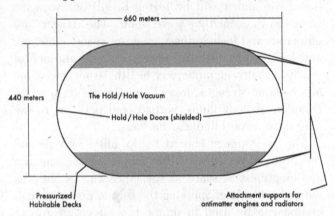

The gray sections of the ship are pressurized, and the cylinder is spun to simulate the effects of gravity. The *Copernicus* spins at a rate of two revolutions per minute to provide 0.98g at the lowest deck and 0.9g in the principal living area. The hold is in vacuum and is used to store equipment, protecting it from micrometeorite and most radiation damage. During the cruise phase, the Ito devices, antimatter engines, and radiators are stored here. It is here where smaller spaceships and shuttles are maintained and even constructed after arrival. It also serves as the "shuttle bay" for the starship with shuttles and small spaceships coming and going through the hold doors. Note that the hold is sometimes referred to as the "hole" by the crew.